Contents

viii • Contents

Founding Fathers

So there is Howard Hughes standing on the corner talking to Bugsy Siegel.

Now this is not just any old corner. According to the prominent street sign, this is the intersection of Las Vegas Boulevard and Flamingo Road.

And this is not just any old Howard Hughes. This is the young HH before he adopted a hippie lifestyle. You know: long hair and fingernails, no clothes and a stockpile of Kleenex for hangers-on. This Howard Hughes looks bathed, shaved and saved. In fact, he is quite natty-appearing in a lime-green zoot suit with matching fedora.

Bugsy Siegel is nothing to hide in your guest closet, either. His zoot suit and fedora are watermelon-pink, and his feet wear two-tone shoes of black-and-pink patent leather. I believe that the pink part is shaped like a flamingo.

Now you may think that Midnight Louie is dreaming, or is still lost in the La-La-bye Land of his last case, which had overtones of the paranormal so loud they might have out-shouted the clothing of the two gentlemen under discussion, or description, here.

In fact, some may dismiss this vision as a nightmare in neon-brights.

I grant you that I have a tendency to dream in Technicolor—how else is a born carnivore like me to see blood? (I admit that in these latter days most of the blood I see has been spilled by somebody else. That is what happens when one trades the role of mean-streets prowler for that of private investigator.)

So now my prey is no longer the puny operators I used to tangle with: fishy small-fry, midnight nibblers and noshers, Dumpster fungus. Now I hunt Big Game, which is carnivorous on a scale to make my poor previous food-gathering expeditions pale. This game usually sports two legs instead of four, and has occasional pretensions of humanity as well as chronic tendencies toward homicide.

Anyway, my new occupation puts me in the way of seeing many strange things, so I greet the vignette of Howie and Bugsy chatting it up with a blasé yawn. Frankly, I wish the pair would knock it off so I can get down to business. I am not here to file my fingernails, you know. I moonlight these days as a media personality. I have more important things to do than watch two dead guys togged out in Popsicle colors, even if they happen to have pretty much founded the town I trot my tootsies through, Las Vegas, Nevada.

Of course, there may be some question of who is alive and sane here: Howard Hughes yakking in the bright lights, or me huddled behind bars in a comfortless cage, watching the proceedings.

I had heard that being a star results in a confined lifestyle, but had no idea it involved long periods of imprisonment.

If Miss Temple Barr, my solicitous roommate, knew in what conditions I were being kept, she would never allow it. Unfortunately, she is off around the town, working at various public relations projects, while I languish here in the lap of lassitude.

The only consolation is my cellmate. Or, rather, the prisoner in the adjoining cage. She is my co-star, and not for her the anonymous plastic shell of a carrier right off the pet-warehouse shelf. No, this diminutive doll is zippered into a pink canvas carrier with her name embroidered on the side. *Yvette,* in fancy cursive letters. (Divine is a descriptive adjective that I alone use to embellish her name.)

I believe that someone has scrawled the name "Louie" on a torn piece of paper bag and taped it atop my carrier. As if enough twenty-pound, muscular, wet suit–black, green-eyed hairy dudes with the acting instincts of Al Pacino were hanging around to confuse the matter of who is who.

Stardom feels more like serfdom, so far.

"Ah, Louie," the Divine Yvette sighs next to me as she lolls on the pink satin cushion in her carrier. "Do not fret. We will have our time in the sun. The acting life is always 'hurry up and get there, then wait an eternity.' "

"Do you mean wait an eternity as in 'for us to get together'?"

"We are together now," she answers demurely.

The Divine Yvette is nothing if not demure, a trait I generally do not care for unless it is accompanied by big blue-green eyes framed in natural black mascara along with a full-length platinum-blond fur coat that would make a silver fox gnash its fangs with envy.

"You know what I mean," I growl, but she does not answer.

The Divine Yvette does not address the more earthy facts of life, I have discovered. I doubt she has ever raised a paw and stretched out a razor-sharp shiv to do more than manicure it.

So we wait, she and I and our director, trainer and stylists; also Miss Savannah Ashleigh, the little doll who claims to own the Divine Yvette. We wait for the gaudy ghosts of

Howard Hughes and Bugsy Siegel to finish their shtick and clear the stage so the real performers can get to it.

For one sure way to save a shekel in an À La Cat commercial is to borrow someone else's set. Once Howard and Bugsy exit, the stage and the spotlight are ours!

There is only one fly in the ointment, in this case a feline in the fetuccine. Either way, you have a pretty unappetizing menu.

The dude's name is Maurice. He is large, yellow in color and used to have my job before I edged him out. There is no reason for him to be present at the filming, other than mischief.

There is definite reason to believe this dude would love to do away with all of my nine lives.

And I am not talking brands of cat food here.

Chapter 1

Voice of the Dark

At one o'clock in the morning, under the overhead fluorescent glare, night was a memory rather than a reality. It was as if a miscegenated moon hung from the bland ceiling, sun-bright yet pale as Dutch cheese.

Matt felt like a hothouse violet being kept under constant artificial illumination, something forced into the unnatural state of flourishing at night, like a vampire. Still, he'd come to enjoy working the night shift, especially in a city like Las Vegas that blurred the lines between night and day at every opportunity.

"One of yours," Sheila sang from the next cubicle, leaning out far enough to show her shy-violet face. "Line four."

Routine callers seem a contradiction in terms for a crisis phone center, but some clients' lives are serial crises, so they become serial callers. Like serial killers, they most often come calling at night. Maybe that's when nerves and negative emotions run hottest.

Matt adjusted his headset and pushed the right button, wondering which of his regulars he would hear. He had more than the other counselors, because he was so "understanding," the supervisor said.

Matt knew that being understanding was merely the result of doing time listening to other people's troubles, and doing an even longer stretch at being too nice to dump those who most deserved it.

"ConTact. Brother John," he said. Tonight, as on some bleary, weary nights lately, he had almost said, "Saint Rose of Lima. Father Devine."

"You're there." A voice both remarkable and unmistakable.

The big, booming basso made the phone line thrum like a contented cat. That voice, so smooth and confident. Hard to believe this man was hooked on anyone else's voice over the telephone. But he was. Matt smiled to feel his spine straighten at the sound of that voice, that Chamber of Commerce, boot-camp sergeant, motivation-seminar leader, preacher, actor vocal command.

In a way, confidence was the core of this man's problems. Too much and too little. And his problems . . . Matt found himself mentally quoting a rabbi friend's "Oy vey." How could the caller know that Matt was the least-qualified person around to deal with his particular hang-up?

That is the beauty of hotline counseling, utter anonymity. An absolute lack of confrontation, of obligation beyond the moment. No faces to prejudge, no fears to detect in person, no reason to dread the other end of the line, either way.

Would safe sex, Matt sometimes wondered, resemble this in a future age if AIDS remained an untreatable plague?

"Don't you ever take a day off?" the caller asked, though the Voice sounded pleased by the idea of Matt being eternally on call.

"Not over weekends, which is when you call most often."

"Do I? God, you got me there! I hadn't noticed. That's what I like about you, Brother John, always there, and you always remember things I forget."

"Not always. I may be accessible, but I'm not eternal, or omnipotent."

"Hey, you are to me, baby!"

Gambler maybe, Matt thought. The Voice thrummed with the gamester's high Matt had heard before.

"I'm here to help," Matt said firmly, "not to feed dependency fantasies. You don't need to know about me. You need to know about you. Have you contacted that psychiatrist in L.A. I referred you to?"

"Oh, thanks, yeah! I got my people trying to set up an appointment, but I'm on the road so much. And the impulse comes over me so . . . sudden. Just when things are going great. Guess that's self-sabotage, huh?"

"Sounds like you've been reading some of the books I recommended."

"Oh, yeah. I can get in a little reading on the road. But I like talking best. That's what I do best."

"I believe you. That's why a hotline could become addictive, as addictive as your main problem."

"An addictive personality just keeps breaking out all over, like hives, huh?"

"Until you deal with the root of the addictions."

"Root is right!" His laugh was as compelling as his speaking voice. "Hey, almost called you 'Doc' then."

"I'm not. I'm not anybody. You've got to seek consistent, professional help."

"But now, right now? 'Cuz it's coming on again. That . . . itchy trigger finger, you might call it." A laugh, man-to-man bawdy. "That sense of impending doom and delight. I'm gonna do something I'm gonna regret tonight, if you don't stop me."

"If you don't stop yourself. I'm an echo, a wailing wall. I reflect back what you need to hear, to see about yourself. Don't give me any credit. You're doing all the work."

"I'd like to meet you sometime." Spoken suddenly. "I mean, you sound like such a together guy. Even, you know? No highs, no lows. That's my business, all highs and all lows. Then I get so itchy . . . gotta release the tension. Then, I blow it. Can't anymore. Got a lot more to lose. A lot.

"Got a wife now. Me, a wife! God, she's a knockout. Body by va-va-va-voom. Every guy in the world would kill to be in my shoes. And we got a little baby. She still kept her figure, after, not gonna let that slide. The wife, not the baby. Never thought I'd go so crazy over anybody else, but that baby . . . Why do I still get those late-night gonna-do-something-baaad blues, Brother John? I'm gonna blow it all, the best time of my life, and I can't stop myself."

"Yes, you can! You said you have before."

"Yeah. You talked me out of it a couple of times. Only times I didn't do anything. You're the only one."

"Is that what you tell your wife?"

A long silence on the phone.

"You punch like Muhammad Ali sometimes. Makes me wonder why I keep coming back for more."

"You don't have to. Just make and keep an appointment in L.A. I gave you three top names—"

"Names! My whole life is Names. Maybe that's why I do it. I find the Nameless ones. I follow 'em, introduce myself and it's so easy. It's done. Then I don't have to remember their names, or anything else about them. Like I've put 'em away somewhere, and I'm at peace. Until the next one."

"What about tonight? Isn't somebody with you? Your wife?"

"Working out of town."

"The baby . . . ?"

"With the wife and nanny in Switzerland."

"Can't you look at their pictures?"

"Oh, man, photos don't do it. Not when I get the itch. Haven't you ever had to have something so bad, so fast, right now, that it's like you're on skis and you see the downhill run and you know you're gonna crash into a great big cedar, but, hell, the ride is everything."

This time Matt was silent.

"Well, haven't you? There must be something that gets you by the throat like that sometimes. A sport? A woman?"

"No," Matt said before remembering an imperative that he could hardly mention, even in this anonymous interchange: the compulsion he felt to find Cliff Effinger. But a mission to locate an abusive stepfather missing for years was hardly what the caller meant. He was talking about pleasurable addictions. Looking at a murdered body that had borne Effinger's I.D. in a morgue viewing room and being unable to say for sure that this was the demon who had haunted his boyhood . . . seeing a presumed-dead man walking in Effinger's cocky lope across the Strip not long afterwards, these were not pleasurable sightings. His hunt for the truth, for Effinger dead or alive, wasn't an addiction. It was only an obsession. Wasn't it?

No, Matt concluded. Nothing pleasurable had ever driven him, only duty and guilt and anger. "No," he said.

"No! No babes. No ballgames. No fun. What the hell are you, man, a monk? That's what they call them, don't they? 'Brothers'?"

"Yes, they do, but no, I'm not a monk." Not quite.

"Yeah, I know. You're nobody. Believe it or not, sometimes I envy guys like you. Probably lived in the same place for ten, fifteen years. Wife and kid. Two cars, one dog. Maybe you mentally play the stock market now and again for kicks. Am I right?"

"No." Matt couldn't help sounding amused. "But it doesn't seem like a bad life. Why can't you settle for it?"

A sigh, dramatic enough for a nighttime TV soap opera. "Never thought I'd settle for the domestic routine, period. Lot of people—women—were pissed when I did, like I'd betrayed them. Women are always taking things personally, aren't they?"

"So they should, especially when so many men class them into one big aggravating category."

"Hey, I like women! Boy, do I like women."

"That's not good enough, though, or you wouldn't be on the phone now."

"Yeah, you're right. I think I like 'em. I say I like 'em, but I guess I like to have had 'em better than I like 'em. They're never enough, and I don't buy that proving my manhood bull, either. But there's a down, after. Maybe I didn't really like the one I was with enough to have screwed her, or maybe she didn't really like me, maybe she liked my Name, or some other little—or not so little—thing about me.

"It's like doing a big gig. You get up for it, the hoopla and the howling and the screaming and swooning. You perform your guts out, you get rave reviews and leave 'em laughing and applauding and whistling . . . and it's still not enough. Afterward, you're alone and you feel hollow. You ever felt like that?"

"Everyone has."

"And then, it's really funny. They all loved you. Loved what you did. And you think, they were so easy. So you despise them for loving you, and yourself for not loving them. Then you end up hating everybody, even yourself. It's like you wish you could scrape yourself off yourself, you know? And shake that slimy skin on the floor and leave it there with the Victoria's Secret Miracle Bras and the stale perfume and your pricey silk underwear."

"You don't want to go through that again, and the guilt, now that you have someone to answer to."

"I don't answer to anybody."

"Except yourself."

"Yeah, except me."

"The self that wants to peel its skin off. You ever have thoughts, at times like that, of suicide?"

"Suicide, naw! That's ludicrous. I'm at the top of my game. I'm a winner."

The Voice kept silent for an unprecedented minute and more.

"I've drunk myself cold out, sometimes, afterward. Maybe that *is* a death wish. Maybe I oughta call that L.A. shrink, or all three." A laugh. "You scared the hell out of me this time. I think I'll make it. You're worth every penny."

"This is a free service."

"Not when I'm calling long-distance."

"You're calling long-distance? You're not in Las Vegas?"

"Now, yeah."

"But before, you've called from out of the area?"

"From out of the country, pal."

"That's . . . absurd."

"No. You're worth it. I've been telling you. You're the best."

"The best?"

"Yeah. I told you."

"You mean . . . you call other hotlines?"

"Sure, all over. Hey, I go all over, and the Devil on my back is ready to ride every goddamn night I'm alive. But, don't worry, you're the best."

"Don't you see? You're playing the same game with me . . . with all of us anonymous counselors, that you play with your wife."

"So what? You're jealous, is that what you're saying? You want to be the only one, or some dumbass thing? Hotline counselors are just like women?"

"No, I'm saying that *you*'re the same, with everyone and everything. Until you see that, and work to change it, you're going to trust no one, not even yourself."

"You can't fool me, Brother John. Everybody wants the same thing from me: attention, time, all my attention and all my time. Well, I'm a busy guy. I belong to the world. I don't need this policing. I don't need your shrink list and your straight-arrow shock over the phone. Forget I called; I won't make that mistake again."

The line hummed like an angry bee. Dial tone. Empty line. Unoccupied. The Voice, exiting on an egocentric, aggrieved note, was gone.

Matt hung up the phone, still wondering what had hit him.

The man was a master manipulator. Matt knew that, had always recognized the fact. He'd encountered such carelessly charismatic personalities before, often in very successful people, very insecure people. Still, this time Matt had been caught off guard. All that sincerely articulated flattery about how much Matt did for the man, how he helped him. But no one could do anything for this particular man, who gaveth and who taketh away. Always he had to take away: you are not really the One. You are not really Unique. You are only One of. I am Unique and you are One of Many who take/want/beg/borrow from me. My time, my attention, my intimacy. I award it everywhere so that you will know you are Nothing Special. Only *I* am Something Special.

Matt shook his head. His callers didn't often leave a bad taste at the back of his mouth. He seldom felt that they were hopeless cases. And he never believed that they deserved their own misery. This man did, he thought with a flare of rare anger. Wasting ConTact's literally precious time, tying up the line when someone truly troubled—and deservingly humble—might have needed to call in.

"Deservingly humble." Matt replayed that phrase in his mind. His own education and experience, steeped in the Beatitudes from the Mount, argued that the meek had a place on the earth, if not over it. Many religions emphasized self-effacement to the point of self-abasement. That wasn't any healthier than a rampaging ego that seduced and subdued every other person around it. Self-serving people were hard to like, in Matt's book of flaws, but they still needed help even when they were stomping your own self-esteem as flat as roadkill.

He knew that. Already the sting of personal betrayal, a form of superego, was fading.

He also knew that the Voice would call again, and ask for him. Only him. Always him. Even from long distance.

Chapter 2

Strange Birds of Paradise

"Nine hundred thousand plastic flamingos?"

Temple Barr wasn't sure of her own name, couldn't be certain she hadn't been transported into an alien universe. She couldn't believe her ears, and she was sure most people wouldn't believe their eyes if they ever saw nine hundred thousand pink plastic flamingos in one humongous flock.

But that's what Bud Dubbs was talking about, right here in his staid but cramped office at the Las Vegas Convention and Visitors Authority. And the flamingos, nearly a million strong, would blanket the Little Town That Could, if international conceptual-artist Domingo had his way.

"Well," she said faintly, " 'Domingo's flamingos' has a certain ring to it. I can't believe the board has okayed this flamingo-wrapping scheme."

"The man is a recognized genius," Bud said, "at publicity, if nothing else. He wanted to cover Hoover Dam, but I convinced him it was too remote to receive the proper media attention."

"So he's going to smother the Strip in flamingos? That'll stop traffic all right."

"He's agreed not to install conceptual artworks anywhere they might impede vehicular or foot traffic. This will be an improvised installation, his first. He will tour the area, get inspired and then . . . put out flamingos."

"Bud! I can't believe all the Strip enterprises would approve this flaky idea."

"Well, they haven't. That's where you come in."

"Me?"

"We need a freelancer to temporarily assist Domingo. Follow him around. If he settles on a site, try to clear it with the necessary honchos. If they say no, break it gently to Domingo. If they say yes, see that the installation doesn't impede business."

"You want a diplomat, hostage negotiator and baby-sitter all in one!"

"Exactly. With all the different clients you handle you're used to the sticky field situations that could come up—"

"Like murder of the conceptual artist in question! Come to think of it, plastic flamingos could serve as headstones in the Truly Tacky Graveyard."

"You have to suspend judgment. Domingo has been hailed the world over for altering the way we look at our landscapes. He's the man who hung a green-and-red spaghetti curtain from the Leaning Tower of Pisa. He concocted the world's largest horizontal chocolate milk shake from one end of the Brooklyn Bridge to the other and got the mayor of New York to suspend traffic for twenty-four hours while it was set up, displayed and eaten. Or drunk. Or slurped."

"What was the message of that: New York sucks?"

"I know it's nuts. Sure the guy's a banana. But he has *Time* magazine photo spreads, *Paris-Match* features, you name it. When Domingo does, the world looks."

"Not every enterprise in Vegas needs or wants publicity nowadays. In fact, some are downright surly about cooperating on even self-serving projects, not to mention more mainstream ones.

The job you're proposing I handle is like being one unpopped kernel of corn in a forest fire."

"We'll pay you well."

"Hmm. What do you know about Domingo that I don't?"

Bud handed a gold foil–embossed, glossy black folder across the paper canyons of his desk.

"Money," Temple diagnosed with a puritan sniff. "This guy must waste tons of money."

"But he has it to waste. People and institutions underwrite his projects. Artsy people. Eyeball those press releases."

Temple scanned letterheads listing a wealth of East and West Coast arts groups. It seemed the middle of the country was much more middle-of-the-road about Domingo's conceptual creations. But then there were all his European stunts . . . er, installations . . . and all the eminent museums arrayed behind the artistic angler.

Color photos showed a white-shirted Domingo directing various of his mammoth enterprises: a flotilla of fifty thousand French horns on the Seine, for instance. The project illustrated the subtle musical tension of moving water, one critic said, making a strong plea for the ecological rights of the planet, per se.

"What about the ecological rights of Las Vegas?" Temple demanded. "We're already considered the Capital of Crass. A million flamingos aren't going to improve our image any. It's a large-scale joke on the entire town, don't you see? It allows the intelligentsia to poke fun at sacred cows, with Las Vegas as the silly old bossy vain enough to be conned into looking like a worse parody of itself than it already is."

Bud shrugged his shirted shoulders, which were nowhere near as broad as Domingo's. "That's the point, Temple. Who can spoof a laughing stock? Domingo can't hurt us, and if he is so blooming artsy, no one can say that Las Vegas didn't have the sophistication to snicker at itself."

"*Some* in Las Vegas. Other quarters will definitely not be laughing. This could be dangerous, Bud."

"To you? Or Domingo?"

"To both of us, and to about one million plastic flamingos. One million—can anyone even make that many?"

"They're extremely popular all over South America and Mexico, I understand."

"How much?" Temple asked, unmollified.

Bud wrote a figure on a notepad and passed it to her.

She nodded. Flamingos were beautiful birds, actually. "That's per day. For how many days?"

Bud Dubbs smiled at her angelically. "As long as it takes to paint the town flamingo pink."

Temple had not been satisfied with the information level and extent of press kits when she was a television news reporter, and she wasn't satisfied now.

As soon as she left the Convention Center parking lot, she pointed her Geo Storm's aqua nose toward the city library.

By computer or by fiche, she would learn all there was to know about this so-called artist, even whether Domingo was his last, first or an assumed name.

The trail led to the periodicals area, where she skimmed glossy art magazines she seldom saw. Inside she found more photos of the artist, who resembled the offspring of a weight lifter and an orchestra conductor. His arms were always elevated in big gestures, waving, directing. Dozens of Domingo's faceless, nameless minions darted around arranging parachute silk or six-story-long strings of spaghetti or twenty miles of *dry-cleaner bags* over hill and dale and under bridges and around revered monuments and locations.

Only one Domingo project had been stridently rejected: a scheme to wrap the Black Hills of South Dakota with ant farms. Not only did Native Americans object, but insect-rights people feared that ants would die by the billions before the project was completed. That was the point, Domingo had protested. A parable of genocide. Weren't these red ants, after all?

"Loony," Temple said aloud.

"Shhhh!" hissed a pasty-faced wimp who was poring over a biker magazine. This *was* the Las Vegas library, after all.

Loony, she repeated to herself, reading that Domingo (no one knew whether it was his first, last or simply latest name, and he wouldn't tell) traveled with his female manager (read mistress between the lines). She leaned close to the photograph to study what would probably be her biggest problem, the Other Woman. She suspected that Verina (no last name, either) would naturally consider herself as the only go-between Domingo should ever require.

The woman was tall, thin and dark, just like Snow White's wicked, witchy stepmother, a chic, handsome forty-something who broadcast a Duchess of Windsor air of imperious command.

Suddenly Bud Dubbs's princely salary didn't look so royal. Did Temple really need this project, with all the other assignments she had to handle? Temple nodded to herself. Yes, to keep her bank balance from bouncing gently now and then. Freelance work was feast or famine. Better to put the pedal to the metal whenever possible than to coast for a while and end up out of gas and stranded.

From the library, Temple headed for the Las Vegas Strip. The sun shone bright on all the glassy hotel façades and unlit featured-attraction signs, but the distant mountains wore their autumnal pales. The air offered the ineffable crispness of November.

Seasonal change in the desert is subtle, which makes it all the more welcome. Now that Halloween was over, along with the disturbing events at the haunted house, nothing but happy holidays loomed, Temple mused: Thanksgiving and Christmas. Temple toyed with the idea of going somewhere else for one of them, like home to Minnesota, or even to New York to visit Aunt Kit. But then what would poor Max do, marooned as he was in the twilight zone of the rogue undercover operative? Or poor Matt, above ground but enjoying it no more than a groundhog who had emerged six weeks too early on February 2.

Groundhog Day. Now there was an unhappy holiday, if you could consider it one. An almost-certain decree of six more weeks of winter, laid on the head of some hapless little mammal subjected to an annual grilling under hot television lights. Not that six more weeks of any kind of weather mattered in Las Vegas, which was mostly fair and sunny, with a long, hot salsa–strength summer guaranteed.

Temple took a left off the Strip to Paradise, where the town's latest hot-cha-cha spot had hung its neon shingle.

To declare anyplace the latest hot spot was always dangerous; so many new attractions were springing up daily. Temple slowed the Storm to cruise past her destination.

Still, you couldn't go wrong naming Gangster's the waning year's newest diversion. Temple eyed the string of indecently stretched black limousines that always underlined the entry canopy.

Lest the uninitiated mistook the pervasive limos for a funeral-home fleet, the club's entry had been designed to banish that notion. Polished black marble, as slick as the elongated Cadillacs, faced the building front, along with neon-lit glass blocks in Art Deco designs. Through the etched-glass blocks the lurid lights flickered as shadows flitted behind them. The murky shadow-play implied action of the dangerous, sensual sort: dancing, gaming, fighting, mating.

Le Jazz Hot and Forties Swing drifted through the open double doors as clients were ushered inside by broad-shouldered men in sinister fedoras who wore pastel ties against dark shirts and suits.

The upper level of the building was shaped into a fedora and gun barrel, both cocked, with veiled red lights visible as squinting eyes in the eaves' eternal penumbra.

In high-rise Las Vegas Strip terms, the building looked as low and sleek and darkly intimate as the shadowed cars, but that was deceptive. Temple knew it also housed a modest, six hundred-room hotel, a four-thousand-seat theater, a giant gaming casino that was "raided" nightly by fake feds, a vintage movie theater that even played newsreels, a museum filled with gats and getaway cars from the gangland days of old, and up-to-date shopping centers in flanking wings: Gents and G-Men on the left, with the Moll Mall on the right. (Some women, when shopping, presumably behaved like Mau-Mau insurrectionists.)

In the area of parking space, though, Gangster's was hardly the bee's knees. Temple drove around to the side lot, which—unlike most Las Vegas car parks—charged a fee.

"Wish you had a courtesy lot," Temple grumbled as she took a chit from the cheeky attendant. "I'm just here to pick up a friend."

"Jeez, lady, keep your garters on. You get a free pull at the Electric Chair million-dollar bonanza slot inside." He spoke with a Brooklyn accent, provoking Temple to wonder how many aspiring actors were finding work at Las Vegas theme attractions these days.

She hustled inside, checking her watch. Six o'clock. She was supposed to have retrieved Midnight Louie from his day's labors at five-thirty.

The doorman was a brute in a navy pin-striped suit, his lapel adorned with a pink carnation. Temple scurried into the marble-floored lobby, meant to echo to the click of women's high heels and the softer snick of men's patent-leather evening shoes.

Her Manolo Blahnik snakeskin pumps provided the proper click, but most of the tourists milling about inside wore tennis shoes that scuffed the mirror-polished floors.

Temple passed the uniformed hat-check girl and the page boy, zoomed past the Hush Money and Speakeasy restaurants and through the casino to descend to the theater.

The placard inside echoed the bigger, brighter sign outside:

DARREN COOKE, LIVE AND IN PERSON, STARRING IN
MAKING LAS VEGAS

Temple paused to evaluate the dramatic black-and-white photo of Cooke. The photographer had mastered the harsh, five-o'clock-shadow lighting that had dominated film-studio portraits in Hollywood's pre-Technicolor days.

Cooke was a man of many talents. Comic, film actor, cabaret performer. He looked as lethal as Sam Spade in his angled fedora and wide lapels, his profile a deep, hawkish shadow behind him. He could have been John Garfield or James Cagney, those

macho masters of menace in a dozen gangland sagas. At first
glance he was Tyrone Power–handsome except . . . his looks just
missed leading man, which was why his format was the spoof,
the takeoff, the almost-serious impression that turns on itself to
go for laughs instead of thrills and chills.

It weren't as if Cooke had Crosby's ears or Hope's nose. Nothing so obvious. But like Steve Martin or Jim Carrey, he seemed
more natural mocking himself. Now he was featured in a revue
mocking Las Vegas's mobster roots.

"They're rehoising, lady." A thug, also obviously from Brooklyn via Central Casting, paused in cruising the casino aisle to eye
her suspiciously as she hesitated before the theater.

"That's okay, bud. I'm here to pick up one of the cast members." *Quite literally "pick up."*

"I guess you can go in, but keep it shut."

Temple wondered whether he meant her mouth or her mind.
She ducked past the entrance curtain (nice touch) and down the
slanted aisle toward the only lights and action in the theater, the
stage with its cast of dozens milling about.

Nothing onstage held anything but a passing interest for her.
She headed for a line of bored and downcast people slouching
in the first row, fencing in two bored and downcast cats.

"Is Louie done?" Temple bent to ask the director in a whisper. Maybe Louie could get her guest passes to the show, now
that he was a card-carrying member of the animal performer's
union.

Kyle Conrad was an acidic man in his forties, whom she suspected of secretly hating cats.

"Apparently," he said. "Mr. Comedy King onstage has called
for so many reruns that they haven't even gotten to the 'Viva Las
Vegas' number on whose coattails we're supposed to ride."

"Don't you mean cattails?" put in one of the commercial stylists, a bouncy twenty-something woman named Marcy Givens.

Temple was amazed. "But this is your second day on the set.
You mean you haven't even gotten a chance yet to block out the
scenario?"

"We're a charity operation," Kyle said. "Charity operations sit around on their cans day in and day out."

"But then . . ." Temple was shocked. "Poor Louie's been confined to that awful carrier all day for nothing."

Temple brushed past the stalled crew members to crouch beside the carrier in question. A pair of resentful green eyes stared out from the dark interior.

"Louie!"

"He's had the three required bathroom breaks." Sharon Hammerlitz, the animal trainer, a jeans-clad woman with an aggressive blond buzz-cut, had followed her. "But he doesn't much care for cat litter."

Temple pinched the door mechanism open and thrust in a hand.

"He growled when I did that," Marcy noted.

"Maybe you had cat litter on your hands." Temple scratched Louie's velvety chin and was rewarded with a basso purr.

From onstage came the inevitable aural chaos of rehearsal: people outshouting each other, set pieces scraping into place and properties in motion clattering.

One voice overrode it all. "Okay, people! We finally got the Big Daddies sketch right. Let's break for today. We'll start with the chorus number tomorrow."

A big chorus of groans came in unison. "Awwww."

"They're all in costume for it now, Darren," a flunky's timorous voice explained.

"Change back. What's the big deal, people? I've got two-dozen changes in a two-hour show. You don't hear me moanin' and groanin'. This is what you get the big bucks for, so hustle the bustles back to the dressing rooms. Everybody'll be fresher in the morning anyway."

"As the chicken said to the egg, 'The yolks won't be any fresher,' " someone threw out in parting.

Nobody laughed.

The tramp of departing feet accompanied by low grumbles indicated that the chorus was in retreat. In the first row, another grumbler added, "These cats won't be fresh in the morning after sitting around for two days."

"They'll be fresh for acting up," the trainer added more loudly. "And they're amateurs on top of it."

"Who's an amateur?" an indignant new voice demanded.

Temple knew that voice and didn't want to. She straightened as a willowy platinum-blond woman came stalking down the aisle on heels so high they wobbled.

The woman brushed past Temple, and Louie, to pause dramatically two seats down.

"How is Mummy's little sweetums?" With one smooth unzipping, little sweetums was swept from her pink canvas carrier and lofted into her mistress's arms.

Normally the sight of the petite shaded-silver Persian cuddled against her mistress's matching hair would have been pretty enough to photograph, as had been duly done many times before.

But on this occasion, the seraphic expression on Savannah Ashleigh's overmadeup face was falling faster than Lucifer exited Heaven.

"Why . . . what's wrong, baby?" Savannah whirled to face the line of numbed crew members. "Yvette is . . . wet!"

"Maybe she drooled," Marcy suggested hopefully.

"She is not wet in the area that drools! How has this happened? Who was responsible for giving her potty breaks? I suppose she hasn't had a dab to eat all day too! And you call yourselves animal handlers? I should sue."

Before anyone in the front-row seats could rouse themselves to a defense, an energetic patter of feet came bouncing down the temporary steps at stage right.

"House lights!" a lusty male voice demanded.

He got 'em. Temple blinked at the sudden burst of high-power light. So did the moles on the commercial crew who'd been huddling in the darkened house all day.

Inside his carrier, Midnight Louie did not blink, although he rose and thrust a furry black paw through the grillwork.

" 'Vannah, that you?" Darren Cooke himself—he who had

commanded, "Let there be light"—came straight for Savannah Ashleigh and her publicly embarrassed cat, squinting slightly from the ordered light. "Haven't seen you for an age, luv!"

She dodged his automatic embrace by turning away, Yvette still in her arms, and offering her cheek.

"Touch not the cat, darling; she's been kept waiting all day and is . . . cranky."

"Not unlike her owner, as I recall," he answered in a stage whisper. With his booming voice, even a discreet comment rebounded to the back wall.

Cooke turned and took sudden notice of the glum people in the front row. "And who are we?"

"We are a television-commercial crew," Kyle answered for one and all. "We have permission from the club to piggyback a forty-five-second spot on your big Las Vegas number."

"Oh, yeah. I heard about that. Savannah oughta look drop-dead gorgeous against the tutti-frutti gangster chorus we've got in that number. Once we get it rehearsed tomorrow, you can take all the time you want to set up and film. The chorus boys and girls are paid for a full day. I'll get done fast, so you guys can go to it."

Sighs and murmured thanks exploded from the front row.

Darren Cooke turned his special crooked smile on Savannah. "Anything for you, dollface." She wriggled uneasily, whether from prolonged cheek-to-cheek contact with Yvette in her disgraced state or from Darren Cooke's embarrassingly wrong assumption it was hard to tell.

"Wrong dollface," Temple couldn't help putting in.

Her comment drew Cooke's direct gaze and thousand-watt, professionally whitened smile. "Who are you?"

"Temple Barr. My cat's in this commercial too, just like Savannah's."

He whirled to the actress. "Your *cat*? Not you?"

"They wanted Yvette desperately. I didn't want to stand in her way."

Cooke turned back to Temple, the charm still radiating on full wattage. "And where is *your* cat?"

"He's the malcontent in the carrier."

Temple took the occasion to spring Louie, then heft him into her arms. He was, thank goodness, dry as a desert, if not as chipper as a chuckwalla lizard.

"All that's just one cat, Temple?"

"Just one. And only. Meet Midnight Louie."

"Midnight Louie. I like it. Might use that name in the show for a minor character. Well." Cooke glanced at Savannah, who pouted while discreetly dabbing at Yvette's posterior with the pink satin cushion from the carrier. " 'Vannah, when you're done catting around, come backstage. We've gotta get together. Why didn't you tell me you were in town?"

"Didn't know that you were, Dare," she said, her voice becomingly breathless. Yvette was unceremoniously returned to her carrier, cushion and all, and zipped away. "I'll just freshen up and be right down."

He nodded, then swept his eyes over the weary television crew. "Nice to meet you, folks. Here are passes for the show." Cooke produced the fanned sheaf of colored pasteboards almost as suddenly as the Mystifying Max could conjure a magical deck of cards, and passed them out, not forgetting Temple.

Then he bounded up the stairs to grab a towel from a stool offstage and vanished into the wings.

"Wish I'd had that towel for Yvette," Savannah muttered. Her penciled eyebrows knit as she surveyed the inactive crew. "I'm going to be here first thing in the morning, and I'm not leaving until you finish filming. Obviously you can't be trusted with a delicate creature like Yvette."

She lofted the carrier and undulated up the aisle, no doubt to the nearest ladies' room, where both she and Yvette could wash away the strains—and stains—of the day.

Marcy bent to pull a litter pan from under her seat. "I put that prissy Persian in the box about eight times today and couldn't get Mummy's little sweetums to tinkle once, much less do anything else. Your Louie isn't a great performer, either, but at least he can contain himself."

"Maybe you need separate boxes for the two cats," Temple suggested. "How long do you think it will take tomorrow?"

"We can do our bit on this set in a couple of hours," Kyle said. "Depends how long Mr. Perfection drills the chorus."

"Well, I'll stay with Louie when we come back tomorrow morning."

Kyle cleared his throat and took off his round, horn-rimmed glasses to polish them. "We really prefer to work without owners present. They can distract their animals."

"Listen, as long as that piece of cinematic cheesecake is here to defend her sweetums tooth and nail, I'll be here to do the same for Midnight Louie."

A martyred sigh. "Amateurs. Maurice was so easy to work with. He didn't have an owner. It's a good thing I have him here on call, just in case."

"In case of what?" Temple asked, highly miffed.

"I have a feeling a lot will go wrong tomorrow. It wouldn't hurt to have a body double on hand."

"Maurice doesn't look a bit like Louie."

"He would if he were dyed black from toe to tail." Kyle turned to his dispirited crew. "Come on, gang. Drinks on me. Tomorrow we'll see action, I promise you."

Temple was left with a heavy cat in her arms, a heavy carrier on the chair seat behind her and an empty stage before her.

"Stardom is a pain in the neck for stage mothers too, Louie," she told him, struggling to stuff him back in his carrier.

Louie fanned his toes, flared his nails and clawed plastic.

"Now don't be temperamental," Temple said, panting. "Fame has its obligations, and if you're too difficult, I'll let a tie-dyed Maurice have all the glory. That Yvette is as much a pain as her owner, anyway, not to mention a bad example in the bathroom department."

Louie's grip on the carrier suddenly gave. He was in and had turned around to face Temple in the twinkling of a green eye.

"Merow," he said, most persuasively, rubbing against the grille.

"I will be good," it sounded like to Temple, but she was a born optimist.

"Ooof!" She heaved Louie and his carrier off the seat to begin the long walk back up the aisle. "I'm going to have to pay a union grip just to carry you."

It wasn't fair, Temple thought. Here she was hoofing it home alone with the Godzilla of the cat world while Savannah Ashleigh was primping herself and her lightweight Yvette for a tête-à-tête with the charming Darren Cooke, who was obviously no stranger.

Not to be catty or anything, but some bimbos had all the luck.

Chapter 3

Curb Service

"Show business!"

Temple let Midnight Louie's carrier thump to the Circle Ritz lobby floor.

"As in: there's no business like—?" Electra, her landlady, fed Temple the first part of the lyric as if they were on a game show.

"I would hope not. Poor Louie was kept sitting around in a carrier all day and never got a chance to go on."

"I hope he got a chance to go."

"He didn't take that opportunity, either. I better get him up to our digs—and I do mean 'digs' in this case—pronto. Although he almost never honors his box upstairs with a deposit."

"Er, what is his location of choice, then?" An alarmed expression grew in Electra's gray eyes.

"Not in the condominium, trust me. He goes outside, I guess, during his many mysterious outings."

Electra held the arriving elevator door open so Temple could drag in the carrier.

"I did meet Darren Cooke, though," Temple added in parting, as the elevator doors slashed shut between them.

Electra thrust a bangled forearm between the doors faster than Bruce Willis on a *Die Hard* rampage, then bumped her way through as they opened again.

"Darren Cooke! He's one of my favorites."

"Favorite whats?"

"Favorite performer, favorite comedy actor—and not a bad dramatic actor, either—favorite male, period. Is he as good-looking in person?"

"Sort of."

"Sort of! He's supposed to be a real ladies' man. What did you think?"

"He's professionally charming. If that's a ladies' man, then he's got the title. He did show mercy on our little À La Cat commercial film crew, though. That bespeaks a gentleman, but appearances can be deceiving, especially when said gentleman is trying to impress the hooker shoes off a certain blond bimbo named Savannah."

"Temple, I wish you wouldn't act so jaded. You're much too young for that. Darren Cooke is practically a movie star, for heaven's sake."

On the second floor, Electra held the elevator doors ajar while Temple and Louie bumped through. Then she commandeered the handle of Louie's carrier and led Temple down the circular hallway.

"What does 'practically a movie star' mean?" Temple wanted to know. "He made—what? Two movies. And one was a bomb."

"It's hard to find the right vehicle for an actor who does both comedy and drama," Electra said to defend her idol. "So what is Darren Cooke doing in Vegas and where did you see him?"

"At Gangster's, where they're supposed to be filming Louie's À La Cat commercial. At least Darren Cooke promised the crew that he'd get his show on the road tomorrow so that we could film, and gave everyone passes to his show. Poor Yvette waited so long that she . . . ah, sprinkled her carrier."

"Persians are high-strung, unlike your average alley cat. Me, I'd take a mongrel every time."

Electra waited while Temple unlocked her door, then slung the carrier to the entry-hall floor.

"But you didn't. Karma is a purebred, isn't she?"

"Karma is a Birman, but I didn't pick her; she picked me. If I'd had my druthers, I'd have picked a little mongrel."

"I think the politically correct term these days is 'random-bred.' " When Temple bent to spring Louie, he charged from the carrier, then swiftly leapt out of sight.

"He seemed entertaining," said Temple, finishing her inter-rupted postmortem on Darren Cooke, "but anybody who appar-ently had a fling with Savannah Ashleigh can't be accused of good taste."

"Savannah Ashleigh and Darren Cooke? No!" Electra plunked her muumuued form down on Temple's pale sofa, a tropical vine engulfing a mushroom. "Maybe Darren just feels sorry for Sa-vannah now that her career is kaput."

"Pity does not appear to be a dominant shade in Mr. Cooke's psychological makeup kit, despite his mercy to the commercial crew. I wonder now if that was because Savannah's cat was in-volved and he wanted to look good in her eyes."

"You've become so suspicious of other people's motives ever since you got involved in a murder or two, Temple. It doesn't become you. Maybe that's why your love life is in limbo."

"What makes you think it's in limbo?"

"I haven't seen any gentlemen callers hanging around here lately."

Temple was tempted to retort that her beaus were to be heard and not seen, thinking especially of Max's surreptitious comings and goings, but pride wasn't a good enough excuse to blow his cover.

So she merely sat on the sofa and swung the empty carrier door open and shut with the toe of her shoe.

"Don't worry about me, Electra. I've got my hands full with work assignments right now. I appreciate a little peace and quiet."

"That's just it. Matt is so quiet lately. Too quiet."

"He always was."

"But he was getting better when you two were—"

"Were what?"

"Well, I don't know what, exactly. That's what's so aggravating. If you're going to be a landlady and have tenants, you should at least have the fun of prying into their private lives, but your and Matt's lives are much too private for any fun."

"How do you know, if they're that private?" Temple waggled her eyebrows significantly.

Electra stood, jerking her shapeless muumuu into place. "I guess I'd find the diary of Mr. Midnight Louie more revealing and entertaining than I would one of yours, or Matt's or Max's."

Temple smiled. "I guess you might. Louie and Yvette seem to have a pretty hot thing going."

"If I'm reduced to feline soap opera, I might as well retire. So, anyway, if you get another show pass, I'd love to see Darren Cooke's revue at . . . where is it?"

"Gangster's. The new casino-nightclub on Paradise. And I bet I'll get more passes tomorrow. I'm going to be on the set until it's all over."

Electra nodded, regretfully glancing around the empty apartment as if in search of hidden hunks, then left.

Temple had risen to slide home the chain lock behind her when the phone rang. She went to the wall model in the kitchen, flicking on the overhead fluorescent light.

Matt Devine's voice came over the line like a baritone shiatsu massage. Temple kicked off her heels and leaned against the wall, letting her expanding vertebrae iron the wallpaper.

"Is this a good time to call?" he asked.

"Best time. Just got in."

"Ah, I'm off tonight."

"So am I."

"I need your advice."

"Oh?"

"And I could use your company."

"Ah."

"But I don't have any idea of what we could do, or where we could go. The guy is supposed to be good at this."

"Not when he's talking to a crack Las Vegas PR lady. Relax. Come down to my place in half an hour and we'll leave from here."

"I hate to stick you with all the driving."

"No problem. No driving. Half an hour."

"Ah . . . what should I wear?"

"Something black would be appropriate."

Temple depressed the hook, then dialed. G-A-N-G-S-T-A. Not much dialogue was required.

"Circle Ritz. Two people." She spoke in a confidential whisper, then checked her watch. "Seven-thirty."

That was all. Temple pushed off the wall, hoping that Gangster's lived up to its advertising, but mostly wondering what Matt's problem might be . . . this time.

Twenty-five minutes later, Electra's LOVERS' KNOT WEDDING CHAPEL sign winked blue-and-pink neon on Matt and Temple as they waited in front of the Circle Ritz.

"Black didn't work out." Matt lifted a foot to show his only trace of the color—shoes.

But his navy sport coat almost looked black when the neon winked off and his light gray slacks were in the black family. And at Gangster's, family was everything.

"I don't wear much black myself," Temple admitted, "but I did dig up this."

"This" was a crinkle-cotton affair with a tiered, ankle-length (on her) skirt and a blouse with ruffled sleeves almost as big as watermelons. Spanish dancer was as close as Temple's closet could get to Mafia mama.

"Here's our ride," she announced brightly.

Matt had mastered the art of disguising surprise early, but the long, long black limousine that whispered up beside the curb nearly ruined a lifetime's worth of practice.

"Temple, we can't afford this! I just wanted a quiet place to talk."

"The back of a limo isn't quiet enough for you?"

Before he could answer, the sable-uniformed driver had come around to flourish the passenger door open.

Temple bent to walk into the dim, capacious interior; Matt could only duck and follow.

The door was shut with the expensive finality of a bank vault as Temple wiggled her ruffles deep into the cushy upholstery.

Matt was slower to settle in, from unease rather than enjoyment. He leaned forward to study the driver as they left the curb.

"He didn't even ask where we're going."

"That's because he knows where we're going. Don't worry! It's a free ride."

Matt's fretful expression deepened as sallow flashes of the Las Vegas lights bored through the dark window tint. "The only free ride you get in Las Vegas is if you're a high roller, and we sure aren't."

"You're whispering, you know. I don't think the driver can hear us unless we push this button."

Matt regarded the indicated mother-of-pearl circle with suspicion. His look turned to horror when Temple started pressing other white buttons: piped-in music began to play, and a lid flipped down to reveal a portable bar.

"This is better than a game arcade!" She poured the contents of a cocktail shaker into two waiting martini glasses. "Except the ride is a lot smoother."

"Nothing for me." Matt was looking around for more trick furnishings.

There was nothing to see beyond the tinted-glass barrier that reflected her and himself as convivial ghosts and . . . a small vase near the car window on his side.

"Why a white lily?" he wondered aloud, still whispering. "Are we going to a funeral?"

"Who knows?" Temple sipped her martini. "Ooh, really different. Try one. I bet it's vintage."

"Vintage gin?" he asked in disbelief.

"No, vintage recipe. Try a sip."

Temple's aplomb required an answering ease. Matt leaned

over to sip from her glass, amazed by how the silk-smooth ride made everything so easy.

"It is different."

"A gin cocktail, I think. I had a gin account once. Orange bitters and straight gin. Don't worry. Everything's on the house . . . until we get there."

"Worrying's a basic tenet of my religion."

"Well, at least wait until we get there."

"Where is 'there'?"

Temple sighed hard enough to stir her sleeve ruffles. "I guess you didn't eyeball the license plate on this limo."

"I didn't notice the car until it was at the curb."

"It's a vanity plate: Mobmobile three."

"That's supposed to be reassuring?"

"We're being taken for a ride."

"Free. Even less reassuring."

"To Gangster's."

"Friends of yours, no doubt."

"Doubt it. They don't know me from Adam Ant, but nothing is too good for us."

"Why?"

"We're customers. Look."

Temple pointed out Matt's window. He pressed his nose to the tinted surface and squinted at the lights looming on the right.

"It's . . . some kind of—"

"Joint," Temple finished happily. "Newest little gyp joint in Vegas. Gangster's. Apostrophe's all wrong, of course, but why should any attraction start getting grammatical now? Look at Caesars Palace. Back to Gangster's: casino; mob museum; theater and revue with Darren Cooke headlining; two restaurants, Speakeasy and Hush Money; and two attached shopping malls."

Matt turned back to her. "Plus a line of limos two blocks long."

"Right. Gangster's makes up for having only a small hotel with a gimmick: importing tourists from other hotels by the load. Call 'em and they'll pick you up anywhere in Las Vegas. First-class and free. Want that vintage martini now? Might be here for a while before all the other uneasy riders disembark."

Matt stretched out a hand while Temple passed the alcoholic ammunition, and talked.

"I peeked into Hush Money when I was there earlier this evening picking up poor Louie. It's really quiet. Old-fashioned telephones at each table and booth; no one speaking louder than a whisper. The waitstaff even wear Hush Puppies. Should be ideal for a civilized discussion."

"And they take us home?"

"Round-trip service . . . unless you end up in cement overshoes in Lake Mead."

Matt shook his head. "I can taste bitters in this drink, that's what is different."

"How does an ex-priest like you know about bitters?"

"Comes with the territory."

Chapter 4

Father Confessor

As soon as I am sprung from my cage, I head for the hills.

When we are talking Miss Temple Barr's condominium, we are talking about up hill and over dale in interior terms. In other words, I dash for the spare bathroom, do the two-step up the commode and then hop high onto the narrow sill. Finally, I am out the ajar window and down to the narrow triangle of patio that is the only thing between me and a twenty-foot splat on the ground-level concrete.

Where is a guy to go when he seeks an upstanding and sympathetic ear?

I examine my options. There is Sassafras, but she might be in stir. She is always being jailed for streetwalking, until she is bailed out by a sympathetic human. (Sassafras is a mighty engaging bit of pussycat.) Then she struts away from her new home as fast as her spike-heeled nails can take her. Unreformed, that is Sassafras's M.O. And that is why there is no chance I will find a sympathetic ginger ear there; she is too hard to locate in a pinch, being that she is so often pinched.

I consider Ingram. Are you kidding? He is so lost in the theoretical world of books that he would not know what to do with a real-life dilemma if it walked up and snapped him in the bow-tie collar, which it often does when I come around seeking information for a case.

But now *I* am the case in question.

I pace the twilight streets, wondering where a guy who solves every one else's problems can go when he has one of his own. Who listens to the listener? And I am a prime-time listener, who nods off on cue, gives out frequent, profound "hmmmms" and flexes all my thinking toes during the long, boring recitals of woes both human and feline.

Now I need somebody to sit still and lend an ear. Miss Temple is not adequate for this service at the moment; she has problems enough of her own.

For an instant the name "Midnight Louise" flashes through my fevered brain. But I am dreaming. My hard-as-nails offspring is hardly one to sympathize with her papa's delicate condition.

I wander the familiar streets, lost in thought if not in direction. I might cadge some human sympathy at the Crystal Phoenix. Miss Van von Rhine and Mr. Nicky Fontana—not to mention the entire Brothers Fontana—might give me a friendly pat on the back, but I need more direct attention.

I walk in circles, until I end up at the Gray Line bus terminal.

Terminal. That is the condition of my search.

And then I see a bus interior glowing warm in the dusk and read the destination emblazoned on the narrow window above the windshield: TEMPLE BAR.

If Miss Temple Barr is too distracted to provide me the proper advice and comfort, a closer relation lies at the end of a long, dark bus ride.

I hop aboard. (I have spent a long time cultivating the Gray Line bus drivers and must say I have them well-trained by now; a private operative can do no better for cheap, reliable transportation in a hurry than his own bus company.)

"This is our company mascot," the driver announces over the intercom. "We are thinking of changing our name to Black Line, he has been hopping aboard so regularly. We think he is a stray with a wandering paw. We call him 'Blackie.' "

I stroll the aisles, accepting coos from middle-aged ladies, a bit of mauling from preteen kids and not much eye contact from adult men. Adult men do not usually have much time for those of my ilk. No doubt they are aware of my awesome reputation with the ladies; jealousy is such a pathetic fault. Only the weak know envy.

Well, we are all soon whisked away on the air-cushion ride of a well air conditioned tour bus, not that we need much air-conditioning at this time of year.

Still, the bus is pretty full, which makes me happy for the operators of the main attraction at Temple Bar, the Glory Hole Gang. With such a colorful name, I am flattered that they would name their restaurant after me, in a sense: "Three O'Clock Louie's." Yes, I am Midnight Louie, but obviously Three O'Clock is kin of mine. My father, to be precise. He is a salty old dog, for a feline, and spent his retirement years in the Pacific Northwest on a salmon trawler until he was pensioned out to Lake Mead. I imagine that a lake, even a large, artificial lake like this one, is quite a come down for one used to the open ocean, the icy, fish-choked waters of the Pacific.

Speaking of icy, fish-choked waters, I can certainly use a carp cocktail at the moment, and Temple Bar landing on Lake Mead teems with them. Carp are quite an attraction for the tourists, who call them "koi" and want to feed them. And why should they not? The carp will be all the more fat-ter for my own delectation. Of course my own delectation must await my own satisfaction, and that is the rub. I am so distressed by my bizarre personal quandary that I can hardly extend a talon for the hunt.

But not to worry. My esteemed sire, Three O'Clock, is unofficial maître d' at his namesake restaurant, and I am sure he can come up with a tidbit or two for an offspring in extremis.

When the bus pulls into the lot, the place looks brighter than a traveling carnival. I see lights on the water. So the Glory Hole Gang's dream of a gambling showboat that straddles the state line which runs through the lake hereabouts has come true. I know they have bigger plans for the site than an eatery and a floating casino, and am diverted enough from my own problems to wonder what is cooking (besides fish fillet).

I hop off the bus first to avoid being trampled in the general exodus. (Being as I am the Sublime Color, black, I am often in complete agreement with the turf, be it asphalt or the black-rubber matting of a bus. So it behooves me to be fleet of foot and out from under nearby feet.)

We now must pass over an arched footbridge (very Oriental and sheik), below which carp lips are positively panting for treats. I gaze down, flexing my fingers and toes. I would have a shiv surprise for them, had I not better things to do, places to go and dudes to see.

I notice Wild Blue Pike, Encyclopedia Brown and other Glory Hole Gang guys on the gangplank, welcoming the landlubbers aboard this restaurant on a peninsula. I would say hello, but am too distracted to put up a brave front.

So I duck under the wooden deck that surrounds the restaurant and go hunting my old man.

I have to admit the old man has sunk to lower levels in his retirement. No more fresh game for him. He prefers it precaught, precooked and delivered to his door. With the alfresco tables surrounding the indoor restaurant, enough

bounty falls through the deck-boards to feed a fleet of re-
tired salmon fishermen.

I find Three O'Clock, attired in a lobster bib, reclining like
a Roman emperor under a party of twelve, half of whom
are having seafood.

"Are you not ashamed of yourself," I greet him, "lapping
up fish flakes as if they were rain?"

"Sloppy eaters, I love 'em," he answers without a qualm.
"How are you doing, sonny boy? I have a shrimp or two I
could spare."

"I am not hungry." I hunker down beside him, beneath
the hullabaloo and the hooting.

"You cannot afford to be 'not hungry,' not in that fly-by-
night business you operate. So what is up?"

"Possibly my life expectancy."

This catches his attention. He actually turns his head and
misses a tidbit of calamari that has snaked down between
the floorboards above us. I hate to see a good piece of
sushi go to waste, so snag it.

"Your life expectancy? Pish, boy. You will outlive me. But
not by much. I expect retirement to be extremely beneficial."

"Maybe not. I may be the victim of foul play."

"That is what you get for messing around the mean
streets. You ought to move out to the country like me.
Crime is down and tourism is up. You know what that
means. Free eats! It is not too bad if you stay out of the
sun; can get a little hot in the summer. There is a whole
crew of us out here. We call ourselves the 'Lake Mead
Meows.'"

"Please! I am not about to join a retirement community.
I merely came out for a little paternal advice and instead I
get a Sun City infomercial."

"And what is wrong with resting after one's lifetime of
labors?"

"Nothing. Only one cannot rest if one is the target of a hit man."

That gives the old man pause. That is to say, he lifts his mitt and licks his pads thoughtfully. "A hit man? After you? Why, lad?"

I hate it when he uses that old-salt talk. His seafaring days were about one-tenth of his lifespan, but you would think he had been on the *Merrimac* or the *Nautilus*.

"I know too much," I reply.

"That is an odd condition for one of our family," Three O'Clock ruminates, picking shrimp remnants from his teeth. "Since when?"

"Since I attended an all-cat séance and was approached by the ghost of Maurice One."

"Maurice One. That some kind of perfume, son?"

"That was some kind of TV huckster. Big yellow tiger-stripe, out of a shelter. Promoted Yummy Tum-tum-tummy cat food."

"Very bad. That stuff is not a dolphin-safe catch. This Maurice should have bought it for lending his name to such an earth-unfriendly product. At least my salmon was dolphin-safe."

"It was not very salmon-safe to the salmon involved," I grit out between my fangs. Three O'Clock is hardly one to point a paw. "The fact is, Maurice One is one dead dude, thanks to the quick thinking of his body double, Maurice Two, who shoved him into a vat of Yummy Tum-tum-tummy."

"What a way to go! Whisker-deep in seafood. That is how I would like to bow out, only I would wish to be set adrift from Temple Bar here, on a barge heaped with salmon and tuna fish, and then set afire. Will you see to it, son?"

"Pricey funerals went out with Erik the Red, Dad. If you want, I can see that your ashes are thrown off the top of the Luxor pyramid. I have Egyptian connections."

"Then why not go to your 'Egyptian connections,' if you need muscle?"

"I do not need muscle. I need spiritual guidance. I am not the Yummy Tum-tum-tummy spokescat—"

Three O'Clock's big paw rests on my shoulder. "I am so glad, son. I would hate to have to tell anybody that. Especially your Aunt Kitty."

"I am the co-spokescat for À La Cat—"

"Now *that* has a ring to it."

"That may be. As spokescat, I get to act opposite the Divine Yvette."

"Ooo-hee, boy. That is not the sleek Persian number I have seen on the old boys' television set hawking Free-to-be-Feline in the past? What a set of whiskers! Can you get me her phone number?"

"Shut up, Dad, unless something is dropping from above, and I hope it is gull guano. I need some advice."

"Oh, I am good at that!"

"The thing is, should I off this Maurice Two before he offs me?"

"Definitely. It is justifiable homicide."

"How do you know?"

"Any homicide is justifiable to save your own skin."

"But what if he has decided that two accidents on a cat-commercial set would be suspicious? I might be exercising a termination with extreme prejudice for nothing."

"Does this Maurice Two look anything like Maurice One?"

"He is the spitting image."

"Well, then, there is no problem. I have seen this Maurice One, or Two, on the tube. I never did care for yellow-bellied tiger-stripes. You would be doing the world, and Miss Silver Persian, a favor by ridding the planet of his ugly mug."

"You are suggesting murder!"

"No, I am suggesting anticipatory self-defense. It would not be self-defense if you did not strike first. Do not be a wimp, Louie. No son of mine would hesitate to do unto be-

fore he was *done* unto. The next time I see you, I expect
to hear that Maurice Two is no more."

With this, he boxes me in the face like some Mafia don.

What an imagination. He is living in the past. There must
be a civilized way of handling the entire situation, and I plan
to find it, or I will have to knock Maurice Two right off the
face of the planet.

And I abhor unnecessary violence.

Chapter 5

Money Talks

Gangster's had a hundred-dollar atmosphere but Hush Money boasted a ten-dollar bill of fare.

That is the great, democratic thing about Las Vegas, Matt thought as he perused the well-illustrated menu. Food and lodging are kept family-affordable even though the atmosphere shouts Big Money. Everyone feels like a king or a queen on a parlor maid's budget.

Now that he was face-to-face with Temple across a table, he felt strangely reluctant to bring up the reason for this meeting. Maybe that was because serious discussions about other people's problems always brought underlying personal issues of one's own to the surface.

"What are you having?" they asked each other in the same awkward rush at the identical moment.

Matt, who had been stewing about food for thought, not for the plate, cast his eye on the first likely entrée. "The, ah, St. Valentine's Day Massacre ribs."

"I'm not that hungry. Or that homicidal. Guess I'll get the Ma

Barker baby quail. I wonder if they serve buckshot with that."

Temple picked up the tabletop upright phone and lifted the vintage earpiece to her modern ear, giving their order directly to the kitchen.

"Everybody has a gimmick," Matt commented, restoring the menus to their slot behind an illuminated jukebox radio that looked as if it had survived the Depression.

Their nook was more of a box than a booth, so high were the dark-wood backs and sides. Green leatherette upholstery cushioned the closed-in effect. Had the booths been horses, they would have been described as springing from Spanish Inquisition out of Gin Joint.

"Feels like an old-time confessional," Matt noted, turning the dark beer he had ordered on arriving. The waiter had worn a shabby tuxedo and a dishcloth apron splattered with tomato sauce—one hoped it was tomato sauce, anyway.

"I think it's kinda cozy." Temple sipped her white zinfandel, whose pinkish hue clashed with her don't-give-a-damn, "frankly Scarlett" red hair. "So. Do you have confessional matters to talk over?"

"Not really. Still, I do wonder if I have a right to discuss this with anyone." Matt found himself muttering, as if in fear of eavesdroppers. Ethical dilemmas always made him sound uncertain.

"So." He was changing the subject, or maybe just delaying the inevitable or else rushing in where fools and forces of nature hesitate to go. "You never said how that Halloween-séance death was cleared up."

"It's still hanging fire. What is the Scottish court's judgment? 'Not proven.' Yet."

"Like Cliff Effinger's alleged death."

"Is this about that?"

"No. This is about the living, or the presumed living. Speaking of which, has . . . Kinsella made any magical appearances lately? I haven't seen hide nor hair of him, but then I might not recognize him without a Hawaiian shirt and a ponytail."

"I've seen him a couple of times," Temple said after a moment's hesitation.

"So he's planning to become a fixture on the Las Vegas scene."

Temple laughed. "Max as a landmark? I don't think so. He's only here to do his Invisible Man act."

Matt contemplated that. "Invisible? Or Invincible? Maybe not seen . . . but also not forgotten. That would suit a magician's ego."

"Listen, this time Max *wants* to be forgotten."

"Will he be?"

Temple shrugged. "Not by us, I suppose."

Matt sipped the imported ale. Bitter, like medicinal brews.

"You wanted to talk about Max?" she went on. "Or me and Max?"

"No!" Too strongly said to be quite true. "I'm . . . avoiding the real issue, I suppose."

"Cliff Effinger? Have you decided what to do about sighting him, or his double?"

"That's not what I want to talk about, and no, I haven't decided what to do. What I want to talk about tonight is a man I've never met."

"What a relief! No stress, no problems, no hidden agendas, right? Strangers are such a comfort."

"Keep me laughing, Temple, and I just might spit out what I want to say." Matt heard his voice lower as he hunched over his glass mug of beer, closer to Temple. "He's a . . . client. Of ConTact. I may be violating a confidence to discuss him with someone else, but his problem is a world away from any I've dealt with, even before ConTact, in the church. He's become like a patient, a parishioner, a regular. Yesterday I learned he even calls me from out of town. I'm not supposed to be someone's private shrink."

Temple nodded soberly. "I can see the reason for that, but I'm surprised. Hotline counselors actually get repeat calls from the same people? I always figured a person called a hotline when they were drunk or drugged out or thinking about suicide. That doesn't seem the sort of thing that calls for repeat contact."

"A lot of people work their way up to doing something about

critical problems. They try out their resolve on us, the strangers at the other end of the line, before they confront people they know. And some callers are chronic reformers, always talking about it, never doing it. Ill people use other people, and they'll use a hotline counselor as fast as they will a friend. As a counselor, I have to avoid being finessed into becoming an enabler. That's what's bothering me. I think this guy is feeding me the same manipulative line he reels out to everyone in his life: he needs help, he wants to change, only I can reach him."

"Professional crybaby, huh?"

Temple leaned away from the tabletop as Guido or Vito or Tony returned to push a mounded platter of hot food in front of each in turn, ladies first.

"He's a mystery." Matt ignored a pile of barbecued ribs as high as a small gopher mound. "A man with such a strong ego is usually impervious to self-inflicted wounds, but this one seems to wallow in his inner unworthiness, all the while perpetuating the behavior that makes him betray others, and himself."

"Wow. Even on my darkest, three-chocolate-sundae blue Mondays I have never, ever 'wallowed in my unworthiness.' You have to think a lot of yourself to have the chutzpah to feel *that* guilty."

"Exactly true, though rather circuitously put. He has a monumental ego. I confess I'm not used to dealing with that sort of person."

"No." Temple smiled gently as she dissected broiled baby quail. "So," she suggested in Brooklynese. "Maybe youse want a crack P.I. to give you the dope on this anonymous caller, all from long distance, sorta like Mycroft Holmes or Nero Wolfe."

"Like Temple Barr would do fine."

"Hmm. What sort of clues have you picked up so far?"

"For one thing, he is Somebody."

"Isn't everybody?"

"Not the way this guy sees it. He seems to think I'd know his name. Little does he realize how out of it I am."

"And he's called you long-distance?"

"He must be some sort of . . . entertainer. He says he's on the road a lot."

"So was Willie Loman, or so is any traveling salesman today, for that matter. You could be talking to an Astro Toilet Company sales rep with delusions of grandeur. Do you think he gambles?"

"Maybe. He doesn't mention it as one of his vices."

"Then if he isn't a celebrity who comes to Vegas to gamble, he's a celebrity who comes to Vegas to perform."

"Or golf."

"Does golf seem to be one of his vices?"

"No. He seems to favor night games."

"Oho. So that's a problem? Celebrities are surrounded by groupies. One who doesn't succumb is the exception."

"This guy is exceptional, and exceptionally sexually active, to hear him tell it."

"Not smart in this day and age of AIDS."

"He claims it's an addiction."

"And you don't believe in sexual addiction?"

"Oh, I know it's a way certain people have of dealing with past problems, like overeating. But I'm not sure that I believe anything this guy tells me. I think he's been lying to people around him so often, he now has to go farther afield to be believed."

"So he's addicted to lying?"

"Possibly. But not in a pathological way."

"Just a garden-variety liar."

"That's it! He's so casual about what he does, and about telling me. He's a garden-variety womanizer, adulterer, deceiver."

"He's married?"

"Recently. For the first time. Apparently he 'escaped' matrimony for years while being the playboy of the Western world, to hear him tell it. Now he can't stop playing around."

"So he calls you. Makes sense. You work at night. He would ordinarily play around at night. While he's talking to you, he's not out playing around. Seems like he's found a likely solution."

"But I'm not supposed to spend all my time distracting a habitual fornicator."

"Fornicator! Ever wonder why there are so many long words to describe simple hanky-panky?"

"It's hard for me to empathize with his kind of problem."

"I bet!"

"Yet, in some crazy way, he seems to depend on me, like he knows I'm a kind of opposite to him."

"Maybe you aren't." Temple was looking particularly analytical as she stared over the tiny pile of bones on her plate at someplace above Matt's head.

He almost wanted to turn and crane his neck to see if something hadn't appeared there on the dark wood, another womanizer like Elvis, maybe, or maybe St. Maria Goretti, the martyred patron saint of chastity, as all saints of chastity seemed to have been. Or maybe a halo. Instead he kept his eyes fixed on Temple's.

"What do you mean?" he asked.

Her glance came back to his, a challenge. "I mean, here we have two men, anonymously connected by a phone line, who have led lives in the extreme—at opposite ends of the spectrum—but both at extremes nevertheless. You two actually have quite a lot in common. Maybe that's why he calls you so much, and from so far away. Maybe he needs an antiplayboy to wean him from the course he's followed so long. Sort of an Angel's Advocate."

"Amusing and creative, but hardly helpful." Matt studied the piled-up ribs on his plate. Smeared with carmine barbecue sauce, they did resemble mounded bodies. "St. Valentine was a priest, did you know that? He cured the blindness of his jailer's daughter. He had nothing to do with love or marriage. If love is blind, it's odd that a man who restored sight should become the patron saint of lovers."

"I'm sure the Al Capone gang wasn't even aware it was Valentine's Day when they set out to knock off the Bugs Moran crowd. Or . . . maybe love *is* murder."

"Love is singularly absent from my caller's vocabulary. The only real affection he expresses is for his baby daughter."

"Love embarrasses men who have a lot of sexual partners,"

Temple said thoughtfully. "It's almost as if they need to prove that all sex is separate from all love."

"Can it be?"

She really mulled over that one. "Supposedly it's women who insist on attaching emotion to what the male gender would prefer to regard as random acts of self-satisfaction, many random acts. Yet who writes all the lamenting love songs: I lost you, you left me, what we had was wonderful? Most human cultures reward men for suppressing all their emotions except anger, but I think most men need love with their sex like scrambled eggs need ketchup."

"Is love always such a bloody ingredient?"

"Okay. Like English muffins need honey. That's something warm and gooey."

"Why food comparisons?"

" 'Cause we're eating? Or were." She grinned at their empty plates. "Seriously, what makes you think this guy is a celebrity?"

"He keeps talking about what everybody expects of him. Even mentioned that his wife's body is famous!"

"Before or after the baby?"

"Apparently both."

"Galloping galoshes! Do you suppose he could be—wow—Bruce Willis? In Vegas to open another Planet Hollywood or whatever?"

Temple was truly excited, but Matt knew he looked blank.

"You *do* know who Bruce Willis is?" she asked.

"Yeah . . . some sweaty actor in action movies. *Die Hard Sixteen.*"

"But you don't know he's married to Demi Moore?"

"Who?"

Temple shook her head. "*Vanity Fair* magazine cover girl, nude and ninety-nine months pregnant. Starred in *Striptease* postbaby."

Matt shook his head. "Never heard of her; never seen her, and not sorry."

"Good God, man! Don't you watch *Hot Heads*?"

"Not before . . . or since your pal Crawford Buchanan became a stringer for it. When would I watch it? Not at six-thirty, when I'm on my way to work. When it's rerun at ten-thirty, I'm on-line, so to speak."

"But you do know what time it's broadcast! I call that a serious slip into popular culture, Padre."

Matt found himself smiling a bit sheepishly. "When Buchanan was bugging us at the Hell-o-ween Haunted Homestead, I had Electra tape the show for a few nights to see if anything ran."

"And did it?"

"No. I think Buchanan was more interested in heckling you than getting footage. Midnight Louie was to be seen slinking out of camera range during the vermin-activists' segment. That did run."

"Too bad. Wouldn't you know it? You look like a movie star and I sassed Crawford back, and he wouldn't use either one of us."

"I wish you wouldn't say that."

"What?"

"My looks."

"It's true. Pretty people get on television more, and move up in jobs faster and get paid more."

"Talk to ConTact about that."

"You must have some fancy advanced degree after all those years in seminary. I bet you haven't even tried finding a position in keeping with your background."

"I thought we were here to talk about my mysterious promiscuous caller."

"That's why *you're* here. I might want to talk about something else. Conversation is a two-way street, you know. I must admit an anonymous promiscuous caller with claims to celebrity status is a lot more interesting than finding lucrative employment for an ex-priest."

Matt finished his beer. "Look. I want to settle this question of my past, of whether my stepfather's dead or not. That was the reason I came to Las Vegas: to find Cliff Effinger. Everything else, including my so-called career path, will have to wait until that's settled."

Temple nodded seriously. "Meanwhile, the hold-body-and-soul-together, easy-to-get low-paying job is eating at your ethical soul."

"Just this one caller. I could blow the whistle on him; refuse to take his calls. Then, every time I pick up the paper and some male celebrity has committed suicide—granted that doesn't happen a lot—I can blame myself."

"Is he the only one of your clients who's been such a pain in the principles?"

"Oh, some are heartbreakers. The abused women who never walk away, the unwanted old who call mostly for company. Some are pains, especially the compulsives. I can handle them. But it's hard to be sympathetic to an obviously privileged guy whose problem is getting too much sex when—"

"You've never gotten any."

"I was going to say, when so many needy people are stuck in horrifying situations because they haven't the money to escape them. There's nothing personal in this."

"Then why are you blushing?"

"I'm . . . not judging the man's sins, only his sincerity."

"There you go, turning big vague concepts like sin into word games and turning your 'client' into 'the man.' Methinks he's getting under your skin. You did call me here to get my opinion, didn't you?"

Matt tried to keep from squirming on the hard wooden seat. Right now Temple was making him feel ten years old and under the thumb of Sister Linus John. And all because she had mentioned the unmentionable . . . sex. As in: his lack of it.

"I just don't understand where he's coming from. Confession is not even called the same thing it was when I was a child, and fewer people use the Sacrament of Reconciliation now that it's face-to-face and so . . . unblaming.

"Maybe you don't understand where I'm coming from. Literally. St. Stanislaus in Chicago is an old-country parish so far behind the times masses were said in Polish once Latin was abolished, but a Latin mass is still said there every Sunday to this day. They even imported a Polish priest so none of this 'modernization' would infect the parish. I may have grown up there in the sixties and seventies, but it was as if I were in the forties and fifties.

"So I take sin seriously, and especially sexual sin. It's different in Western Europe, France, Italy, or even in the rest of the Americas, where priestly chastity is an often-flouted convention, not a conviction. But Eastern European Catholics—and the Irish too—are fanatically nineteenth-century Catholic, with zero tolerance for sexual immorality."

"Is that why Pope John Paul the Second is Polish? Isn't he the first non-Italian in decades?"

"In centuries," Matt said. "The church grinds even more exceedingly slow than justice. That's why an Iron Curtain cardinal became the first non-Italian pope; he was stoutly out of touch with modern times and mores; he was more nineteenth-century than twentieth because of his isolation and having had to fight for the right to practice religion in a godless state. The Curia will never let a loose cannon like Pope John the Twenty-third slip through again."

Matt could see that his reference to Pope John meant nothing to Temple. She hadn't been born during the brief "open window" tenure of the late, lamented pope of ecumenism. Religion could still be as deep a dividing chasm as race or gender.

Temple was thoughtfully sipping her wine, which was almost untouched.

"You know, someone like your caller, the Don Juan type, usually is afraid of real intimacy."

"After all those . . . conquests?" Matt couldn't keep the incredulity out of his voice.

"If you can believe him." Temple smiled wryly. "That's another thing about Don Juan types. And you said it: conquests. That's what it is for these guys, like winning at poker, or getting a hole in one or . . . oh my, listen to me! I'm knee-deep in double entendres despite myself."

Matt frowned. He hadn't been listening that hard and had evidently missed some subtlety.

"What do you mean that 'conquests' are the key to it?"

"From his point of view, proof of virility. From the woman's point of view, proof of attractiveness. He may win the one-night stand, but even a professional party girl likes to think that there's something special about her, that the union was more than just a scorecard. Unless she's a competitive player too, of course. And then you have the duel of titanic egos."

"If that's the case, what's sex got to do with it?"

"Aha! By Jove—a very promiscuous god, by the way, the great-granddaddy of promiscuous gods—he's got it! I don't think that sexual record-setting has anything really to do with sex. See, that's your hang-up. You're thinking this guy's having all this lurid fun. And he isn't. Every conquest is a failure, because there are more women out there he hasn't converted. Everyone has to adore him, and prove it. His charisma has to triumph over and over. Woman after woman."

" 'Converted.' You make his quest-and-conquest routine sound like a perverted vocation."

"Exactly! He's a high priest of his own Godhood. Which is his Manhood. That's why insecurity has to be at the bottom of it. He doesn't love women. He's a man who simply can't resist a lovely, or a willing or a resistant woman. He's got to prove himself over and over, every day, every night. He's a little boy who's never believed in himself, no matter what worldly success he has achieved. He needs trophies: golf trophies, award trophies, automotive trophies, female-flesh trophies."

"You do make him sound pathetic. And what you say about charisma . . . Did you know that's a religious word? That we talk of Charism as a favor especially granted by God. A grace, a talent. A vocation. And chrism is the oil-balm that is used for anointing; that's why the sacrament for the dying used to be called extreme unction."

" 'Unction' as in 'oil.' I never would have thought of that! That's what I saw you . . . applying to Blandina Tyler's wrists and forehead."

"The anointing." He nodded, trying not to let the aftertaste of the beer, the memory, twist his lips with bitterness. His last priestly act had been performed when he was not a priest any longer, in a situation of extreme need, of extreme unction, for Blandina Tyler certainly. And perhaps for himself.

Matt sighed. This wasn't going as he had expected. He did a hasty examination of conscience on his expectations: sympathy, agreement, shared distaste for the man he had to talk to on the telephone. He had not expected: question, challenge and compassion. Temple Barr was much better at matters of conscience than she knew or than he wanted to admit.

Chapter 6

The Other Side
of Paradise

Although armed with any number of esoteric facts about Domingo's lifestyle, artworks and former projects, Temple was a bundle of nerves at the thought of their first meeting.

She could tell from the magazine pieces that Domingo himself was as much of a performance artist as his projects were what used to be called "happenings" back when she was busy being born in the sixties.

Besides, as at home as she was with set designers, choreographers, actors, singers, dancers and the occasional freak-show attraction, *real* artists, *fine* artists, *art* artists, scared the flesh tones right out of her already pallid coloring.

They tended to be an egocentric, tyrannical lot, from what she had read of the great ones. The less-great, from what little she had seen, were even more egocentric and tyrannical. So many of them were people-eaters, plain and simple, from Picasso to Warhol. Temple had a real distaste for being eaten, particularly since she was small enough to serve as an hors d'oeuvre for some Monster of Monomania.

She was even more nonplussed to be meeting said unknown ego at a most unusual hostelry. The Blue Mermaid Motel downtown, once an avant-garde motor inn in the thirties, was now, quite simply, a dump.

Her several-years-old Storm looked like a million-dollar baby in the motel's shabby parking area. She hated to leave it alone without an alarm system, a thought that had never occurred to her before.

Her high heels speared food-stamp chits and greasy burger wrappers as she minced over the litter to the designated room. Above her, like some shabby madonna thrusting up from the prow of the motel-office roof, loomed the huge plaster statue of the Blue Mermaid herself.

Where brass numerals had once indicated the proper room, all that remained was the dirt-etched outline of a one and a six. Temple didn't quite know where to place her white-knuckled knock, so she lifted a foot and rapped with her shoe toe.

The door exploded inward before she could lower her foot, so there she was, introduced to Domingo like one of his blasted flamingos, standing on one foot. At least she wasn't attired in pink feathers, or plastic.

"Isn't it marvelous?!" he demanded in a voice that could have been announcing the Second Coming, or his first one. "Fabulous! Don't just stand there gawking. Turn around and look. The Miss America of Las Vegas. Right behind you."

Temple turned. (What else could she do when Domingo seized her elbow and spun her around?)

All she saw were the cluttered, low buildings of downtown.

"Magnificent!"

She followed Domingo's dark, adoring eyes upward to the plaster figure. "Very Art Moderne . . . ," she began.

"No! You are wrong. Art Now. I will cover the roof with flamingos, make this into a temple of fecundity and fantasy."

"Uh, it probably already is." She hadn't wanted to think about it, but some of the items she had carefully stepped around and over included used condoms, and needles.

"Yes, you see it!" Domingo's eyes narrowed as they returned to her face. "Who are you?"

"Temple Barr. Your liaison with the Convention and Visitors Authority, what passes for a Chamber of Commerce in this town. I have an appointment with you for eleven A.M."

He smiled suddenly, at her. "And is it eleven A.M., pretty lady?"

Temple cast a nervous glance at her watch. Somehow she did not want to take her eyes off Domingo. "Seven to eleven."

"Then you were on time. Domingo does not wear a watch."

He swept his arms wide, nearly knocking Temple off her feet, to display white shirtsleeves rolled up to his elbows and hairy forearms bare of watch, bracelet or any accoutrement.

Bully for Domingo, she wanted to say, but overpowering personalities turned her into a clockwork Shirley Temple, all manners and no guts.

"Then how do you keep appointments?" she asked.

"I do not, but appointments, like you, come to me, and *they* keep me on time. Don't worry, we won't stay here." He had caught her eyes wandering over the less-appetizing details of the Blue Mermaid.

"I did want you to see what I'm looking for. The ambience, quintessentially American. That is where my million flamingos will blossom. All over this city. They will give it color, wit, warmth, excitement."

Temple wanted to point out that Las Vegas already had plenty of all that, but Miss Shirley fluffed her butt-length circle of crinolines, curtsied and kept a demure, dimpled silence.

"Look!"

Apparently Domingo spoke only in imperatives.

"My car comes. We will lunch someplace else."

The car (of course) was a fifties flamingo-pink Cadillac convertible, with a flamingo hood ornament, driven by an Asian man. In the backseat, riding alone, sat the dark woman from the photographs, wearing black.

Domingo opened the huge front door and Temple skipped over the fallen private-dancer flyers into the perfectly preserved white-leather interior. Settling in the backseat with Verina was like being one of two dice in a coffin. They would have to shout to speak from their distant sides of the wide bench seat.

Domingo took the front passenger seat, pulling a flamingo fedora from the glove compartment, along with a pair of flamingo-bearing sunglasses.

Temple had to smile. A man who was not afraid to look ridiculous was hard to come by. Max came to mind.

"One last look at our figurehead—will she not look splendid with a nest of flamingos in her hair?—and then we go have lunch."

Temple turned to her seatmate, still feeling very Shirley. "I'm Temple Barr, the PR woman. We haven't met, but I've read so much about you—"

"Then we don't need to meet now," the woman snapped. "The driver is called Martin."

Just like the artist is called Domingo? Temple wondered. Is that what artists really did: call things by names of their own choosing? She wondered what Domingo would call her.

Evidently this artist believed in going from the ridiculous to the sublime: the pink Cadillac pulled into the entrance to the Mirage, its high, coppery glass curve of rooms sparkling like a Hoover Dam of fool's gold.

The party of three, Domingo and the two women, threaded through the tropical entryway teeming with trees and flowers, until Domingo stopped.

"I love this!" Again the shirtsleeved arms cast netwide and drew in a small school of tourist attention. "Embalmed palms. Yes!" he announced to the dazed onlookers. "These trees are real, and not real. Mummified. Preserved. Quite dead, but looking eminently alive. Like you! Boo!"

He laughed as they scattered like little red hens fleeing a falling sky. He was the Sky, with his eye that took in everything, his flailing arms that took in so much and shut out so many.

"Is he always like this?" Temple couldn't help asking Verina.

"Genius is always like this. Domingo . . . sometimes he is other ways." Her tone was knowing, almost bitter.

Temple was not sure she was equipped to deal with genius, not with her cotton-piqué pale yellow pantsuit and her black-and-yellow Charles Jourdan pumps and black-patent tote bag. Not with Shirley Temple taking over inside and twirling a little curl in the middle of her forehead. The trouble with Shirley was that she was always, unlike genius, predictable. Always good. Never horrid. Temple had a feeling that only someone with a capacity for being horrid could stand being around genius for very long.

Domingo led the expedition, describing the process of preserving palm trees in a loud, museum-guide voice. Actually, it wasn't a museum-guide voice. Such guides always spoke in hushed, inaudible tones that made one nudge one's neighbors to get closer and hear. Domingo's tone was that of a carnival barker whose overriding emotion was contempt for what he hawked and those who bought it.

"Fade-proof, fire-retardant," Domingo announced. "Fiberglass beneath. Preserved leaves, preserved bark. Pasted and glued and wired back together like a bionic tree. No water, no bugs, no growth. Wouldn't people be superior if so reconstructed? What do you say, Verina?"

She said nothing, merely walked behind the artist like an Arab wife in chador, her long dark hair hiding the expression on her face.

"And you!" he barked. "What do you think?"

Temple jumped at the sudden shout. Then she guessed that she was "you!"

"I prefer my people—and trees—organically grown, even if they are a bit messy to take care of."

Domingo laughed, swinging his flamingo sunglasses from one forefinger, and walked on.

They passed the hotel fish tanks and lobby, the casino and restaurant, making for the elevators.

In silence the trio rocketed up in the elevator to the top of the copper tower. Not far down the hotel hallway, Verina unlocked a door and stepped aside to let Domingo enter the quietly luxurious penthouse suite first. Here was no sunken black marble

Jacuzzi off the living room, no mirrors and naked statues, that passed for luxe at some of the older Vegas hotels.

Domingo held up his bare wrist and grinned mischievously at Temple. "You look so much better without your sunglasses on. Room service is sending up lunch at twelve-thirty." He squinted at his wrist, laughed and disappeared through the sliding glass doors to the patio.

Temple checked her own, very visible watch. Eleven-forty-five. That meant forty-five uncomfortable minutes wondering what Domingo would do next and what on earth she could say to the chicly hostile woman beside her.

Verina solved both problems.

"He wants to be alone. People . . . tire him. You'll want to see the plans."

Temple couldn't argue with any of that, so she followed Verina into an adjoining room. Once a bedroom, its usual furniture had been pushed to the walls, with the bed replaced by a pair of banquet tables bare of tablecloths.

Instead they were covered with stand-up cardboard cutouts of miniature flamingos, dozens and dozens of them. Several Las Vegas landmarks were also represented. The Luxor's pyramid rose like a shark fin from the foaming sea of flamingos. Leo the MGM Lion was surrounded by the creatures. The Camelot's fairy-tale towers sported flamingo guards; even its wizard now wore a flamingo-pink robe.

Something sparkling caught Temple's eyes: Dorothy's ruby-red slippers redone in flamingo-pink sequins.

She turned to Verina. "You're not going to change Dorothy's shoes in the MGM Grand vignette?"

"He is. We're negotiating with the management. He also wants to decorate the artificial lawn surrounding the Oz figures with the artistically placed lawn-ornament flamingos."

"They will go for this?"

"The huge corporations that own such major attractions are noticeably lacking a sense of—"

"Humor," Temple finished, nodding sympathetically.

Verina looked daggers at her, daggers dripping flamingo-pink blood, no less. Maybe she had pinkeye.

"I was going to say, a sense of artistic license, of the absurd and the profound, which, as Domingo says in his lectures, often occupy the same sacred ground."

"Domingo lectures, formally?"

"Domingo speaks to prestigious groups: think tanks, university presidents, governmental bodies. He believes that art should be public, that it should have scope and thrust, that it should inform every corner of our culture, pathetic as it is."

Temple nodded. That's what Shirley would have done.

"I'll just study this architectural model, then, until lunchtime," she said. "That should give me a better grasp of the project's scale and purpose."

"Oh, I doubt that. You can't be expected to grasp the artistic aspects of the installation. All we ask is that you inform us of the personalities involved at each of the project manifestations. I really don't think that we need you, but Domingo insisted on someone local to run interference." She lowered her sunglasses for the first time to let Temple see her ice-blue eyes. "I hope you're good at it."

Then she left, shutting the door so silently that not even the turning knob clicked audibly as it slid into place.

Temple sighed and wandered toward the floor-to-ceiling windows covered with vertical blinds. Through the thin fence of the edgewise slats, Las Vegas was laid out far below like a body on a dissecting table. From this height she could see the straight spine of the Strip, the vertebrae of cross streets.

On second thought, the city was more of a Gulliver stretched upon the sand while millions of Lilliputians thronged like parasites over its roads and sidewalks and identifying marks. Here she stood on the mole of the Mirage, there lay the bruise of Bally's and there the curving vein of the monorail running to the MGM Grand. Arteries, veins, bruises and also birthmarks, such as the vast construction site for New York–New York.

How could you satirize a parody? How could you vulgarize Vegas? How could an overpopulation of plastic flamingos make any more monumental an adult fairyland founded on one keystone hotel, the first and only Flamingo to set foot in Las Vegas? Bugsy Siegel's bouncing-baby hotel-casino, the font of all this, which would soon bring forty million people a year to a wasteland turned Wonderland.

Maybe this time, Temple thought, Domingo had bitten off more than he could chew. Maybe this time he had picked the one national monument mad enough, and mean enough, to bite back.

Temple was summoned into the main room when the room-service lunch arrived. Domingo ate hurriedly; it was a necessary task rather than a pleasure. The women followed his lead, Temple picking at her vegetable pasta and soon calling it quits, Verina doing likewise with a fruit plate.

Domingo looked significantly at Verina, who left in a rustle of discarded napkin and exiting robe. Domingo rose as well, abandoning the table, and leaving Temple only one role: to follow him to the window-wall looking down on a dusty, daylit Las Vegas.

"I have a dream," Domingo said.

The bright daylight from the high, hotel windows turned him into a silhouette, a speaking silhouette with arms thrust wide. Temple couldn't tell if Domingo were a frustrated actor, or a frustrated Christ-figure.

"You've seen it. Now I'll tell you about it." He strode to the bedroom that housed the model, and Temple followed. Verina awaited them like a dark bronze statue. Once there, Domingo prowled around the huge display table, waving his arms, telling his dream.

Temple didn't need long to understand it. If Los Angeles were known as the City of the Angels, Domingo would make Las Vegas notorious as the City of the Flamingos, at least for a brief, shining moment. An ambition to make Las Vegas more notorious than it was and is struck Temple as oddly touching.

Why flamingos, she asked.

"Excellent question. No one has thought to question me before. I am too famous, too successful, too outrageous. Yet there is method to my madness."

He proceeded to identify his method. "The first truly visionary hotel-casino was founded on the Strip in nineteen forty-six by Bugsy Siegel. It was called the Fabulous Flamingo."

"Why?" Temple asked.

"Why what? Why found modern Las Vegas?"

"Why name a hotel in the middle of an empty desert the 'Flamingo'? Flamingos are long-legged, shallow water–dwelling birds. They belong on African lakes and in South American jungles and maybe in Florida souvenir shops for tourists. So why name a desert hotel after a flamingo?"

"How do I know?" Domingo was beginning to sound frazzled. "The flamingo is a bright, sinuous bird. Great for graphics. Perhaps a man nicknamed 'Bugsy' wanted to be associated with a more elegant creature than an insect. Why is not important. *What* is what art is all about. *What* is what I do.

"I do not explain myself, I present my concept. The world explains it, defames it, photographs it, deplores it and myself. Editorials rant about the waste of good money, about how much water could saturate the desert for the cost of importing these thousands of cheap plastic birds, these lowly, mass-manufactured foreign imports that spear into good soil all over the Americas—South America, Central America, Mexico and the United States. These homely lawn ornaments that will not die! This is not for me to explain."

"All over the Americas? Canada too? And what about Alaska?"

"*What?!*"

"Do plastic flamingos populate these more-northern turfs, so to speak?"

"No! The actual flamingo does not breed beyond the snow line, or the timber line or even the sun belt. They are creatures of sunlight, that is the point. They are gaudy, New World storks; they represent fecundity and fashion. They will wrap Las Vegas in their otherworldly reality, in their shoddy, hollow shells, in their bright, impossibly lurid color. They are very spiritual things, these humble lawn ornaments."

The artist's model was neither particularly spiritual nor humble, but she stood looking on at this performance like an iron madonna.

During this exhibition, Temple had come to realize that what Domingo said about himself was more important than what others said about him. His real object was performance art. Wheedling civic big wheels into endorsing his wild, wicked schemes was half the fun. He was, at heart, a con artist.

And he was ideal for the role. In his photographs he looked like an odd combination of hipster, hippie and nineties guru, and no more than thirty-four. In person he was ambiguity personified. His age might be fifty, or even sixty, or a well-worn thirty-four. His brooding dark eyes, hedged by shaggy black hair, suggested an exotic foreign origin—southern Italy, Greece, Central Europe, perhaps even Turkey. Or Native American.

His voice had an almost-foreign formality, but no accent, not even of a regional U.S. locale. Domingo was a blackboard, a blank slate for the eyes and ears and hearts of his viewers to fill in as they wished, or felt impelled to do so. Con man, genius, gypsy, thief of time and pretension or merely a crazy artist? Who was he? Or, more important, *what* was he?

As Temple watched Domingo strut his stuff, seemingly for her alone, she realized that they were collaborating on a work-in-progress that Domingo started all over again with each city, each person, each landscape and landmark he drew into his whacked-out remodeling schemes.

"Now, Miss Barr!" His domineering voice demanded her full notice. "Which place in this city do you wish to see inundated with birds of a feather called flamingo?"

She jerked her attention to the toy Las Vegas on his conjoined tables. That was a work of art in itself, or certainly a high order of craftsmanship.

"I can't say right off. I've never thought in terms of flamingos before."

"No! That is why you are considered sane and safe, and I am

not. That is also why I am a good deal richer than you, aren't I?"

"I have no idea of your personal finances."

The Dark Lady finally spoke. "Domingo is a multimillionaire for weeks at a time . . . before he reinvests in his artworks."

"Yes! I have reversed the art-world stereotype. I invest in my own art, rather than leaving that important function to others, to kingmakers and hangers-on and frauds."

Temple had been musing over the small-scale layout of Las Vegas. She felt like a Greek goddess, up at this Olympian height, gazing down on the puny affairs of mankind.

"Of course the obvious is the existing Flamingo Hilton hotel."

Temple pointed to the bright horizontal band aping the wrap-around neon sign of flamingos imitating fan-dancers on the hotel's entry façade.

"Obvious, yes." Domingo came to brood over the tiny mock building. "Still, the finest sign of the old school left in Las Vegas. Is any of the original building left standing?"

"I'd have to find out."

"Then make it so."

"Oh, you watch *Star Trek: The Next Generation* reruns too."

Domingo's brooding intensified. He could have given the young Marlon Brando a run for his acting money.

"Popular culture must be watched with only half a mind. Garbage in, garbage out. I would like my flamingos to pay true tribute to this benchmark site, but I will not have them outshone by a nervous flock of neon flash-dancers. I must think. Where else do you see flamingos?"

Temple considered it bad PR to say that she could die happy never seeing a single plastic flamingo in Las Vegas, no, not even atop a swizzle stick.

"A fleet of wading flamingos in the Treasure Island moat might add a subtropical touch to the proceedings," she offered hesitantly.

Like most artists, Temple was sure, Domingo did not appreciate kibitzers.

"A pirate ship is sunk during the hourly sea-battle, isn't that the case?" he asked.

"No, a British Navy ship is sunk, briefly. Like the British lion, it only lies down to rise again. Law and order go down to the pirate ship's guns."

"Then Domingo's flamingos will rise, in a sunset cloud, along the verges of the moat. It will be a Kodak moment for all the tourists. Do you think the hotel will agree to my installation?"

Temple decided to unveil her own piece of performance art. Unlike Domingo, she did not require a booming voice and big gestures, just the facts that were her job to know, and tell.

Her shrug was rueful and vague. "I have your press kits. The installation of a miniature Alps of soldered-together lira in the Trevi Fountain in Rome should impress them, along with the hundred herds of sheep in the courtyard of the Louvre. That the French would tolerate the droppings alone speaks well of the importance of being the object of your attentions. I know the hotel's hierarchy, and should be able to bow and scrape my way up it.

"But you must understand something, Domingo. This is not some hundreds-of-years-old city with a flagging economy and tourism business, and a need to sacrifice its ancient monuments to the latest international artistic whim. This is Las Vegas, a back-lot Baghdad-on-the-Mojave thrown up almost as fast as the pyramids in a Cecil B. DeMille epic. Bugsy Siegel may have given it a kick in the pants, but the mob and Howard Hughes built this city and now the corporations own it. Corporations don't need anybody.

"Maybe in the sixties and seventies Las Vegas was still hungry enough, or greedy enough to court good—or even better, bad—publicity. Now Las Vegas doesn't even bother. Anything lavish and large that the mind of humankind can produce, Las Vegas can reproduce for three times the money in one-thousandth the time. This is not a real city, it's an open-air carnival, and it doesn't need flamingos, or Domingos. But I can ask, and maybe they'll say yes."

Domingo had listened, hands in pants pockets, head lowered like a bull's.

"This is half my point. Everything is owned. Every artwork must be begged for. There is so much empty land in the United

States, near Las Vegas, but it is all owned. The artist is owned. If they say 'no,' they become a part of my art."

"And if they 'yes' ?"

"They become a part of my art." Domingo smiled for the first time. "How will a small little thing like you broach all these lords of Las Vegas and get anything?"

"I'll do my best. And you do have a pretty impressive reputation."

This time Domingo shrugged, both his shoulders rising like snowcapped mountains moved by a volcanic emotion.

"When you get to the top of the hierarchy, arrange for an appointment with me. I speak best for myself, but have no time to hack my way up the mountain."

Temple nodded. She had expected no more, nor no less.

"Verina will get you all that you need. Our office is off the Strip."

He waved them both away, going to the window to gaze down on the real Las Vegas in miniature, the cluster of grandiose buildings laid out like Tinkertoys on a barren stretch of desert ringed by mountains. For all its multimillion annual visitors and staggering construction projects—Temple wouldn't be surprised to see an Ark Hotel go up with two of every animal on earth except the gambling, overpopulating human kind—for all its hubris, Las Vegas was still a sand-castle city, a puny architectural pretension huddled in the center of nature's most life-hostile, wide-open vista; cheek by cheeky jowl with wind-sculpted scarlet stones of the Valley of Fire, which in the ruddy gore of a desert sunset outshone all the neon that Hoover Dam could electricize. It was an oversize dollhouse, maybe, for boys instead of girls. Marzipan and mirrored glass, air-conditioning and laser-lights, stuffed toys and cotton candy.

Step right up, folks. You pays your money and you takes your chance.

Even Domingo.

Chapter 7

Call Again . . .

"I've been thinking about you," Matt told his most devoted caller.

"Oh?" The Voice sounded intrigued, even pleased.

Matt smiled grimly. Manipulating back was too satisfying. Man was the only animal that could become his own tormentor.

"You've only been calling me for the last eight months."

"You counted. I'm flattered."

"No, I checked the logbook."

"Logbook?" A tinge of panic.

"As a nonprofit agency, we have to account for ourselves." This was an off-white lie; in reality, the book logged crank callers. But Matt wanted his caller to see the larger network beyond the lone counselor on the phone. He got quite a reaction.

"More than anything, you have to remain private. Discreet. Isn't confidentiality what you promise, what you sell, what you get paid for?"

"Is that how you think of us, as hookers? As an intimate service you pay for?"

"Why not? I've done it all my life. Paid for service. Nobody ever does anything for free, one way or another."

"That's a cynic's self-justification."

"What's this 'we' all of a sudden, anyway? I thought it was just you and me. You trying to hide behind an organization, Brother John?"

"Isn't everybody nowadays?"

"Not me. I stand alone."

"Except on the phone."

"Not fair! We're supposed to be talking about me, not about what you think of me."

"I don't think anything of you. I'm an organization man, remember?"

"I don't care who you are. That's the beauty of this arrangement, isn't it? We don't have to know each other. We don't have to like each other. But you have to answer the phone."

"You don't have to call."

A pause.

"There's where you're wrong. I do."

"Is it another addiction, then?"

"Life is an addiction, Brother John. You ever think of it that way? That if we're not addicted to staying alive, we die?"

"You say you're not suicidal—"

"It's a phone! You say a lot of things on the phone . . . that you're interested in somebody's deal, or body. That you won't be late for an appointment you have no intention of keeping. That you wish somebody a 'Happy Birthday' or a good life. None of it's necessarily real."

"I'm not a debating society. I'm here to help. It seems to me the only help you need is a twenty-four-hour on-line baby-sitter."

"What is this, tough love? You used to just listen. I could hear you being nonjudgmental. Then, a call or two back, it changed. Why?"

"At least you're thinking about somebody besides yourself."

"Is that it? I'm too self-centered? Why shouldn't I be? I'm famous for it. That's why I liked talking to you. Usually I have to give people a certain amount of time to spout off about themselves, but you . . . you would just listen. You could be a robot for all I know."

"Is that your ideal partner for a heart-to-heart, a robot?"

"You don't get it. That's not an insult. That means you're good at what you do. You don't let you get in the way. Talking to you is like talking to myself, and then I see things . . . "

"Insight is important, but—"

"No, you listen, listen to me about what you should do, for a change. Don't judge. You never know what circumstances made me the self-involved pig I am. You never know how much I might hate this wonderful famous self of mine, or how many people around me might hate it too. You never know when my talking to you might be a matter of life or death. Do you? Do you, Brother John?"

What could he say? Nothing. Matt felt his shoulders sag.

"Now, listen . . . "

Chapter 8

Breaking the Carrier
Barrier

"Stone walls do not a prison make, nor iron bars a cage," but a cat carrier makes a pretty good chastity belt. Like the Cavalier poet-dude, Richard Lovelace, I speak from painful experience.

And I am not feeling very cavalier right now. There we are, the Divine Yvette and me, together on a glamorous assignment; workmates, co-stars. There are our separate carriers, into which we are placed for hours on end without even an opportunity for a little sniff and whisker-tickle.

And there is Maurice, the Yummy Tum-tum-tummy spokescat who was originally supposed to have had my part (that of lovestruck swain) in the new À La Cat commercials. He should be back in some Sherman Oaks compound chatting it up with the other trained animals. But, no, he is along for the ride. On the scene of the crime, so to speak. In the wings. I wish those wings were the real thing and on his back.

For this is a very dangerous dude. I have it on good authority (albeit incorporeal) that Maurice Two is an imposter, like I told my old man. Poor Maurice One!

Imagine drowning in Yummy Tum-tum-tummy! What irony. All those dead fish doing you in. Poetic justice, I suppose, but I have no intention of falling into a carp pond stocked with piranha. And when Maurice Two is around, any set piece or prop is a potential murder weapon.

I am seeing potential for disaster everywhere I look.

Take the human chorus line that is supposed to back up Yvette and me when we finally get our few, brief moments on the stage. All those size nine and ten shoes (and I am talking just the girl hoofers here; the boys probably wear elevens and twelves), all those tap shoes, armed with steel plates. Say I slipped (or was pushed) coming down the long flight of stairs on which I make my dramatic entrance.

I would make a dramatic exit under a hundred tapping feet. They could then market a new brand of cat food: Midnight Louie Pâté. To think of it is to shudder, save there is no room in this cramped crate to so much as sneeze.

So, in one respect, my incarceration offers a certain protection.

But is life worth living under a constant threat? More than one human has pondered this question. I suppose I could seize the moment and endeavor to off the miserable Maurice Two before he offs me. This was the suggestion of Maurice One's pathetic shade. (Shade is a fancy word for ghost.) This dude came to me in a séance-dream. Although all the cats at the séance were actual felines, not another present was honored with a vision of Maurice One, so I know that our karma is irretrievably mixed. (And I am not speaking of the psychocat named Karma who shares Miss Electra Lark's penthouse at the Circle Ritz. Okay, Karma is a psychic cat, but I prefer the other spelling.)

Anyway, what to do? Watch my back, obviously. Take out Maurice Two if given time and opportunity, well . . . no. I have spent too much time of late on the right side of the law. I am not a vigilante, just an ordinary street dude who happens to have a nose for trouble. Still, it is hard to play a sitting duck when you would rather be eating one.

As for the Divine Yvette, she is happily ignorant of the dead-serious byplay. She gives me the baby blue-greens at every opportunity, although I detect a subtle change in her attitude. Her glances seem to be more of an appeal than a come-on. I think that she has sensed the tension and feels a corresponding distress.

All of this does not bode well for the À La Cat commercial. But then, can a television commercial that combines a purebred Persian with an alley cat and a human chorus line in Easter egg–colored zoot suits possibly go right? Especially when said Persian is wearing a diamond collar and said alley cat is forced to have a flamingo-pink fedora affixed to his head in ways that are too embarrassing to mention. And must it tilt down over one eye, so I cannot see when I am pussyfooting down all those stairs in front of a tidal wave of tap dancers also wearing fedoras tilted over one eye so they cannot see when they run me down and pound me into chopped liver? And kidney and tongue and tail.

If you want a recipe for disaster and murder most musical, you could not find a better formula than at an À La Cat commercial filming in Las Vegas.

Color me History.

Chapter 9

Call Her Stage Mama

If ever a child of hers were in the school play, Temple would never show up at rehearsal to embarrass the poor thing, be it boy or girl.

But Temple didn't have a child, she had an it. A cat.

And supervising a cat's participation in a television commercial was more akin to being an animal-rights activist than a stage mother.

Stage mothers were the pond scum of the earth and the dust-ball under Sir Laurence Olivier's bed, for good measure. Animal-rights watchdogs were assertive, altruistic people.

Why, then, did Temple feel like the fifth wheel on somebody else's little red wagon just for being back here at Gangster's, hovering over Midnight Louie's carrier like a loan officer expecting an imminent repossession of the family farm?

Maybe it was the stormy look on the face of her competition for the stage-mother sweepstakes.

Savannah Ashleigh, chic in an acid-green satin spandex jumpsuit, glowered at Temple and Midnight Louie's humble discount-store carrier as if they both were infected with the plague.

Temple wished that it were so, but only for the privilege of passing on the lethal germ to the film star. On the other hand, a nice dose of plague might spring Temple and Louie from the tedium of waiting for the hours and hours it took to set up a TV commercial.

Temple flipped down the empty theater seat to the left of Louie's big beige carrier and sat. Savannah Ashleigh, glaring, did likewise on the right side of Yvette's carrier, a small pink bit of baggage like her mistress.

"I'm here," Savannah announced to no one in particular, and thus to everyone, in her breathy ersatz-Monroe diction, "to see that my Yvette gets the proper number of potty breaks."

"Funny," Temple said. "I am here to see that my Louie doesn't get pointless trips to the box. He has such terrific self-control, you know, due to his sturdy proletarian roots."

"He is a Communist cat?" Savannah's heavily powdered brows, clashing together, raised a small dust poof of disapproval.

"I was speaking of his vigorous bloodlines."

"You mean alley-cat stew!"

"Exactly. Louie's genes have not been watered down by generations of overbreeding. No wonder your Yvette . . . wets."

"Yvette is a sensitive, delicate creature who takes her responsibilities before the camera to heart. Has your cat had any on-camera experience?"

"Quite a bit, lately," Temple said loftily, thanking her unlucky stars for the recent Halloween-séance filming that had put Louie in the spotlight. For once Crawford Buchanan and his cursed *Hot Heads* kamikaze camera lens were good for something. "And, of course, Louie's done a good deal of still work." Like the newspaper photos recording his exploits in the body-finding and death-defying departments.

"Still studio work means nothing these days." Savannah's dismissive shrug further dislodged her off-the-shoulder neckline.

"I guess you should know," Temple conceded politely.

"At least Yvette can benefit from my vast experience in the

film field. Your Louie is not so blessed. Cats are not often called upon to do—what is your line of work?—oh, yes. PR."

Savannah might as well have articulated the childishly dismissive word, "Pee-yew."

"Somebody has to do it," Temple said cheerfully, "and Louie is actually quite good at it. Guess he was born with cat charisma."

"We shall see when the film begins to roll," Savannah retorted dubiously. "No director can afford expensive delays and reshoots for an amateur."

"You should certainly know," Temple answered again, much less politely.

An even more impolite silence ensued, just as a lull in the onstage action arrived. The previous day's dress-rehearsal cast was scattered around the dramatically tiered set, a symphony in sherbet-colored costumes.

Temple didn't care much for revue-style shows, and Las Vegas versions were more bloated than most: bloated with dancers and production numbers, with chorus girls attired as God made them, except for pounds of glitz everywhere on their persons that immodesty permitted, with ponderously written jokes as ponderously delivered.

Still, the Darren Cooke show, from what she had glimpsed of it, seemed determinedly snappy. Its star sucked energy from being onstage as greedily as every little lightbulb in Vegas siphoned off the millions of kilowatts generated by nearby Hoover Dam.

Hoover Dam. Temple pictured that Cinemascopic curve of mighty gray wall, plastered with pink plastic flamingos, twisting gently in the breeze like rearview mirror trinkets. A monumental achievement . . .

An assistant mounted the stairs to the stage, Yvette's pink carrier in hand. Apparently she had no stand-in, poor overworked little thing.

Temple glanced across the two in-between seats at the other bereft owner. The shared stress of waiting helplessly while one's beloved pet was carted away to the crowded stage had done nothing to melt the Iron Curtain between the two women. Savannah rose to stalk away on Miami Beach, wood-soled high-heeled sandals. Their slender straps carried a cargo of enough fake fruit to make Carmen Miranda's neck snap.

Temple shrugged to herself and scrunched down in her seat to watch the forthcoming action.

"May I join you?"

The tone was low, but the timbre thrummed with excitement. Temple glanced up to see why, amazed when Darren Cooke, every razor-cut hair precisely out of place, pushed down the flip-up theater seat to sit beside her.

If she'd been Little Miss Muffet and he had been a tarantula, she couldn't have been more surprised. Glancing around, she saw that they alone sat in the house seats. Everyone else was clustered up on the stage to watch the rehearsal.

Cooke's smile revealed Hollywood-white teeth and a perception of just how much his fame and reputation nonplussed her.

Oh, what white teeth you have, grandfather, Temple thought. And big eyes for another conquest maybe.

"I understand your cat is the star of the coming big scene."

"Co-star. Savannah Ashleigh's Yvette actually was contracted for the commercial before Louie."

"Louie? I still love it. A great name for an alley cat."

"Midnight Louie," she reminded him.

"Even better." He peered politely into the dim carrier, but Temple would bet he didn't give a fresh fig about cats. "I assume he's black. Black animals are usually harder to film. How did he get the part?"

"He, ah, crashed the site of the last commercial shoot. Louie seems to have an abiding interest in Yvette."

"He's not a tomcat?"

"I'm afraid so. I meant to get him fixed, but . . . things keep happening."

"What things?" Cooke's face was sober now, one of those unusual men's faces that look more handsome when they're not smiling. Like the young Brando or Beatty.

Temple was reluctant to explain all the ins and outs of her and

Louie's careers in crime. Her hesitation seemed to please Darren Cooke.

"The Divine Savannah called you 'Nancy Drew' the other day. Why is that?"

"That's what you call her, 'the Divine Savannah'?" Temple found that a scream, attaching an adjective coined for the Divine Sarah Bernhardt to a strictly B-movie actress like Savannah Ashleigh.

"Not to her face," Cooke added with a slight smile.

"And why would she be talking about me to you?"

"Savannah is like Scarlett O'Hara. She sees herself as greatly wronged by the inequities of the world. Apparently your alley cat coming out of nowhere to share the billing with her purebred is beyond her endurance."

"Too bad. She'll just have to hope that tomorrow is another day."

"But what's this Nancy Drew stuff?"

"Silliness. Why do you want to know?"

He frowned, a nice manly frown that would come across well on camera. Film actors knew their every bad angle, their every winning expression; they practiced hiding one and flashing the other daily. Temple sometimes wondered how they survived without a flunky carrying a mirror around for them. She had seen young actors that could no longer look someone they were talking to in the eye. They were that busy searching out a mirror, or any reflective surface.

Cooke was a veteran; the mirror was internalized by now. He could feign concentration on another person pretty well. No wonder he was a ladies' man.

Now he was looking sincere, but decently reluctant. "I have a delicate problem I don't want to discuss with the usual . . . professionals. I would trust an amateur more at this point. And a woman. If you are a grown-up Nancy Drew, and you are a fetching candidate for the role," he added with a rapid sizing-up, "I might—want your advice. For a professional consideration, of course."

"Mr. Cooke, I've never been paid by anybody for stumbling onto the scene of a crime. As a public-relations person, I have a responsibility to see that events I'm coordinating are efficiently run."

"And murder is so inefficient."

"Exactly. Not to mention bad press. The sooner it's off the books, the sooner the status quo is restored. That's how I got involved in what I got involved with."

"Fascinating. Crime-solving as good PR. It makes sense. I know you might not want to take on a commission, but it's really advice I need, and badly. Tomorrow's Sunday. I throw an eleven A.M. brunch for friends and crew in my suite at the Oasis. Come up for a bite, and we'll find time for a talk. That's all I ask."

Temple was a veteran PR woman. She'd had her fill of celebrity socials where everyone used the mirror of her spectacles for a looking glass. Still, this was the first time she'd been invited by the host celebrity before. Even more interesting, he was a notorious womanizer who seemed more interested in her little gray cells than her crimson curls.

As she hesitated, he said something astounding.

"Please."

Temple nodded mutely. The last time she had turned down a man she suspected of lascivious motives, he had died before her eyes. Only then had it occurred to her that she had a certain reputation in this town for getting to the bottom of things. She wasn't just a young, single woman in Las Vegas anymore, she was P.I. PR woman, supersleuth!

Just like Louie was about to become Mr. Midnight, TV star!

As Darren Cooke discreetly slipped away to rejoin the cast onstage, another low voice was at her ear.

"Miss Barr."

Sharon Hammerlitz, the hostile animal trainer (not that the animals were hostile, just the trainer), leaned over her.

"Keep Louie calm. Frank is going to do a run-through on the sequence with Maurice, but we'll need Louie backstage now to slip in for the final take."

"Why Maurice first?"

"He's a stuntcat, so call him Midnight Louie's body double. I know how to make Maurice go where they want, so they can get a quick fix on the entire action sequence. Then I put Louie in, and hope."

She sounded crabby and Temple, watching Sharon walk off with Louie's heavy carrier, couldn't blame her. A perfectly adequate and trained pro, Maurice, had been pushed aside by a rank newcomer who probably would muff his business. Luckily, Louie had no lines to blow, as far as Temple knew.

Temple trained her attention on the stage, and noticed Savannah Ashleigh at stage left, glaring out at the empty seats. Empty except for Temple.

She was obviously wishing either Temple or Midnight Louie dead, and probably both.

Chapter 10

Tripping to Stardom

So. What indignity can the mind of director invent?

I am soon to discover.

I most resent being carted away from my dear Miss Temple so soon after the approach and departure of Mr. Darren Cooke. But the so-called animal trainer has come to collect my carrier without as much as a by-your-leave. And poor Miss Temple is so perplexed by the recent request of Mr. Darren that she hardly notices my withdrawal! I must say that she is at times irritatingly susceptible to male ploys coming from the wrong species. I am the true gentleman of the lot, and would make no untoward demands.

So I leave her alone in the theater seat, mooning over who knows what, as I am borne to my fate. I have heard, of course, every bit of dialogue that has transpired in my vicinity, from the hiss-and-spit between Miss Temple and my darling's obnoxious mistress, to the strange request from the star of the show.

I fear he is less interested in Miss Temple's sleuthing abilities than in her scarlet hair and trim little ankles. Oh, that I could escape this assembly-line carrier and tend to business!

However, I have worries of my own. It also has not escaped me that Maurice Two is not only usurping my rehearsal role, but he has apparently been freed of confinement for some time, while I still languish in the calaboose.

Not a good sign. This dude has gotten away with murder before on a cat-commercial set, and that was not even on location, but at the Yummy Tum-tum-tummy plant. Now he has all the confusion and clutter of a backstage production number to disguise his nefarious doings, the exact same cover that made the romance convention such an ideal site for serial murder. Naturally, I would be Maurice Two's second victim (that we know of, I add ominously), so he is a practiced paw at murder most feline.

I am lugged, rather clumsily, up the thirty-nine steps of the set. (I do not actually count the number of steps, but it feels like a lot, and thirty-nine is a nice mystery number.) The chorus has parted for my arrival, so I have an honor guard of flashy dudes in lurid suits. Once I arrive at the pinnacle, I see an assistant hovering with a loathsome object in her hand: it is a miniature fedora in a color I can only call blushing-salmon pink. In other words, even a sockeye salmon would cringe to see an article of clothing in that extreme shade of pale orange-red called flamingo. No wonder these birds often hide their heads under their wings. I would too if I had to run around all day looking like a sunburned posterior. Schiaparelli did not call it "shocking pink" for nothing.

I am removed from my carrier while the fedora is tilted over my right eye and held on with a black elastic. Out of the corner of my left eye, which is the only functional one at the moment, I see Maurice sitting on the sidelines snickering. He is footloose and fancy-free and could have arranged all sorts of booby traps for me during the perilous descent ahead.

For the script is simplicity itself. I look far below to see the Divine Yvette being primped by her personal stylist as well as Miss Savannah Ashleigh. Someone has wrapped an ostrich-feather boa dyed in this same flamingo-pink color around her fluffy little ruff and diamond dog collar. (You would think the truth-in-advertising laws would prevent using ostrich feathers in flamingo guise, but I suppose no one besides me cares about the fine points anymore.)

Besides aggravating the cast by clothing them in interspecies articles, the producers of this little epic are calling for me to speed down the thirty-nine steps, half-blind, right toward the Divine Yvette.

They have imported a number of barbarian devices with the supposed purpose of encouraging me to follow stage directions whether I will or no. Little do they know that I do not need to be a Method actor to zero right in on the Divine One as fast as my four lightning limbs will permit me.

Perhaps you have heard of a "cold bolt" of lightning. I understand that this is a rare phenomenon: a gray-black lightning ball that streaks through a room. Well, put the Divine Yvette wherever you wish, give me a glimpse and Cold Bolt Louie will be there in a flash. They do not need their ostrich-feather whips, their bell-laden bouncing balls, their clickers, their crouching trainers and assistants huddling along the camera route to herd me back onto the right path. I can take direction without being hit over the head with it, especially if it is something I would want to do anyway.

I see that they have mounted a track device on which the camera can coast alongside me, capturing every graceful, cheetah-like leap as I run down the thirty-nine steps.

I also see that it would have been easy for Maurice to plan some dirty work. The steps are painted black, and smudged with the tracks of many human hoofer feet. A bit of spilled oil in the right place would do wonders. My sharp eye (remember the foolish fedora!) does not spy any slick places, but Maurice Two managed to leave no trace at the site of his last job, or rather, Maurice One's last job. If it were not for the feline séance that took place during my previous case, I would not even suspect that Maurice Two is not the original Maurice, but the successor who moved up through caticide.

To be forewarned is to be forearmed, as by taking arms against a sea of troubles we end them. My sea of troubles is the rank of human faces in the chorus, who will all be doing their tap-dancing thing on the sidelines as I and the camera hurtle past.

I watch like a hawk when the director cues the animal trainer to send Maurice down the steeply inclined gantlet. I feel a little like an Aztec priest high on my step pyramid watching the feline sacrifice plummet to the deadly ground below.

A plastic ball is set bouncing down the stairs, then the trainer at the bottom whistles and rattles a plastic container of Yummy Tum-tum-tummy. You notice that the operative word here is "plastic." Such is the falseness of show biz. Then a clicker sounds.

Maurice takes out after that pathetic plaything like Pavlov's pussycat. I watch his rump bump and grind down all thirty-nine steps while the camera keeps pace on its elevator glide mechanism. Now *that* is how I would like to make my entrance! This running one's gaiters and mittens off is for the birds, preferably flamingos. I am not much fond of flamingos at this point.

But, no, I am expected to risk life and limb on those damned steps. The camera is hauled up to the top again. Maurice, panting, is carried back up and placed beside me. As if there were anything that I could learn from this bozo besides murder methods.

"Piece of cake," Maurice says between huffs.

"Yeah? Frosted with arsenic or strychnine?"

"You are a suspicious sort, Louie. How would I be able

to hurt you with so many witnesses looking on, including a camera crew?"

"You managed to do in Maurice One in equally public circumstances. I will warn you now; if anything happens to me, my little doll will be all over this stage with a laser-light. She will examine every centimeter of film and find the means and the culprit. She is my insurance."

"Your little doll is an amateur who got lucky a time or two. Besides, she will not be suspecting feline felony."

"Maybe not, but if you should by some odious chance be successful, I will come back to haunt you, and so will Maurice One."

"I do not believe you! Who saw this ghost besides you? Only some bats in the haunted-house attraction, which is a pretty good assessment of your mental state . . . batty! Okay, sucker. Time to play your part. Break a leg, buddy!"

By now we are snarling and the crew is hushing us and acting as if I am somehow responsible for it all.

"That," the À La Cat honcho harrumphs loudly, "is what we get for working with a *tom*cat."

I cannot tell you in what degree of loathing the word "tomcat" is spoken. Hey, were it not for tomcats, there would be no cats, although there are a few million too many, I grant you. I tell you, we middle-aged, unfixed, free-roaming dudes are a downtrodden minority these days. It is almost enough to make one go off and join a survivalist clan out in the boonies.

But social criticism is not my main problem at the moment. How to save my skin is. When the director yells, "Quiet!" everybody shuts up except the chorus, who clatter around like nervous horses. They are supposed to lip-sync their number, the À La Cat jingle, which will be recorded in the studio later.

"Action!" cries the director.

The trainer at my rear swats my posterior with what feels like a baseball catcher's mitt embedded with thorns.

I rocket down the aisle of empty stairs, chorus costumes

a nauseating blur of melted sherbet as I pass, the camera dolly cranking and creaking away alongside me. Then I see it. On about the twenty-seventh step down, a little figure eight of steel wire like they wrap newspaper bundles in.

Momentum is not allowing me to pick my step placements. I am bound to get tangled up in that treacherous loop like a calf in a roping contest. The Divine Yvette's little face is growing large, a look of horror widening her dark pupils. What can I do but improvise?

I carom off to the side, into the chorus line on my blindside, and snick out my shivs. In a split second I am climbing a mandarin-orange suit (ick!) until I am perched upon a mandarin-orange shoulder.

I tilt my head against the warbling chorus boy's face, although no sound is emitting from his lips and his eyes are rounder than the Divine Yvette's. I am no lightweight, and remain on his shoulder only because of my superb balance and my fully extended shivs curving into his shoulder pads and the underpinnings below, which may be epidermis. I do so hate to get human skin under my nails!

Before he can react enough to give a howl that would ruin the take, I bound down to the stairs again, weaving in and out of the tapping choristers' rainbow-colored legs. I might even look like I am dancing, were I not running for my life.

When I think the treacherous spot is well behind me, I bound into the center space and continue my insouciant descent, straight for my baby's feather-dusted arms.

Except that I must stop first, on a dime, and fall back in awe.

There, posed before the Divine Yvette, is this crystal wine glass, heaped with the homely gray glop of À La Cat. Except that a food stylist has been at it for hours, and every little flake sits up like a fox terrier in a circus act. Every flake has been hydrated and teased until it shines like a salmon in the sunlight. It looks pink and pale and plump. It looks downright tasty as the Divine Yvette, following her cue, edges back from the dish, bats her long eyelashes and permits me a sample.

This will be the hardest part of the entire ordeal. I stop, box my nose with a couple of hardy gestures then bashfully jam my nose into the stuff. I figure if my nostrils are blocked it will not smell so bad, and what does not smell bad, does not taste half-bad, in my experience.

So I wolf down this masterpiece of inferior design, finally stopping to step back and bow to the Divine Yvette. She simpers and minces closer. We end up, whiskers entwined, lapping up À La Cat cheek to cheek.

The camera at the bottom is probably zooming in for a nauseating close-up.

"Cut!" the director yells from somewhere far away, and I know I am safe until the next take, at least. But I will survive.

There is one motive, and one motive above all, that will see me through any perfidy that the murderous Maurice has up his stripes. I am sorry to say that it is not the round-eyed face of the Divine Yvette so near, staring up at me with limpid adoration.

The fact is, I would die before I would allow myself to leave the planet while wearing this ridiculous headgear.

Chapter 11

Picture Perfect

When the phone rang, Matt was standing in the kitchen eating his usual noon brunch of cereal, yogurt and an orange.

He stared at the instrument, usually silent. When his phone did ring, it was rarely a friend—he had practically none—or a relative—they were all distant or dead. Usually it was unwelcome news.

Chewing, he took his time heading for it, wondering if the high-tech yodel would stop before he could get there. With no answering machine, the caller would forever remain a mystery. Mysteries didn't bother Matt. He was used to keeping a respectful distance from the Unknowable. Knowing too much was the enemy.

He picked up the phone, mouth clear. "Hello?"

"Molina," was all she said, and all she had to say. "Got a pencil handy?"

"Pen." He patted his shirt pocket for the drugstore Rollerball always clipped there. A pen was an employee's best friend at ConTact.

"Take this down: Janice Flanders," she went on before he could even click the point out. "Sixteen Forty-nine Wilder Lane. Five-five-five, seven-two-four-eight."

Matt scribbled the information one-handed on the phone-book cover's skimpy white border. "What—?"

"Most of the time we use computer identification programs. Used to rely more on actual artists. This is one of the best. You might try her on your phantom stepfather."

"Thanks, but I thought—"

"Just let me know if this leads anywhere."

He jerked the phone away from his ear. The dial tone suddenly buzzed there like an angry hornet. Whew. Molina wouldn't earn any public-relations awards with her tone on that call.

He felt dully resentful, like a kid who's had to deal with a teacher who's snappish for no known reason. He felt punished rather than assisted. He would have mentioned her rudeness, but she was gone too fast to challenge.

The name and numbers he had slashed down were barely readable. He almost felt like forgetting them. Help this surly he didn't need . . .

But, then, guardian angels don't always come clothed in feathers and cumulus clouds; sometimes they wear sackcloth and ashes. Matt smiled wryly. Molina probably hated helping him out on what she judged a wild-goose chase. She probably hated being helpful. Heck, she probably hated *him*. That was a new thought; people usually liked him. Matt considered. Maybe he was losing his polite seminary edge.

No sense in putting this off. He dialed the number, waited a decent number of rings, and was rewarded on the fifth one.

"Flanders Folios." The voice was friendly but briskly businesslike.

"I'm calling for Janice Flanders."

"Speaking."

"My name is Matt Devine. Lieutenant Molina at the Las Vegas Metropolitan Police Department recommended you. I'm trying to find someone I glimpsed a few days ago."

"Is this police business?"

"No, personal. Private."

"Who did you say—?"

"Matt Devine."

"No, the officer's name."

"Oh. Molina."

A pause. "Don't remember working for a Molina. He been there long?"

"It's a she, and I don't know."

"When do you need the sketch?"

"Whenever's convenient. I, ah, work evenings, so it'd have to be during the afternoon hours."

"Great! All my clients are on opposite schedules. Listen, why don't you come over now; we can discuss details when you see what I've got in my studio."

He agreed, she told him rough directions and that was that. Matt hunted up his checkbook, then tried to find a place to carry it. A moderate climate called for casual dress and checkbooks fit best inside jacket breast pockets. He settled on taking his nylon windbreaker and stuffing the checkbook in the side pocket. Before he left, he consulted the slimmer book under the tabletop phone book, a street guide to Las Vegas/Henderson.

From the squirmy lines of her neighborhood streets, it was a newer development. He prayed his checkbook was up to commissioning the first portrait Cliff Effinger had ever had. For the first time since Molina's call, a chill of excitement gripped him. Would this artist really be able to conjure an identifiable likeness from the scattered motes of Matt's memory?

The neighborhood lived up to his expectations, and had been that way for perhaps fifteen years. The lots were larger of lawn and the homes lower of roofline than the trendy new homes sprouting ski-slope roofs and winking expanses of Palladium windows in nearby Henderson.

Still, the watered grass and clipped bushes rustled of California-ranch affluence. The Hesketh Vampire's raunchy motor seemed obscene on this decorously deserted street. Matt turned the motorcycle into the long concrete driveway and parked it behind a red Jeep Cherokee.

The walkway led to a roofed portico. White tatters of Halloween ghost figures fluttered among the front plantings. Inside the front window, a kitchen-witch figure with a twig broomstick peered out.

When Matt rang the bell, he waited a long time; so long that he began the useless debate of wondering whether it worked, and how long he could decently wait before trying it again.

The wood door swept open as if presenting a jack-in-the-box, only this was a Janice-in-the-box. He wondered if the box contained chalk, or Crayolas.

She opened the outer glass door. "Mr. Devine?"

At his nod she stepped aside to admit him. The darkness inside was disorienting. In bright climes, houses are always shadowed shocks of unseen terrain.

"Come on back to my studio."

He followed, glimpsing a formal living room and dining room before going down a long hall, turning into another hall, passing closed doors and finally emerging into what must have originally been a back bedroom.

Now it was a combination solarium/studio, the back wall and ceiling pushed out and up into two massive wings of glass. Everything was white—the composition floor, the painted walls, the slip-covered daybed in one corner. An outside patio, its boundaries marked by hanging baskets of bright flowers, extended beyond the sight line to parallel the family room and kitchen, he would guess.

"Quite a contrast, isn't it?" she asked with a grin. "I hate these Sun Belt houses—all dim hallways and plantation-shuttered windows. It makes sense to keep out the heat and the sun, but back here I wanted light, and I'm willing to pay to keep the studio cool."

"This part of the house is below the peak of the roof, facing north, isn't it? So you get indirect light, anyway."

"You have an artist's eye. This assignment should be easy."

"Not an artist's eye. Maybe a sense of direction. I grew up in the frozen north, where we're always trying to face things south. Here, the opposite applies."

"Amen. Have a seat."

The seat was white vintage wicker, with a floral-covered pad and a round, framing back.

"This is charming," Matt couldn't help commenting, his eyes finally adjusting to the lavish spill of daylight.

He could have said as much of his hostess. Janice Flanders sounded like an accountant, someone plain and no-nonsense who did people's taxes. This woman was not particularly frilly, but much more feminine than her name. She wore fashionably faded jeans that looked as if they'd gotten that way through wear rather than manipulation. Her shirt was loose and vaguely Native American in its soft, desert colors. Long supple beaded earrings in iridescent earth tones undulated like small, personal serpents from her ears. Her ash-blond hair was anchored at her nape in a silver clip. And a slim belt of conchos circled her narrow waist.

He remembered to look at her feet last, shame on him! Temple would definitely find nothing there to envy: soft chamois moccasins, also beaded and probably Native American work.

"It's kind of you to see me so quickly," he said.

"Kind, nothing." Her earrings shimmied like a sandstorm around her lightly tanned skin. "I can use the commission. I do a lot of family portraits now. Mall caricatures now and then. Mostly evening and weekend work. I enjoy consulting during the weekday hours."

"What will this involve?"

"Me asking questions, you answering, describing. Who do you want me to sketch?"

"A man I knew years ago, and thought I saw a few evenings ago. It may be impossible—"

"Don't even think that." She laughingly leaned forward, fanned a hand with long, thin tanned fingers. Her left hand. Ringless.

"All right. But I don't know what this . . . project will cost . . . Miss Flanders."

Her hands fanned and gestured again. Rings circled the fore-finger and fourth finger of her right hand. Amethyst, amber. "I usually get two hundred. It takes, maybe an hour. I draw as you talk. Is that okay?"

"Fine. If a check's all right—?"

"Sure. You were referred by the police, weren't you?"

"By a particular police lieutenant."

"A woman." She sounded impressed. "Would you like some-thing to drink before we begin? It helps to have something to worry at while you're trying to remember. Lemonade? Iced tea?"

He requested the iced tea. Sipping it might disguise any bit-ter twist of the lips as he described Cliff Effinger to this sunny, sophisticated woman a world away from harsh Chicago winters and harsher domestic realities.

She vanished through a doorway he hadn't noticed, one that connected to the kitchen and family room he had theorized. Nei-ther were as sun-infused as this room, but when he stood to see the vista, they were as clean, cleverly accoutred and inviting.

"Decorating must be a hobby of yours," he called into the kitchen, seeing no one, but hearing the pleasant clatter and clink of glassware.

"I'm a compulsively visual person," she caroled back. "My fellow students at RISD would blanch at the western mode of design, but I've grown to love it."

"Risdee?"

"Rhode Island School of Design."

She came back into the room on that explanation, bearing a Coca-Cola tray topped off with tall glasses of amber tea.

Matt took the tray from her to place it on the low table before the sofa/daybed before resuming his seat. He nodded at the empty easel in the room's far corner.

"You paint as well as sketch, then?"

"Does a duck waddle? I'll show you some of my work after our session." She sipped some tea, curled her long legs under her on the muslin-covered daybed and picked up a large sketching pad leaning against the daybed leg.

The sketching pencil was one of many fanned in a tall ceramic vase, like an arrangement of dried leaves.

Before Matt knew it, he was launched on his artistic inquisition.

"A man. Does he have a criminal record?"

"A . . . petty one."

"And you saw him at twilight."

Matt nodded, then realized that she was already slashing in lines and curves and watching him only intermittently. "Yeah, that dusky time when you don't know whether the semaphore lights are on or off."

"I know just the moment you mean! One of my favorites—if you're off in the desert looking at the horizon, instead of in Las Vegas waiting on a traffic light."

Her laughter was infectious. Matt found himself relaxing, even though he was reliving one of the more traumatic moments of his current life.

"So why were you at that particular traffic light?"

"I was on my way to work."

"Right. You work nights. What kind of work?"

"I'm a hot-line counselor."

Her eyes, hazelnut-golden, flicked up with approval. "Great! But you're used to hearing people, not seeing them."

"True. Very true. I had only a glimpse, that's the problem—"

"There are no problems when you're working with a sketch artist. We thrive on reconstruction. Where was he?"

"Crossing the street in front of me."

"How old is he?"

Matt had figured this out long ago, and contemplated it every birthday. "Sixty-three."

"Tall man? Short? Walk with a stoop?"

"I thought you . . . that the idea was to get a face."

"Face it is, but it helps to know context."

"Medium height. Except he had that loping, rangy, sort of swaggering walk."

"Sweeney among the nightingales?"

Matt was dumbfounded. "You know Eliot?"

"Not personally." She looked up to grin. "A wonderful image, though, isn't it? Neanderthal man swinging those calf-dusting fingertips among the fragile-throated birds fit only for an emperor. Eliot is so visual."

"I thought . . . cerebral."

Janice shrugged, her sketching hand never still.

What could she be sketching already, Matt wondered. Her eyes darted up, to him, for only a moment, as swift as the fan of butterfly wings. Her eyes were hard and concentrated, and her smile looked fixed. Still, her face was a pleasant mask that he couldn't read, as if a god had inhabited her.

"Sixty-three. And still vigorous."

"I suppose. He was walking fast. The Strip is wide but he kept up with—was ahead of—the crowd. And he wore a hat."

"Hat. Hard hat? Baseball cap?"

"Western hat."

"Stetson?"

"I don't know. Uh, pale, but dirty pale. Dented crown."

"And the brim?"

"A hat brim. Average. For a cowboy hat, I guess." Matt felt as if he were failing elementary spelling.

Janice smiled and tilted her sketchpad toward him. He could see the apt, rough lines of a Western hat above an empty oval of face. "That it?"

"No. The crown was lower. There were some . . . gewgaws on a hatband."

She tilted the pad back to her, left hand working rhythmically. Left-handed women were rare, especially left-handed women artists, he would bet.

He became aware of a *click-click-click* noise somewhere in the house, and lifted up his head to hear better. She didn't look up.

"Nothing to worry about, Matt. The kids are off at computer camp for two weeks."

"I hear . . . clicking."

"Or ticking?" She smiled, still not looking up. Her earrings trembled with the slashing movements of her cocked left arm.

"A clock?"

"I collect old clocks. I like that sound of time tsking away."

"I didn't hear it before."

"Time's like that. Sneaks up on you. Like this Cliff Effinger. What kind of nose?"

Nose. How often do you study another person's nose? Maybe once, after you've punched him in the face and he's lying on the floor, groggy, not quite focusing on you . . .

"Ah, average nose. A little crooked in the middle."

"Fighter?"

"Loser," Matt said before he could stop himself. Calling what Cliff Effinger did with his fists "fighting" was like saying a rooster sang Mozart opera.

Janice nodded. "Face showed it?"

"Yeah. It had . . . battered edges, some partly age and drink, some . . . abuse. Maybe self-abuse, maybe not."

"Drunks fall on their faces a lot. They get a certain look. Kinda . . . smashed." She grinned at her double entendre.

"How do you know these things?"

Level, sharp eyes looked up. "I watch. That's my job. I like sketching criminals. Their faces are living rap sheets. They are types, you know. How you live shows in your face. Not everyone can see it. That's why I'm asked to do criminal reconstruction sketches."

"Does it bother you ever? Seeing so much in faces."

Janice seamed her lips shut as she shook her head, making the bead-snakes in her ears shimmy. "I rarely have to confront the faces I draw from descriptions. I only see their damage in the people I interview."

He nodded. He had dealt with the aftermath of other people's acts too. Always the real perpetrators were faint and far away, lurking somewhere beyond the victim's taut vocal chords and shuddering breaths and shrouded eyes. You weren't supposed to call them victims, but "survivors." Yet they were both, and always would be, just as he was.

Matt hadn't realized he had sighed until he heard it between the ticks of the hidden clock.

"Eyes," she said, demanding each fragment of face in piece-meal order.

Eyes. Color? Like roiled water, maybe, half mud, half some viscous venom. "Hazel," he suggested, trying to remember if Molina had ever mentioned Effinger's rap-sheet statistics. He thought not. "I should have asked the lieutenant for those details."

"Doesn't matter." Janice kept her expression pleasant, peaceful. "I don't sketch in color. I meant their shape, size, expression."

"Small eyes. Lost in himself. Squinting all the time, angling, maneuvering, sizing up the situation."

"Shifty? Like in the old detective stories."

"Yeah, shifty. You coming up with a cartoon?"

"Not quite." She hummed as she sketched. "Any identifying marks?"

"Nothing, unless you'd consider sideburns that."

"Sideburns? Shades of Elvis. Did he wear sunglasses, by the way?"

"Yeah. I forgot that. Aviator-style, like a million other guys in Las Vegas."

"Maybe three million," she suggested gently. "I'll do a small inset with the sunglasses on."

"Thanks. Guess he only wears them outside. He was duded up in Western; that's how I saw him."

"A new look for him?"

"Very." But then Matt's memory had fixed this man in the amber flypaper of the past.

Janice turned the pad toward him again. The oval was no longer blank. Matt was ambushed by a resemblance he recognized. "That's amazing."

"Not done yet. What needs changing?"

He studied it hopelessly. That there was even a ghost of a resemblance to Cliff Effinger struck him as a miracle. That it could be better struck him as impossible. How could he remember details of a face that had aged sixteen years since he'd last seen it up close and personal?

"Teeth," he remembered suddenly. "A gold one at the left upper rear. And his lips disappeared when he smiled."

"Bet he didn't smile often."

"You'd win. But the upper lip was longer, or the space between the nose and the upper lip, kinda horsey. And his chin wasn't that strong. It sloped down into his neck."

"Ah, Mr. Sweeney's really coming along now. Get those nightingales into their cages."

She flashed him a smile as warm as the iced tea had become in its glass. Melted ice had thinned the drink to the washed-out color of river-water.

She finally turned the sketchpad toward him again. She had taken each feature and seamed it sixty-three years' worth. Finally they came together. An old man now, Matt thought with some wonder, some resentment at the unswerving tick of time. He's an old man now. He shut his eyes to picture the body in the morgue viewing chamber. Right age, right build, vaguely right face. But this . . . Matt blinked at the pad, then took it as she relinquished custody. This was a nightmare come to two-dimensional life. If his mother saw it—

"Great," he said, meaning it. "I can't believe you did this so quickly."

The clock promptly bonged the quarter hour. She glanced at the turquoise-and-coral-banded watch on her right wrist. "Quickly? You've been here just under two hours."

"Really? It seemed like minutes." Then he stopped, because her smile had softened and become . . . what? Conspiratorial? Knowing? What had he said? What had he said wrong?

"Time flies when I'm sketching," she said. "It's my form of therapy." She flipped the top sheet over Cliff Effinger, wiping away his sneering (how did she know that?), seamed face with the previous page, with . . . Matt's own likeness.

"When . . . how did you do that?"

"To warm up when we were first talking." She tilted her head to study her work, his face. "Usually good-looking people are a bore to draw. Everything is surface, and the kind of charm that goes with good looks freezes into a kind of mask early on."

"It doesn't look like me," Matt said, almost to himself, then caught the implication. "I mean, it does, but I don't see myself that way."

"Good. I feel most successful when my subjects see themselves in a different way. You can have this one too."

"I'll pay extra," he began, plumbing the windbreaker pockets trying to remember where he'd put the checkbook.

Her beringed right hand waved away his offer. "I only take money for sketching the absent on these assignments. Come on, I promised to show you my paintings."

He reluctantly left the studio to follow her, left behind the naked sketchpad with its incriminating likenesses, of Cliff Effinger, of himself.

In the hall she pushed a button. Track fixtures all along the ceiling splashed slashes of light on the huge canvases lining the walls. It was like touring a Byzantine gallery—formal figures, almost totemic, men and women touched with barbarian flashes of gold leaf. He couldn't tell if they were shamans or saints, often if they were male or female, but all shared the trait of great personal power, of a brooding bitter spirituality that was quite the opposite of the sunny studio with the flower patterns splattered against white wicker.

He followed her into the main rooms to find the painting sequence commanding the wood-paneled walls there like Easter Island colossi flattened into pigment and then pressed onto canvas, like relatives who came to call and were impaled onto the walls.

"These are such inhuman figures," he commented.

She stopped, and smiled over her shoulder. "Funny, I used to know them all. I think maybe they were even more inhuman then."

"Do you have a theme? A—" He couldn't think of anything else to ask . . . a reason, he meant. An explanation for such a strong and bitter vision.

She shook her head and led him into another, smaller room. They were in the opposite wing, a bedroom wing, and this was a child's room. A little girl's, to judge by the row of stuffed-animal figures on the single bed.

"That's the kind of family portrait work I do." Janice pointed to a pair of pictures at the bed's head.

He went closer to see. Full-faced children, the boy about eight, the girl younger. Their noses, chins, cheeks were plastic yet round and damp and undefined. Grave black eyes occupied almost all of their sockets as if their adult selves were imprisoned behind the mushy façades, peering out from peepholes a size too small.

"Lovely," he said, "but sad."

"Of course they're sad. They have to grow up."

Beyond the window Matt could see a corner of the yard, bright and pale in the autumn sunlight. Inside, the house was shadowed, secretive somehow.

Down the hall, the clock ticked.

Janice leaned against the pale lavender wall, hands behind her so she looked like a prisoner too. "I love them dearly, but sometimes—these computer and summer-camp times—I appreciate the freedom."

"You're . . . alone with them?"

"Divorced, yes." Her look was direct. "Single parent is the proper oxymoronic expression, I believe. No Sweeney on site."

Until then he hadn't seen it, guessed it. He felt cornered, although she was the one who had her back to the wall.

He felt the immaculately kept, charmingly decorated, empty house all around him, holding its breath. This was a child's bedroom, there would be others, another, all empty, charming, waiting.

The clock ticked, measuring moments, and this one was trembling on the brink far too long. His fault, of course, for being so stunned, for wondering if he were imagining things, for thinking what he was thinking . . .

Which was that she was even more charming than her house, an artist full of energy and compassion, a quite-attractive woman who probably had far too few occasions to prove it . . .

Which was that no one was expected here for some time, maybe hours, maybe days . . .

Which was that adults did these things, acted on impulse, forgot that the clock always ticked and that one was supposed to be someplace else . . .

Which was what harm would it do if care were exercised and both were certain to keep it timelessly exciting and distant, and if loneliness got lost in the shuffle and no one would know and no one would be hurt, least of all the parties involved who were strangers and therefore risked less even as they risked more . . .

And he almost could see it, could see safety in a stranger, could see disguise in nakedness, could see *just getting it over with*, suddenly, for once and for all, in circumstances that could be called a dozen different things, not one of them premeditated . . .

And he could see how nothing could be said and everything, and how no one could be to blame and everyone, and how people could do it all the time, maybe not the same people, but the same thing happening everywhere all the time . . .

And why not to him?

"Thank you," he said, and left the room.

Chapter 12

Midnight Munchies

This just missed being my unlucky last chapter, set at a feline funeral parlor, which is to say an anonymous little bonfire at Smoke Rise Farm.

While I am dying to learn what others may say about me once I am dead, I am also willing to leave this terminal bit of feline curiosity unfulfilled for quite some time. Nor am I ready to don the ashen mantle of the late Maurice One and his ilk. Besides, I have never been one to leave a feather or a fur unruffled, so for me Cat Heaven would be Hell, as bad as the state pen for a cop gone bad: a place full of old foes waiting to make my Afterlife as miserable as I made their Forelife.

But those who hand Midnight Louie a banana peel to slip on usually have to watch me dance my way out of danger and come up singing, with a banana split.

And so it went at Gangster's. While I nearly did the splits avoiding the trip wire Maurice Two laid in my path, I managed to land on all fours (on my proper mark too) and am the cynosure of all eyes. (I am not sure what this cynosure is, but being a long, odd word, it must be hot stuff.)

The director has flipped his toupee over my agile escape antics, only he interprets it as a "cat soft-shoe."

The dude whose suit I ruined while using it for a ladder to his shoulder is not complaining, as he will now have a close-up in the À La Cat commercial, for which he will have to give permission and therefore get paid. He is babbling to his fellow hoofers about his "big break" while the costumer is trying to pull snagged threads smooth and whimpering about having to resew from scratch, so to speak.

Meanwhile the Divine Yvette has taken advantage of her freedom and the resulting flurry to rub back and forth most provocatively against my ruffled suitcoat, purring, "You are such a natural performer, Louie. What an improviser! You must teach me that little jazz step you did on the way down; we would look great together and I would get more close-ups. This is my commercial, after all, big boy."

There is a bit of a subdued growl in her last words, but I do not blame her for coveting more camera time. So I turn my skin-saving routine into a simple cha-cha-cha, and she picks it up right away.

"Film that!" the director barks. "We can save a pile on computer animation if these cats keep up the good work."

So I get to do a little victory dance with my honey. Even the stupid flamingo fedora does not seem so bad at the moment.

"Get Louie's face tight," Kyle orders. "He looks like the cat that swallowed the canary, and that is how a consumer of À La Cat should look. What a natural!"

Natural nothing! Although I show my usual savoir faire and aplomb, my stomach is in imminent revolt, not from my shocking plummet down the stairs, but from the lump of À La Cat I was forced to consume on camera. Ugh! It feels like one of those fabric-stuffed mice people are always forcing on undiscriminating house cats, a soggy, cotton-flannel wad in my stomach. I burp and the director goes ballistic.

"He burped! Did you get that? Great. We can put some really macho sound under it—after all, this is the alley cat—and intercut it with a shot of the blonde licking her dainty whiskers. That burp really says 'satisfied customer.' Hey, this is gonna work."

Well, nobody likes a happy director more than a performer, but I suspect that Miss Temple will be the beneficiary of a humongous hair ball on her coverlet around 3 A.M. this morning.

While I am the center of all attention, I cast a glance to the top of the stairs.

Yup. There he sits like some bronze statue out of antiquity, deceptively still. Maurice Two has witnessed his murderous scheme backfire. I have no doubt he is already dreaming up the second installment. I start up the stairs toward him.

By now, though, the director has ordered the cameras to back off and there is a race up the stage stairs. Two sets of high heels pound in tandem as the Divine Yvette's and my respective stage mamas each strive to be first to congratulate her darling.

Miss Temple wins by a nose, and a rather endearing, short nose at that; and sits beside me on the fifteenth step. Maurice lucks out again.

"Louie, are you all right?"

"Of course he is all right," Miss Savannah Ashleigh snaps from below. "He nearly crashed into my adorable Yvette while doing all that fancy footwork. What a showoff."

"A natural gymnast," Miss Temple corrects, not too gently, meanwhile tenderly probing my anatomy for sore spots.

I do not doubt that tomorrow my lean torso will feel the effects of those aerial acrobatics, but for now, all is clover.

The director is still babbling about what a great segment this is, and how he wants to get a bunch more shots on the set when possible. Even the human star of the show has wandered over and is now deigning to notice me.

"Clever fellow," he tells Miss Temple. He bends down so Miss Savannah Ashleigh cannot hear and also tells her, "Do not forget about coming to my Sunday brunch tomorrow."

She nods, paying him much less attention than a star like Mr. Darren Cooke is used to, all the while feeling the flexibility in my limbs, which are the usual wet noodles.

"Darren," Miss Savannah Ashleigh says, following him into the wings, my lovely Yvette trapped in her grasping arms, "was not Yvette wonderful?"

He can only agree, but I see that his heart is not in it, nor is Miss Savannah much in his heart or mind. I am happy to say that I and Miss Temple seem to have replaced her in his regard. I begin to wonder how I could drop in on his brunch on the morrow, for I am sure he would have asked me had he realized that I am willing to attend these little career-building social affairs now and then. Although Miss Temple is touchingly concerned about my welfare, she does not view me as quite the asset I am. She is clearly underestimating the scope of my future performing career, not to mention my many previous contributions to her dabbling efforts in the crime-solving department.

Miss Temple has become so carried away by my athletic exertions that she picks me up and actually attempts to rise. I see that I am to be toted back down to my carrier, and am much touched by her efforts, but fear she has overestimated her toting power. I am no lightweight normally, and with half a pound of À La Cat turning to concrete in my gut I am even more unwieldy than usual.

Miss Temple's dainty shoes kick the almost-fatal trip wire to the bottom of the stairs. Nothing like stumbling over the evidence. She misses the second-to-the-bottom step on the set and teeters for a moment before she gets her balance back. Then she cranes her head over my swollen stomach to examine the floor.

"Tsk. Someone left a piece of wire onstage. How careless. I'll have to get it once you're back in your carrier."

No, no! I look up. Maurice is slinking down the stairs unnoticed, like any second banana. I am helpless to resist, although I do offer Miss Temple a few delicate pricks of warning.

"Louie! Don't fight. I'll let you out as soon as we're in the car. Union rules require you to have a container."

Of course by the time she has carefully minced down the steps to the stage, dumped me in the carrier and returned to do her good deed and pick up the rogue wire, it is . . .

"Gone," she mutters to the empty stage and house. "I could swear I stepped right on it."

By now Maurice has batted it a few dozen yards away into the wings, and if he has any smarts, into the nearest waste receptacle.

I swallow a growl of frustration, but it is a small one. I doubt he left any pad prints on the wire, and besides, no human would think to look for them, anyway.

If one is going to commit murder, an innocent façade is the best disguise, and fur is fail-safe in that regard. However, that works both ways, and if Maurice persists in trying to turn me into cured ham, I may have to fix his bacon.

The expression makes my stomach growl, but first I have to be rid of that À La Cat. I believe I will shock and overjoy Miss Temple by gobbling down that awful Free-to-be-Feline when I get home. A few swallows of that ought to make everything come up in a most satisfying way.

Chapter 13

A Cooked Goose

"Oh, Louie!"

The cold, wet lump under Temple's bare foot told her she needed her glasses after all.

She hopped one-legged (like a flamingo) back to the bed and its companion table. Putting on her glasses, she examined the suspect part of the parquet floor. Yes, a damp grayish glob, like a wet cigar, defaced the wood.

Temple sat on the bed edge and wiped the bottom of her foot with a tissue. She pulled six or seven more tissues from the box, then went back to collect, wrap and deposit the giant hair ball in the bathroom wastebasket.

Through all of this, Louie sat majestically on the zebra-striped coverlet, licking off more hair to end up in yet another Major Hair-Ball Production.

"I suppose because you're a TV star--to-be now you think your hair balls are cashmere."

Louie stopped licking to regard her thoughtfully. At least Temple assumed his manner was thoughtful. She would hate to think it was possibly disdainful. He pushed up on his front legs, then leaped to the floor, carefully treading around the damp area. But he limped a little.

"Louie, are you all right?"

She trailed him, barefoot, to the living room, where he took a turn into the kitchen. There he paused over the Free-to-be-Feline bowl he had actually honored last night by consuming some of the contents thereof. After a sniff he turned back to the living room and finally hopped up on the sofa.

His limp had evened out on his travels, so Temple opened her door to collect the fat Sunday paper and left it on the coffee table while she returned to the bedroom to contemplate her options.

What to wear to a Darren Cooke Sunday brunch was the problem. Temple didn't usually fret over what to wear, except to worry about forecast rain or unseasonable cold. But Temple didn't usually hobnob with the city's influx of celebrities. And Savannah Ashleigh would probably be there. For some reason, ever since they became dueling stage mothers, she felt rather competitive toward SA. At least she didn't want to embarrass Louie, who was now known even to Darren Cooke.

Maybe she should follow his example and always wear black. A muumuu like Electra, but black. Except . . . Temple wasn't that fond of wearing black. And white was too summery now and her closet was a bore, along with everything in it, and half of that everything needed dry cleaning or drip-drying or small repairs with needle and thread, which she had not laid hand to in months.

Of course her scheme to replace all her wire hangers with smooth plastic ones had fallen apart half accomplished, so every other outfit she wanted to examine was tangled with something else. What Temple bought depended on her mood that day as well as what was on sale, and given her theatrical background, her wardrobe had multiple-personality syndrome.

When Temple complained about her lack of a signature style, Electra said that at least she didn't have a range of six sizes to consider, and no notion which she would fit into on that particular day, as Electra had faced until she had converted to the all-accommodating muumuu. Temple guessed that would happen to her in a decade, when thirty became forty.

She decided to do Hollywood chic out of the Beatnik fifties—a huge white shirt (discreetly touched with eighties rhinestones, like fallen crumbs) cinch-belted over black leggings. For shoes . . . she bent to dig among the pairs impaled on a chrome rack . . . something Savannah. Aha! A pair of vintage high-heeled mesh sandals with flamingo-pink feathers on the toes . . . just the thing! This would subtly (or not-so-subtly) combine her current two assignments: supervising Louie's film-world debut and running interference for Domingo's flamingo fandango.

A pair of thin black-enamel hoop earrings completed the Arlene Dahl look. "Bet you don't even remember Arlene Dahl, dahling," she told Louie as she scooped up her favorite black-patent tote bag, grabbed her car keys from the inside-cupboard hook in the kitchen and headed out with about seven minutes to spare. "Neither do I."

Arriving too early for a Hollywood bash was haute gauche, she was sure.

The Oasis's fabled towers looked flat and faded in the daylight, but the giant pair of entry elephants stood at attention, one foot and two tusks each raised in welcome.

Sabu the elephant valet pulled his tasteful brocade turban firmly over his ears as he bent to squirm into the Storm and whisk it away. Temple felt the car at least deserved valet parking on such an occasion, and she didn't think that she or the flamingo shoes could take a long walk from the parking garage.

It was already a long walk inside the Oasis to the elevators.

Like all Las Vegas PR people, Temple had attended an occasional high-profile press party. She had been among crowds invited to hobnob with the newest semifading star to make a long Las Vegas engagement part of an attractive retirement package. Amazing how you almost never ran into the guest of honor at those wingdings.

This was the first time she had been personally invited by the host of honor, and she didn't know quite what to expect. Darren

Cooke didn't want her flackery skills, but what Savannah Ashleigh dismissed as her "Nancy Drew" proclivities. Temple was a teensy bit impressed that Cooke would take her seriously, and apparently he was in serious trouble. She wondered if she had a right to step in.

The elevators were glass bullets, Hyatt-style, but fashioned like bejeweled Indian caskets. As her car rocketed smoothly up to the penthouse region, Temple was able to watch the lobby of greenery and temple ruins, exotic live birds and curtains of waterfalls slip past.

The hall she entered was plain in comparison, although eastern fretwork shadowed the walls of many doors. Doors were fewer and farther between on these elevated levels than on the steerage floors below, which packed in tourists like desk keys.

A door announcing itself as THE TAJ MAHAL SUITE bore the right number. Temple looked for a bell before she knocked, and found a gong affixed to the wall, with a mallet attached by a rawhide string.

A modest rap produced a deep, mellow call . . . and no answer at the door. She could hear nothing through it, either the result of the Oasis's superior construction or evidence that she had gotten the date, time or room number wrong (or all three).

Oh, great. Temple hit the gong again, harder.

The door parted, then paused. A subdued clink and chatter leaked through the inch-wide opening. Then a hand with very long, very thick fingernails painted Passion Fruit Purple undulated through.

Oh golly, Miss Germaine Monteil! She had forgotten that the fashionable set these days was wearing weird-colored nail enamels; her fingernails were a discreet flamingo tint. How remiss.

The door widened and Savannah Ashleigh's face peered out.

"Oh, it's you. Dare wanted me to see who it was." With that she shut the door.

With that, Temple reopened the door and stepped in, ready to dip her flamingo polish in Ashleigh blood, which was probably purple to match her nails.

Since the one person in the room Temple knew had vanished,

she edged along the room's fringes until she got her bearings. There was a good deal of gel- and mousse-mussed hair going in all directions and a lot of heavy metal masquerading as jewelry on both sexes. Actually, Temple realized that she should think in terms of *all* sexes, as in he, she and it. For besides the apparent hetero- and homosexuals present, another rara avis pecked around the premises, the anorexic, androgynous figures Temple saw in fashion magazines, either boys in makeup or muscular girls in tattoos.

The older set, of course, was much more conventional and therefore much less interesting. Some men actually wore blazers, in such succulent desert tones as melon and sage green, with open-necked yellow shirts. Some of the past-forty women sported diamond jewelry instead of the usual toolbox accouterments.

Then Temple spotted an old friend she recognized from many a press party and made for that spot like a camel in need of an oasis at the Oasis.

The buffet table. Here the scene and activity and dramatis personae were old pals. Plates, paper napkins, platters full of . . . European crackers and beady black caviar, lox and olives, layered extravaganzas of tomatoes and capers and sour cream and chutney, everything that would look absolutely awful if it dropped on a Big White Shirt.

Temple didn't care for caviar (too fishy) or chutney (too sweet-tart) or dry-cleaning bills, so she poured herself a ginger ale and nibbled crackers and waited to figure out what she was doing here.

As she studied the room, which was much like Domingo's suite down the Strip: large, furnished with bland Hotel Ritz, walled with windows that showed only the blue-pink distance unless you went right up to them and looked down, she realized that the host was missing.

Temple eyed the other guests again. No one was better at barging in and making herself at home than a PR woman, but these people were grouped into tight twosomes, like sets of Ken and Barbie. Savannah Ashleigh was negotiating an intense tête-à-tête with a partially shaved guy in his midtwenties who wore jeans and a spruce leather jacket with no shirt under it.

Just then someone sidled up to Temple.

"I'm Mr. Cooke's personal assistant. I don't believe we've met."

The tone implied accosting a gate-crasher. The speaker was all of twenty-five herself, a tall, willowy young woman with artificially wine-red hair wearing a strapless spandex tube dress with a safety-pin dog collar. One multipierced ear dangled a cascade of silver charms to her collarbone. Yet despite the theatrical getup, she seemed all business.

"I certainly would have remembered," Temple said with her most charming smile. "I confess I'm new to the Sunday-brunch set. Mr. Cooke invited me only yesterday at Gangster's."

Two tiny frown lines defaced the pale complexion. "He never mentioned you."

"How can you be sure? You don't know my name."

"He tells me everything," she began, with an odd combination of stridency and uncertainty, "but he's been on the phone in the master bedroom for, oh, minutes and minutes."

"I suppose it wouldn't hurt anything if I waited until he came out."

"Only . . . you don't know anyone here."

"Only . . . Savannah Ashleigh. And I see she's lost in conversation with that yummy young mugging victim in Claude Montana leather."

The girl jerked her messily teased red poll in that direction. "That's Mosh Spiegel, the famous dirt biker."

Temple had never heard of any famous dirt bikers, unless you counted Evel Kneivel.

"Well, I'm Temple Barr, and I'm here at Mr. Cooke's request. I'll just have to entertain myself while I wait for him, unless you want to entertain me until he comes out."

"Uh, I have things to do." A long, bony hand with gnawed fingernails waved toward the buffet. "Eat something, or . . . whatever."

Whatever seemed the only option, so Temple prepared herself

to hold up the wall for some time. Sitting solo in a standup crowd like this was isolating and awkward. Most guests were either very young (which meant even younger than Temple) or quite middle-aged (which to Temple meant over forty-five). But that made sense. Darren Cooke was easily in his early fifties, no matter how much the plastic surgeons pinned his ears back year after year. Of course he would still attract the young and trendy; all stars did, even when their twinkle was mostly in the surgeon's laser-light.

Temple nibbled on what resembled a mutilated carrot. She hoped it was a carrot. She switched walls. Then she ambled to the windows to look out. Usually at a party, looking out attracted another looker-outer. Not here. She could have been invisible, in fact, was, because she was unknown. Should have brought Midnight Louie. He was a great conversation-starter.

And then, staring at the great nothingness beyond Las Vegas, at unchanged easygoing mountains whose brown summits snagged clouds as airy as biplane pilots' long, fringed white silk scarves, Temple realized the obvious.

Darren Cooke had consulted his "Nancy Drew" because something in his life disquieted him. Why wasn't he coming out?

Temple set her ginger-ale glass on a table and turned toward the closed door at which the personal assistant had cocked a dyed-red eyebrow.

She met the assistant on an intercepting path.

"You can't go in there," the woman said.

"You ever wonder why he's left his guests alone so long? Mr. Cooke didn't strike me as the reclusive type. Not at his own party."

The frown returned, rather deep for such a young forehead. "He did seem . . . surprised by the call."

"Maybe you better check on him."

A blank stare.

"A shocking call. Heart attack maybe."

"No." The young woman seemed truly alarmed. "Not a heart attack. He's too young—" She turned and ran for the door.

Temple shook her head. Darren Cooke was way past "too

young" for a lot of things. She discreetly followed the woman.
No one else noticed; they were too busy performing the latest
chitchat.

Temple paused outside the ajar door. Only silence seeped
through. She pushed it slightly, encountering a barrier.

The girl was standing two steps inside, frozen.

Oh, my god, Temple thought. Not at his own party.

She pushed the door until it butted the girl, then pushed harder,
until the girl gave way. Temple stepped in, shutting the door behind her.

She didn't see what she expected, but neither had the personal
assistant.

Darren Cooke was alive and well, sitting on the massive
emperor-size bed, by the telephone. A bottle of tall, clear liquor
guarded the tabletop receiver. The faint drone of a dial tone
wafted all the way to the door.

Cooke was slumped over, elbows on his knees, a bathroom
water glass tilting in one hand. The other hand was clenched in
his perfect two-hundred-dollar razor-cut.

"Darren, what's the matter?" The personal assistant sounded
like a hysterical teenager.

Cooke turned toward the door. He seemed to have heard the
girl, but he focused on Temple. The Hollywood tan, whether
from the sun or a bottle, looked like a waxy yellow buildup on
his too-taut face.

"Good," he said, straightening. "Keep the guests happy, Alison. And you"—he was lost for a name, then found one—
"Nancy! You stay."

Temple exchanged a puzzled glance with Alison, who tucked
her glossy features into a disapproving pucker suitable for a
nineteenth-century old maid, and left.

Temple took the seat Cooke indicated with a sweep of his manicured hand. It was a biscuit-colored suede chaise longue worth
about three grand.

He pointed again, now to the travertine bedside tabletop.
"Ouzo. My favorite private stock. Straight from Athens. Want
some?"

Temple nodded. She didn't, but finding a glass would help the man pull himself together.

He lurched up and disappeared beyond a set of double doors that likely led to a palatial bathroom. While he was gone, she studied the master bedroom, which was as close as she'd ever come to High-Roller Heaven. Not for real VIPs the garish, gaudy excesses of lower-level suites, the ones that make the magazines and newspapers, the ones everybody likes to snicker at, for their sunken Roman baths, built-in waterfalls and tacky theme-park decor. Everything here was expensively plain and simple, boring even.

She looked down at her feet and wiggled her toes. The absurd flamingo-pink feather pom-poms on her toes fluttered and flirted back. That was *her* reality check; that's what kept her feet on the ground, the sweet eternal extravagance of shoes. Sole on ice. Not ouzo.

He came out finally, empty glass in hand, an ordinary heavy hotel glass, thick and clumsy. "I'm not drunk, just . . . stunned."

"Maybe you need more help than I can give." Temple started to rise.

"No. No Papa Bear of police. No Mama Bear of shrink. You're like Baby Bear's bed and chair and porridge, just right. You won't scare the house." He sat on the bed's edge, then poured a couple inches of what looked like water into the glass. "Besides, Savannah hates your guts, and Savannah hates only people with class."

"If you know that, why do you know Savannah?"

He pointed wearily at the bottle. "My favorite private stock. Women without class."

"Aren't you married?"

"Oh." As if he had forgotten. "Oh, yeah. To a classy lady. Did that right, when I finally did it." He glanced up through ruffled eyebrows, the thicker lintels age offers fading eyesight. A remnant of boyish charm trickled through. "You don't care. What can I do? Pay you? Give you comps? Why are you even here?"

"I'm curious."

"Like your cat. Midnight Louie. Light-Foot Louie." He

laughed until the room rang. "What a performer, that cat. Knows how to hog the spotlight, and that's what fame is all about. Ask O. J. Look. I'm not drunk. I know what you're thinking. I know what I'm thinking." He pointed to the abandoned phone receiver, still droning. The warning yodel that it was off-the-hook had long since given up the ghost. For some reason, Darren Cooke wouldn't—couldn't—break the connection with that dead phone line.

"Phone's a best friend to a guy in my game. Traveling. Alone. Phone home, if you got one, or got anyone there. Phone room service. Phone Athens for ouzo." He snapped his fingers. "It's the geezers' Internet."

"Sometimes people phone you."

"Yeah. Not often. Fans. Don't want fans on the phone. Letters are okay. Letters are distant. Impersonal." He frowned. "Usually. The phone is personal."

Temple sipped the ouzo for lack of anything else to do. Never had it. A sharp licorice tang and the sting of almost-pure alcohol. She had heard ouzo could knock out a sailor, and she had never been to sea.

"What's wrong?" she asked.

"I don't know." He opened the bedside-table drawer and pulled out a manila envelope.

An ordinary manila envelope. Temple took it when he offered it, amazed at where common ground existed. He was a star, but he stuffed the secrets of his shredded life into an ordinary manila envelope just like everybody else.

She pulled the papers out slowly, feeling them first. Stationery, that slightly soft weight. Serviceable, store-bought goods, nothing expensive, unlike everything else in this room.

"I've been getting those letters for the past couple years. From my daughter."

"I didn't know—"

"Neither did I."

His left hand—ringless—ploughed through his dark hair. The ruffling gesture never revealed a glint of silver. Washed away, rinsed away. He drank from his glass and spoke again.

"Neither did I. No one ever said I had a daughter, or a son, or a goddamn golden retriever. Not one woman, asking for money, asking for marriage, asking for anything. The women have never asked for anything. I guess I was enough."

"Or you weren't worth asking for."

He looked up. "I'm a rotter, aren't I? Never married, never wanted to . . . until lately. The man women love to love, and love to hate and maybe both." He pointed to the phone. "She hates me. She's never met me except through tabloid TV but she hates me. I've been sitting here listening to the drone of her disconnected hate for half an hour. Look at those letters."

Temple didn't want to. This wasn't work for Nancy Drew. This was the dregs of someone else's life, not clean like a dead body you don't know. This was a live body on the dissecting table. She didn't need to crawl over it like a maggot.

"Listen. I don't have any friends," he said. When she looked up, his smile was crooked, but working on being charming again. "Just girlfriends. I can't tell my wife. We have a daughter. It would scare her to death that some . . . stranger from my past is out there, hating me, hating us. Maybe hating our kid. I love that little girl." His voice almost broke. "Me now . . . maybe Padgett later."

"This is way over my head."

"I know. But for right now, I need to talk to somebody who's totally outside of it. Nobody I know, nobody I don't know. Don't you see? You're just right, like Baby Bear. I need somebody who's over their head, like me. Until I can sort it out, and then, I'll do the right thing and I'll tell the police and hire the bodyguards, but right now I need Nancy Drew, you know. Somebody normal, who's as surprised as I am, but just a little bit objective."

Temple had started to skim the letters. They weren't what she had thought. The envelopes were sealed with fanciful stickers. The letters themselves were illustrated with rubber stamps and multicolored inks. Artworks of a sort, expressing admiration and connection and a desire to be friends. Like letters a foster child in a foreign land would write a sponsor at first, crude, reaching-out letters, eager and innocent. . . . The handwriting changed,

Temple saw as she shuffled through them, carefully organized by date and rubber bands. Organized by his hand, this man who had someone to do everything for him but solve his life puzzles.

"What's your name again?" he asked.

"Temple Barr."

"Temple. Good name. Like all my friends are naming their kids. We're old hell-raisers and late-life dads, but we can afford it. We can afford to give our kids weird wacky names, and the position and money to live 'em down. They don't have to be Tom, Dick or Harrys; Joanne, Marjorie or Marys. Padgett. It's got class. It says I'm somebody unique, right?" He frowned as he glanced at the droning phone receiver.

"What name does she sign?" Temple asked, turning to the letters' second and third pages.

Nothing. *Your daughter.* No name other than that.

"I called," he said. "Called them up, called them all up, everybody I could think of, or whose phone number I could find. No, they said, no abortions, no hidden clauses, no kids. I was careful. I knew to be careful. Wouldn't you think the woman would know?"

Temple nodded. "Weren't there other women, not-famous women who maybe didn't know how to be so careful?"

"I didn't exploit anyone. They knew what it was. They were of age. They were smart, attractive women. So what's the sin in that? I didn't want to be tied down. The house, the car, the dog, the wife, the kid. Everything a 'the.' Me 'the' husband. I wasn't cut out for that. So they called me a playboy. The guys always leered and the women, they kept coming. It was so easy."

Temple sighed. "Maybe she isn't your daughter. Maybe she just thinks so."

"Does that make her any less . . . worrisome. Or dangerous?"

"No. Maybe more so. Look, Mr. Cooke. Call the police, call a crack private-investigative agency. Don't sit here in a hotel room with a bottle of ouzo and a stranger."

His head lifted. "I feel better."

"Is that all it's about? You feeling better?"

"No. But that's something. I tell you, I was ready to jump out of one of these tinted-glass windows when that call came through."

Temple felt an awful clutch in her stomach, a sense that she was standing on a road alone, watching a train wreck about to happen.

"Look," she said. "I've gone through these letters, but I've used a tissue to touch them. There could be fingerprints. Go to the police, or to an investigative agency with policelike powers, and I imagine a few are well-known in Hollywood. You do have friends! You have all those aging guys you used to party with. They'd understand. They could be in the same fix. They'll help you. They're powerful people—"

"No! We're not powerful. We just got seduced into thinking we were because we were rich and famous. In a way, I want to meet her. I want to see what kind of girl she is, maybe explain."

"That's the worst thing you could do." Temple replaced the letters, handed back the envelope, stood. "I can't help you. I can only tell you what you already know."

He nodded, looked down, finally picked up the receiver, ponderously, in slow motion, and hung it up.

"You could stay," he said, slyly, like a dying man who enjoys bargaining with the Devil, even if it's the devil within.

Temple felt the room rock. If she'd had the manila envelope still in her hands, she would have crushed it.

"Is that, really, always your only bottom line? Haven't you learned anything? Hasn't this taught you anything? I could be your daughter's age. I could be your daughter."

He shrugged. "I'm lonely. I'm lonelier than I've ever been. Is it so bad to want to be not lonely?"

Temple tried to think back to when she had been the teensiest bit flattered to be invited to Darren Cooke's hotel house party. She had, and it was not that long ago.

"Maybe not," she said finally, "but there are better ways to work on being not lonely. Propositioning strangers isn't one of them."

"So you need rings and regulations to sleep with someone."

"No, but I need . . . self-respect, on both sides."

She turned before she picked up her ouzo glass and did something B movieish like tossing it in his face. That face was too tormented, even as it resorted to what had always worked for it before.

"Nobody's ever turned me down before," he called after her, as an afterthought, a warning, a plea.

She turned from the closed door. "They will." Then she opened it and walked out.

Chapter 14

Partners in Crime

"I am never," Temple told Louie when she returned to her condo and peeled out of her Hollywood-brunch garb like a snake shedding a particularly loathsome skin, "going to involve myself in possibly criminal matters again. And you can quote me."

Louie blinked to indicate that the message had been received. He then watched wide-eyed while Temple disappeared into the bathroom for an unprecedented midday dip. She left behind a trail of knee-high hose, a tangle of shed leggings and a tent of white shirt.

Also two tipsy shoes leaning against the wall, black with extremely pink and fluffy feather arrangements on each toe. Feathers, oh my.

Louie jumped down to the floor.

The bathroom door opened.

"And leave my shoes alone, you unreformed feather freak!"

Temple snatched the heels into the bathroom with her, shutting the door with an emphasis that was second cousin to a slam.

Louie sniffed the place where the prey had been, hunting that indefinable avian essence, then lumbered out into the main room, where he presumably could pursue predatory thoughts without being subjected to ESP.

Beyond the closed bathroom door, up to her neck in hot water, as usual, and up to her nose in mounds of bubbles, Temple regretted taking out her bad temper on Louie. Poor little guy had worked hard the past two days, then when he craved a little feather-sniffing, she had treated him like a pervert.

Temple often turned to baths as her own private think tank, especially in this old fifties tub that was deep and wide enough to float in. Thoughts somehow grew as airy and improvisational as the sudsy coverlet of clouds that shifted on the water's warm surface.

"Might as well have tried to help Crawford Buchanan with his sulky stepdaughter," Temple addressed the admirably echoing tile walls. "At least I would have known enough to just say 'no' in his case, under any circumstances. But Darren Cooke was a star, he really needed some nobody's encouraging words and savvy insight into human behavior. Savvy, huh! Insight, huh! Suckered again."

Temple grabbed the barge of Ivory soap that obligingly floated as advertised, and smashed it on the water. Tile walls wept tepid tears. "What a skunk. That guy will use any excuse to hit on a female. I can't believe that I thought he possibly could care about anything besides the notches on his Calvin Kleins! I hope the Daughter from Hell chases him from here to Pago Pago."

Of course no one could hear her fine denunciations; nothing could view them except the mirror above the sink, and it was fogged over. An apt symbol, Temple thought, for her recent perceptions. Well, nothing had been lost except a tiny remaining strand of illusion and a couple hours of a Sunday morning. Getting back to work with Domingo tomorrow would be a refreshing contrast. At least he flaunted his mistress, so he was hardly about to try anything tacky with Temple. Right?

Imagine, using the letters from that poor demented child to gain female sympathy as a preseduction ploy!

Temple rose from her steamy cleansing ritual, wrapped herself in a huge white bath towel and pattered across the black-and-white tiles to the bedroom, which was empty and cool. She stashed her retrieved shoes in the closet, safe from tooth and claw . . . and, even worse, saliva.

Then, still wrapped like a mummy in the ankle-length towel, she decided to raid the refrigerator, given how few of the buffet's expensive tidbits she had been able to eat.

Louie watched her from the sofa, the unread Sunday paper beside him and now beneath a proprietary paw.

"That's mine when I come back," she warned him.

Cats made excellent company. They received comments with grave attention but no overreaction. They were rarely anxious or milling underfoot, like dogs. Instead, they surveyed matters with supreme calm from a lordly or ladylike distance, which is why some people disliked them.

Temple was not in the mood for catlike detachment at the moment. After she made a mug of instant hot chocolate, she skittered out the kitchen's other end to the spare bedroom/office, where her answering machine was set up.

Sure enough, the little red Rudolph-nose button was winking, blinking and nodding. Her finger hesitated over the playback lever. Did she want to hear from somebody unwelcome today? Did she really want to know about something she would have to do tomorrow? Did she care to tend to any kind of business at all?

She shrugged and pressed the button.

After some rewinding and squeaking, the thing settled down and replayed . . . Matt's voice. Thank God. The intonation of calm and reason. "Temple," it said, "I've got something important to show you. I know it's early Sunday morning, but could I drop by later?"

Early Sunday all right, only 11:30 A.M. Matt's call must have come after she'd left at nine-thirty. What was he doing up so early on a Sunday, other than habit? If she'd been at church like other good Las Vegans, she would have avoided the debacle at the Oasis. Temple picked up the receiver and dialed Matt's number, pleased to realize she now knew it by heart.

He answered on the second ring, completely amenable to cocoa and cinnamon rolls. Fifteen minutes.

Temple scrambled to claw the packaged rolls out of the freezer, then ran to dig culottes and a knit top out of her bedroom closet. She even had time to read the funny papers before he arrived.

And he arrived bearing another roll of paper: naked newsprint in the bland, oatmeal color of pulp.

"What is it?" Temple asked. "Not a treat for Louie?"

"If it becomes one, I'll have his ears for it," Matt announced gravely. "It cost me a lot." The second sentence was even grimmer than the first. He glanced at Temple to make sure she was fully awake. "Sorry I called while you were asleep. I was pretty anxious to show you this."

"Wasn't asleep, silly. Was out."

"Out? Already? What's happening in Las Vegas before noon on Sunday besides gambling and church?"

Temple shook her head. "You forgot the other part of Las Vegas's trinity of eternal verities, even on a Sunday: food. Obligatory brunches. Cocktail wienies instead of sausages, caviar instead of coarse-ground pepper on your scrambled eggs, mimosas instead of grapefruit juice."

Matt made a face, before sitting on the sofa with Louie. Actually, right beside Louie. In fact, so close that Louie struggled upright and moved down a foot. Matt edged right into the empty spot, so he sat dead center on the sofa. He laid the rolled paper on the coffee table, then waited for Temple to come stand beside him for the unveiling.

She sat beside him instead. "Well?"

He unrolled the top, setting the crystal ashtray that was never otherwise used on one corner. Then he unfurled the rest like an old-fashioned parchment window shade, turn by turn, so the face drawn on the paper appeared inch by inch.

Temple held her breath from the top of the western hat to the dented collar points on the western shirt at the bottom.

"Is that really him?" she asked.

"Close enough for discomfort." Matt shook his head at the

likeness. "I don't know whether to tape it on the wall and heave rotten eggs at it, or what."

"Shoot it down in size on a copier and make flyers, even a few laminated 'wallet-size' copies you can flash in person. Then start asking people if they've seen the party in question. So this is Cliff Effinger."

"In disguise," Matt cautioned her, "and aged by an artist's guesstimate."

"Who's the artist and how did you get onto him?"

"Her," Matt corrected swiftly. He kept his eyes focused on the sketched face floating above the clutter.

It must be like looking down at a body in the morgue viewing room, Temple thought.

"Molina called me yesterday, out of the blue, appropriately, and suggested I try a police artist."

"You barely glimpsed the figure you saw on the street."

"But I never forgot the man he used to be."

"And this is the result. Does it look . . . right?"

Matt nodded slowly. "A remarkable job. She's really very good, this woman. Makes you remember things you didn't even know you'd forgotten, like a bump on a nose."

"That is some hokey getup."

Matt nodded. "Hokey like a chameleon maybe. Didn't your friend Max say that extremes are a disguise in Las Vegas?"

"Friend Max said that naked was no disguise in this town, only noisy was; loud clothes, loud pose. This dated urban-cowboy getup does it. You remember the hat and the sideburns more than you do the man under and behind them."

"If I hadn't known him from before, I'd have been hopeless at providing a description. Janice aged him to the right degree after I'd described all his features."

Temple clasped her elbows and nodded as she studied this likeness of a dead man walking. Cliff Effinger was not a savory customer, no matter what he wore or whether he were dead or alive.

"At least you accomplished something this weekend. I got sidetracked and, boy, am I sorry."

"What happened?"

"My brunch was more like a 'crunch,' and I was the main course. I'm still kicking myself for going."

"What could happen at a brunch?"

"Darren Cooke."

Matt finally looked up from the pinched, sketchpad face he couldn't tear his eyes from. "That name sounds familiar."

"He's a quasi–movie star. A comic actor who's done road shows and now is headlining the new Gangster's revue about Las Vegas's colorful past, that is, the criminal elements we love to sentimentalize once they've safely rubbed each other out."

"That's right! I saw a placard when we came in to the place. So you had brunch with this guy? Why?"

"Because of Savannah Ashleigh. You've heard me mention her?"

"Have I ever. Mother of Louie's Persian playmate and she-devil of Hollywood."

"Well, Ms. She-Devil apparently bad-mouthed me to Darren Cooke."

"Why?" Matt sounded indignant that anyone would bad-mouth Temple.

"She's an ex-fling of his—he's as famous for flings as for his throwaway lines—and apparently the competition was too much with me around the À La Cat commercial. It's being partially filmed on the Darren Cooke set."

"I see," Matt said, looking confused.

"So she called me 'Nancy Drew' to Darren Cooke, which got him wondering why. When he realized that I had been involved in a . . . situation or two, he decided he needed my expert assistance."

"But you don't really . . . do anything. You just happen to be front and center at crime scenes."

"Thanks for the vote of confidence. I thought I actually had some insight. So when he sat me down in an Oasis-penthouse suite, I was prepared to do what I could."

"What was his problem?"

"Pretty personal. I don't want to betray his confidence. Lord,

I sound like a priest! Anyway, he beat his breast with remorse for his past wicked ways, then ended up propositioning me."

"On Sunday morning?"

"The day of the week isn't the point! The point is that his distress call was only an elaborate ploy to hit on another female victim . . . me!"

"You mean his problem wasn't real?"

"Oh, he may be genuinely disturbed about it, but the man is such a knee-jerk Romeo that even his weaknesses become a pretext for chasing some new female on the scene. *Any* new female on the scene. I can't believe I fell for it."

"What did he do?" Matt looked like he really didn't want to hear.

"Nothing overt. He didn't have to. Made a veiled suggestion I saw right through, at which point I gathered up my Sherlock Jr. mail-order detective kit and left in a fairly discreet huff."

"So now you'd like to see his head on a platter at Hush Money's?"

"No, you can't blame a human hyena for having carrion tastes. If he exposed his tomcat ways, I exposed my own stupidity. I really do think I can solve people's problems. That idiotic Savannah Ashleigh isn't half wrong. I *do* think I'm Nancy Drew. I told him it was a police matter. I begged him to have it looked into professionally, even if he has to use some pricey Hollywood agency. He lost interest because the object of the game had never been his problem daughter. He uses everything to excuse his promiscuous social life."

Matt was looking at her oddly.

"What? You're surprised that I could be such a self-important fool?"

"No . . ."

"Thanks, counselor."

"I'm thinking, if this man is as famous as you say, he could be the one who calls me."

Temple slapped a hand over her mouth in shock, which did no good, because she managed to talk through it anyway. "Ooh, I never thought of that. I was so caught up in my part in the prewritten drama, I couldn't see the sex addict for the stardust. You're right! He's exactly the kind of guy who could be calling you. Thanks a bushel and a peck, Ned."

"Ned?"

"Never mind. I feel a lot better now that someone else has profited from my little walk on the wild side. Do you know when you got his calls?"

"We keep a log at ConTact, yes, but this guy even called from out of town. The dates wouldn't necessarily jibe with Darren Cooke's Las Vegas schedule, even if it is he."

"There must be some way to check it out."

"I'm sure you'll have some insight into a method any second now."

She looked hard at him to make sure he wasn't razzing her, but he was smiling, so she did too.

"You've had a banner weekend," she said. "First you nail Cliff Effinger to the wall in oatmeal-and-charcoal and then you figure out I've been brunching in Bluebeard's castle."

"It's been quite a weekend, yeah."

Matt's smile had faded. Temple picked up her tepid mug of cocoa. "I'd better microwave those rolls, and a cuppa chocolate for you."

As she rose, Louie picked that moment to make an imperious change of position. He lofted himself onto the coffee table atop Cliff Effinger's preciously recalled features.

"Lou-ie!" Temple screeched, tilting her cocoa and almost adding chocolate freckles to the already mottled Effinger mug.

Matt jumped up to corral the cat, but by then Louie was showing them the underside of his tail as he darted to the floor and out of sight.

"Is it all right?" Temple babbled. "How much did it cost? Can she do it again if need be?"

"Looks okay." Matt shifted the drawing away from Temple's mug. "Couple hundred. And I don't want to see her again if I don't have to."

"Oh, gosh, the paper's separating." Temple felt the sick feeling of any hostess whose guest's goods have been damaged in her house. "Matt, I'm sorry. Louie almost never makes sudden moves like that; he's just too big."

Temple fingered the peeling corner, and saw the paper curl back. "Wait! It's only two sheets on top of one another. The drawing's okay. Worthy of any post-office wanted wall. See?"

She carefully held up the top sheet to demonstrate. Then she spotted the portrait under it.

"Hey. It's you!"

Matt moved her cocoa mug to the coffee table's far side. "Apparently."

Temple sat again. "A real drawing, not a sketch. Good too. Not signed, though."

"She did it to warm up," Matt muttered. "She said. I didn't even know she was doing it."

"And she just gave it to you?"

"Well, I paid two hundred for . . . him."

"Matt, this drawing bugs you. Why?"

"I feel like the Native Americans, I guess. It's a stolen image. I don't know what to do with it."

"Frame it."

He frowned. "I've got better things to do with my money."

"And send it to . . . your mother."

"For Christmas or her birthday—" He visibly brightened at the idea, so Temple guessed that he was always at a loss for an appropriate present. "Maybe—"

"Or—" she went on. He waited hopefully for her next good idea, and she couldn't resist. "Give it to a girlfriend to frame."

"You don't really want it?"

"Why not? It's obvious that you don't, which means you won't take very good care of it, and it's too nice to waste. She really did a fabulous job for an off-the-cuff session. Even caught that cute little worry line at your left eyebrow. Come on, Matt, you have to feel a little bit flattered! You look mah-velous! I bet she thought so too."

He reached for the paper. "I don't want it—"

Temple kept it in custody.

One corner tore off.

She stopped smiling and he suddenly sat back on the sofa, far from the two pulp-paper portraits side by side on the coffee table.

"I haven't had a photograph taken since I left St. Rose of Lima. I'm not used to seeing myself. Or to seeing how other people see me."

"You need to get over that," Temple said seriously. "You can't know somebody else until you know yourself. You really need to be a teensy bit vainglorious about being so handsome. It's only human."

"I know that. I know what I look like. But I don't like seeing what it does. It's not just the portrait, it's the . . . context."

"What happened?"

"Nancy Drew is right. You know something happened. You're worse than a mother or a . . . a nun."

"Thank you. Actually, after my almost-close encounter with Darren Cooke, it's rather reassuring to be compared to a mother or a nun. I was beginning to think I was a bimbo."

"What did you really resent about that, Temple? That he thought you were cute?"

"Aha, that's just it. I didn't have to be cute, I didn't have to be me, I just had to be female and to be there."

"So if Darren Cooke had fallen instantly in love with you, it would have been all right."

"Well, better. But he didn't, and it wasn't."

"How do you know he wasn't genuinely attracted to you?"

It was an honest question. Temple thought about it. "His reputation. His lack of constancy."

"But that can change."

"Not for him. He's a confirmed womanizer. Woman, generic term. Not me, not Savannah, not his lovely wife. Who, by the way, is a famous model."

"How do you know? How do you know what someone is feeling, and why and how genuine the emotion is?"

Temple spread her hands. "From living and watching, and trying to sort out the fake from the real in yourself as well as in others. From being a fool sometimes, and being too afraid to be a fool other times."

Matt nodded at his portrait. "You think she liked me."

Temple studied it more intently. "I think she was attracted to you. That's why you shy away from the evidence. She made you look a little too sexy for your own peace of mind."

"But not yours."

Temple grinned. "Never. So who, or what, is she? And what did she do to you?"

"Nothing, I imagine, which only makes it worse. Do I get any of that cocoa or not?"

That sent Temple to the kitchen to warm up her now-cold cup and make a second mug. By the time she came back, the two drawings were rolled together, both safely out of sight.

"I mean it, Matt. I don't want you abusing that drawing. Most of us never get captured in pen and ink."

"Maybe it's just as well. It's funny. You know what she said her business consisted of? Family portraits and criminal reconstructions. Pretty extreme, huh?"

"It's like Chekhov said about happy families: they're all alike. I bet she enjoys putting criminals on paper more."

Matt looked at the rolled drawings. "Speaking of extremes, we both have had similar reactions to extremely different situations. Maybe you should tell me about life and love and sex in the secular world. I think I'm ready."

Temple tilted her head and narrowed her eyes. "It'll be what I think, what I've seen, and there won't be anything religious about it."

Matt nodded. He knew what prescription he needed when he heard it.

Temple grinned. "You're not really ready, but you never will be if you don't figure this out. Okay."

She sat forward in her usual presentation posture: outwardly composed, professional, possibly even a tad perky. Lou Grant on *The Mary Tyler Moore Show* had hated perky almost as much as he had hated spunky, but what was a single working woman to do but put a bright face on an uphill struggle?

Recalling that show brought back memories of her and Max, bad ghosts to haunt a serious discussion with another man in another place and time.

Temple took a deep breath. "Look at us. We're both unmarried, relatively young—will you grant attractive? Me, at least?"

"Oh, yeah! You're fine . . . you're ah—"

"And you're searching for words other than 'cute.' "

He made a defeated face. "You are pretty cute."

"Okay, but I don't have a face that would launch a thousand magazine ads, that makes people stop dead in their tracks. On a scale of one to ten, maybe a seven. You, whether you like it or not, are a nine and a half."

He made another distasteful face, but waited for her point.

"So here we sit, free to be anything but celibate, and what are we whining about? Being surprised by unexpected sexual overtures. Why? We ought to be at least flattered. And maybe tempted. We certainly shouldn't be surprised. What is the matter with us?"

Matt frowned as if trying to get a tough test answer right. "These were . . . spur-of-the-moment situations with virtual strangers. We're not that casual."

"Why not?"

"My background, religious and social."

"Obviously. But I don't have your background. So ignore yours for a moment. You said you liked this artist. You admit you found her attractive. You almost admitted that you might have liked the idea if you hadn't been so shocked."

"I can't ignore the fact that it doesn't seem right—"

"But it did seem a little exciting?"

He was silent for a while. "It showed me a world I'd never thought about. Nice people meeting and moving right to the bedroom. Ordinary people. For a moment that looked easier, maybe even more romantic than going through all the stumbling steps of building a relationship."

"Instant attraction. Instant love affairs. It's in all the movies. And it's out there. You haven't seen it because your vocation was a shield."

"Not from everything. Women were always trying to flirt with me."

"But . . . now you're noticing that you can flirt back."

"You mean, before I never would have noticed what she was implying? No, I'm just a vain fool. I must have imagined the undertones."

"No. Darren Cooke only had to say, 'You could stay,' in a certain way, and I saw the whole scenario from beginning to end. You can't build a court case on body language, or tone of voice or unsaid messages. But anyone who's been around a while, who's available, will notice them. It's only natural."

"I've never thought of myself as available. But you were going to make a point about being available and not being available."

"Yes. Anyone who's really committed to someone—or something—else won't hear or see the signals. You won't be looking, so people will sense that and won't look at you that way. Even if they still indicate an interest, you'll deny it, dismiss it, show surprise. Because you really aren't in the market. Happy longtime paired couples are like that. Priests and nuns make vows to be like that. And then there's everyone else."

"So why were you as surprised as I was, even offended?"

"Were you offended?"

"No." He thought again. "Scared."

Temple laughed. "Someday you won't be scared anymore, and then what will you do?"

"You're dodging the issue of Darren Cooke."

"I suppose. Maybe it's because girls are hit on by guys they'd never date, much less sleep with, at an early age. Maybe it's because in the working world, women are still considered fair game. We get touchy. We demand sincerity. We just want to do our jobs and not get hassled. Most of us tune out to sexual feelings on the job.

"I have to admit that I was flattered to be invited to Darren Cooke's Beautiful People brunch, that I was flattered to be consulted by him. I thought I was being taken at face value, not Face value. So I was angry at his sexual suggestion, and the fact that his way of life relies on using women like facial tissues, one snatched from the box after another, then discarded.

"If he's your caller, and even if he isn't, he's a sexual addict. Anyone involved with such a person becomes a victim. I don't like being singled out as a potential victim. He's a sick man, and part of his sickness is that he's so charming about it."

"You don't criticize Janice like that."

Temple shrugged. "That's different. Personally, it annoys me, but what happened, or what you think almost happened, is understandable."

"Understandable? You walk into a woman's house, and two hours later she's ready to sleep with you?"

Temple sipped cold cocoa. It was hard to give sex-education talks to a man you were attracted to. It made her feel like a big sister, at least. She could see where parents went white at the idea. Ethics and realism had to blend, and the result couldn't help but be confusing.

"Look at what you told me about her. She's divorced, probably had a decent financial situation before, but now is struggling to keep up the house and take care of the kids she got custody of in the divorce. Maybe her husband was well-off, but a jerk. Maybe he was a nice guy but they changed in different ways. Maybe he abused her. You can't know. But she's attractive and spending all her time being Mama and Artist. Maybe she can't consider a serious relationship because of the kids and the ex-husband and bad examples. So the kids are away at computer camp for once, right? And in walks this nice guy, nice-looking too, and maybe the physical type that pushes her buttons, which are getting a little rusty. So . . . she could do worse; what would it hurt?"

"Leave out the morality, what about disease? She didn't know my background. The risk—"

"—was maybe worth it to her. And from the persnickety house you described, you can bet safe sex would have been practiced. She's not crazy, just lonely. Maybe she hasn't had sex in a year. Or two. Or more. And there you are, looking like the angel Gabriel."

"But, why me? Why not the delivery man, or an old friend?"

"Different social class, or maybe her old male friends are all married. Look at your hands. No rings. Besides, most men your age have developed some line or another, something slightly false to get through. You're absolutely honest. Oh, baby, you are the answer to a maiden's prayer." Temple tented prayerful fingers. " 'Course *they* don't know you've got some growing-up to do."

"Is that why you . . . showed an interest in me? Max was gone and you were alone, and I was there, this naively honest fool?"

"Partly. I felt guilty about being attracted to you. Yes! Non-Catholics feel guilty sometimes too. I felt disloyal to Max, even though he'd disappeared without a word, which is fairly disloyal behavior in a relationship. But there's that third factor, besides opportunism and personal emptiness. There's Mother Nature's little elixir: hormones, infatuation, inexplicable instant rapport.

"Society says it should operate only under certain conditions for certain available people, but it doesn't.

"And," she went on, "because it's always there, we could all be playing with fire all the time. People like Darren Cooke get hooked on the built-in excitement of the first time so much that their first times are also always the last times. Then it's always the hunt and the capture and surrender, then the next game. That way everyone is a challenge, everyone strikes sparks, and these people are always in a state of sexual anticipation. It dominates their lives like cocaine. They need more and more, and end up emptier with every hit. It's a fun fantasy, but a bad trip in real life."

"I don't know if I want to live in real life," Matt said glumly. "The choices are worse than I imagined, even in the confessional back at St. Stan's."

"Worse in what way?"

"Not clear-cut."

"No-no's are always clear-cut. It's saying yes to life that's sticky."

"You and Max . . . have you—?"

"No. I've thought about it. He says he was faithful when he was gone. I believe him about that."

"That's trust."

Temple nodded solemnly. "That's what we had, before."

"And now?"

"Now . . . something valuable's lost."

"That's sad."

"Yes, it is. And every relationship is that delicately balanced."

"About my . . . encounter. It occurred to me I might be able to get it over with easily, with no second thoughts or stricken conscience until afterward, and that it would be worth it to be on equal footing with him, with you. To not be this . . . freak anymore."

He finally looked up at her, worried.

"You really considered sacrificing yourself to this woman for me?" Temple was rhapsodic. "That's the sweetest thing I've ever heard. But sex is much too good to ever just 'get it over with.' Or to spend on an uncaring stranger. You're being human, Matt. Insecure and anxious and a little competitive. That's a very good sign."

"If this is progress, I may not survive it."

"Teenagers do."

"Are you and Max surviving it?"

That one she couldn't answer.

Chapter 15

To Yvette, in Prison

Miss Temple may be prepared to mope her days and nights away, but I do not intend to stick around to be her crying pillow. Saltwater has never done a thing for my topcoat.

Also, I am not torn between two felines. There is only one polestar in my cat heaven, one feline in my firmament, one star on my astral plane, one comet on my tail and one meteor in my mind.

I refer, of course, to the Divine Yvette.

These last few days of working together have been sadly lacking. Here we are, the image of onscreen togetherness, yet offscreen we are kept behind convent grilles (okay, it is just a carrier grille, but the effect is the same).

Although we are to emote next week in various "location" shots around town, I am no longer willing to settle for a whisker-rub under six-thousand kilowatts of spotlight. I decide to break my darling out of her unnatural confinement for a night on the town.

This will be one of my hardest assignments.

By keeping my ears open while appearing to doze, I have learned that Yvette and her mistress, Miss Savannah Ashleigh, are sharing a suite at the Goliath, paid for by the Yummy Tum-tum-tummy/Free-to-be-Feline/À La Cat conglomerate. (Can you imagine, one company makes all these different products? Hard to believe that the loathsomely nutritional Free-to-be-Feline and the tasty Yummy Tum-tum-tummy spring from the same corporate culture, so to speak.)

I am most indignant on my mistress's behalf. Simply because she is a Las Vegas resident, she is being bilked out of expensive accommodations during the shoot. I think the cat-glop people owe her at least a good dinner out. But that is her problem.

Mine is more insurmountable, quite literally. I will have to breech the Goliath security system (which I hope consists only of stone knives, in keeping with their ancient-civilization theme), discover which rooms house my petite princess and spring her without anyone being the wiser. And let he who casts the first stone be called Michelangelo's David.

Getting out of the Circle Ritz is the usual snap. Getting over to the Goliath on the Strip is the usual car-, bus- and van-dodging trip. Getting into the Goliath is the usual hanging out by the kitchen service door and darting in under cover of a cart. Just call me cat À La Carte.

Luckily, I am making my moves at night, when my dark topcoat makes me all but invisible. Unluckily, the lobby is one of those overlit, open expanses of white marble, saffron carpet, gilded lilies and upholstered furniture so pale that a shaded-silver Persian cat hair would show up on it, not to mention my own svelte dark form.

So I attach myself to various arriving parties, dashing along in the shadow of their duffel bags and rolling valets, wishing for a brief, minor power failure from Hoover Damm to the Valley of Fire.

Besides, such a power outage might inspire some work

CAT IN A FLAMINGO FEDORA • 139

of cinematic art. If they made such a fuss about the night the lights went out in Dixie and the night the power failed in New York City (resulting in a higher birthrate nine months later), think of what would happen if the lights went out in Vegas, the city that never nods off? Now there is a disaster-flick plot for any bright bulb who wants to take it from me.

Some might say that I am a trifle selfish for wishing a townwide blackout so that I can visit an amour, but whoever they are, they are not here and I do not worry about them.

What I worry about is finding Miss Yvette's room number, particularly since she is not registered under her own name.

As in most Vegas hostelries, the registration desk is a hornet's nest of activity.

However, since this hotel, in particular, wishes to convey an atmosphere of desert luxe, a number of potted palms are sprinkled around the tomblike lobby. The pots actually serve my purposes better than the palms. It is from the shade of just such a gargantuan container that I spot a subspecies on the premises.

This is a terrier known as a Westie, a brighter-than-the-usual-dim-bulb-dog, that is also something of a terror, being from a rather bossy breed. I ankle over to the party, which also consists of a man and a woman who are checking to see if they have any mail. Ah, veterans. Just what I need. I force myself to rub ingratiatingly on the Westie's furry white side.

"Hi, fella. Been staying at this dump long?"

I get a growl and a snort (a Scottish snort; I recognize the accent from my association with Baker and Taylor, the Scottish fold cats, on a previous case). " 'Tis no dump, you blathering numbskull, an' verra expensive as weel."

"Just wondered if you spotted a sleek little number who travels in pink. Shaded-silver Persian a little darker than yourself."

"More of your sort? I had no idea the hotel provided so

much sport for its canine guests. I have, in fact, sniffed some sort of vermin being carted to and fro. I took it for an Angora guinea pig."

With great self-control, I refrain from turning Westie into Scarface, from now to eternity, for calling the Divine Yvette vermin.

"And where did you see this creature coming and going?" I ask sweetly.

"In the elevator. A great imposition. Your kind smells, you know."

"So does yours," I growl back, "and if you want to retain a sniffer to smell with, I would watch your lip."

I dart away before the little sucker can do me any damage, leaving him bouncing up and down on his short little legs and barking up a storm.

"Wescott, be quiet!" his mistress urges, looking around to see what might have got him yammering.

Of course I am invisible behind my palm pot once more, and a good thing, because I think if Wescott spies me, he will take off after me and drag his mistress right along for the ride, he is that mad. There is nothing like a Scot for making much over nothing.

Vermin, indeed!

I straighten my coat sleeves, then ponder another route to my destination. Elevator encounters hardly betray the floor and room number of my sweetie.

I manage to dive beneath the long marble registration desk, which is done up to resemble a banquet table decorated with goblets of fake wine and dishes of wax grapes set here and there. The reservation staff is dashing back and forth attending to a long line of eager guests, and I have to keep a sharp eye on all five of my extremities. There are few occasions that I envy human beings anything, but the facility for strutting around on two legs, with only ten toes to get stepped on, does sometimes make me a teensy bit jealous.

I pace back and forth, dodging the swift and unpredictable footsteps of the personnel. I hear many names bandied about above me, but none that make my whiskers quiver: "Costner, Branagh, Schwarzenegger . . ." These bunch of nobodies are wasting the desk clerks' time when the staff could be answering inquiries for Savannah Ashleigh, the movie star.

Alas, the bell does not toll for her, probably because she is already checked in. And the Goliath has forty-eight hundred rooms. I will check out each and every one, if I must, but it will put me sadly behind schedule. At this rate, I will see Yvette on the set Tuesday sooner than I will find hide or silver hair of her here.

I have resigned myself to curling up on a box of Goliath maps (the hotel is so big each guest gets a map to follow around), and am yawning widely when my ears come out of the temporary deafness a good yawn induces to hear the magic word: " . . . leigh."

Now that could be Lee as in a last or first name. Or "lee" as in Levi's jeans. Or it might even be somebody talking about what nobody doesn't like, which is Sara Lee the dessert maker. Or someone could be discussing the Kennedy assassination and have dropped Lee Harvey Oswald's name into the hopper. Still, hope is a frail thing with feathers, and I go for things with feathers. I perk up both ears and smother my second, world-class yawn.

"Photos for Miss Ashleigh? I'll have a bellman take them up."

Yes! I leap up with joy, forgetting that I am reposing under a marble counter. Ouch! Then I hear the sharp ping of a bell. I wiggle down the underbelly of the counter and keep a sharp eye out for a bellman uniform.

Here I almost make a fatally wrong calculation. I am hunting for the usual uniform, navy with gold buttons, or perhaps a tasteful maroon or hunter green. What have I done? For a moment, I have failed to remember that I am in Las Vegas. Here a bellman can look like a bodybuilder and often does.

So I almost miss the guy in the thong sandals, the thong diaper and the sheet-swathed head. But he is carrying a manila envelope and I have seen containers of that description all over Miss Temple's desk, full of photos, documents and what have you.

What I have is a lot of catching up to do before this desert-dude hops aboard one of the palanquin elevators and leaves me below, watching him defy gravity through the elevator's glass façade.

I make the same flight by the skin of my hocks and heels. Of course I am noticed, but I act like I know where I'm going and when a woman near the control panel asks, "Can I hit a floor for anyone?" I merow a very clear "four."

She apparently does not hear me, which is lucky as the manila envelope is going much higher. In fact, it is going so high that all the other passengers exit beforehand, so while it is really hard to hide from the bellman, no one else is aware of me.

But the bellman begins doing muscle flexes in the rear mirrored wall as soon as everybody has exited, concentrating so hard on his biceps that he does not look down far enough to notice me. Miss Temple frequently bewails her short stature, but I must say that sometimes it is better to keep a low profile in this town, and this is one of them.

Once the elevator doors open at the twentieth floor, the bellman struts out, looking in every hall mirror he passes. There are quite of few of these, as the passage is tricked out like the Hall of Mirrors at Versailles.

(Some may wonder how an exceptionally short P.I. in Las Vegas, who has no formal education except what can be picked up on the street, can know about such ritzy foreign attractions. Quite simply, I am an autodidact, which means that I taught myself all I need to know and a good deal that I do not, but the non-need-to-know comes in handy to throw into my conversation now and then. I have read a lot of books in my time, under the pretext of snoozing on them. I use a technique called feed-reading. First I consume a meal generous enough to make me drowsy. Then I curl up on a newspaper or any old tome I can find. Once I am suspended in a state of absolute relaxation, I absorb the contents at my pawtips by a kind of osmosis.)

This is a tricky bit for me. I must "shadow" the bellman while remaining far enough behind that my mirror image does not show up in his view. This I manage until he stops at a door and knocks. Then only boldness will work. I sidle up right behind him, counting on the dim hall and the dark carpeting to camouflage me.

The resident is slow to answer. I wait, twitching my whiskers with impatience. So near and yet so far from my Divine Yvette.

At last the door is cracked open, with the chain lock still on!

"Miss Ashleigh."

"Yes," comes the breathy, foggy reply.

"The front desk sent up a manila envelope for you."

"Slide it through the door," she requests throatily.

This will not do! It has been years since I have been able to shimmy through a door crack that is only as wide as a chain. Perhaps if I had been more dedicated to working out, I might manage it. But I have never embraced unnecessary movement.

What to do? I reach up with an unadulterated mitt and snag a claw on the glued flap at the envelope bottom. As the bellman reaches up with the envelope, I drag down. Bicep-pumping aside, I win, thanks to the surprise element coupled with my fighting-sharp talons.

"I dropped it, Miss Ashleigh, and the envelope is partly under the door. Maybe you could open the door just a little bit?"

"Oh, rats. Did you have to be so clumsy?"

But the door shuts and I hear the chain-lock slide being operated. The bellman bends over to lift the envelope (thus giving me an unwanted close-up of his thong diaper). By the time he straightens up, Miss Savannah Ashleigh is standing in the open doorway in a flowing black chiffon negligee bordered with black marabou feathers on every edge.

The bellman is so startled he forgets about his own anatomy for perhaps two seconds.

That is all the time I need, especially with the made-to-order camouflage I see before me. I dart through the door as the envelope exchanges hands above me, and dash into the shady shelter of Miss Savannah Ashleigh's floor-dusting negligee. In my haste I allow my tail to brush her leg, but she merely twitches a bit, no doubt assuming that the tickling marabou has wafted against her epidermis. That is the trouble with wearing clothes trimmed in the fur and feathers of animals and birds. The wearer grows accustomed to the feel of foreign bodies, and cannot discriminate between the lifeless outerwear and the real thing.

Now I must navigate the area in perfect tune with the Ashleigh doll's high-heeled baby steps. (I notice that she is wearing satin pumps with more marabou on the toes.) Tickling her gams with whiskers or tail is not my biggest problem now; I will have to be nimble to avoid being speared by those lethal satin heels. Miss Savannah minces over to a desk, where she sits to slit open the envelope.

I sit beside her, naturally, trying to make myself as small as I can, which is akin to compressing twenty pounds of muscle and bone into a five-pound bag of liquid litter.

At this juncture, when things are very cozy under her skirts, Miss Savannah Ashleigh commences to tap her dainty foot.

"Of all the nerve," she huffs, tapping the other toe.

I switch my tail from side to side like a metronome, trying to avoid a painful pinning to the floor. Unfortunately, Miss Savannah Ashleigh has not a rhythmic bone in her body. There is no rhyme or reason to her toe taps. I decide to make a break for the far wall under the desk and whisk through a fragile curtain of see-through chiffon.

"Ooh! Yvette! Is that you, sweetums?"

Any expert would never confuse the coarser, shinier texture of my black topcoat with the airy, fluffy feel of the Divine One's silver fur. But I fear that Miss Savannah Ashleigh has the sensitivity of a sponge, not to mention its capacity to retain water.

I slip along the wall while she is lifting her skirt to hunt for a phantom Yvette. Soon I am patting open the door to the boudoir. My pulse races. Here the Divine Yvette must lie. Lay? Languish? Sure enough, I spot the familiar pink carrier and race for it. Empty! Has my lovely flown the coop before I could play the hero and release her?

I survey the fringes of the room, then leap atop the dressing-table stool for a better look. On the king-size bed, smack dab in the middle, the Divine Yvette reclines in a faint pucker of coverlet.

My heart leaps up and so do I. Despite the treacherous footing on the down comforter, I wade my way toward the feline of my dreams. Those round, aqua eyes widen at my approach. The Divine Yvette rolls onto her back and draws her curled dainty forefeet up to her chin. What a pose! I would even buy Free-to-be-Feline from the little doll.

She yawns, exposing tiny sharp white teeth and rosy tongue and palate.

"Louie! What are you doing here so late?"

"It is never too late for us, my love," I tell her. "I have come to free you for a night on the town."

The Divine Yvette puckers up her adorable face. "I would so love a few hours of frolic and sight-seeing, but my mistress is exceedingly distraught, and I dare not leave her at this critical moment."

"You will excuse me for saying so, but Miss Savannah Ashleigh is often distraught about this or that. If one were to put off one's own pleasures to wait for her to experience a few of her own, I am sure that one's whiskers would go white and drop off in the interim."

"That may be true, Louie, but this is a genuine crisis. My mistress visited her Las Vegas plastic surgeon yesterday and apparently the news is rather dire. I believe that he found it too soon for another laser wrinkle lift, but gravity and the desert sun wait for no woman." The Divine Yvette sighs. "These are the times I thank Bast that I was born in furs, not flesh. I would have to be shaved for any wrinkles to be visible."

"Do not speak of such a travesty! I have heard of a case where a cat was shaved, and the result was not a pretty sight."

Yvette's plumed tail pats the down comforter beside her. "But stay and talk awhile, Louie. My mistress is drowning her wrinkles in the astringent called alcohol, which must be taken internally. She gets even more boring than usual at such a time. I do long for a good bit of street gossip."

I leap into place beside her, letting my tail entwine with hers. She stretches out her long front gams and bats her eyelashes. I know that I would be getting the blue-green light if the rotten Miss Savannah were not in the adjacent chamber. I wish on her the sudden explosion of a nasty zit—that ought to have her sprinting to the hotel health club for a facial.

"So," asks the Divine Yvette, "where would we have gone if we could have escaped for a few precious hours together?"

"Nothing earth-shaking," I reply.

"Good." The Divine Yvette's ruff shakes wholeheartedly. "I spend most of my time with my mistress in the better neighborhoods of Los Angeles. I face a good deal of earth-shaking there, and prefer a more quiet climate."

"Exactly, my dear. I thought we could take another peaceful ride on the Love Moat. I could show you the spot where my signature shoes were found. Then we could trot around to the Crystal Phoenix, where I have an in, and we could nibble on steak tartare fresh from the meat cleaver of Chef Song. For dessert, we could hie to the Desert Inn, to relax in their A-one spa area, where we could give each other body massages and finish up with a tongue-bath."

"Sounds divine! Perhaps my mistress's unhappiness is somewhat catching, but I find myself out of sorts too, and evincing strange, obsessive behaviors, like sudden headaches and a certain mental restlessness. I cannot think what is the matter with me!"

"Nothing is the matter with you," I pronounce confidently. "You are perfect! And you would be even more perfect were you able to slip away for some feline-to-feline resuscitation."

"Your confidence is so inspiring, Louie. I do not doubt that I am being infected by my mistress's discontent. Does your mistress not transfer her burdens to you?"

"Not really, but then I am not around long enough to function as a transferee. And Miss Temple's burdens are pretty small stuff, just like her, though she would be furious to hear me say it. Fortunately, we do not speak the same language."

"Yes, it is a comfort not to have to speak to humans. Imagine how they would burden us with their troubles if they thought we could understand them. It is bad enough that they sniffle into our freshly washed fur on occasion."

"Indeed. But their weakness is part of their charm."

We are thus contemplating human behavior in perfect harmony, each emitting a gentle, back-of-the-throat purr, when we hear a clatter and crash and our ears flatten as one. I leap to the floor in one cheetah-size bound.

I am not a second too late. The bedroom door is flung fully open to frame the black-draped figure of Miss Savannah Ashleigh. She stamps her foot on the thick carpeting, nearly breaking off a heel on her satin slides.

"Imagine!" she tells the room and the Divine Yvette (and me). "That rat had the nerve to turn me down. What an ego! Who does he think he is? Who does he think he can get, at his age and with his track record? We go way back, but I'm not about to forgive a snub on the grounds of old times."

She stamps her way to the bedside table that holds a clock, and picks it up to squint at the tiny dial inside double rings of blue rhinestones. "However, the night is young yet," she snarls. "When Mr. Darren Big Deal finds out how hard it is for an aging Romeo to find the proper Juliet in Las Vegas nowadays, perhaps he'll settle for Hamlet's mother!"

I can see that I had better scram, especially when Miss Savannah Ashleigh starts mixing metaphors. I slither out to the other room when her back is turned, and find a sheltered hunkering-down spot near the entrance doors. Surely someone will come or go one of these hours, and then I will skip out the door to my former freedom.

"Ooh, Mommy's sweetest 'ittle pussums," I hear crooned from the bedroom. "You would never let Mommy down, 'ould you? No, no, no."

I am afraid that the Divine Yvette is getting one of those saltwater baths that are so damaging to her fur coat.

Will humans never learn the proper care of their boon companions?

I think on other dark and disagreeable subjects for a couple of hours. Imagine my surprise when the person that finally frees me rustles, fully dressed to kill, from the bedroom. Miss Savannah Ashleigh does not even look down, her nose is so high in the air. She jerks open the door and struts out of it. I have to be quick to avoid getting a tailectomy as I bound through the door with her.

Well, I was thisclose to the Divine Yvette, and once again her puzzling devotion to her straw-headed mistress has foiled our perfect union.

I am beginning to think that the Divine Yvette and I are not meant to be. That is such a depressing thought that I hurry back to the Circle Ritz, planning to snuffle on Miss Temple Barr's shoulder.

Chapter 16

Fly on the Wall

Eleven o'clock on a Sunday night, and the ConTact help lines were still.

Matt sat facing the three white sides of his cubicle. He watched a fly crawl over the hole-studded soundproof tiles, adding a random element to the perfect pattern of perforations. Matt kept waiting for the fly to crawl into one of the round black holes, and disappear.

But it didn't. Its splay-footed legs moved delicately over the aisles of white between the perforations and never made a misstep. If only people had the discriminating instincts of a common fly!

But they didn't, and that's what made his job interesting, even on tedious nights like this.

"Want me to call you up and pour out my troubles?"

Matt leaned back in his stenographic chair to eye the only other counselor on duty right then: Bennie Cordova.

Bennie was grinning over the plastic frames of his glasses, highly magnifying half lenses that made the bags under his sixtyish eyes look like they were packed for an around-the-world cruise.

"You have troubles?" Matt joked back.

No doubt Bennie—whose baptismal name was Bienvenido, "Welcome"—had been a cool guy during his sixties heyday, probably thumbing his nose at authority when it wasn't busy inhaling pot. If anyone had told Bennie then that his dark hair would gray and retreat screaming from his forehead with the inevitability of an ebbing tide, that he'd someday wear grandpa glasses and cardigan sweaters to work on a chilly Las Vegas night, Bennie probably would have beat him up. Now, time had beaten up Bennie, and his knees and neck were stiff, but he still had his sixties insouciance. No sweat, man. Stuff happens, even growing old instead of up.

"Everybody has troubles, man. What about yours?"

"Minuscule."

"Min-a-school. Where'd you get words like that?"

"In a school."

"Very funny, man. Say, when dullness walks in the door around here, it doesn't fool around." Bennie sipped from the mug of coffee constantly at his right hand. The mug's design commemorated Earth Day 1983. "Sheila still trying to get you to dial her line? I miss all the good stuff, being a substitute. It's like missing a week in a soap-opera plot; everything's different."

Matt shook his head. "Not here. Sheila's still working here, but that's about it."

"Still working on you, I bet. Man, when I was young, chicks were prettier and people knew how to groove."

"It was safer then too."

"Naw. We just thought it was. The power of positive thinking kept us from bad trips and ugly consequences, that's all. We were just lucky."

Matt nodded. Ignorance was bliss, he understood that more every day, as his ignorance inched away as subtly and irrevocably as Bennie's hairline had retreated. Growing old but not up. Bennie would snort to hear that Matt felt that way at thirty-three, but every generation had its twisted time frame and its own values.

"You still live at that far-out Circle place?" Bennie asked.

Matt nodded.

"Man, that must give you willies. Every room ends in a curve, the halls are curved . . . I suppose the elevators go up in a curve too, huh?"

"Not that we notice. You seem to know the building pretty well."

"Did some work on it back in the seventies. The outside marble facing needed some spit and polish; that was when I still did construction work. Now I'm ree-tired."

"So you volunteer to come in here nights and listen to sad stories."

"Right. Doan wants miss what's happenin' out there. Besides, I'm a pretty good drug counselor." Bennie winked over the Santa Claus glasses. "Oughta be."

Matt noticed that the fly had settled on a spot dead center of four holes to clean its face. Maybe he'd get some more coffee and—

And answer the phone. His line. He pulled the earpad on his headset into place and let his focus on the fly fuzz out.

"ConTact. Brother John."

The idea behind pseudonyms was to guard the counselors' privacy. The use of "handles" also gave a stressed caller something to focus on, and personalized the counselors while still letting them keep the necessary distance. Matt's handle got a lot of initial reaction. It was more than a name, it implied a relationship. "Brother John" sounded like family.

The caller must have thought so too.

"Brother, can you spare a dime?" he began.

Matt tensed as he recognized the strong, confident voice. He was used to hesitaters, or nervous "spillers," not to a man who sounded like he should be giving advice instead of taking it.

"I thought you were through with us," Matt said.

"With you, buddy, not the organization. But . . . I'm feelin' blue and like doing something foolish on a Sunday evening and

I thought I'd better call my buddy at ConTact. Great name, Con-Tact. I have its card right here before me. See, you can take the name two ways: 'Contact,' as in connection . . . phone connection, personal connection, and 'Con' as in the Spanish 'with' and 'Tact' as in knowing what to say, or maybe just knowing what people want to hear. Same difference, right? I do it all the time myself. Tell people what they want to hear. That makes us peas in a pod, I guess. So, you make up that name? 'ConTact.' "

"I had nothing to do with it. Whatever thought went into it, happened before I got here."

"Now, that's hard to imagine. I think of you always sitting there, eavesdropping on us lower Slobovians, like God."

"You're feeling a lot of hostility tonight."

"Yeah, I'm hostile. People think I'm joking all the time, and most of the time I am. They think that I'm all pose and no sincerity. They never ask themselves if that's not exactly the way *they* want me to be."

"How do you want to be?"

In the pause, Matt heard angry ice cubes rattle, as if they were being slammed into an empty glass.

"The way I am, without everybody coming at me complaining."

"What do they complain about?"

"What I say and do, who I see. What they think I'm thinking."

The ice-cube, feisty-castanet chatter softened to muted clinks, probably sinking under a potent sea of hard liquor. Since he began his phone nightlife, Matt had become adept at inventing faces and settings for his callers. He might be totally wrong, but it helped him sense their hidden messages, the heartbreaks they weren't mentioning.

Only, with this caller, this frequent phoner, the imaging trick had backfired. The caller had used it on Matt, assigning him attitudes and a posture Matt didn't possess. People who had lost touch with their own inner burns and dodges often misinterpreted other people, usually those they were most closely involved with. That this particular caller would play this game with "Brother John" meant that Matt was perhaps closer to him than the man's intimate family, or at least knew more about his worries and weaknesses, even if he didn't particularly understand them.

"What's the problem tonight?"

"Tonight. Making it sound like I have problems every night. Well, I don't, Brother John. I don't need to call you like a whining puppy trying not to pee-pee on the rug. You're lucky I justify your job. First some little nobody treats me like I was the worst turd on the eighteenth floor. Then this old squeeze of mine gets huffy. Then my *wife* calls wondering why she couldn't reach me *last* night. Listen, I didn't *have* a wife longer than she's been alive! I don't answer to nobody! Especially not you."

"No, you don't." Matt kept his voice calm, his manner cool in reverse proportion to his caller's heat. His own heart was racing with recognition. If "some little nobody" was quite literally Temple, the caller must be Darren Cooke, the man she had rejected earlier today. Matt wasn't supposed to know who he was talking to. That broke the rules, changed the balance, and maybe bothered him more than it betrayed the caller. He needed distance, to fight fire with its opposite element, ice.

"Is there anything I can do for you? You could call one of those three psychiatrists' answering services, leave a message."

"I don't want to leave a message! I don't want to be passed on like a dirty shirt. You sound high and mighty tonight. Tired of talking to me, are you, Brother John? Some brother! Haven't you ever had it up to here with women? You can't satisfy them, and when you do, they all come around wanting to be the only one. Even your own little kid. I wish I had a son. I'd teach him how to avoid the bad raps and the traps. We'd be buddies."

Matt hesitated. He could hear the grind of escalating anger and depression, which always made a dangerous triumvirate with alcohol. Yet to suggest that Cooke . . . his caller stop drinking would only infuriate him more.

"I thought I was your buddy," Matt said soothingly, mirroring the man's own insecurity.

"Hey, you are! Don't think for a minute because I bad-mouth you a little we're not pals. I'm just an ordinary guy like you.

Except . . . I'm famous. So I have to act famous, act like some big wheel. I stop the act—and I crash, career and all. The act is all part of my act now, get it? I just had a rotten day, is all. And—"

The line was suddenly silent. Matt sucked in his breath. Something was happening on the other end that he couldn't visualize. He didn't like it. The man was in a dangerous mood, to himself, and maybe to somebody else.

Then he heard sounds again. A glass set down hard on a tabletop, the last brittle slosh of melting ice cubes. Motion. A man in motion . . . using a portable phone, that was it.

"Somebody's here," he sang out in a tone of slightly drunken playfulness. "Eleven-thirty. Must be the maid coming to get laid. Let's look through the peephole, huh, Brother John?"

The phone sounded like it was underwater as the caller disengaged to view his visitor.

"Say, this could turn out okay. Sorry, BJ, but I'm gonna have to hang up now. I don't go for threesomes. Thanks for the listen. Talk to you sometime . . . Hel-lo, baby! Just what the doctor ordered. Come on in—"

Matt heard a bolt click, heard the warm, strong voice at full, confident power.

The line choked off right there, as if the lights had gone out on a play in midscene. Matt knew that, somewhere in the glitz and glamour of Las Vegas, a woman was walking into a man's room for what used to be called "immoral purposes" an eon ago.

Was she a friend? A former lover? The woman who'd spurned him earlier coming back? A call girl some buddy of his had sent to cheer up his friend? Any or all of those scenarios were perfectly possible in Las Vegas, and in this man's busy, empty life.

Matt felt cheated again, like an alcoholic's AA call-buddy who has to hear him fall off the wagon. He felt used, more used than that unseen woman would feel probably. Presumably she knew, or knew of, this guy. Knew what to expect. He had never claimed to be a one-woman man, not even to Matt.

They were just one of hundreds of couples. It was a terribly common interaction, sometimes for money, sometimes for fun, rarely ever for love.

Matt shook his head as he disconnected.

"Lose him?" Bennie wanted to know from the adjacent booth.

"Yeah. Lost him."

Chapter 17

Hats Off to Homicide

After her semisexy, stressful and ultimately frustrating weekend, Temple fled back to the normal world of flamingos as fine art.

Domingo's minions had shown up, a trendy ragtag bunch of earnest young snobs-to-be enjoying a brief adolescent rebellion before moving into the ranks of the twenty-first century's top museum curators. No wonder modern art was in retrograde.

The entire project gave Temple the feeling of a student-assisted archeological dig on some remote foreign soil that hid the architectural bones of a vanished but mighty civilization.

Except that Las Vegas wasn't very vanished and the mighty civilization to be unearthed was whatever flavor-of-the-month seeped out of the developers' bag of theme attractions.

The last thing Friday, Temple had paved the way for the first of Domingo's flamingo flings: the site of the former Sands Hotel and Casino, a fifties icon recently razed because it simply couldn't keep up with the neighbors, like the Luxor's King Tut, Leo the MGM Grand Lion, the New York City skyline and other Nouveau Flash installations on the Strip. The old, softer romantic fantasies were literally falling one by one to the laser-edged hype of the New School of Stripography. Restaurant names told the story of Las Vegas development themes as succinctly and sourly as news headlines: good-bye, Sands Hotel and your old-style exotic Shangri-La and Xanadu restaurants, hello Planet Hollywood and Hard Rock Cafe. Harley-Davidson on!

For now, the former Sands square footage was only a construction trench from which a one-and-a-half-billion-dollar, six-thousand-room behemoth would shortly rise, like the movie monster Mothra leaving its unsuspected cocoon. Temple had suggested that a showy ring of rubbernecking flamingo-spectators would add an air of anticipation to the project. Domingo had liked the idea so much he now thought it had been his.

Thus developers and Domingo were as one in their emerging ecstasy. The construction project would make history as the first local site to sprout its plague of flamingos. Domingo had a massive, flat canvas of desert scrub to impale with imported lawn ornaments, émigrés from a Massachusetts plastics company.

Even the modest origin of the inexpensive decorative birds made a statement, in Temple's opinion. She had done her homework. Half a million of the molded pink birds sold every year, dotting the landscape from the Canadian border to Tierra del Fuego at the tip of South America, at only nine ninety-five a pair. You couldn't get two of anything for just nine ninety-five anymore, not even dish towels!

Once Domingo's dream was giving media people nightmares, Temple had plans to import members of the Society for the Preservation of the Plastic Lawn Flamingo, as well as the flamingo manufacturer's flamboyant artist, whose signature is captured in molded plastic on every pink flamingo body: a guy named Don *Feather*stone, of all things. Despite a classical-art background, Featherstone managed to compete with his birds for popular attention, his wife and he having dressed exactly alike each and every day for twenty years. Perhaps marketing the flamingos in pairs was catching. Nor was Domingo the first on the conceptual-art scene to seize onto flamingos as a metaphor for what have you: a Maryland woman rearranges and attires thirty-four lawn flamingos every week, attracting a crowd of regular gawkers.

So, in a sense, Temple was beginning to catch flamingo fever. Nature writers grew tongue-tied trying to describe thousands of the Greater and Lesser Flamingos of Africa settling on the salt flats like a mobile sunset. Mere plastic could not dim their in-born shrimp-pink luster. Flamingos en masse, and especially in plastic—accessible and indivisible to all—really did have something to say. Further, Domingo was convinced that the visual statement of a flamingo infestation in Las Vegas, with its many social and psychological connotations, was far too rich a subject and effect to be ignored by anybody who was anybody, such as art critics, who were mostly nobodies outside the pages of their slick host magazines, anyway.

And, of course, the tabloids—print and electronic—would have a flamingo field day.

"There is no middle ground," Domingo announced to his followers as they stood like explorers stunned silent by the equatorial sun as well as the blazing noonday emptiness of the land they surveyed.

The vast vacant lot did resemble a bland, sand-blond blot amid the bright and lurid fantasy constructions of the Strip. "No middle anymore. Only top and bottom. Developed nation and Third World. Rich and poor. Wise and foolish. Cadillac and Kia. Gaming palace and plastic flamingo. Keep this in mind as you plant your subversive symbols."

Domingo had studied the site over the weekend and drawn an elaborate master plan, a kind of Da Vinci cartoon for the major massings of the flamingo flocks around the perimeter of the great empty hole from which Mothra would arise, girder by girder, glass wall by glass wall, laser-light by laser-light.

In honor of the day's desert-expedition atmosphere, Temple had worn closed-toe canvas wedgies, a khaki suit (Bermuda shorts and safari jacket) and a hat against the noonday sun and any mad dogs and Englishmen who might take exception to her exceptionally red hair. It wasn't a pith helmet, since she didn't own one, but it was a sporty brimmed affair, also khaki, that looked quite at home on a blasted Las Vegas lot.

"Very nice," said Domingo when he saw her. He snapped his fingers and his photographer groupie, a tall, stork-thin young man who was already turning pink in the warm November sunlight, came rushing over, clanking the cameras slung around his long white neck.

"We will have a picture of me directing the team, with Miss Barr beside me." He raised his voice to a stentorian shout: "People, gather round for documentary photos. And you, keep those camcorders running at all times. I wish every aspect of the installation recorded."

Domingo then proceeded to wave his arms as he indicated the master plan, while Temple nodded sagely in her savage-sun hat. The kids mopped their sweatbanded brows or tossed their braided and ponytailed heads, looking like nothing so much as a herd of coltish wild horses dressed by Esprit.

When they went to work, though, it was in an industrious flock. Three-foot-tall pink flamingos positively flew off of flatbed trucks and hit the sandy soil in tens and twenties, like so many oversize and gaudy thumbtacks.

Temple had timed her arrival near the lunch break, so they soon transformed into a scratched, sweaty, dusty crew of fairly androgynous boys and girls gathered around the food van.

They sat where they could: on parked vehicle hoods, a large and friendly rock that could keep their posteriors from the fire ants, on a couple of beat-up aluminum lawn chairs, on their haunches on the insect-infested ground.

"This is the best time of year to do this. Cooler." She had grabbed any old sandwich from the van and joined them in munching. Nothing united strangers like a common appetite, which was the behavioral fact behind everything from sports fans to twelve-step recovery programs.

They nodded, chewing, as Temple found a dusty but unoccupied fender and tried to hop up on it.

"Let me take that," another fender-sitter offered, relieving her of the wrapped sandwich so she could use both hands to boost herself up, as always. How humiliating!

Once installed, she drummed her soft heels against the truck's side like everyone else and munched without comment. Behind her Kmart sunglasses (she was *always* losing them), she summed the crew up in the thoroughly wicked detail she could exercise when no one else could see her eyes.

"What do you do for Domingo?"

Temple couldn't quite tell where the question had come from, given a scraggly circle of fourteen or so workers, but she noticed sly smiles and heard snickers as she looked over the group.

"You could call me a scout," she said finally. "I'm a Las Vegas PR freelancer, so I've been designated to ask potential flamingo beneficiaries for permission to adorn their frontage."

"Beneficiaries!" The snorted word came from a lanky guy wearing the expedition uniform: loose T-shirt and shorts, sports socks and expensive tennis shoes. "That's putting whipped cream on a rotten banana. The only entity one of these shebangs benefits is Domingo International."

More sniggers erupted among the burps as the crew downed soft drinks and beer. Apparently Domingo's loyal followers expected him to have liaisons with any and every woman around.

"Really," she said. "An embarrassment of flamingos is great publicity for a coming attraction like this." She waved at the bare lot, large sign and cyclone fence that hailed forthcoming mega-construction in Las Vegas. "But the established hotels can be . . . unimpressed."

"Unimpressed? By Domingo? Shame on them!" The speaker was a sharp-nosed and mushy-chinned woman, so tanned that the freckles blended on her arms and face.

Temple tilted her head to better catch the bitter undertaste to the words. "How come you guys work for Domingo? It's hot, hard labor, and I bet you don't get paid much."

The lanky guy looked up from tearing into his Subway sandwich, which shed lettuce curls onto the barren ground.

"A season in hell with Domingo and French horns or spaghetti or flamingos looks good on our résumés. He's a worldwide fig-

ure and his stuff gets lots of media. We're all under- or postgrad
art students, and could use a little sex appeal on our *vitae*."

"So Domingo plays the part of professor on a field expedition?"

The silence that greeted this summation told Temple a lot. Exchanged glances told her more. Domingo was a necessary evil
in the face of the advantages of having worked for Domingo.

"Domingo doesn't teach; he uses."

The young woman who said that was poured into cutoff jeans
and a tank top, and not to either garment's advantage. She was
downing slices of pizza fast enough to add another fifty pounds
to the overweight that crammed the clothes, but her angry black
eyes were incisive.

"Bren-da!" The girl beside her didn't give the admonishment
much energy.

This one was Domingo-meat if Temple had ever seen it:
smooth gilded hair pulled back into a clip, California tan, pastel
shorts and shirt that made her look cool as iced sherbet in Hades.

"You guys love to speculate about the Maestro's love life,"
Baywatch Blondie went on, "but he's really most interested in
putting his energy into the project. Did you really look at what
he came up with for this site? It'll be awesome. Some people
have nothing to do when they're on a break but sit around and
gossip."

Temple's lifted interrogatory eyebrow was wasted behind her
oversize shades. (She would never wear those icky little round
frames, no matter how fashionable; they made her look like a
twelve-year-old.) So she led the class forward to the next topic.

"I guess you workers get something out of it."

"Screwed," came from her left, another female voice.

Waves of uneasy laughter rippled the circle.

Temple studied the guy who had accused Domingo of using
them. Despite his T-shirt's tenting graces, his adolescent overweight teetered on obesity. Thick glasses and a seriously wracked
complexion didn't help.

The girl who had put the word "screwed" on the table was
slim, earnest, and also bespectacled, though hers were the fash-

ionable small round metal ones Temple abhorred. She looked and sounded like a woman scorned. If so, no wonder Domingo had dumped her; the wonder was that he had been interested in her in the first place. Or had he been? Young infatuations often steamroller older cautionary urges.

"Don't you guys like Domingo?" she asked as innocently as a thirty-year-old among twenty-somethings can manage.

The freckled woman sighed. "He's okay. A little full of himself, but that's his job."

"Self-appointed job," the lanky guy put in.

When he got up, the others also rose. Temple saw her prey slipping away, so she finished her . . . ugh, had she really been eating a tongue sandwich? Luckily, her question-and-answer session had distracted her from such essentials as . . . taste and texture. Yuck.

"What about you?" The slender girl in round glasses stood before her, dusty arms crossed.

"What about me?"

"Are you this big fan of Domingo's, or just a hired hand, or a soon-to-be mistress or what?"

"Since none of the specifics above apply, I guess I'm just an 'or what.' "

The girl's tennis shoe kicked rock-hard sand. "Better watch out what you ask around here. Domingo always picks a 'project girl.' He hasn't had one for this flamingo thing yet."

"No doubt the elegant Verina—"

A frown, deep enough to bury BBs in, wrinkled her brown brow. "He's never shown up with some la-di-da female like *that* before."

"Yes, it's so unfair with these foreign females coming in all fresh and dolled up when you installers are filthy and tired and hot," Temple said demurely.

"You mean we might be jealous? Well, some of us, maybe. And especially the guys who had an eye on the girl Domingo picks."

"Does this 'project girl' always go along with her new status?"

"Oh, no. Then there's hell to pay. Domingo gets in a bummer

mood. And some of the girls are actually miffed to be considered second choices. Can you believe that?"

Gazing into the defensive eyes, Temple definitely could.

The girl bit her lip and looked around. The others had dispersed back to their forest of pink legs and necks. She spoke again, more softly.

"We have this pool going, the group. On who will be Domingo's Clingo for the project. You know, his squeeze. Some of the guys are pissed that nobody's emerged as a clear favorite yet. That's why they were asking about you."

"I'm a candidate? I am honored. But Verina has a headlock on him for now, alas."

"Don't be too sure. He really likes younger women, and you're much closer to us than she is."

"*I* am a younger woman? Bless you, my child!"

"Well, like . . . you can't be more than . . . twenty-five, right?"

Temple took a deep breath. "I'm afraid I can. Try . . . thirty."

The girl's sunburned nose wrinkled. "Gross! Then our pool still has a ghost of a chance. I'll tell the others."

Off she hustled, as fast as her clumsy hiking shoes would take her, to report far and wide that Temple was thirty.

Temple remained seated on the warm fender, kicking the tire with her rubber-soled shoes and thinking.

Successful middle-aged men tended toward two prime hobbies: golf and girls. Was Domingo just an artistic CEO on the rampage? Did being an artist instill no respect for other persons, for the human soul, for restraint from sexual games?

Apparently not. Remember Picasso. Temple jumped down, automatically flexing her knees to disperse the shock. Every small hop down was a giant step for one of her height, or lack of it, rather.

She dusted her palms off as she considered who looked like the biggest gambler in the group. No contest: the shrimpy chain-smoking guy who had boldly accessorized his baggy gray shorts with a Hawaiian shirt. Shades of Max, quite literally.

"Hi."

He looked up from planting a spike-footed flamingo in the

sand. A soggy unfiltered cigarette clung to the saliva slick on his bottom lip.

"Yeah?"

"Say I want to join the project-girl pool?"

"Can't. You're in the running."

"Suppose I told you that the girl in glasses running around to everybody is telling them that she found out I'm thirty."

He glanced around. "Amanda." Sweat trickled past the rolled bandanna on his forehead. "Hey, babe, you don't look that bad to me."

"I'm too tall for you," Temple said, her voice even steelier than her eyes, which no one could see because of the dark glasses. Pity. This was a Molina-class look.

"Yeah?" He glanced up, then thrust another flamingo into the ground. "I guess you're right."

"So . . . uh—"

"Jeff."

"So, Jeff, who are the leading contenders?"

"Amanda for one."

"But didn't she—?"

"Don't let her disgusted act fool you. She's disgusted that she might not make it. This is her third year on safari with the Great White Hunter. She's out of grad school next spring and out of the running."

"And?"

He nodded to the blonde, naturally. "Steph would be the guys' lead choice, but Domingo doesn't like blondes."

"Doesn't like blondes? What kind of kinky cradle-robber is he?"

"Doesn't like blondes, and hasn't had a redhead for a while. That's why we put an outsider into our pool. Then there's that Ice Age ice-chick, Verina. Who would have thought he'd show up with that Vampira babe?"

"Maybe he's outgrowing the Lost Boys and Girls."

"Naw." Another flamingo bit the dust. "So you wanna toss five bucks in the pot? Pick your front-runner. You could even bet on yourself. The competition does get, shall I say, hot?" He eyed her as if having produced a terribly suave come-on.

"I'd have to know more about the full field of candidates. Maybe later."

"Later it'll all be over but the celebrating. Domingo doesn't usually wait this long." Jeff looked up at her again. "Speaking of long, I kinda go for tall women."

"Do I know a great one, and I bet she'd really go for you!" *With handcuffs and an unlawful-gaming charge,* Temple added to herself.

Temple departed with a friendly, but not too friendly, wave.

So Domingo was a Dirty Old Man. She felt vaguely disappointed, but didn't let that stop her active mind from churning.

Why, then, was Domingo breaking tradition? Why was he snubbing the panting project girls, making the jealous project boys nervous, putting Temple in the running for a race she didn't want to enter? Temple had assumed that a woman like Verina was the typical Famous Artist's accessory, but she was decidedly past forty. Poor thing! Why was she here, and why had Domingo broken a long, proud tradition of girl-chasing? Didn't he know his natives would be getting restless at his uncharacteristic hesitation?

Didn't he care?

And, if so, why not?

The man himself was currently the center of a squall of flamingos on the move, so Temple went over to rubberneck.

Some local-news cameras also homed in on the flutter. Temple saw why Domingo was always making like a traffic cop with his arms. He was always being photographed on-site, by still and motion cameras. Either way, he came off as a central figure in his white hero's shirt, full of energy and command.

She seemed to be his designated right-hand woman today. Perhaps it was only because he approved of the safari outfit, or because she made him look bigger since she was so (sigh) small, or . . . Temple didn't want to think about the deep discussions of Sunday afternoon, but it was all too clear that, like many powerful men, Domingo had eyes for any available female, including her, as the crew had speculated.

She was not the only one ruminating in that direction it turned out. As the day wore on, the flamingos propagated like a rash and even the young gung ho groupies wore out.

A shadow fell over Temple. She looked up to see Verina, bearing bottles of Evian water from the refreshment van. (Domingo's operation was used to on-site hardship in the middle of nowhere. Obviously, Las Vegas was considered to be equally absent of civilities like bottled water.)

"Wonderful!" Domingo wiped his fevered brow with a shirtsleeve and accepted a bottle.

The cameras zoomed in. Action that wasn't a pink blur.

"It's so hot," Verina complained. "And in November."

"Las Vegas cools down at night," Temple pointed out, "but by day the temperature can reach the eighties, even in the winter months. Besides, black attracts heat." She eyed Verina's twill designer bell-bottom pants and belly button–showing top, a long-sleeved, shrunken-midriff jacket. Socko in *Elle,* but a heat sink on the Strip.

Verina glanced at Domingo, handing Temple an Evian bottle, then patted delicately at her forehead. "The sun is so hot on my hair, I'm burning up. I had no idea." She lowered her voice, so only Temple could hear her. "And skin cancer runs in my family."

"Oh, gosh. You really shouldn't be out here, then."

Verina again eyed Domingo, who was flapping his wings like a living model for one of his flamingos. "He expects me to be here."

"Maybe you could wait in the refreshment van."

"It's so hot." Verina's husky voice was almost a child's whine. Her dark eyes fastened on Temple as if suddenly seeing a savior. "But your hat would shelter me from the rays."

"Well, ah . . ." Redheads weren't exactly made for overexposure to the sun, which is why Temple had worn the hat, knowing there would be no shade. She was more worried about contracting freckles than skin cancer, but she supposed she should be more worried about the latter than the former.

"If you could lend it to me, just for the afternoon—"

"Sure." Temple wasn't about to argue with a family history of skin cancer.

She handed over the hat and watched it waft to the top of Verina's elegant form, where it sat quite handsomely, being a charming if casual hat, after all.

Verina sidled off, following Domingo, cameras en train.

"Jeesh!" came a male explosion from behind Temple. "What an operator."

"Huh?" Temple turned to face a freckle-faced cameraman from a local TV channel. She thought that his name was Sean.

"You and that hat were getting too much attention for her taste, from her boss and from the cameramen. Why'd you hand it over?"

"Who can argue with skin cancer?"

"Say, you and I are bigger candidates for that than that spoiled broad. Just make sure you get it back."

Temple frowned through her sunglasses. Cameramen and photographers always saw the bigger picture, quite literally.

"Thanks for pointing it out. I guess I missed the obvious."

"She's gonna be on the cutting-room floor in my footage, after that ploy." Sean winked and moved on, focusing on flamingos.

The sun beat down on Temple's red-hot head while she considered kicking herself with a rubber-soled wedgie toe. Once again some slick out-of-towner had suckered her, this time a femme fatale. Why should a Woman Who Has Everything—a towering, thin, fashion-magazine body with the properly sexy androgynous look, a famous boyfriend, the latest designer wardrobe—have to scam a twelve-dollar hat off a working woman who has more to worry about than being the center of attention?

Maybe because all that Everything added up to Nothing.

Temple didn't move, but she stepped back mentally, like a cameraman, to pan the entire scene. She tended to immerse herself in her assignments, to get lost in the hype and the hullabaloo, and that made for myopia. Domingo's workers scurried like ants bearing trophies from the Flamingo Hilton chorus line. Domingo ranged ahead of the installation, like a scout, ignoring the sun, moving with a kind of Mediterranean passion; Zorba the Greek translated into a man for all nations. Verina, she of the ambiguous name and gender, followed along like an elegant black stork, picking her way among the squat, gaudy plastic birds, all pose and no purpose.

The famous always attracted hangers-on, but did they have to become addicted to them? Was there anybody who became a household name who didn't divorce a spouse, drop old friends, who actually despised the hollow trappings of fame, the easy decadence of getting everything free, from groupies to drugs?

Maybe Einstein. Maybe. Maybe Mother Teresa. She remembered a shallow, callow girl she'd met at a Women In Communications, Associated, meeting a while back. She'd chattered on about how she knew it was a sexist world, but that she had to use it while she was young and slim. She'd boasted of the red-devil satin catsuit cut up and down to *here* she'd worn to some national convention, and how a gray eminence, an author whose work Temple respected, had flirted with her and pulled her cat-tail at a cocktail party. And Temple had thought, did either of them really need to do that? Did she need to be Somebody so much she had to become a *Playboy* Bunny for old men? Did he so need to feel potent, despite all he had achieved, that he could be flattered by a vacant girl in search of big names to tease with her firm, unreachable anatomy? Was it all so unreachable, after all?

Temple shook her hatless head in the noonday sun. Knowing Matt had made her into a Hamlet of modern mores, ever-ready to question the small seductions of everyday life she used to take for granted. What was just being playful, and what was being manipulative? Look at the games Darren Cooke played, pulling the little red devil's tail at every opportunity! Maybe one day some little red devil—or some little red devil's big bad boyfriend— would pull the plug on ole Darren's serial seduction act. Maybe he was flirting with death, not just decadence. Maybe that was the real thrill of the chase for him, the endless pas-de-deux with self-destruction. She still couldn't answer her basic question. When it came to socio-sexual maneuverings, what was inoffensive fun and what was a very nasty habit on the way to becoming harmful to the health and happiness of all concerned?

She knew one thing. The greater anyone's fame and fortune, the nastier, and more lethal, everyday seduction became. From hats, maybe, to homicide.

Chapter 18

Dead Time

At 4 P.M. Temple returned home from the flamingo installation hot, irritated and hatless.

When she'd been ready to leave the site from sheer exhaustion, she had politely suggested to Verina that her hat should go with her.

No dice, and that was unusual in a town like Vegas.

Verina, downcast, alluded again to her skin cancer "situation." Temple didn't feel up to wresting a lifesaving possession from the top of a rival's head. Besides, she couldn't reach the top of Verina's head without making a fool of herself.

Since she didn't want to leave the empty lot wearing a fool's cap and bells, she simply left her hat and hoped for the best. Perhaps Verina would tire of the charade and return it to her tomorrow. No, not tomorrow; that was Midnight Louie's location-shooting day. Between flamingo overpopulation and cat commercials and hat thieves, Temple was feeling pretty put upon.

"Louie!" she said on unlocking her front door and finding

the cat sprawled on her sofa, looking like a dog waiting to welcome her.

She bent back to the hall floor to retrieve the two newspapers awaiting her attention, the evening *Sun* and the morning *Review-Journal*. Then she shut and locked her door, plucked a can of Diet Dr Pepper from the fridge on the way to the living room and plopped down beside Louie.

He reciprocated her attention by stretching his long black front legs to touch her thigh, and began kneading his nails in a fond—if somewhat hazardous to her pantyhose—gesture of cat satisfaction.

Temple put her shod feet atop the glass-topped coffee table, a rare desertion of decorum for her, and began skimming the two papers. She almost never got behind on her daily reading.

"Oh, Lordy, they're going to put up another megahotel and casino. Will this flagrant imitation of distant landmarks never end?"

Louie blinked and flattened his ears as she looked at him.

"I agree with you, boy. It's too much to keep up with. My Jersey Joe Jackson plans already sound like small potatoes, and I haven't even had time to write up a detailed proposal for the project. Nicky and Van are being very patient. If they knew I was out consorting with flamingos—!

"Hmm. Another drug bust on the north side."

She switched to the evening paper, scanning the front page. STAR FOUND DEAD IN HOTEL ROOM caught her eye, but not as much as the word FLAMINGO in a below-the-fold headline.

Reading the bottom half, she saw that Domingo's first flamingo installation was already making waves. Vandals had removed or paint-spattered some already in place. Some Vegasites were calling them "an eyesore."

Well, Vegasites ought to know!

The police expressed concern that such a massive flocking of the plastic beasts would cause traffic accidents. And Domingo was quoted—she had to follow the jump to page six—as saying that the installation was intended to have an impact on casual spectators. That was the entire point of outdoor art. Were billboards distracting to drivers? No.

"A front-page jump story. Not bad, Domingo."

She was not the one who had gotten the coverage; her job, for once, did not include that. Maybe Domingo was naturally newsworthy. Doing something loony in this town, even if you tried to dignify it by calling it "art," always caught the media eye.

Temple set the paper on the coffee table, so she'd remember to clip the story later, then recalled the tantalizing headline on the top half. What aging performer had died with his feet on the stage this time?

She retrieved the front page, flipped to the above-the-fold stories, and scanned the text. When the name "Darren Cook" (they'd omitted the terminal "e"; so much for stardom) leaped at her, she jumped to her feet so suddenly that Louie, in midtoecurl, snagged her shorts. Temple didn't care.

She was reading avidly. " . . . found today after noon by a hotel maid." Then he died . . . "Police estimate death occurred after midnight Sunday." But, she had just seen him Sunday noon! " . . . bullet to the head." Oh my! "Evidence of a last visitor, but the scene suggested suicide to the preliminary investigator, said a police source who declined to be identified."

Oh, yeah, the always-unreliable phantom source.

"Suicide!" she squeaked in disbelief at Louie, who looked utterly indifferent to her parroted revelations.

Why would a man as egotistical as Darren Cooke kill himself? Even if he were unnerved by letters from an unknown daughter? Even if he needed reassurance so much that he had hit on her, Temple.

Who had turned him down. Had she underestimated his sense of desperation? No! No. Famous men did not commit suicide because little old her had rebuffed a seduction attempt. Maybe no one *had* rebuffed him before. Maybe the letters had broken down his self-regard. Maybe she *was* to blame.

Temple sat down again, slowly, forgetting to look for Midnight Louie. Forgetting Midnight Louie entirely, until his indignant howl as she squashed him reminded her to jump up again. She read the story once more, but the body had been discovered (by whom?) too late for many details to make today's newspaper.

What about Gangster's revue, she wondered? And the À La Cat commercial built around it? She should call the director and see if tomorrow's location shoots were still on.

Temple scurried for the phone, the folded paper still in her hand. But when she began dialing, she found she was punching in Matt's number. Four-fifteen. He should be home. He should have about forty-five minutes before he left for work.

"Matt," she began as soon as the receiver was lifted. "There's been terrible news. Could you come down and help me interpret it? I'm pretty amazed, and dazed."

"News?" he asked. "From your family?"

"No, no, nothing personal. Not really. More professional. I just don't know what to make of it."

"I'll be right down," he promised, obviously having given up on getting any details over the phone.

Temple wandered to her door, reading the short article for a third time. She still shook her head in disbelief. She had seen the man only a bit more than twenty-four hours ago. It was hard to picture him dead. And if the suicide theory fell through, would anyone from the brunch remember that she had been closeted in his bedroom with him? Temple winced. What a compromising position. She wondered if she should have called a lawyer rather than an ex-priest.

Matt's knuckles rapped once and she had the door open.

"Thank you for not ringing the bell! I think it would have sent me up the wall. Here's the paper. That's the article. Come sit down, then tell me what you think."

He read as he walked, his white-blond brows knit into a small frown. Absently he bumped into the coffee-table leg, then just as absently compensated his direction to stumble around it to the sofa, where he sat.

This time Midnight Louie, also frowning, skittered away before anyone else treated him like a seat cushion.

Matt sat without incident, still reading, or rereading, the article. He looked up to find Temple sitting on the edge of the next cushion.

"This is the performer at Gangster's," he said.

She nodded gravely. "Imagine. I actually sort of knew the man. I almost feel guilty for turning down his proposition."

Matt looked shocked, perhaps as much by the circumstances as the fact of Temple's association with Darren Cooke.

"Look. He'd asked for my help."

"You never said what kind of help."

"Mystery-solving of a sort. Anyway, he took me into the bedroom."

"You went? And you never mentioned the bedroom before."

"He said he had something to show me."

"Etchings? Temple, I may have been out of the swing of things for years, but even I've heard of that old ploy."

"Oh, the proposition was probably just an afterthought. A tension-reliever after the main course proved unpalatable. Because he did have something pretty serious to show me. I guess I can tell you now."

"What?"

"I don't know whether to call them blackmail letters, or threatening letters. They were from a young woman who claimed to be his daughter. As far as he knew, he'd never fathered a child, but given his impressive list of women seduced, it's possible one gave secret birth to a child."

"What did this . . . child want?"

"Hard to say if it was recognition, or money eventually. She seemed disturbed. It's even possible she's an adoptee who fantasized that Darren Cooke was her father."

"So how could you help him?"

"I couldn't. Or I did, by telling the truth. I told him this was a job for the police, or for a discreet private detective. He didn't want to hear that. When I tried to leave, he suggested I stay for horizontal consultation."

She glanced apologetically at Matt. "I'm sorry I didn't take your own recent encounter with seduction more seriously. Women get to expect it, but in this case I found it insulting. I mean, I shouldn't have; there I was, this nobody turning down this famous performer. Except I felt used; that pretext about me helping him, it was all so manipulative. I think he would have gladly taken any solid suggestions I had. But the bottom line was still . . . my bottom line."

Matt smiled. "You warned me that I was unlikely to correctly interpret Janice's motives. Now I'll tell you the same thing. Sounds like Darren Cooke was under a lot of pressure. I'd bet he wasn't as debonair a proposer as usual."

"Maybe." Temple sighed and clasped her upper arms. "But now I've got to wonder if I—my rather uppity turndown—contributed to his death."

Matt had bent his head to read the article again, searching for revelations among the tersely worded statements. That wasn't going to happen, but she smiled at his earnest profile, the boyish way his blond hair brushed his forehead. He looked like a dedicated student puzzling out a particularly difficult problem.

Sensing her observation, the schoolboy looked up to reveal the dark pessimistic expression of a thousand-year-old man.

"Temple, if you were right, and my mysterious caller were Darren Cooke, I may have been the last person to speak to him alive. I may have heard him inviting the woman who drove him to suicide, or was his killer, into the room."

"You!"

"My caller got through to me around midnight. He was railing as usual, gibing me, in a really foul mood. I sensed that I shouldn't let him off the line, despite the abuse, and then he had a visitor. I heard him walk to the door. He sounded . . . pleased. Invited her in and hung up. Now I've got to wonder if something I did pushed him into an uncustomary vulnerability."

"Matt! You're saying we both might have had a hand in Darren's death! I asked you down to ease me off this guilt trip, and you heap a bigger one on yourself!"

His twisted smile was still engaging. "Yeah. I'm a real success as a counselor. Should we tell Molina or somebody?"

"No! God, no. It's speculation on both our parts. Someone else may have been calling you. Maybe it was Darren's lost daughter's call that drove him to self-destruction. Those letters of hers did not sound well balanced. We'd be nuts to insert ourselves into this case on hasty conclusions."

"Maybe the police could allay our suspicions."

"Right, and charge us as accessories before the fact, or something. I do not trust the police to put our guilt trips into perspective. They don't have the time to take weird little exercises in blame into account."

"But we'll probably never know if our suppositions are right if we don't present them to the police and get their reactions."

"As for me, I don't want police reactions in a sticky celebrity death, do you? It wouldn't help your counseling career."

"Maybe not, but that job is worth nothing to me if I blew it and drove a man to suicide."

"Matt, I'm sure you didn't. You're much too conscientious for your own good. You said your caller sounded happy about his visitor. That doesn't sound like an imminent suicide victim."

"Nooo—"

"And maybe you could say something cheering to me now, like I should take it as a compliment that Darren Cooke asked me to do the bedroom tango. Like . . . he really had been turned down before, and so just laughed at my indignant act. Besides, he didn't die until twelve hours after I kissed him off. It's obnoxiously self-important to think that what I did and said at noon would kill a man at midnight."

Matt was smiling again. "I don't know why you called on me. You can talk yourself into something better than anybody else. And, in the meantime, you've also managed to convince me that the coincidence would have been too much. I couldn't have been talking to Cooke. There must be thousands of sex addicts in this town."

"Right," Temple said with a brisk nod. "And thousands of eager flamingos in the flock for Darren Cooke. No sense brooding over the one that got away."

"I'm glad you got away."

"Ditto."

They smiled at each other.

"I suppose you have to rush off to work now."

He checked his wristwatch. "Yup."

"Darn, no time for seduction. It'll have to wait until later."

Matt stood. "Still, I'll be waiting for another call from my man. If he never calls again—"

"We can't second-guess the living any more than we can the dead."

"I've certainly seen that in the case of Cliff Effinger. Can you get me a copy of that clipping?"

"Sure. I'll keep a few for myself too."

"Molina might—"

"No. I especially don't want Molina to know I walked into that Cooke setup thinking I was Nancy Drew."

"It'd be handy to know what the police were thinking."

"You think you can get that out of Molina?"

He shrugged. "She did suggest I contact a police artist about Effinger."

"And look how that turned out! About as well as my going to Darren Cooke's brunch and listening to his tragic tale of the letters from an unknown daughter."

"People do catch you up in their own agendas, don't they?"

"And you better realize that Molina is better at that than most. Why'd she point you to a police artist? She wanted you to do her footwork for her."

"But I might have heard something on the phone Sunday night that means more than I could guess."

"Do what you want. But don't expect to get from Molina anything like what you give to her."

"You're probably right. I wish I'd heard the mystery woman's voice."

"No, you don't. Besides, you can't get a sketch on the evidence of voice alone."

Matt stood. "Looks like we're stymied."

"Stymied, stalled and hip-deep in slush," Temple summed up as she walked him to the door.

There he turned to her. "Don't worry. I'm sure you had nothing to do with Cooke's suicide." His hands rested on her shoulders.

"I'm sure you said nothing to encourage his self-destruction, either."

"We're both absolving each other," he noted.

"That keeps it between friends, at least."

His hand lifted from her shoulder as his face bent down. Temple expected a religious gesture, a blessing, even a sign of the cross.

She was confused when his free hand cupped and tilted up her chin, even more shaken when he kissed her. Not the way Max kissed her, but long and sweet and so deliberately she thought it would never stop, which was fine with her.

But it was over, and he was gone, in the same empty instant.

She had really hamstrung herself between two men, between two hot-and-cold-running relationships, Temple thought soberly. She felt like one of those insipid classical ballerinas, tippy-toeing en pointe from one side of the stage to the other, from one male partner to another. Back and forth, to and from. *Make your mind up, girl!* she admonished herself, always a fruitless exercise.

Kisses only confused her more, like too many hors d'ouvres before the main course. She would have to put her little arched foot down someday soon, stamp a definitive high heel and choose a dancing partner for real. But then somebody would get hurt, and she couldn't abide the idea of leaving either man out in the cold.

Brrrr. Temple shivered with indecision and self-disgust. She shut and locked her door as if to bar the north wind, then wandered into the living room. Louie had resumed full possession of the sofa, stretching out over all three cushions.

Temple picked up the newspaper again. Nothing in the story had changed. Darren Cooke was dead, and she was sorry. Matt's conversations with his mysterious caller might be over as well. Temple was sure that he would be sorry on some level too. Their separate but similar guilt probably made them the best mourners Darren Cooke would ever have.

Chapter 19

Gossip Never Dies

The next morning, Temple returned to Gangster's, Louie in his carrier beside her.

She was on time, 11:30 A.M., but she didn't expect to see much action today. Surely they would have to reshape the commercial tied into Darren Cooke's opening number.

She had not taken into account another famous musical number: "The Show Must Go On."

Everyone was there: the chorus line, the choreographer, the commercial director, even the Divine Yvette in her pink tote bag, with her airheaded mistress, Savannah Ashleigh.

Savannah looked as shaken as anyone with so much plastic surgery could. The apples in her cheeks had slipped and the sagging skin around her eyes, normally drawn back into a slightly Asian tilt, looked as if it had been carved from sun-melted suet.

"Don't look glum," Kyle counseled Temple. "The show's not down yet. Gangster's is negotiating with a substitute."

"Are there any substitutes for the likes of Darren Cooke?"

"How about Steve Martin?"

"Steve Martin? Really?"

"This is Las Vegas, dearie. Dreams come true here, especially after nightmares."

"On such short notice?"

"Not Martin Short; I said Steve Martin. All show biz thrives on short notice."

"I heard the name right the first time. He's a bigger star than Darren Cooke."

"Extreme emergencies require extreme solutions. Gangster's is not about to choke on spending money for its first revue. When fate hits you in the guts in show biz, you've got to bounce back swinging."

"And the cat commercial?"

"Same deal as before. Today we'll get some establishment shots in the car museum. Want help toting your cat back there?"

Temple actually didn't feel like going it alone today. She nodded, so Kyle whistled over the cat stylist. The trainer was watching sullenly from under her Nazi-like hairdo, definitely not a willing cat-toter.

"Gosh," Marcy said as the carrier exchanged custodians. "I swear this guy gains weight between assignments just to be ornery."

"Louie is never ornery," Temple said, defending her mute young. "Sometimes he's just too big to move easily."

"Let's go," Marcy said with a laugh. "This big guy gains weight just by sitting here, wishing."

She was off, the carrier bumping her jeans-clad legs on every step.

Temple hustled after her, glad to be leaving the theater behind, where the ghost of Darren Cooke had sat beside her, requesting help. Maybe she *should* tell the police about the letters from his reputed daughter.

It was while the commercial crew was parading through the lobby on the way to the old-car wing that a briskly moving figure intercepted them.

"Miss Barr," came the salutation of a familiar voice.

The entire party stopped to stare at Temple.

"Lieutenant Molina, Las Vegas MPD," the tall, advancing woman in a navy pantsuit added, producing a verifying badge. "I understand you cat-commercial people had brief encounters with Darren Cooke in the past few days."

Molina included them all in her roundup glance, but her eyes ultimately fixed on Temple.

"He came down to the seating area to welcome us," Temple conceded.

"And some he welcomed more than others."

Molina's assertion brought no answer but a guilty silence. Everyone resisted glancing at Savannah Ashleigh.

"I think," Molina went on, "the female contingent could answer that best. I understand that Darren Cooke was quite a ladies' man."

When no answer came, Molina flipped back her notebook cover and began to scan the contents. "I should say that some of you were spotted at his hotel suite in the past few days."

Temple felt her high heels turn into carpenter's nails and impale her to the floor.

"I'll have a word with you over there." Molina waved the notebook at the mostly deserted Prohibition Bar. "Kyle Conrad." The director. "Savannah Ashleigh." Savannah looked as guilty as Temple and twice as rebellious. "Sharon Hammerlitz." The animal trainer from hell, now that was interesting. "And Temple Barr. The rest of you can go do what you were planning on doing. I don't believe I'll need to interrogate the cats."

"Yvette does not leave my side," Savannah burst out in a hysterical falsetto. "You will have to wait to shoot her until my grilling is over."

"Miss Ashleigh." Molina's smile was so tight it resembled a rigor-mortis grin. "If you were truly getting the dreaded 'grilling,' it would be downtown in a bare, tiny room and no cats would be allowed. Keep Yvette with you, if you wish. But I will accept no whining and screaming from either of you."

"Oooooh," Savannah's shaky little moan came perilously close to a whine.

Temple waved Louie and his carrier on. He didn't like incarceration, but he was a perfect gentleman about it: no howling, hissing *or* pissing.

The group drew up chairs around an empty table for six. Molina plunked her notebook on the table and drew out a tiny pocket recorder.

"I'm compiling a roster of who was with the deceased the past few days. Since he entertained so often, it's hard to get a complete guest list. If any of you recall other attendees you knew, I want their names. This is all routine, I assure you."

Yeah, Temple thought. A homicide lieutenant on a suicide investigation. If suicide were the cause of death, with no reservations, Temple doubted Molina would even be here . . . unless to harass Temple.

Paranoia, Temple reflected further, was the curse of the thinking class. Like Hamlet, she thought too much, and look how that had ended!

"Mr. Conrad." Molina began with the director. "I understand you were present at Mr. Cooke's Friday-night cocktail party at his hotel."

"Yes, purely a professional courtesy. I only met him when we began working on this cat commercial. He was a generous man, and so included me on his guest list. I was hardly on a level with most of his guests, who are recognized 'names' in the business."

"Was anyone else from the crew or associated with the cat commercial present that night?"

Kyle eyed the table as if to refresh his memory. "Only Miss Ashleigh. But she had known him for years."

"For years," Molina repeated unnervingly, jotting the information down.

"Not that many years," Savannah corrected. She had removed Yvette from the canvas carrier and was holding the slim little cat to her chest and cheek as a child will cuddle a favorite teddy bear.

"How many?" Molina was as cool as a frosted beer mug.

"Years? Well, I don't know exactly. I first met him when I was doing *House on Heavenly Isle.* That was released in nineteen eighty-four, so . . . eight years ago or so."

"At least twelve," Molina corrected.

Savannah puckered her blond eyebrows and rubbed her prominent cheekbone (probably an implant) against Yvette's pretty Persian face. Yvette rubbed back.

"I can't be sure. I'm only thirty-six and I'm sure I made that film when I was about twenty, maybe?"

"We can check the film dates," Molina said, hiding a smile by forcing her mouth corners down.

Obviously, Savannah Ashleigh was so used to manipulating dates in her favor that she was hopelessly lost in a tangle of wishful lies when she discussed her career and its longevity.

"And you are—?" Molina asked the animal trainer.

"Sharon Hammerlitz. I train animals. I never knew Cooke before this project. I don't know why he invited me to his Friday-night party, but it was too good an opportunity to miss. We animal handlers are rarely invited to high-level parties, or any parties at all."

"So you went out of curiosity?"

"Like a cat." Sharon smiled for the first time in Temple's memory.

"You didn't sense that Mr. Cooke took a personal interest in you?"

"Me? I'm just a twenty-four-year-old animal trainer. What would a famous older man have an interest in me for?"

"You're attractive. Mr. Cooke never failed to notice an attractive young woman. How did he happen to overlook you?"

"Dozens of prettier types at the party; real starlets. I was just a lowly extra. I drank one margarita, nibbled some crackers and crab and left by nine."

Molina lifted an eyebrow at Kyle Conrad.

"True. I hardly saw her, and only stayed until ten myself. Nobody was much interested in talking to me. It was a closed crowd. They knew each other."

"I'm impressed by all your moderate hours and abstemious ways. And was Miss Barr present?"

Kyle and Sharon exchanged glances, shaking their heads in tandem.

Molina's eerily blue eyes finally rested on Temple again. "You weren't invited, Cinderella?"

Temple shook her head, wondering if she should volunteer her presence at the Sunday brunch, a much more incriminating day.

While she debated, Molina snapped her notebook shut and turned off her tiny tape recorder. "Just checking on the decedent's last days. He strike any of you as suicidal?"

More head shakes, very definite.

Temple sat there biting her tongue. If she didn't volunteer her presence in Darren Cooke's suite, admitting it later would look very bad. Perhaps if she had a private word with Molina—

But the lieutenant had stood and was thanking them perfunctorily for their time. The chance, now lost, would be awkward to reclaim.

"Well, are you coming?" Savannah Ashleigh demanded beside Temple. "We're back in business as usual, and your big tomcat must be gnawing at his carrier grille to get another chance to sully my little Yvette."

"Louie doesn't sully anything," Temple answered, hastening after the others and leaving Savannah to reinsert Yvette in her carrier, zip it up and come trailing after.

Chapter 20

Louie Goes for a Ride

I am a tad peeved with Gangster's.

Their advertisements claim they will pick up anyone anywhere in town. They certainly pick up Miss Savannah Ashleigh and the Divine Yvette, and bring them to the set every day that we are shooting. They certainly return Miss Savannah Ashleigh and the Divine Yvette from whence they came at each day's end.

Why, then, am I suffered to be "dropped off" and "picked up" by Miss Temple Barr? It makes me sound like dirty laundry. Of course, I realize that Miss Temple is a working mother (so to speak, especially if it is Savannah-speak, though Miss Temple has never called me "Mummy's little darling baby." Thank Bast!).

Still, I think I would look most elegant arriving in the passenger seat of a long, black limo.

And it appears that I am finally going to get my due. The Divine Yvette and I are about to be portrayed as passengers of some fancy vintage mobmobile. We are also going to be fed again (the best part of the commercial racket). As I overhear it, this sequence is a takeoff on that mustard commercial where two old British snobs roll up to the stoplight in their chauffeured Rolls-Royces, each of them slathering something they call Great Poop-on on their wienies. This strikes me as a strange name for a product meant for public (if not proletariat) consumption, but those Brits have some weird names for things and I do not always hear too well as I snooze during every commercial I am subjected to.

I do not get to slather Great Poop-on on my wienie for this commercial. I must scarf down more À La Cat from a sissy dish without a dab of Great Poop-on to make it palatable. (This Great Poop-on has a spunky, spicy taste, though its name is for the birds, or rather something that went through the birds. I think it is the same "Poop-on everything" they are always asking people for in the advertising biz. If these Madison Avenue hucksters can sell that poop goop, they can certainly unload a lot of À La Cat with two glamorous types like myself and the Divine Yvette hyping it from here to cat heaven.)

The car the Divine One and I will share is no limo, but one of those cavernous, beetle-back black numbers from the thirties. We do at least have a front-seat driver, a dude who looks like he escaped from Alcatraz. Dis is one tough-looking dude, let me tell you, and the Thompson submachine gun poking a steel nose under his zoot-suit lapel only adds to the ambience.

We are stuffed in the backseat, which is then hit with about two million kilowatts of spotlight. Now I know what they mean by the phrase "being on the hot seat," for those lights could broil an ice cube. I inquire whether my lady friend is suffering due to the heavy fur coat she wears at all times.

"No, Louie," she tells me while lolling on her side to cool off. "Being overheated is one of the prices of natural beauty." Va-va-varoom!

All around us sit polished, stalled cars of a similar vintage, though some are more colorful than our hearselike vehicle, like tan or even cream-colored. But most are the same basic black as our car.

Of course we are back in costume: I in my flamingo-pink fedora, Yvette in her feathers and diamonds. Our À La Cat servings are salmon fricassee, so the color goes well with my dashing but ridiculous headgear. If Bast had meant me to wear a hat, she would have made them all with earholes. A massive picnic hamper reclines on the car floorboards. Its open cover reveals such niceties as silverware and china plates, cans of paté and long loaves of French bread, none of which appeal to our predators' palettes. But I suppose it adds some eye-appeal to the human viewers who actually buy the glop that the poor house cats are forced to eat.

I glimpse my mortal rival, Maurice, on the sidelines. He is out of his carrier and in the cat trainer's arms, apparently quite the favorite. I realize that the animal trainer has a big stake in her alley cat's mangy hide. Favoritism is an ugly tendency.

The next thing I see I do not like one bit. The crew is rolling another humped, black car alongside ours, with another punk-looking driver and—who do they plunk in the backseat but His Majesty Maurice Two, the Maurice One slayer? That is like Macbeth giving King Duncan a friendly ride home in his Rolls while his missus lurks in the boot with a knitting needle.

Miss Temple has dawdled behind, no doubt questioning the boys and girls of the chorus about the demise of their leader. I know it is important for her to feel useful by making her little inquiries, but I do think she should be here protecting our contract from infringement. In my understanding, this was to be the Midnight Louie/Divine Yvette show. Maurice was nowhere mentioned.

And he also has footloose privileges while the DY and I are locked up. This kind of favoritism will only give him a chance to booby-trap the commercial. He has deceived this same set of subcretinous humans before. So he is only a body double who offed the celestial body he was substituting for, i.e., the star. They do not know nor care.

At last my ears hear tiny heels clicking on the hard-composition floor paving the car-museum area. I leap up and put my paws on the sill created by the rolled-down window.

You should hear the screeching! You would think a colony of bats were abroad.

"No! No pawprints on the finish!" the crew screams, descending on me in a raving horde. "Ugly damp pads."

They are lucky that I make my protest only with pawprints. There are other, even more corrosive ways of damaging prized human property, if I make myself clear?

Miss Temple does not help my cause.

"What has he done now?" she asks, clattering up to the car door I am desecrating.

"He was sitting in the backseat nice as pie," the trainer explains, "then he was up on his hind feet looking around."

Miss Temple, to give her credit, examines the scene of the crime by walking around my car.

"Maybe he's upset because this other male cat is hogging the backseat of the neighboring vehicle. I thought Louie and Yvette were the focus of the commercials. What's Maurice doing here?"

Way to go! Keep those legal beagle tough questions coming.

On the seat beside me, the Divine Yvette bestirs herself. "Is that nasty Maurice causing problems, Louie? I do not like him. He is a bad boy!"

My heart glows to hear my rival dismissed by the one who counts.

"Do not flutter your furs, my dear," I return in my manliest swaggering tone. *"My* mistress will make Vienna sausage out of him, with no Great Poop-on to ease the transition."

The animal trainer comes to loom over Miss Temple, which is not hard to do even when she is wearing high heels, which only make her a feisty but tottery five-feet-three.

"Listen, lady, your cat is completely untrained. At least Maurice knows some tricks and responds to clacker signals."

"Louie is a natural performer, from what we saw of his improvised dance down those stage stairs. And what about Yvette's contract? Is she supposed to be shoved into third place by that camera-hogging yellow mongrel?"

Miss Temple's germane inquiries have even stirred Miss Savannah Ashleigh from flirting with the twenty-five-year-old cameraman. She undulates over in languid irritation.

"What is this about another cat intruding into what is already an imposition on my Yvette, who was to star solo in these tawdry commercial epics?"

By now the director has come over, patting shoulders, even mine.

"Calm down, everyone. The trainer suggested a spoof of the mustard with the two old gents commercial, and I thought it was a good idea. Maurice is simply in the scene as a loser, the cat who carries a no-name brand of cat food that Louie and Yvette can sniff their noses at as they partake of À La Cat. We will only see a flash of his swill and his hide, I promise."

"Just so he is not as prominent as my Yvette."

"Just so he does not get more airtime than Louie."

The director keeps nodding and crossing his heart and patting the ladies' shoulders. There is nothing like a good pet for soothing the savage beast. Not to mention Miss Savannah's savage breasts, of which the like I have never seen.

The ladies calm down and back off the set, but their two sets of eagle eyes watch director's and cameraman's every move. I notice both men's hands shake ever so slightly as they set up camera angles.

"Is the rude interchange over, Louie?" *ma petite*'s voice mews from her recumbent form.

I must say that these Persians are very laid-back cats, except when they are mad.

"All is well," I reassure her, adding a lick or two, including a slow tour of her shell-pink ear.

"Louie!" she simpers with feminine delight. "That could show up on camera."

"Let it," I declare. "This scenario could use a little more spice, and that certainly will not come from Maurice, so it is up to us to uphold the standards of the species."

"Whatever you say is so sensible. You may lick my other ear, if you wish."

I waste no time taking up her invitation, and hear the director telling the cameraman to "catch that."

But they will not catch anything from us, as we are both exceedingly clean, especially after all this ear-licking.

So the action begins. I mean the commercial-filming action, of course.

The two cars' facing back windows are rolled down. I am tempted to our car's inside window by a feather on a stick peeking up over the windowsill. Frankly, this tired feather, dyed a disgusting orange, would not lure me into a bordello of Birmans. But I do know what is expected of me, and bound to the open window, planting my broad black paws on the surface. No cries of pawprints on the wax job now. This is show business, and this pose is my business.

"Good boy," the director croons as the trainer crouches below the opposite window with the same tawdry toy.

And, lo! The awful Maurice puss pops up in the opposite opening like an ugly jack-in-a-box. It is all I can do to refrain from sticking my tongue out at him, but I know that this would be an unflattering pose for the camera. I am trapped by fame and fortune from following my basest instincts. This is not a good trade-off.

We make faces at each other for a minute or more. The computer geniuses will add lip movements in the studio to

fit the script. I have read the script, and know that I am supposedly boasting about the superiority of my brand of cat
food, so Maurice must be singing the praises of some real
poopon stuff.

The cameras pan past us to focus in turn on dishes of
glop on each of our backseats. I do not know what ugly stuff
is showcased in the ugly Maurice's ugly container, but our
set features an Irish-crystal bowl heaped with this stylized
À La Cat that has been plumped and toothpicked until it
resembles a beehive hairdo from long ago—if hair were
usually salmon-pink.

I do my business by pushing the bowl of À La Cat toward
the reclining Yvette. She reaches out a dainty paw to pat
the bowl, then leans her little face into the mess and begins nibbling away.

I sigh in a way that is not detectable on camera, then insinuate my face into the bowl, so our whiskers interweave
as we sup.

At the director's call of "Cut!" this particular segment is
history.

"Look at how Louie stops eating the minute the director
calls cut," Miss Temple points out with fond maternal glee.
"It is like he knows he is off camera."

"Maybe he just does not like À La Cat," Miss Savannah
Ashleigh says as she sashays over to wrest Yvette from
my tender custody.

"Then he fakes it pretty well," Miss Temple crows, also
drawing me out of the vehicle.

I try not to interfere with her magic moment, but I am a
lot more pussycat to lift straight up than the Cotton-Puff
Queen, the Divine Yvette. Miss Temple's dramatic recla-
mation of myself is less than graceful, and there is nothing I can to do prevent her further embarrassment.

"I think Louie's getting enough À La Cat to gain weight!"
she announces to one and sundry.

And in this little moment of owner hubris, she loses her

grip on me. I slide back to the car seat like a sack of potatoes.

"I will get him," the director suggests gallantly.

But, before he can move, the car I am stalled in does.

"Clete! Hit the brakes!"

"Where are they on this antique?" Clete yells back as he
and I roll toward a very long, low, expensive-looking convertible covered in chrome.

A good question. I hop over the high front seat with my
usual agility and find myself staring into the dark cavern of
the floorboard, which bristles with gear sticks and other
strange equipment. It resembles no car of my acquain-
tance, and I have motored extensively. Maybe my old man
would have a tip or two on how to stop this rolling death
trap, but he is not here.

"Oh, Aunt Kit's kaboodle!" Miss Temple exclaims, the
only one with the sense or guts to run alongside the moving car. "Clete, can you hit anything on the floor to the left
of center? The brake must be there."

"I cannot feel nothing but the gas pedal, lady, and you
sure as hell do not want me flooring that by accident."
Clete, wrestling with the giant steering wheel, overturns
it in a panic that has us weaving right and left like a
shuttle-bug.

I jump into the dark at his feet, hoping to avoid a crush-
ing. The pedals look confusing even to me, just faint
shapes in the dark I am used to seeing in. I identify the gas
pedal, though, and hurl my full weight on the pedal left of
it. Nothing happens, except that I am jostled to the floor. I
leap upon the next pedal and feel a slight hesitation in our
progress. Bingo! Now to get some human muscle on
the job.

I insinuate my forelimbs up the guy's right pantleg. He
begins giggling, partly in panic, partly because my light
touch tickles him. Then I snick out the shivs and claw down
hard. He screams and tries to stomp me as if I were a bug.
Maybe a foot-long centipede. I wait until the peril of the last

moment, then leap aside onto the center hump. His combat boot stomps the brake so hard that both our noses hit solid surfaces. His head impacts the center of the steering wheel, which sets off a terrible sustained honking note; I bump into the center hump, sorely abrading my second-best sensory organ on the console.

Despite my cosmetically tragic injury, I clamber up and over into the rear seat, glad the Divine One had been removed before the rough stuff started. I also begin licking my nose, imagining how delightful it would be were the Divine Yvette loose and able to tongue my wounds.

Everyone outside the car is agog, helping the driver exit, asking if *he*'s all right and how *he* stopped the car. The injustice of the moment stings worse than my skinned nose.

A museum attendant runs up to study the car that has stopped . . . oh, maybe six inches from the sleek little vintage convertible's side.

"I cannot believe this happened. The emergency brakes are set on all these cars every day we open, but this one has its emergency braked pulled up and out. It was useless!"

"How much strength would it take to disengage the emergency brake?" my mistress's curious voice pipes up from somewhere very near.

"Not much. A two-year-old could do it."

I plant my mitts on the open windowsill and glare back into the once-adjacent vehicle our slo-mo rush to oblivion has left behind. Maurice is in a mirroring position to mine, except that he is grinning whisker to whisker. I am beginning to bet that a well-trained eight- or nine-year-old could do it too, and did.

"I got the footage," the cameraman is yelling. "Louie going over the seat into the front compartment, Clete yowling and hitting his head."

"Yeah, Clete," the director asks. "Why did you scream like that?"

"I do not know." Clete rises from his dazed seat on the

running board. He inches up his right pantleg. "Felt like a dozen scorpions stinging me, and I stomped down on it so hard I hit the brake. Sure couldn't see it."

"Well, look at that," the director says.

They look, even Miss Savannah Ashleigh, who has minced over to eavesdrop on everything.

"Cat scratches," the director says in an awed tone. "The cat scratched you so you'd stop the car."

"I do not think so," the dazed Clete says. "I think the cat was just trying to hide under my legs."

"It does not matter," the director replies, stepping back to view the car and me in it. "We will shoot some new stuff to intercut with what the cameraman got now. Louie finding the brake and doing his scratching-to-save routine. We will put some catnip on your leg, that ought to do the trick. Then Louie leaping into the backseat again—we have got that—and perhaps getting cozy with Yvette. Or she could push the À La Cat bowl to him this time. I love it."

"What about Maurice?" the trainer asks in a grating tone.

"Huh? Oh, him. I guess we could close with a shot of the Louiemobile taking off and shooting a cloud of dust into the back of his car, all over his inferior brand of cat food."

"Great work, Louie." The director reaches into the backseat to pull me out.

He even scratches my ears, but I do not admonish him for this liberty. I like the way he thinks. I also watch the animal trainer quietly collect the disgraced Maurice.

Missed again, buddy. Too bad the cat is not out of the bag—and the commercial—entirely.

Chapter 21

An Inspector Calls

Matt felt as serene as the blue rectangle of cool water in the pool three stories below. He had just been beside it in the warm November sunshine, doing his tai-chi routine and then a more conventional Western meditation on the blue mats.

His panicked feelings about the ConTact caller had receded like a high tide. His head and emotions were clear; he felt exonerated, forgiven. Having just gotten up an hour before, he was hacking together a cold breakfast: cereal, milk and half a cantaloupe, when the doorbell rang.

Who could that be? he wondered, discounting Temple. She was off turning Midnight Louie into a TV star, and landlady Electra had lots of weddings scheduled for her attached wedding chapel, the Lovers' Knot.

So he opened the door, cantaloupe cleaver still in hand.

Lieutenant C. R. Molina stood there, looking like an enlisted woman in navy blue.

"C—" he began to greet her.

She held up a hand he was surprised to see was not white-gloved. "None of that Carmen stuff, Devine. I'm here on official business."

Her officer act was second to no one else's. Crisp, authoritarian, humorless, she could have been an archbishop. He gave way as she entered, glancing sardonically at the large kitchen knife.

"Just, ah, butchering the breakfast cantaloupe. You care to see?"

"No. Put your food away. This will take only a few minutes. I hope."

He reluctantly left her in the barren living room, looking at his things—or the lack of them—in her see-all, know-all way. In the kitchen he threw his partially assembled breakfast in the refrigerator. The cereal would get soggy, but that was hardly a major loss. ·

He glanced down at his white gi and bare feet. Hardly formal enough attire for an official police visit, which is no doubt why they love to make them unannounced. Control is the name of their game, and they are used to getting, and keeping, the upper hand.

He hurried out again, wondering how many conclusions her penetrating eyes had drawn from his few possessions.

"Coffee?" he asked.

"No. For me it's lunchtime, which I usually don't have time for, except at my desk." She was studying every piece of furniture frankly, the phone on its wobbly secondhand table, the single and ugly floor lamp, the odd book, the sparse wall ornaments.

"Looks like a class photo," she commented when pausing before a huge horizontal black-and-white picture.

"Eighth-grade graduation photo. St. Stanislaus."

"And you are . . . let me see if I can pick you out of the lineup. Hmm, there. Second row, far left. Cute as a little blond bug."

"I don't know about the cuteness, but I am on the left, I remember."

"You hang up a photo and don't know where you are in it?"

"I didn't have much to hang up, and I haven't much looked at what I did hang up. Too busy."

She turned from the wall. "I'm impressed," she admitted. "So uncluttered, even ascetic. I would have thought ex-priests would go in for material possessions after years of not having very many."

"Rectories are usually crammed with parishioner hand-me-downs, dark heavy old pieces, rather depressing. And I haven't had time to furnish this place. Temple wants to take me to the resale places, but—"

"But you'd see more of the same you saw in the rectories. Can I sit?"

"Of course. I forgot to make it plain. Have only the one sofa, though."

"This one will seat three or four. It ought to do for us, don't you think?"

"I can stand."

"I'd rather you didn't."

Matt shrugged and followed her over to the plaid sofa, wincing upon remembering that only one cushion was unsprung. If he could maneuver her onto the good one— But Molina was not one to be maneuvered, even for her own comfort. She sat on the second-from-left cushion (sprung), forcing him to select the end one (also sprung).

"I'm investigating a death," she began.

"Not a murder?"

"Not . . . yet. Have you ever heard of a man named Darren Cooke?"

"Not until very recently."

"How?"

"Temple mentioned him in connection with a cat commercial her Midnight Louie is in. Apparently he's some sort of entertainer."

"*Was* some sort of entertainer."

"Sorry. I know he is dead, but I knew so little of him when he was alive, that it hasn't really hit home. His death, that is."

"Maybe this will hit home."

Molina drew a business card from her side jacket pocket and threw it down on the empty seat cushion between them. This was the unsprung cushion. The card lay on the tautly plumped cushion as if on a presentation pillow. It was a ConTact card.

"I-I recognize the card, but what has that to do with Darren Cooke?"

"It was found in his possession. If you'll turn it over, you'll see the name 'Brother John' written on the back. In Cooke's handwriting, I might add. Was he a phone pal of yours?"

"I don't know. All my callers are anonymous."

"You must get some clues to their backgrounds, though: ethnic, regional, education level, and so on."

"Yes. Most don't call more than once."

"But some do."

"A rare few."

"—who would therefore stick in your memory?"

"Possibly."

Molina narrowed her eyes, letting their electric blue diminish to two slits, like in an armored tank. "You're being fairly evasive for the good, honest ex-priest you are. What are you hiding?"

"Uncertainty."

"Yes, priests aren't trained to deal with that."

"Listen, Lieutenant. I'm not a priest any longer. I'm not hiding behind a clerical robe."

"I can see that." Molina eyed his gi with some amusement.

It made Matt feel like a twelve-year-old playing at martial arts. He understood that part of her interrogation technique was to juvenilize subjects so they would respond to her as an authority figure. He'd had enough of playing an authority figure, but guessed that if Molina wanted to go head-to-head with him in this mode, he could pull up enough experience to outgun her. She had gone to Catholic schools herself, after all.

"Lieutenant," he said, donning his parish-priest demeanor that cowed the faithful and drove the preteen girls wild, despite his best intentions, "you must understand that I cannot jump to hasty conclusions. My job is to help people, not hunt them down. I accept them for what they say they are, and we go from there. There was one repeat caller who had delusions of being Somebody. He was a sexual addict who hated himself for his addiction, as so many addicts do at times. It's possible he was this dead man. I'll just have to wait and see if he calls again, and since his calls have been so erratic, that may be quite a while."

Molina sat forward on the sprung cushion, oblivious to its discomfort. "Was your frequent caller suicidal?"

Matt nodded. "At times. He was older, had more at stake, including a marriage, his first. I referred him to three top psychiatrists, but he delayed contacting any of them. A common denial mechanism. He was using me as much as he used any woman; he's an inveterate manipulator, too hooked to stop."

"Hmm. Could be Darren Cooke. If we got a tape of his voice would you recognize it?"

"Maybe. It was distinctive, strong. But a lot of men with strong voices call me, and claim to be big winners or Somebody, and they're compulsives, all right, but gambling is their game, or drinking or drugs. Our callers are really anonymous, given the huge base of troubled people here in Las Vegas."

"But he was suicidal?"

Matt nodded again. How many ways did he have to say it?

"Cooke's death certainly looks like suicide. Was your caller distraught enough about his addiction that he would have killed himself after having . . . entertained a woman?"

"Very much so. He was trying to follow the straight and narrow, had a new wife and a baby daughter that he adored. All addicts build their fantasy worlds on a foundation of self-loathing. I hope I do hear from him again," Matt added in a burst. "I hope my man is not your man. That mine is alive and still has a chance to beat his addiction."

Molina nodded, picking up the ConTact card and slipping it back into her pocket.

"Why did this man keep calling you?"

"He said I helped him."

"You sound dubious."

"The trouble with all addicts is that they'll say anything to win the world over to believing that they don't have problems, or that they've got their situation well in hand. You must know that. Deception is their stock in trade. They're so used to it, they hardly recognize it as deception. It's called 'delusional sincerity' in the textbooks. They believe their own lies."

Molina nodded as she stood and walked toward the door. "I've dealt with a lot like that in interrogation rooms." At the door she turned back to him. "Listen, don't get your Catholic conscience in a wad over this guy. My guess is suicide will remain the diagnosis. But he's a famous guy and we have to investigate his last days just to be sure. You any good at martial arts?"

Her last question caught him off guard.

"I've studied for years, but I've never had to use it. So I guess I don't know. I like it for the mindset, the meditative quality."

"A pacifist to the core," she said, laughing.

"Maybe," Matt conceded sheepishly.

"Maybe not," he told the door after it had shut behind her.

Chapter 22

Flamingo Tango

The empty lot was a sea of that indescribable shade of pink called flamingo when Temple stopped by the first installation site in the morning.

She could hardly get near it for the rubberneckers slowing their cars to ten miles an hour to gawk at the latest imitation life-form to descend on the Strip.

Since it would take her at least fifteen minutes to come abreast of the driveway into the vast sandy parking lot the site was, she followed Mad Matt's example with the Hesketh Vampire and drove over the curb. An aging Geo Storm was not a motorcycle. Two sets of wheels jolted over the barrier, nearly knocking Temple's big plastic eyeglass frames off her retroussé nose and giving her a very French nosebleed.

She parked as soon as all four wheels were on sand, ignoring the indignant honks of people who had no business being there anyway.

By oncs and twos, at close range, the plastic yard ornament

was a cheap thrill. Two for nine ninety-five. You could see the manufacturing seams and the molded-feather shapes.

But here . . .

Domingo's plan was more than a two-dimensional layout on paper. He had made sure that certain flamingos were propped up higher than the rest, as if standing on hillocks, or walking on water, if one were paranormally inclined.

The effect was of waves of flamingos. Through the sun shimmer came an odd illusion that they moved, that feathers ruffled and long necks bobbed. Temple could sense what a real flock of thousands of flamingos would look like in the wild. There were few library books devoted to the subject. One ancient text—so old it was illustrated with black-and-white photos!—written by a British explorer who nearly lost his life pursuing the haunts of Great and Lesser Flamingo tribes in Africa, said that the sight was so overwhelming that he could hardly describe it. And considering his long and precise descriptions of alkaline mudflats, that was quite a concession to loss of words.

Now Temple glimpsed his awe. She actually was impressed by Domingo. If art was getting people to look at their world in a different way, he was a genius. There they bloomed en masse, like so many cactus flowers, unreal as anything around them, yet representing a form of natural life seldom seen in its glory.

The display both mocked and celebrated the artificiality that was Las Vegas. It looked as if all the half-million plastic flamingos sold in both the Americas every year had marched here in protest at being parceled off two by two. This was a flamingo convention, and surely not the oddest birds to descend on Vegas over the years.

"You like?"

Temple started to find Domingo beside her, his showman's arms lowered for once.

"It's . . . amazingly lovely," she said.

"Much that we do not look at closely is lovely." Domingo had no accent, but he phrased his words like someone foreign to the English language. Somewhere in that tone was flattery.

Temple tore her eyes from the flamingos—and it was an

effort—to view their assembler. Domingo was smiling at her, looking far more human than she had ever seen him.

"Here is your hat. I understand it was forcibly borrowed the other day." He bowed (another foreign affectation) as he handed it back.

"I wasn't expecting it back."

"A shame. I have had a word with the . . . mynah bird who took it. She will not trouble you again. Or me."

"Verina? But she—"

"She had attached herself to me. I rely on others to help me with my work. I had not looked closely at her. I work so long and see the results only infrequently." He began walking toward the installation, and Temple fell in step with him, amazed. "It is not good to have those around you who are more selfish than yourself. She is gone, back to where she found me. I am in love with my flamingos for the moment, anyway."

"You have so many helpers," Temple marveled, watching college students move among the flamingos like body servants, adjusting angles, tilts, postures.

"I rely upon the passions of others to complete my own, whether professionally or personally." Espresso-dark eyes seared her face. "It is a terrible, heartless lifestyle, art. It attracts terrible, heartless people, who in turn draw terrible, heartless hangers-on." He stopped and turned to Temple. "You are refreshing. I am glad to have met you. Now I do not need only plastic flamingos to restore my faith in life and the living. We will celebrate the return of your hat and my optimism. With a late lunch at my hotel this afternoon. And without Verina."

Temple may have been in a flamingo-daze, but she was not oblivious to the obvious.

"Domingo, if you're hitting on me because your girlfriend skipped town—"

"So refreshing." Domingo took her arm to lean companionably closer. "I wish to find out how you have kept your charming optimism, and your charming skepticism, in such a place as Las Vegas. I am sorry, Miss Temple, but you are my flamingo of the moment. I like your ideas. I like your honesty. I cannot afford to ignore reality when I encounter it. To me, at this moment, you are as real as they are."

This was the most dubious compliment Temple had ever heard, so of course she was flattered by it. Besides, she had a rather wild idea about where Darren Cooke's bad seed might be lurking. After her experience with Cooke, she would have to be demented to go off alone with another known ladies' man. But just saying no did work in certain areas, if not with addictions. And if she couldn't decide to say yes to two perfectly attractive men her own age, she didn't see herself succumbing to another midlife charmer.

Domingo swept a hand, finally, in a grandiose gesture, toward the wonderful parliament of birds.

"Your suggestion. And it looks marvelous. Several major hotels that had already rejected me out of hand are reopening negotiations. You will have to help me nurse along their revived interest, otherwise my project will make a fool and a failure out of me. You do wish to contribute to great art, don't you?"

"That, Domingo, is a loaded question, and I never answer those. But I will join you for lunch, mainly because I'm curious to hear about Verina's downfall."

He laughed, facing the sky as if it would laugh with him if it could. "Women! Revenge is always more interesting to them than love."

Chapter 23

The Wronged Woman

Temple came home tuckered out, and a bit confused. Domingo had played the perfect gentleman at lunch, more sheepish than wolfish.

She became even more stupefied when she listened to the message on her answering machine.

"Miss Barr, this is Michelle Bonard," said a soft, slightly French voice. "I wish to speak to you most urgently. I am at the Crystal Phoenix, room seven-eleven. Could you please call as soon as possible?"

Temple absently reset her machine to receive.

Michelle Bonard. The name was vaguely familiar, but she couldn't imagine why. Perhaps she'd been working too hard lately and every name was starting to sound familiar. There was no arguing with the fact that while the voice was polite and businesslike, an underlying strain invested the request to call immediately with a sense of urgency.

Temple dialed the Phoenix, whose number she knew, and

asked for room 711. Next to the Ghost Suite, which was 713. Was Jersey Joe Jackson playing a trick on her?

" 'Allo?" answered the same voice that had left the message, so quickly that she must have been sitting by the telephone.

"Temple Barr. You needed to speak to me?"

"Oh, yes! Have you eaten? We could dine in my rooms at six."

Everybody on earth wanted Temple to eat with them, except Max Kinsella and Matt Devine.

"May I ask what this is about?"

"It is about my husband. My late husband, Darren Cooke."

Temple's heart almost stopped and began running backward. What could his wife—widow—want to say to her?

"Of course I'll come. I'm so very sorry about his death."

"Yes." Said a bit too abruptly, as if that was all she had heard for a while. "Yes." A sigh. "Unfortunately, we must discuss his death. I have some questions about the circumstances."

"But . . . why call me?"

"I will explain when we are face-to-face. I would much appreciate your coming without knowing more. It is a lot to ask of a stranger, but I am . . . in a difficult position."

"Of course." Sympathy was Temple's greatest motivation for complying with Michelle Bonard's strange request. Curiosity was a close runner-up.

Six o'clock at the Phoenix gave her just enough time to fork more treats over Louie's mound of Free-to-be-Feline and to dash into the bedroom to don something appropriately sober and sympathetic.

Unfortunately, Temple owned few clothes that could be described as sober. Even the black number from her outing with Matt to Gangster's was entirely too frivolous, with its ruffled sleeves. She came across a gray linen suit she seldom wore, teamed it with a yellow silk top and her yellow-and-black patent Charles Jourdan heels.

Feeling like Little Mary Sunshine on a very gray day, she grabbed her black patent tote bag and hit the road.

Pulling into the Phoenix driveway felt like home nowadays. She had unlimited valet-parking privileges now that she was working so much for the owners, so she waved at the parking girl→a nice touch—in her neat peacock-blue uniform trimmed with silver, and left the Storm in her capable hands.

The lobby was the usual throng of people checking in and people heading for the adjacent casino area. Temple scooted straight ahead for the elevators.

"Hey, Miss Temple!" came a deep baritone voice.

Only ten people besides choreographer Danny Dove would dare to call her Miss Temple. She stopped, turned and faced one of them. But which *one* of the young, suave Fontana Brothers was she confronting? They looked so much alike they could pass for double quintuplets.

Whichever one he was, he was dressed for attending a funeral. Gone was the trademark pale Italian designer suit, replaced by a *dark* Italian designer suit. Pin-striped, navy and sober, lightened only by the flamingo-pink tie against a navy shirt.

"Who died?" Temple asked.

"Huh?" He followed her gaze to his jacket and tie, then grinned. "Ermenagildo Zegna."

"Never heard of him."

"You wouldn't have. He's a guy guy. The designer. Ermenagildo Zegna. I won't tell you what it cost, because then you would fall over and you might get stomped in this crowd."

"Thanks. But why the new look?"

"Don't you like it? Nicky says we should look like bankers. That it suits our new role."

"You and your brothers have a new role? I never knew your old one. So what's your new role?"

Aldo or Enrico or Emilio proudly smoothed his long lapels. "We are partners in a business enterprise."

"Not the Phoenix?"

"Naw, Nicky would never let us muscle in here. Might taint the Pieman-pure rep he's aiming at."

"I think you mean 'simon-pure.' "

"No, that's the guy that tells you what to do in that stupid game I wouldn't be caught dead playing."

"Simon Says," Temple said, "turn around so I can see your

new suit in three-D, then tell me what new business you're involved in."

Enrico (she arbitrarily decided) obliged. Temple did have to admire the long, lean, somehow-foreign construction of the suit.

"Can't you guess? You been hopping in and out of our place all week."

"*You*'re gonna build the megahotel on the old Sands site?"

"Aw, Miss Temple. I don't see how you solve so many murders and then make an outta-the-ballpark guess like that. It's Gangster's."

"The Fontana Brothers own Gangster's?"

"Well, part of it." Enrico held out his arms in turn and meticulously adjusted his cuff lengths. "Anyway, we thought we should look the part too."

"You are gentlemen of many parts, certainly," Temple said with a dazed shake of her head. "Whose idea was the limo service?"

"Uh, Nicky's. He thought it would add class to the concept."

"Nicky's the king of class, all right."

"You here to see him and Van?"

"No, I'm visiting a guest."

Enrico leaned his head close to Temple's, which was quite a feat, given the difference in their heights.

"Is it about a case?" he inquired in a whisper.

"Maybe," she whispered back.

"You going to see someone you think might be a murderer? I can escort you."

"No, I'm probably visiting someone who thinks *I* might be a murderer."

"No!" Enrico drew back and up to his full almost-six-feet. "Whoever it is does not know you."

"That's true. And now I must be running along."

"I'll watch."

Temple looked a little nonplussed.

"You are so cute when you burn rubber on those high heels of yours. Kinda reminds me of those little fluffy dogs they call a . . . a Pompadour."

Temple was not going to tell him that the dog's breed was Pomeranian. She'd rather be compared to a French mistress anyday, than a lapdog on the hoof.

She resumed her course, striving for a sober, serious walk more reminiscent of a mastiff. When she turned back at the elevators, Enrico, who was still watching, waved.

She waved too, and entered the elevator, pressing the seven button. As the doors met in the middle, she thanked her lucky stars that the Fontana Brothers had so little to do with the Crystal Phoenix's operation.

Temple knew right where to go when the elevator doors spit her out on the seventh floor. As she passed number 713, the Ghost Suite, she knocked on woodwork. Nobody answered.

Not only was 711 next door, as she had anticipated, but this suite bore a number famous as a gambling password: seven come eleven. Temple thought that if she were a suicide's widow, she'd stay far away from the unlucky number thirteen and its cousin, seven-eleven.

She knocked, then waited nervously. Who was Michelle Bonard besides Cooke's widow, and what did she want with Temple?

A slight young woman answered the door. Her mousy brown hair was cut in the messy shag au courant for Smart Young Things. Though she looked ultra-French in her faded tight jeans and her skinny black top, she couldn't have been more than twenty-three years old.

"Dana, is that Miss Barr?"

Dana cocked a cocky eyebrow at Temple, who nodded.

"If you'll take Cookie for a while—" Another woman appeared in the open doorway. As tall as Lieutenant Molina, but thin enough to read the classified ads through.

In her arms was a pretty brown-haired child, perhaps two or three, dressed in fragile embroidered cotton.

The mother transferred her to the girl's rangy arms, then smiled at Temple. "Her name is Padgett, but we call her Cookie for now. Say hello to the lady, Cookie."

"Hello," the child, at the Bambi-shy age, mimicked.

"Take her in the bedroom while I speak to Miss Barr. Ah!" Michelle Bonard craned her already-storklike neck as she looked beyond Temple down the hall. "I hear the room-service cart coming now. I ordered for you, if you don't mind."

A little late to mind, Temple thought, wondering if the on-coming clank was the cart . . . or the ghost of Jersey Joe Jackson in chains.

Ushered inside, Temple had a chance to eye the suite while Michelle directed the bellman in placing the cart.

Though the same venerable age as the adjacent Jersey Joe Jackson suite, this set of rooms, dating to the forties, had been stylishly redecorated. The look was highly Continental: spare, elegant furniture upholstered in cream and chamois colors, with the occasional touch of an English floral.

Michelle had directed the cart into a window niche, and had seen that two Hepplewhite desk chairs were placed beside it. With the cart's long white tablecloth and plethora of dishes under heat-retaining aluminum domes, the scene reminded Temple of dining on a train long ago. Not that she ever had, but she had seen photographs and wished she had.

Her hostess was wearing orchid silk slacks with a pale blue stretch-satin sleeveless top reminiscent of the fifties, even though it was hot stuff in the designer nineties.

Temple was fascinated by the hostess's angularity. When she sat she folded herself like a flamingo; she seemed all acute angles, knees and elbows. Yet she moved with an almost supernaturally fluid grace.

Michelle Bonard.

"Your name is so familiar," Temple said, shaking out the heavy white linen napkin. "I'm embarrassed to say I don't know why."

Michelle laughed lightly. "It's because my face and body are more important than my name."

"You're a model! You do the series of ads for . . . for—"

" 'Secret, the scent that lulls your senses. You can't keep a man if you don't have a Secret.' "

Now the breathy, slightly accented voice raised an image of magazine ads and television commercials.

"And you were married to Darren Cooke; you were the woman who made a mate out of the world's most . . . famous bachelor."

"You were going to say notorious."

"No, I was *thinking* notorious."

Michelle's weary smile grew a little warmer. Despite her outward calm, she was taking Darren's death poorly. Her skin, pale and perfect, looked almost transparent. Like many very thin women, her face quickly reflected her emotional state. The prominent cheekbones stood out starkly and the hollows beneath them were unhealthy-looking. The thin skin beneath her famous pale blue eyes looked sooty with fatigue.

"It's pasta and vegetables, is that all right?"

Temple started at the question. She had been thinking pasty complexion and rutabaga eye-circles.

"Sure," she answered, taking a serving of the dish Michelle uncovered.

Michelle transferred a half cup of spiral noodles and perhaps three small clumps of broccoli and two of cauliflower to her own plate. Temple wondered if this were the successful model's diet, or the model-in-mourning diet.

"You've done PR in Las Vegas for some time, Miss Barr?"

Temple nodded while the forkful of deliciously seasoned pasta clogged her mouth.

"Almost two years, which is a long time to stay in Las Vegas."

"Darren and I were married three years ago, in December, in Paris."

Temple nodded politely. The waiter had poured them each a glass of wine so red it was almost bloody. Michelle sipped hers.

"No one dreamed he would ever marry, least of all him. No one believed that it would last, though it did, to his death. We spent time apart, given our various commitments on two continents, but . . . the marriage seemed good. He adored his little Cookie-snookie." Michelle's hands covered her face.

Temple went silent, afraid Michelle was crying.

But she was smiling, and the smile lingered when she lifted her head again. "I'm glad he had that opportunity, to know the joy of a child, and that Padgett had an opportunity to know her father. She'll remember him. She's young, but she'll remember him, even if only vaguely."

Temple did not openly disagree, though she wasn't so sure. What did she remember back to the age of two or three? Darn little. She still didn't know why she was here, but figured that Michelle would let her eat most of the meal before she brought up rhymes and reasons, and maybe recriminations. She was a classy lady, and Darren Cooke hadn't deserved her. Maybe that's why he'd killed himself: his insatiable urge to cheat on even the world's nicest, most photogenic bride.

Temple gummed down the main dish as best she could, and picked at the salad. Eating hearty in front of a skeletal widow seemed as bad as giggling at a funeral. Besides, anxiety was turning her stomach into an acid chamber.

"All done?" Michelle observed sadly. Perhaps she felt their somber moods had slighted the food.

Temple nodded and sipped the velvet-soft warm wine. Perfect. "Why did you call me here?" she finally asked.

"You knew my husband."

"Very slightly. 'Knew' is too strong a word. Talked to him briefly on a couple occasions."

"And one of them was the day of his death." The faintly blue eyes rested unblinkingly on Temple's face.

"Yes. But how do you know about me?"

Michelle Bonard bit her bloodless lip, then reached into a side pocket of her lilac pants, which were so tight that Temple was amazed she would store anything there, or attempt to extract it. Ruins the designer lines, you know, like (shudder) cellulite.

What she withdrew was a business card. Temple's card.

Temple studied it, perplexed. "How did you get that?"

"I did not. Darren had it. And, see, he marked the date down himself."

Temple saw the scrawled numbers: eleven seventeen ninety-six. "I don't understand, I gave him this card on . . . Saturday at Gangster's. So why did he write Sunday's date down?"

"Because Darren had a . . . what you call a system. He always took a trophy from his conquests, then marked it with the date of their . . . encounter. He couldn't stop using the system any more than he could help having these encounters. I knew where he concealed his 'evidence.' Not even the police have seen this."

"Wait a minute! I did give him my card, I did attend his Sunday brunch on his invitation, but I never was one of his 'conquests.' "

"You needn't spare my feelings, Miss Barr. I knew all about his past, and his present obsession. I simply want to know his mood on that last day, that last night. Find some reason why he would do it, throw his life away after all these years of struggling with his obsession. As long as the sex was safe, and he assured me it was, I understood that he couldn't stop, and I couldn't let jealousy destroy Cookie's life, and ours."

"I'm not 'sparing' you. I was not Darren Cooke's last lay, that's all. I spoke to him at the brunch, and I do have a clue to why he might have despaired that night. But it doesn't have anything to do with sex, believe me."

Michelle frowned. "He only marked the belongings of women with whom he had sex."

"Well, maybe it was wishful thinking in my case, because it sure didn't happen. Listen, I am currently caught between two men. I do not need any other liaisons cluttering up my already-subdivided heart, mind and body."

She leaned back in her chair, as if to reassess Temple, then sipped her silken wine. "For some reason, I believe you. He never much cared for petite women, or redheads. Then why were you at his brunch?"

"He'd heard Savannah Ashleigh"—Michelle rolled her eyes; that one she would never believe innocent of anything—"call me Nancy Drew."

"Nancy Drew?"

"All-American girl detective from the century's earlier decades. I've . . . stumbled into cases of wrongdoing and have a bit of a reputation as a crime-meddler, if not a crime-solver, around town."

"Crime?" Michelle's back straightened into a ramrod.

"Your husband thought I could help him; I said I'd try, but I

warned him I was an amateur. He took me into the bedroom"—
Michelle's back stiffened even further—"to show me some letters he kept in a manila envelope."

"Blackmail."

"In a sense. Maybe just vitriol. The writer claimed to be an
adult daughter of one of his earliest liaisons. She was bitter, of
course, and taunting. Sounded quite obsessed, and was certainly
hounding him from city to city. I told him he needed the police
to handle this, or a very expensive and discreet detective agency.
He was . . . quite broken up about it, that he hadn't known about
her and that now she hated him. I told him she could be a twisted
fan who only imagined she's his daughter, but I agreed she might
be dangerous, and must be found and charged with harassment."

Michelle had clapped her corded hand over her mouth early
in Temple's recital, her eyes darkening with deep emotions, disbelief, regret, fear and sorrow.

"I don't know why he marked me a conquest," Temple said
softly. "Oh, as I left, he made some sort of veiled suggestion,
which I rather huffily rebuffed. But it was half-hearted, and nothing more than that ever happened between us. I maybe spent forty
minutes with him, between some chitchat at Gangster's and the
tête-à-tête at the Goliath."

"I disagree with your self-assessment, Miss Barr; you seem
to be quite sensible on matters criminal. As for the date on your
card, perhaps, I now think, it was wishful thinking. If he would
do it once, I must wonder how many times since we have been
married it was wishful thinking too. He was no longer young and
perhaps other young women turned him down. How tragic, that
he would keep up the lie of betrayal to me! But then, I always
knew his obsession was more pride than need."

"Why would you take on a man with such a handicap?"

She shrugged in a graceful Gallic manner that said more than
any number of sentences. He was as he was, it said, and I loved
most of that.

"I know," Michelle added, "that he was an excellent father. Of
course, having nannies takes much of the burden of parenthood
away. But he loved our Padgett Cookie like no one on earth, not

even me. She was so innocent, so trusting. She gave him what you call 'unconditional love.' It made him feel secure, and I sense that he was making a genuine attempt to change his ways.

"Then, to hear of this unknown daughter who so reviled him! It would have hurt him very much, because he didn't know. He perhaps began to feel that Padgett would turn on him someday, no matter what he did. Yes, you did have a clue to his state of mind. It must have been very tortured." She turned her bland glance on Temple. "And so have I been, since learning of his death. Suicide. I would never have suspected it of him."

"I don't think that my turning him down was enough—"

"Of course not, Temple." She laid a cold, bony hand on Temple's forearm. "He had ego enough to bounce back from such a shock, and I suspect he'd had more than one such shock of that nature in recent years. As you said, he was automatically reverting to his seducer self. But these letters—have the police got them?"

"I don't know. They don't confide in me. I assumed they'd be found in his room."

She shook her head. "Darren was very clever at hiding things, from everyone. He had to be. These he would have safeguarded more than anything. But I will ask the police. I will at least have them look for this . . . pathetic daughter."

"And how will you say that you knew about them?"

"Do not worry, my dear. I will not implicate you, not after you tried to help Darren with his problem. I will say he mentioned a letter once, casually, and that now I wonder."

"You're pretty clever yourself."

She nodded. "One had to be to marry Darren. Now—" She settled low in her chair and brought the mostly full wine goblet to her bloodless lips. "Tell me about these two men who divide your loyalties. Oh-la-la! What a love life. It sounds fascinating. Perhaps I can be of help."

Chapter 24

Fall of Another Card

Molina wanted to see them downtown. Now. Then she hung up.

Temple and Matt hung onto the phone in her kitchen, ears jammed against the shared earpiece, cheek to cheek, with a bundling board of molded plastic between them.

Temple had done all the talking. Not that there had been much to say. And now the line was dead.

"You're sure we have to do this?" Matt asked Temple.

"You're the arbiter of right and wrong. I thought you'd be cheerleading me to sell myself down the river."

"I'm in worse shape. I might have heard the last person to see Darren Cooke alive arrive at his suite."

"At least you're not the one his wife invited over for pasta only to confront you with evidence that you were the last person to sleep with her husband."

Matt's light tan turned ashen. "Molina's going to ask us why we didn't volunteer this information before."

"We were cowards, plain and simple. You couldn't be sure that your information was relevant to the case, and I was all too sure that mine was, except that it made me look like an idiot."

"You could call it a case of Prejudice and Pride."

"That version of the title does not have a ring to it, and our excuses won't soothe Molina's wrath. In her place I'd be pretty put out with us too."

"You know, that's the first empathetic thing you've said about her."

Temple hung up the dead phone, tired of the guilt-inducing drone of the dial tone, although it perfectly suited her mood.

"There's one thing I'm not going to tell her, even now."

"What's that?"

"It's pure supposition. I'm convinced that Darren's daughter has been stalking him. I bet she's in Las Vegas, and I'm going to find her."

"Temple, that's worse than a needle in a haystack, that's one young woman among one million."

"She wouldn't be far away; she'd want to watch him sweat. I keep thinking that Domingo the flamingo artist being in town just when Darren Cooke was working up his show was perfect timing for someone. Domingo's legion of volunteer flamingo-planters, all with undocumented backgrounds, would provide a perfect cover for a twenty-something Jill the Ripper. I'd really like to nail Domingo's ex-mistress Verina with the role, but she's past forty."

"Why do you have it in for this Verina?"

"She took my hat."

"Remind me not to sit on your cat. I can't imagine what revenge you'd think up then."

Matt ambled into the living room to sit beside Midnight Louie on the ivory sofa. He was wearing khaki and almond; with his blond hair and brown eyes, that made him look both cool and warm at the same time. Temple was starting to regret she'd insisted they confess to Molina. There were much more personal matters to discuss this evening.

Temple joined him on Louie's other side.

Matt rested an elbow on the sofa arm, his face on his fist. "You know, this demented daughter writing ugly letters to her father, calling it stalking, makes me wonder if that's what I'm doing to my stepfather. Whatever he's up to is none of my business. Why I am dogging his trail? Am I a stalker?"

Temple perched on the sofa arm behind him.

"Sure," she said cheerfully. "I don't think you've even figured out yet what you'd do if you actually found him. You might even be a violent stalker."

"That's the scary part." Matt looked up.

"You wouldn't send him hate letters, though."

"Hadn't thought of that. But, no. I'd want to see him face-to-face . . . and then I might strangle the bastard."

Temple tsked. "Not fit language for Our Lady of Guadalupe Church, I imagine."

Matt looked amused. "You can imagine all you want. Priests use strong language in private to express anger, just like anybody else."

"Not all priests."

"No. Some are perfect practitioners of every commandment. When it came to language, I was more often among the lambs than the sheep."

"I don't doubt it," Temple answered, patting his head.

Matt looked up at her again, visibly trying to decide if the gesture was motherly, comradely or something else.

She stood with a grimace. "No time to wallow in comfort and examine our consciences. We've got an appointment at the police department. Hey, I'm wearing leggings. Why don't we take your motorcycle."

"It's Kinsella's motorcycle."

"That's no reason not to take it; besides, Max gave it to Electra."

"Some things you can't give away."

Temple stopped by her front door. "Some things, or some people?"

"It's a rather intimidating machine."

"That's why I want to ride it, silly. Conquer my fears."

"That knit jacket won't cut it; I finally had to find something to replace my windbreaker. The street gets cold these November evenings."

"I've got a great little leather jacket that should be just the thing."

"You don't have a helmet." ·

Temple paused, then lit up. "Electra's not using her 'Speed Queen' number."

"I've never had a passenger before. The new weight might throw things off. I might dump you in the street."

"I'm little, as I often lament. I won't add much weight. Mister, please, I ain't heavy."

"You aren't my brother," he answered sardonically, "but you're sure acting like a whiny kid sister."

"You never had one of those, although I admit I was everybody's kid sister in my family. Consider this a making-up-for-lost-time experience on your part."

"Bratty, demanding kid sister is more like it. I'll run up and get my jacket while you get yours. And sturdier footwear is advised."

Temple pranced into her bedroom. What, did he think these dainty heels were all she owned? She had some kicky ankle-high boots for horseback-riding-if-it-ever-came-up hidden somewhere. She hadn't ridden a horse in years, so it was only in the farthest, lowest, darkest part of her closet that she found the tumbled boots and the cream-colored leather jacket.

What had replaced Matt's unexciting navy nylon windbreaker, Temple wondered as she kicked off shoes and struggled into boots. Was she going to be visited with Electra's vision of Matt-black leather? Temple shrugged into the elderly jacket, which was a teensy bit snug. Eek! Just touch thirty and your weight was creeping up already.

She hurried back to her door as Matt arrived from upstairs. Her prediction had been right, no macho black leather for golden boy. He wore a sheepskin jacket, and looked a little sheepish.

"It's synthetic," he explained. "The real stuff is pricey, and I don't like to know a sheep died for my sins."

"Radical, and politically correct!" Temple took his arm as

they walked to the elevator. "Looks good on you too. Molina will swoon and Electra will be rabid that I got to see it before she did."

He shrugged her arm off, embarrassed as usual by the thought that what he wore might attract attention. Or women. "I needed something warmer and inexpensive."

"So practical," Temple cooed, unable to resist teasing.

Yet Matt's sternly practical instincts had steered him right to the most flattering item. As far as Temple was concerned, black-leather, Marlon Brando motorcycle chic had just been dethroned.

"Molina's working late," Temple noted as they stepped out into a Maxfield Parrish twilight, the sky a warm indigo-blue bowl in the distance.

"Do you think she ever stops?"

"Only to sing for her supper."

Mutual memories of encountering Molina as the house thrush for the Blue Dahlia made them smile.

Matt unlocked Electra's shed and tossed Temple the racy silver helmet labeled SPEED QUEEN.

"I love it! I feel so kicky, right out of *Blackboard Jungle.*"

"You weren't even born when that movie came out. I'll start the cycle and ease it out of the shed. You relock the shed and hop aboard," Matt suggested.

Temple skittered outside, just happy to be there. The motorcycle was so huge close up. It dominated the small shed like a rodeo bull temporarily trapped in a chute before breaking free to kick loose in the arena.

And the noise! She quickly pulled on the bulbous helmet and fastened the chin strap. She knew when she lowered the sinister, tinted visor that she'd see night all around her and that nobody could see her face. Cool.

"These helmets don't have transceivers built in," Matt shouted, visor up, from amid the sound and fury of the revving Hesketh Vampire.

Temple nodded broadly. They'd be unable to communicate. Verbally.

The Vampire came *rhur-rhur*ing out, then paused to gargle disgruntledly. Temple ran to padlock the double shed doors, then turned to face her moment of truth.

The motorcycle seat was longer and broader than she had thought. But she had ridden horses, great huge beasts, so this would be a piece of coconut cake. Maybe. The lift-over was as thigh-stretching as a horseback for her short legs, and she settled onto the hard leather seat with an unintentionally punishing slap. Next, she couldn't find the footrests, not until she stretched her legs way out and pointed her toes. Of course there was nothing convenient to hang onto but Matt, and her passenger position wouldn't really work unless she scooted up right behind him, which she did, snaking her bare hands into the faux sheepskin side pockets of his jacket.

"Ready?" he shouted.

She just tightened her grip and then the Vampire leaped into the street like a runaway horse.

Galloping gallons of gas! She had never noticed that motorcycles tilted this way and that so much. As they turned into the street, Temple felt almost parallel to the pavement and clutched onto the flannel pocket linings until she thought they would rip out. The wind, absorbed by Matt ahead of her, still had plenty of pummel left in it for her.

And the traffic loomed all around them like an encroaching herd, pale circles of headlights and highly polished rumps . . . er, rear fenders . . . of neighboring vehicles.

Temple curled her fingers into the lining of Matt's pockets for dear life.

Luckily, nowhere was far from anywhere else in Las Vegas, which still adhered to its simple desert-town layout.

"Oh, look!" Temple couldn't help shouting to the wind. "Domingo's flamingos are lit up at night!"

She actually unclutched and removed a hand to point, but a Ford Taurus sped by so fast she was almost about to be known as "Knuckles" for the rest of her life.

She replaced her hand in a hurry, remembering that Matt couldn't hear her no matter how well she projected. A motorcycle was no bicycle built for two; it was the eye of its own howlingly cold hurricane. No matter how cozy motorcycle couples look, pasted to each other as they are, she was finding it to be a solitary ride.

Soon, though, the Vampire turned into the deeper dark of the parking ramp behind the Las Vegas Metropolitan Police Department—again almost scraping Temple off on the concrete floor— and purred into an empty third-level space.

Temple sighed her relief as the engine rumbled to a muffled roar, then quieted entirely when Matt turned it off and kicked the stand into place. Temple wasn't sure her legs would ever desert their wishbone position; she would be doomed to bowleg around like a broncobuster forever. Her lovely shoe collection would look laughable at the ends of her pathetic, hooped legs. She would be drafted for croquet games the rest of her life!

Unbending, she tried to hop off; Matt caught her before she could fall over.

"Took me two weeks," he said, "to get comfortable on this silly thing."

"Will it be safe here?" Temple wondered, eyeing the impressive machine as they walked away.

"I locked it; that's the best you can do. If I ever have to tell Electra it's been stolen, I'd hate that."

"You'd most hate having lost something that was once Max's," she added astutely.

Matt stopped to stuff his buff leather gloves in his jacket pockets. "Yeah. I should have told you to wear gloves."

"That's okay. I had to hang onto your pockets anyway. We better forget about our mode of transportation and start thinking about how to handle Molina."

"She'll handle us, as always," Matt said dryly. "I never saw anyone so seriously devoted to her calling, except maybe me. Who wants to go first?"

"I should. I have the guiltier secret. She'll be mad, and rightly so."

"Temple. Don't look like an abandoned basset hound!"

"Oh, thanks! But I ain't gonna like this."

"I'll be there." He put his arm around her shoulder.

A sudden warmth and confidence spread through her chilled frame. This was better than a motorcycle ride anyday.

Inside the garage stairway, signs directed them down to the entry level, where they had to check in with the desk sergeant. One just didn't waltz into the back door of a police station; that would mean too many could simply waltz out.

The large entry area was brightly lit, a shock after the darkening night and the parking ramp's blackness. Its wall of windows faced onto the concrete area between this building and the Hoover Dam–sheer face of the opposite building.

The sergeant gave them no guff, being a disappointingly pleasant, helpful type. He called up, and they were duly instructed that someone would be down for them.

They had been here a couple of times before, and knew there was nothing glamorous about a police headquarters, except its lack of glamour. That's what gave it flavor, the sense of overworked people coping as best they could, with littered desktops and crowded offices and squad rooms, with busy bathrooms and eternally plugged in coffeepots.

Matt and Temple followed their uniformed guide into the elevators in silence, and were finally shown into a long, narrow office cramped for space but crammed with file cabinets and folders.

Molina sat at the room's far end, behind a desk covered with neat paperwork piles.

"This feels like going in to see the principal," Temple gritted through her teeth to Matt.

"Wouldn't know," he gritted back.

"Goody Two-shoes," she gibed.

Molina put her fingertips to both sides of her eyes, as if acknowledging a headache, or the sight of two such approaching.

"Sit."

The chairs she indicated were plain and wooden, a lot less comfortable than the Vampire's hard leather seat.

"From your call, apparently you both failed to tell me relevant information about the Darren Cooke death. It's not really my case, but when your"—she nodded at Matt—"hot-line card was found in the deceased's possession, someone had to check it out and I had the overriding interest."

Her vivid blue eyes floated in pale maroon circles of fatigue. Her abstract tone of weary disappointment was even more marked.

"I won't do it again, Mother!" Temple was tempted to shout. She glanced at Matt. He was giving Molina his rapt, polite attention, like a perfect student.

"I'm surprised you would hold back relevant information," she told him. He winced ever so slightly.

"Matt felt he couldn't violate the confidentiality of a client," Temple said.

"Unfortunate, but understandable. And what is your excuse for keeping my daughter at the sitter's long past suppertime?"

Now Temple winced. "I thought you—the police—would find it. I didn't realize until recently that you hadn't."

"And what didn't we find?"

"For one thing, my card, which Darren Cooke had possession of at the time of his death, apparently." Temple was falling right into the police patois. *Had possession of* indeed.

"You think this card is a witness, or what? And how did you learn that he did have it?"

"From his wife. She found the card, and incorrectly assumed that I . . . was an inamorata of his."

"Again, please. In English."

"Oh, you know what inamorata means, all right! A musical person like you, Lieutenant. You just want me to squirm. I was attending his regular Sunday brunch, at his personal invitation."

"Why should he invite you?"

"We were working on the same set at Gangster's. Theater people make quick acquaintances and slow friends."

"And this happy crossing of paths made you bosom buddies with the late Mr. Cooke."

"No, but he had heard Savannah Ashleigh, who once was very bosom buddy with Mr. Cooke, refer to me as 'Nancy Drew.' So—"

Molina pushed back her seat and almost laid her cheek on the desk. She laughed. Finally, her head lifted and she examined the objects hung on her wall as if inviting them to participate in her merriment. She even glanced at Matt with tear-filled eyes, expecting him to join her hyena act.

But of course he didn't. He was too anxious about his own confession to enjoy another's discomfort.

"Nancy Drew!" Molina was still laughing. "Perfect, and here I thought Savannah Ashleigh's brains were all in her pure-bred cat."

"They are," Temple snapped. "And she had a very hot fling with Darren Cooke a couple years back, if you're interested."

Molina the Poker-faced could sober up instantly once she had fallen victim to humor. She composed her expression to the usual deadpan. "Yes, Nancy?"

"I'm not gonna call you Bess. But I will tell you what I should have told you three days ago. His wife thought I was . . . the other woman. *A* other woman," she corrected. "*An* other woman?"

"And why would anyone think Darren Cooke would proposition you?"

"Because he did! But, don't worry, I left in a huff of injured virtue."

"Is that why his wife thought you and he had—?"

"The fact that I was there, that I went into his bedroom for a few minutes . . . it was perfectly innocent, but I knew people would smirk and rush to the wrong conclusion, which was why I kept quiet about the other thing. It's enough to have a widow ringing you up because she thinks you were her dead husband's last lay and she wants to know his state of mind—"

Molina was her old, stoic self again. "Why was she so sure?"

"He always kept a trophy of his . . . inamoratas, on which he wrote the date of their one-night stand, as a kind of keepsake, or scorecard. For some reason, he'd written Sunday's date on my business card, so naturally his wife assumed—"

"Where did he hide that card? We searched that suite from whirlpool to coffeemaker."

"You'll have to ask Michelle."

"Michelle?"

"Yes, we became quite good friends once she realized that I wasn't his last stand, so to speak. She's French, you know. Michelle Bonard, a world-famous French model, but she's a wonderful mother and she even advised me on my love life."

Oh! She had been rattling on and then . . . Temple didn't dare look at Matt. Or Molina. She studied the framed document on the wall over Molina's shoulder. Some kind of degree, or award, with thick, tortured calligraphy.

"She's at the Crystal Phoenix," she finished.

Molina leaned forward to prop her elbows on what free space remained on the glass-topped desk. "Miss Barr's love life. Now *that* I'd like to hear. Wouldn't you, Mr. Devine?"

"No, I don't care for idle speculation."

"Then you're not cut out to be an investigator."

"I know I'm not. I was trained to hold other people's confidences as sacred, no matter what."

"And this is where your part of the confession comes in."

"No, not yet." Temple drew the harsh spotlight of Molina's attention back to herself. "You see, Darren Cooke really did need a Nancy Drew. That's what he told me in the bedroom. He showed me a manila envelope, an ordinary nine-by-twelve-inch envelope, but inside was an extraordinary collection of letters dating back, oh, a couple of years."

"Love letters?"

Temple shook her head.

"Blackmail letters."

"No, hate letters, pure and simple. From a young woman who claimed she was his daughter. She was bitterly angry, blamed him for everything that had gone wrong in her mother's life and her own. I was sure the police would find something as big as a manila envelope. But Michelle told me that you hadn't, as far as she knew, and that even she hadn't known about the letters. Michelle said that you didn't even find my card because her late husband was exceptionally clever at hiding things. That was his whole life: hiding things, especially from himself."

"And yet he told *you,* a virtual stranger, all about the letters."

"He was feeling the pressure. That's why I think he was

calling Matt. He really wanted to change, but his obsession with seduction was too strong. His wife knew about it, and thinks he was no longer able to attract the foxy young things he'd been used to. He was really anguished about those letters. And sorry that this 'daughter's' mother had kept her existence hidden from him. A couple of years ago, he and Michelle had a first child, a baby daughter he adored; maybe he would have adored this adult daughter if he'd had a chance. He wasn't as afraid of her as I thought he should be. I told him he had to contact the po-lice—"

"Thank you for that." Molina inclined her head as slowly as Queen Victoria. Tall, dark-haired women with morning-glory eyes can get away with those sorts of gestures, Temple had found. She couldn't.

"I told him that if he wouldn't contact the police, he should try some pricey, discreet Beverly Hills private-investigation agency."

"Astute, if not forthcoming."

"He wouldn't have done it. I could tell. And, then, when I was leaving, he made a veiled suggestion."

"Aha. The wolf pounces on the helpful little lamb."

"I was so angry. He was ignoring my advice, but apparently he could find me horizontally useful. I told him a no-shilly-shallying no and got out of there. I wanted to forget about the encounter. I both felt sorry for him, and despised him. So pathetic and so true-to-form. So when I heard he'd killed himself that very night, I figured that you'd find the letters."

Molina remained quiet, doodling on her legal-pad deskmat for a moment. "So you think he could have been murdered—?"

"Maybe. Though, the mood he was in, having struck out in his half-hearted seduction and worried sick about this disenchanted daughter, suicide could be likely."

"And what do you think?"

Molina had spun to drill her memorably blue eyes into Matt's.

He refused to bolt, speaking in a flat, reportorial tone. "You know I've been receiving calls at ConTact for several weeks from a sexual addict. A man with an impressive speaking voice. He's also an impressive manipulator, which comes with the addict's territory."

"You've concluded this was Darren Cooke?"

"This could have been Darren Cooke. I don't know for sure yet. If he never calls again—" Matt shrugged, and then shrugged the sheepskin jacket, which was much too hot for a small office, onto his chair back.

Molina, Temple noticed, was riveted on his every move.

"The incident that Temple wants me to tell you," Matt went on, "was one I was reluctant to report to anybody. I'm simply not sure who I've been talking to all these weeks. This call came Sunday at about midnight."

Molina was no longer riveted on Matt, but on his testimony. And she didn't interrupt him as much as she did Temple. *Sexist!*

Matt toyed with a leather button on his new jacket. That way he could look down and talk more to himself.

"I tried not to judge him, but he would never take positive steps to work on his addiction. I found out last week that he was calling me not only from out of town—I was supposed to think I was vital to him—but that he'd been calling other phone counselors." Matt smiled sadly. "He had to know more than whomever he was dealing with. A tragic personality."

Molina could wait no longer for the tale to tell itself. "So. Sunday night. At midnight."

"I got another call. He alternated between dependency riffs and angry rejection."

"Of you?"

"Of course of me. In these situations, the counselor is the punching bag. He is everybody the caller thinks failed him in life. And then, his tone suddenly changed. I could hear him moving around with his portable phone, answering the door. Apparently what he craved was standing right there. 'Hello, baby,' I heard him say. 'Just what the doctor ordered. Come on in!' He hung up before I heard his visitor speak. That's all."

"That's all? You could have heard the arrival of the last person to see Darren Cooke alive."

"Yes, but what good does that do? I don't know who came to

visit, or why or what happened next. Temple's main concern is that you find the missing letters. Perhaps his widow would know where to hunt for them. She found Temple's card quickly enough."

"Temple's card. Marked with the ritual seal of successful seduction." Molina smiled conspiratorially at Matt. "Is our little Miss Temple as innocent as she would have us think? She has a nasty habit of withholding information from the police. See the Mystifying Max."

Temple jumped in. "I never knew where Max was or why he might have been gone."

"But now that he's returned . . . don't you know more?"

Temple hesitated. "Not enough," she muttered.

Molina hit the flat of her hands on the desk in dismissal.

"I've made what notes are relevant. Miss Barr, if we find that missing manila envelope, I'll have to ask you to identify the contents. Mr. Devine, I presume your hot line doesn't have caller ID?"

He shook his head.

"Why didn't you simply refuse this tiresome sexual addict's calls?"

"I didn't have the heart to cut him loose. He was genuinely troubled, and trying to find a way to help himself, albeit falteringly."

"Albeit. An old-fashioned term. Bet you learned that in seminary." Molina nodded. "Okay, youse two disreputables can go. Frankly, I don't think either one of you concealed anything worth spit, but don't do it again."

"Yes, ma'am," Temple said.

"Thanks," Matt added with a slow smile

They left, both feeling quite virtuous.

"Confession *is* good for the soul," Temple said en route to the parking garage.

"That's what I was brought up to believe."

"I'm glad she took it so well."

"That's because she doesn't think that what you saw and what

I heard are important, thank God. I hope that this doesn't turn out to be one of your murders."

"What do you mean, 'my murders.' "

"Only that you are a verifiable murder magnet. Suicide would be a nice change of pace; though, speaking from a religious point of view, it's the far more tragic death."

"Can't go to heaven, and all that? That's the Holy Roman Catholic Church for you; kick even the dead when they're down."

Matt stopped under the low, dark concrete beams. "The sin of suicide is in the enormity of denying God's will in your life by taking your own life. A great sin. Granted, the suicide himself is a pathetic soul, often under the influence of severe depression."

"Then why punish him after death? In absentia. Seems cowardly to a mealy-mouthed Unitarian like me."

"We'd have to go into about two years of theology to examine all the issues."

"That's it. Why can't religion be more accessible than that? Why can't mercy be the operating system, instead of right and wrong as written down somewhere by self-proclaimed holy men who are afraid to let women and children and suicides speak?"

Matt shook his head as he buttoned his jacket. "I'm not going to argue theology with you; it's too darn cold. Better bundle up for the trip back."

Temple suddenly produced a wicked grin. "I will."

The Vampire coughed before the engine released its full power and took the motorcycle by the throat.

Temple donned Electra's helmet and hopped aboard, only wincing slightly at the stretch. This time she wrapped her arms all the way around Matt until they met in front.

If he found their riding arrangement more claustrophobic than before, he couldn't say a thing over the warming engine's roar. They swooped down the corkscrew exit ramp, Temple wanting to scream as if she were on a roller coaster. She caught her breath while he paused to pay the ticket. Matt got the financially short end of the deal. Temple, clinging like a leech for the chilly ride home, couldn't get to the money she had jammed in her jacket pocket when leaving her trademark tote bag behind.

Outside, stars gleamed high in the sky. Except for a red lash-mark along the horizon, the sun had vanished, letting the lights of Las Vegas perform their nocturnal magic.

Temple did feel she was on a roller coaster as streetlights streaked by. Passing cars became greased lightning as the wind pulled and pushed the Vampire to top speed.

Matt didn't go straight home, but headed into the dark desert, where the highway eventually became a road that swelled up and down, that curved right and left. Temple's bare fingers stiffened in the brunt of the wind, but that only locked them tighter into position, and pressed her closer to Matt, thigh to thigh, chest to back, warm cheek to chill faux sheepskin.

Not being able to talk over the windrush and the Vampire's lonely howl in the wilderness underlined the ride's strange intimacy. After only a few minutes, the Vampire etched a semicircle in the empty, sand-dusted highway. In front of them, the lights of Las Vegas now beckoned on the horizon like an electrified bonfire.

The Vampire sped straight for that tropical, topical warmth. Temple no longer considered the motorcycle a machine under human control, but an animate, metaphorical beast, a steed . . . a warhorse or a dragon or something so old that nobody alive knew its name anymore.

She knew that Matt had not known where they were going when he had headed into the darkness, that neither he nor she could say where they had been and that even the Vampire didn't need to know how to get back home. Click your heels, close your eyes and follow the Strip's bright afterimage searing through your lids. The road became arrow-straight as they neared the city. Cars came crowding around again, like moths hungry for the Vampire's pale, gleaming silver skin and hypnotic howl.

Watch out, she thought. *Vampires bite!*

A more mundane mob of cars, vans, trucks and taxis finally slowed the Vampire to a docile speed. When they arrived at the Circle Ritz, Temple felt as if she had been trapped in an icy, crystal-clear bell jar amid a maelstrom of sound and speed, unnaturally alone in a vast natural world and yet not alone. Maybe this was how the Biblical prophets had felt when they saw God in mountain peaks and fiery bushes.

She dismounted, disoriented, to rejoin still, solid ground, and let Matt put the Vampire to bed alone. When he came out and locked the doors, she turned with a smile.

"That was scary, but it scared away all the anxiety too. Have you ever driven out into the desert like that, Matt? Just for fun?"

"I've never done anything just for fun," he said. "But I might be up for trying it."

"I'm sorry I criticized your religion's positions. They just seem so set in cold, hard stone."

"Don't be sorry. Maybe that's what religious positions are for: to be questioned, ridiculed and sometimes thrown out."

"Goodness! I think that's exactly what happened to us in Molina's office tonight."

After a pause of agreement, he laughed.

Chapter 25

Under the Volcano

I am beginning to chafe at my lack of freedom.

The Divine Yvette, of course, is used to being cooped up for her own good. I am used to being out and about for my own bad.

Also, I am concerned about the welfare of my other little doll, Miss Temple Barr. It has not missed my astute observation—despite being aswamp in the trappings of stardom and its ensuing problems, such as fratricidal envy—that Miss Temple has been not only unusually busy, but rather blue lately.

For this I blame myself.

I have been neglecting her and her trivial concerns. In my rejoicing at the recent absence of the Mystifying Max, I have not considered that another individual might actually miss the Mr. Question Mark. Although I spot traces of Mr. Matt Devine (namely a certain scent unmarked by any bad habits on the living-room loveseat—pardon me, sofa), I also scent that Miss Temple has been out and about in new terrains with new people. It can mean only that she is on a case, nose to the trail. Yet how can I help her out if I am chained to my cameras and my crew?

I decide to disrupt the proceedings in such a way that shooting will stop for a time, and the only possible path to this goal is one that involves a mishap to the Divine Yvette. If my darling should so much as crack a razor-sharp nail, her mistress will scream and carry on and remove DY from the set to go off and pout and not come back for days. Well, maybe a day or so.

A day or so may be all Midnight Louie needs to discover Miss Temple's case secrets, ferret out the perpetrator, nail him or her and get Miss Temple onto more wholesome projects, such as seducing Mr. Matt Devine. (I am not crazy about his presence in my home, but he is far more palatable than the Mystifying Max. That guy is a real upstart, and no respecter of territories.)

Today we are filming under the volcano.

I kid you—not!

The Divine Yvette has been wrapped in some sort of floral sarong, with a delicate lavender orchid behind one ear that really brings out the lilac tone in her shaded markings. I would not need a little grass shack in Hawaii to shack up with this doll; though, of course, I would not be so crass as to take advantage of a co-star.

Anyway, this volcano, the streetside attraction at the Mirage, goes off on schedule like a baby with croup. Wham, bam, up shoot the flames, down pours the water into the lagoon below, where the Divine Yvette and I recline on a nest of leis.

Those flowers get sticky when crushed, and my weight is turning them into marzipan. So my coat is sticky, not to mention stinky, and even the Divine Yvette is showing the slightest bit of temperament.

"Get me out of this flower graveyard!" she yowls to all and sundry. "I do not like blossoms, only greenery and only when I can eat it. Louie, my love, help me! The scent is overpoweringly awful."

I am a wee bit surprised, as the scent in the Divine One's powder (not her selection, of course) is a bit strong for my sensitive sniffer, employed as it has been of late on murder scenes and such. Give me a reek of fresh blood and I can follow a trail anywhere!

The crew has devised this nasty tippycanoe I believe they call an outrigger, on which the Divine One and I are to float like Caesar and Cleopatra.

I am well aware that if there is one thing that will send the Divine Yvette and her mistress into a screaming fit that could pass for an operatic aria, it is if the Divine Yvette should Get Wet.

What kind of cad, you may ask, would get his ladylove wet, especially if that ladylove has a particular allergy to moist surfaces? A cad indeed. But I am torn between two females exceptionally dear to my heart: Miss Temple Barr, who needs my immediate assistance (for she will get nowhere without me, though she will not admit it), and the perfect pearl of Persian pulchritude, the Divine Yvette.

I can swim, having been introduced to water at a very early age, in a sack.

So I can ensure that the Divine Yvette is perfectly safe (as she is perfectly everything else), and even do the feline water rescue, which involves biting the back of her neck (yum-yum) and holding her afloat as I paddle us to shore.

By the way, I would not advise dudes of ordinary weight, strength and endurance to try this trick. I am specially trained at rescue attempts. (Some may remember my death-defying aquatic acrobatics during an escapade at the Treasure Island's ship-dueling attraction.)

So there I sit when they plunk us two in the tippycanoe. (Did I not mention that I am wearing a Hawaiian shirt of most nauseating color and design, the kind Mr. Mystifying

Max dons as a disguise—he says, but I think he likes them.)

Ye gods! First hats, then shirts. What will they hang upon this long-suffering hide next? Three-piece suits? Do not give them any bright ideas.

Anyway, the DY and myself on our tippycanoe look like we are asail on a florist's funeral barge.

"I do not like water, Louie," the Divine Yvette admits in her most private purr. "The Love Moat at the Goliath was all right because I knew the water was shallow and you were there, but this is a huge lagoon—"

"Hush, my silver seductress." (You have to use this smoochy language with dames to get their attention.) "I am here also. Nothing will happen."

That is when my toes feel the infringement of a liquid element. I wriggle them, thinking that they have gone asleep. The cold wet feeling moves up my lower limbs. No doubt the close, powdered presence of the Divine Yvette has turned the blood in my veins into water. Cold water.

I look down. It is dark despite the camera lights focused on our every move. Still, I see wavelets nipping at the edge of the Divine Yvette's sarong. I look out at the water on which our tippycanoe rides. Those waves are bigger, but of the same ilk.

Apparently, someone else has figured that this is a tippycanoe and has helped my plan along, quite inadvertently.

I look to the shore, crowded with camera crew, lights, the animal trainer with the evil Maurice in her arms.

In the night light his pale whiskers shine like ectoplasm. The artificial lights all around paint a fiendish expression on his vapid puss face.

Our vessel is much farther out in the lagoon than I had planned as the site of a sudden dip in the Deep. In fact, I sense great depths around us, perhaps even fifteen feet.

I glance at the Divine Yvette.

"Can you swim?"

"Certainly not! That would involve dampening the hairs of my coat with other than the dry shampoo my mistress employs a groomer to use. I might get a . . . "—sniff—"cold."

"You will get cold. Observe."

The Divine Yvette's perfectly round aquamarine orbs widen as they focus on the boat's bottom.

"Louie! That is water!"

"I am aware of what it is."

"And we are—oh, my dear mistress!—miles from shore."

"Only yards."

"Louie, you must get me out of this! Immediately!"

At last she has given me permission to do the unthinkable. I throw my full twenty pounds from one side of the tippycanoe to the other. In a moment the outrigger and bottom lift out of the lagoon.

The Divine Yvette emits a piercing cry, which is matched by a wail from shore.

"Louie!" my Miss Temple bellows, using all her lung power and wisely eschewing screaming, "swim for the far shore."

I glance across the light-polished wavelets. Miss Temple is right. We are now closer to the far bank. With a last desperate lunge, I take the nape of the Divine Yvette's slender neck in my teeth and roll us both into the cold, wet, dark water.

Above us the tilted tippycanoe hangs for a moment like a shelter before crashing down on us.

I remember my daring dive from the flaming deck of the Treasure Island pirate ship. That scene flashes before my closed eyes as the Divine Yvette and I plunge deep into the lagoon. The Divine Yvette is a petite thing, but she has a lot of hair to absorb water. Now, I must reverse our swift downward, drowning descent and paddle us both to the surface.

I have never worked so hard in my life! My teeth are

clenched in a death grip on the Divine Yvette's neck, in the hold her pedigreed mama used to cart her to and fro as a tiny kitten.

She is not so tiny now, nor am I. In this situation my fighting weight works against me. I can only windmill all four limbs, waiting for our freefall through the water to reverse its pull and let us pop to the surface like a cork. Er, like a cork from the finest bottle of French champagne, in case the Divine Yvette recovers and asks me to refine my figures of speech. How can a dude who does not talk have figures of speech? You got me.

And right now the water's icy, dark hands are wringing the strength from my body. I flail, and finally am rewarded by a sudden waft upward. And upward and upward. And upward and upward. I wish I could see light, but all is dark, and I am no longer sure whether we are drifting upward or plunging down.

Even when my head breaks the water's surface and I see and hear a lion of a volcano shooting flames into the black Vegas sky, I cannot believe it. In a minute the Divine Yvette's head bobs up alongside me, her eyes squeezed so shut a crowbar couldn't open them.

"Can you paddle?" I ask.

"I do not swim."

"Can you spread your toes and move your feet up and down?"

"Spread my toes? Louie, please! I only do so for the most intimate grooming rituals."

"Get intimate and get grooming, or you will drown like an unwanted kitten," I growl.

"I was never an unwanted kitten! I am the product of decades of the finest and most precise breeding techniques—"

I haul a mitt out of the water and smack her in the kisser. Sometimes dames require a firm hand, particularly when they are hysterical, or on a genealogy kick.

Turning my head (and inadvertently the Divine Yvette's

unconscious one) I do the hardest thing I have ever done. I spot Miss Temple's fiery red hair in the crowd by the cameras, and I run for all my might away from her. I am running in water, you understand, toes spread, so what I am doing is swimming.

The Divine Yvette is a terrible burden. My jaws are frozen with strain. But I cannot let loose of her. My long, luxuriant tail has become a liability that could pull us both under. I struggle on, my head never high enough above the waves to see the shoreline for which I aim.

I can see the volcano, though, coughing up its bloody fire and rock, reflected in the water all around me.

I am swimming through icy fire, every limb aching with effort, my mind numbed by cold, even the Divine Yvette a mere memory. If I live through this, I will kill that Maurice!

Still, in my benumbed brain I hear an encouraging refrain: "Come on, Louie! Come on, boy!"

You would think I were Lassie.

The thought of being mistaken for a dog is so repellent that my flailing legs find new strength. I feel more light hitting the top of my head as the surrounding water seems punctured by stars.

In another moment human legs are splashing into the water around me. Yvette and I are lifted, her neck still clenched in my teeth, out of the water.

Miss Temple's face hangs over mine. "He is alive!"

A camera flashes beyond her, and all I can think is, I am still wearing that damn Hawaiian shirt.

This mishap could kill my career.

Chapter 26

Matt's Off Night

Walking the Strip resembles being lost on a carnival midway. Like a moving sidewalk, the Strip gives the impression that the people are standing still while the earth moves beneath them. No matter how long Matt kept walking, he felt he would never reach the end.

It reminded him of Sartre's brilliant play, *No Exit*, and its rather cynical line that "Hell is other people."

Even when pedestrians deserted the sidewalk for a long trek toward the dazzling entrance façade of a major hotel-casino, Matt suspected that they soon recycled back onto the Strip's implacable length and unquenchable brightness.

Somewhere in this milling mass of Thursday-night humanity, Cliff Effinger might be stepping on and off the merry-go-round like everyone else.

Matt studied the passing parade, mentally reminding himself of the facial features of the man he was looking for. He found it hard not to be distracted by the fascinating variety of fellow strollers.

Tourists, of course, made up the bulk of the walkers, their clothes casual despite the cooler night air. Walking is the economy class's favored mode of transportation. Those who can afford to taxi up and down the Strip do so.

Did that mean Cliff Effinger, seen on foot, was pinching pennies? Or hiding his loot from various scams? That was the trouble with supposition: every conclusion generated another legitimate possibility.

Matt saw fallen trashy magazines littering the sidewalk edges. Waiting men jammed fistfuls of the pulp paper at passersby. Never at women, only men, and never at a man alone.

Crushed underfoot, revealing photographs offered private dancers and total fulfillment. Matt wondered whose grown-up little girls and boys these nakedly seductive people were, and what kind of people those parents were.

Not so easy to dismiss the seamier side of life nowadays, when the villain wasn't that easy-to-blame old devil Sin so much as dysfunctional family cycles. What fun was there in stoning someone who had to be analyzed unto the fifth generation backward in time?

Did Cliff Effinger have a grim family history to excuse his pathetic bullying? Was he more to be pitied than condemned? Matt felt his fists ball in his jacket pockets. No. Some people were just bad. Evil. In the power of that old devil Sin.

He veered onto the long, curving sweep of sidewalk that approached the megahotel rising in the distance at an oblique, coy angle. The straightaway was for King Car, the contraption that had first made Las Vegas a feasible resort for Hollywoodites three hundred miles away.

Who would have suspected that the hoi polloi, not Hollywood, would make this desert gambling oasis rich? Even a lowlife like Cliff Effinger had come here to make his fortune.

Long walks were a form of meditation. Once inside a casino, meditation was not an option.

Noise and light bloomed around Matt like a migraine headache as he pushed through the darkened entry doors. The slot-machine jingle sounded like Christmas, but the spirit of Las Vegas's eternal gambling season was receiving, not giving. People, machinelike themselves, sat before clanking, gear-spinning mechanisms that spit back the occasional coin like bad change.

When Matt removed his gloveless right hand from his pocket, his palm was damp. But the plastic-laminated sketch of Cliff Effinger was impervious now to heat and moisture, preserved.

Matt wondered who to approach. Was he expected to tip for attention? If so, he'd be broke within days. Once more he mentally rehearsed his story. Lying, or even bending the truth, still took a lot of rehearsal. He was the opposite of a con man, he wanted to sell the truth even when he knew there would be no takers.

"Excuse me."

The waitress wore something shiny and slithery and scanty, but her face beneath the cheap, harsh makeup was even bleaker.

"Yeah, hon?" Bright tone, the better to cadge tips.

"I'm looking for someone. You might have seen him." Matt flashed the sketch in the insufficient light that was always bright but as tremulous as a firefly.

"Somebody cared enough to do a portrait," she commented. "Relative of yours?"

"My . . . brother."

"You're a lot younger than he is, hon. A lot cuter too." Her blackened lashes lowered to the sketch, her comment a fact, not a flirtation.

"My mother . . . married twice."

Her eyes rolled. "Mine too. And believe me, number two was no improvement. Hey! At least they married." She frowned at the shiny plastic. "That cowboy type is rare these days. They're up in Colorado now, all the Stetson boys. This guy looks a lotta years behind the times."

"He did . . . drop out of sight."

"Maybe. I mighta seen him, oh, couple months ago. Not a regular, though. Want a drink?"

She tilted her round glass-laden tray to him.

"Isn't that somebody else's?"

She shrugged. "I can get 'em another one of whatever you take where that came from. They're all free in the gaming area. You look like you could stand some warming up. It's cold out there on the Strip tonight. Stay here and run the slots a while. I come by regularly."

Matt shook his head, closing his fingers over Effinger's too-good likeness. Should he ask someone else? Maybe.

The waitress had minced away on her Temple-like high heels. She was old for the outfit, and probably knew it. It was cold out there on the Strip.

Matt wandered away from the clattering slot machines into the blackjack and craps areas. He couldn't envision Effinger playing baccarat. The dealers watched the cards, the cameras hidden in the ceiling above watched the dealers and the players and the pit bosses kept an eagle eye on everybody.

He'd talked to one before and found him forthcoming. Older men, seasoned in smoke-filled rooms clinking with ice in glasses. Heavyset usually. The casino's authority figures, not unlike bishops. On a chessboard, he remembered, a bishop could move diagonally. In the church, the bishop's only option was up . . .

If he thought of these men as bishops, he would get on with them better. But no "Your Reverences," only an inner air of respect. Perhaps that's what the heads of crime families expected too.

"Excuse me. Has this man been in here recently?"

The man eyed Matt, ruling out cop and P.I. with expert speed. "Lost relative."

"Right."

"We get a lot of those. And they appreciate it if we don't mention it even if we did see 'em. That's why cameras aren't allowed in the casino area."

"The reason isn't security?"

"Nah. Not our security, anyway. It's theirs." He gazed out on his rowdy flock with a shepherd's satisfaction. "Don't want the folks back in Pineapple Junction to see 'em."

"This guy's a gambler, all right." Matt weighed his forth-coming lies, wondering which false tack would be most effec-tive. "We lost track of him, and now Mom's gonna die. She's all we got left. And there's . . . a lot of money involved."

"And you're lookin' for him? I would think you'd want the lost sheep to stay lost."

"Oh, no. I'd never do that."

"What are you? Jehovah's Witness or something? You're way too straight for this town, kid."

"I know," Matt said with a sad smile.

The pit boss grabbed the sketch to hold it up to the light. He might also have been holding it up so a hidden camera lens could record it.

Matt's fingers itched to reclaim the likeness. Someone might want Effinger to stay lost.

But now he was stuck surrendering his passport to Effinger to some unknown factor. Maybe other people didn't think Effinger was dead either. Maybe someone still wanted him dead, if he weren't already.

"What's this guy's name?"

Matt shrugged. "I guess he would have used whatever worked. We're hoping if we can get him home, we can get him into a re-covery program."

"Sure, sure. I get a finder's fee?"

"I'm sure . . . Norbert will be very generous when he finds out what's waiting for him at home."

"Norbert! They all have dumb names like that, the losers."

Matt flushed. He should have had a fake name on the tip of his tongue, not whatever his subconscious chose to dredge up. St. Norbert.

"Not your fault," the guy said, handing back the sketch. "Saw him a couple months ago, but he moved on. Used to get sloshed and talk about coming into big money. Lousy craps player, which is the way we like 'em. Ended up on the nickel slots. What a piker. Maybe when he gets home and grabs some of that moolah he'll come back and improve his rep around here. Try up the street at The Slottery. He was tapped out when he left here."

"Thanks."

Matt walked away through the crowds and the clatter, mentally repeating the key phrase like a sin that needed confessing. "Used to talk about coming into big money." If the big money wasn't Effinger's to come into, someone might have wanted to kill him. But why fail? Why plant Effinger's ID on a corpse close enough to his own physical description to confuse matters? And why hang around town when he was supposed to be dead? Even an imbecile would know enough to get out of sight and keep out of sight.

Matt felt like an imbecile himself. Maybes weren't good enough. Maybe he needed a new set of maybes, like maybe he needed something he didn't have: Cliff Effinger's rap sheet. Maybe Molina would let him see it, or at least sum it up. Matt stomped down the Strip sidewalk, finding his new boots clunky and clumsy.

The Hesketh Vampire was an evil influence. It was changing the way he dressed as well as the way he got around town. Maybe it would change the way he thought too. Maybe that wasn't so bad. He suddenly wanted the details of that rap sheet so badly he itched all over with impatience. He was a blind man, stabbing in the dark. If Molina was going to sic him on Effinger indirectly, he needed more than he had. Under the bright lights, his watch read 10:15 P.M. Where would Molina be now? Home, probably.

Discouraged, he dragged his way back to the Vampire, blazing like irradiated platinum under the bright light it was parked beneath for security reasons, the presumption being that thieves wouldn't mess with such a visible target. Max Kinsella was right, maybe. Bold and noisy and brash is the best disguise in Las Vegas.

Matt finally knew where he should go, and unlocked the Vampire. The boots were tough enough to kick back the steel stand and come away unscuffed.

He knew where he was going now, and suddenly feared he

might be too late. It was a long shot, but after all the tepid inquiries tonight, he suddenly felt lucky.

Odd that his arena of luck was so far from the Strip.

The restaurant lot was half empty. A week night didn't keep people up at all hours, even in Las Vegas, and especially in the residential areas where the nine-to-fivers lived.

The Vampire was embarrassingly loud about its arrival, and Matt knew his usual relief in switching it off.

The neon sign still burned its pink-and-blue image into the night, a real standout here where the only lights were sodium-iodide street lamps that poured watery Mercurochrome shadows down on everything.

Matt studied the cars as he walked to the Blue Dahlia's entrance, wondering what Molina drove when she wasn't ensconced in a department Crown Victoria.

Impossible to tell, although Temple would have made a game of guessing the car, and probably would have guessed right by now.

But this wasn't Temple's affair; it was his.

He opened the door and glimpsed the smoky dining room beyond. The trio itself was smoking, running a hot riff out for a trial ride and then reeling that buggy back on home. Maybe . . . she wasn't on tonight. It had been a risk, a gamble, an impulse, everything Matt had never relied on.

"Table for one, sir?"

The hostess's long black crepe gown reminded him of an old Susan Hayward film. His nod rewarded him with a seat in the back where he could watch, unnoticed, the figure perched on the stool onstage.

He ordered a Coke and asked the waitress how long the set would last.

"Almost over. Sorry, sir."

"No problem. I want to see Carmen afterward. Could you let her know?"

She eyed him like he was suddenly suspect. "You have a card?"

Matt paused in digging out the ConTact-house card with his name handwritten at the top. Instead he withdrew one of his laminated sketches of Cliff Effinger.

The waitress raised an eyebrow. "I'll see she gets it when she comes off."

The waitress thought he was weird, probably, but then the whole place was weird, a kind of time machine. The trio picked up the melody and then Molina—Carmen—joined in, her voice dream-dusky. He didn't know the song, but the words were sedately old-fashioned and the melody was deceptively sophisticated.

He felt he should be wearing a fedora and nursing a gin fizz. "Of all the gin joints in Las Vegas . . . ," that kind of thing. Matt leaned his head against the wall until all he could see were the shuttered black backs of the spotlights, and then he just listened.

The song had ended and the music had ebbed and died before he snapped out of his reverie. The Blue Dahlia was empty except for a couple lingering over their after-dinner coffees. The hostess came around the corner to his table.

"You can go backstage now." She gestured to his half-full glass. "That's on the house; you can bring it with you."

Matt scooped it up as expected and followed her around the front again, and down a narrow hall. The restaurant's tortuous innards reminded him of a labyrinth; it must be almost as old as the era it evoked.

The hostess paused at a door and knocked. "Come on in, the water's fine, and the whiskey isn't too bad, either," a voice Matt didn't recognize called.

But the woman who waited inside, sitting at a Goodwill dressing table with delusions of Sunset Boulevard, was indeed C. R. Molina.

She spun on the bench, having just removed the trademark blue silk dahlia from her hair.

"You're a cheap date," she said, nodding at the Coke in his hand.

He noticed a plain glass, half-full of amber liquid, on the blue mirror–topped dressing table. Perhaps the whiskey of her greeting. He backed onto some sort of chest and sat.

She nodded to something on the dressing table surface. "I like to wind down after a gig, but apparently you had other ideas. How'd you know I'd be here?"

"I didn't."

Her eyes met his, showing some surprise. "Took a chance, did you, Father Matt?"

"Not a very big one, Carmen."

Gone were Lieutenant Molina and Mr. Devine. Matt realized they had somehow fallen into a double-decker relationship, because of what their guarded, often-invisible personal lives had in common. A religion, an ethic, a burden.

"I almost feel I should smoke in this room," she said, eyeing the small space nostalgically.

"It would be bad for your health and your voice." He hesitated. "You would need a long enameled cigarette holder, of course."

"Of course." She smiled, then picked up the object on her dressing table.

Effinger's sketched likeness. •

"How did you like Janice?" she asked.

"Janice? Oh, the artist. Fine. She was great at digging out all the little details." Matt felt an unfortunate flush coming on. He felt guilty, as if he sat before Mother Superior after having been caught writing mush notes to a fourth-grade girl.

"She's quite a psychologist, in her way. Well, this is a thoroughly unsavory character. Can I have a copy?"

"Sure. I should have thought of that." Matt leaned forward on the chest. "Actually, I'd like a copy of his rap sheet, or a description, if a copy is not allowed."

"Oh, Matt." Molina shook her dark head. "The police department is as riddled with bureaucracy as the church. I can sum up; I can't hand over. But you're used to limitations, aren't you."

"Maybe, and maybe not enough used to getting around them. I bet you are."

She looked at her watch, a slim band with a vintage look. "Look, I've got to get back to Mariah and let the sitter go." She sighed and picked up the blue silk flower. Her eyes met his in the big round mirror, and the indirectness of the look was oddly exciting.

"Want to follow me home? We can discuss this in more natural circumstances."

He stood. "I've . . . I've got a motorcycle."

"A motorcycle, you?" Her eyes, which exactly matched the silk dahlia, widened. "You've got Max Kinsella's motorcycle."

He nodded. "Electra lends it to me. It's hers now."

"Bullshit! It was Kinsella's and I bet he'll have it again. He wouldn't let go of anything that belonged to him."

Matt didn't argue.

"He know you're riding around town on it?"

"I don't know."

"I do. He doesn't miss much. Neither do I. So. You've got a motorcycle. I imagine it can roll right into Our Lady of Guadalupe's neighborhood."

"Not very quietly."

"It's not a very quiet neighborhood."

Molina approached, making him wonder why, then lifted the Coke glass from his hand and put it on the dressing table.

"Wait up front by the hostess station. I'll be out in a wink."

Matt doubted that, given the complicated cut of her vintage velvet gown, but he could wait patiently. That was the first thing he had learned in seminary.

"You're a friend of Carmen's," the hostess stated when he took up a post on one of the waiting benches.

"More like a business associate."

"What business are you in?"

"Counseling."

She nodded, tucking stray hairs into her blond French twist as she closed down the cash register for the night.

Not even Muzak drifted through the restaurant, just the distant clink of dishes being done. For a moment, the place felt like a happy home after a big holiday dinner.

"That's the neatest thing about this job," the hostess commented.

"What?"

"Hearing the music from in there. Carmen sings like, I don't know, like something else."

"She has a lovely voice." He hated stilted comments, and most of all when they came from him.

"Thank you."

Molina was there, a garment bag draped over one crooked elbow, a knit headband holding back her short bob, in flat-heeled shoes, dark slacks and a sweater. Carmen had dissolved like the Wicked Witch of the West in *The Wizard of Oz*.

Matt found himself on the brink of stammering with surprise. This was a halfway Molina he didn't know, and didn't know how to relate to. She looked normal almost, almost . . . casual.

He followed her out into the lot, the Vampire a diamond solitaire shining against the empty black asphalt. Molina went right to it, her car keys jingling like a winning slot machine in her hand.

She stood staring at the motorcycle, fists on hips, as if challenging it to a silent duel.

"I don't like it," Matt said.

"No, of course you wouldn't." She walked around it. "It's Max Kinsella's, all right." She flashed a glance over her shoulder. "You ever search it?"

"Search it? No! It's Electra's now, and none of my business. I'm only using it until I can afford my own car."

"Probably secondhand at that."

"I'm not used to better, and I certainly can't afford it."

Molina tore her attention away from the motorcycle. "Neither can I. That's mine."

She pointed to a well-used Toyota station wagon. "Perfect for hauling giggly eleven-year-old girls on all sorts of expeditions, but no beauty."

"Columbo did all right with his junker."

"Right. Call me Columbo. Okay. You know where the parish church is; I'm about four blocks northwest. Just follow my taillights."

Matt nodded.

Molina stopped halfway to her car and looked back. "You do have a helmet for that thing?"

"Of course." He mimicked her earlier words down to the tone.

Following a police officer is a nerve-racking task, Matt found. He kept straining to read the speedometer, fretting when she slightly exceeded the limit, gritting his teeth when she slowed down enough to make the Vampire snap at its figurative bit.

The neighborhood was only fifteen minutes away. The dark streets thrummed with the high-volume bass of the occasional cruising low-rider. He wondered what this neighborhood would be like on a weekend, and how safe the Vampire would be here then. Already he was fretting about leaving it outside Molina's house.

She had anticipated him, pulling into the driveway but leaving space along the side for him. The garage door elevated on vibrating rails while Molina got out and waved him inside.

She locked her wagon, then followed him into the attached garage, hitting the remote-control close button so soon that the door nearly clipped her as she walked in. She didn't seem to have noticed.

"Your bike is safer inside. Come on."

He followed her into a dark utility room and then into a kitchen lit by a pale overhead fluorescent light.

He sensed age and small spaces, just like at the Circle Ritz, but on a much more modest scale. Somewhere a television set blared through a closed door.

"Bedtime for you, young lady," Molina's voice ordered as she disappeared down the hall. "We've got company for a little while. No, you don't need to see who. I'll be back soon."

She came back down the hall trailed by a stocky Latina girl with long, curly almost-black hair.

"Yolanda, this is Matt Devine." They exchanged nods. "How'd everything go?"

"Fine, fine. Mariah is such a fine girl. *Muy sympatica.*"

"*Gracias,*" Molina bid her at the front door, presumably after an exchange of money.

She returned to gesture Matt to an easy chair, then moved into the square little kitchen.

"I could use a drink. Your unexpected arrival cost me half of my usual whiskey and soda. What would you like?"

Matt was, as usual, flummoxed by trying to anticipate what she'd have available.

"What you're having will be fine."

"Fine, fine," she mocked. "You and Yolanda are two of a kind, a good Catholic kind. Everything is fine."

"No, it often isn't," he finally answered when she brought him a drink that was the twin to the one abandoned on her dressing table.

She threw herself onto a big Naugahyde recliner and took a generous swig of her drink before the ice could dilute it. Then she took Cliff Effinger out of her pants' pocket and slapped him down faceup on an end table, like someone producing the Knave of Hearts.

"You can get me an original-size copy of the sketch?"

"Yup."

"Is this a good likeness?"

"Uncanny, when you consider how long it's been since I saw him face-to-face."

"You're satisfied an ordinary observer could recognize him from this?"

"Are all police officers used to asking the same question six different ways?"

"Sorry." She grinned and leaned back against the recliner headrest. "I'm not used to subjects who are quick on the uptake. Good work. Have you tried it on anybody yet?"

"Some casino employees at the Stardust. Only—"

"Only what?"

"It isn't easy, to approach strangers with no special authority, to ask questions and get answers."

"Now you appreciate the dubious talents of your Circle Ritz neighbor."

"I've always appreciated Temple."

"Watch out that you don't get used to that. Kinsella's back in town."

"You make him sound like Mack the Knife."

"Isn't he? Used to dodging them at least—knives, that is, and the police. Seen him around?"

"No."

"I'm only trying to warn you. You've never known a man like him."

"No," Matt agreed, sipping the drink and finding it strong. He was used to watered-down rectory brandy and restaurant drinks. "But I'm beginning to, I think."

"You? And Kinsella?" Molina cocked a bold black eyebrow. "Saints protect us."

"Kinsella certainly has enough saints' names to do the job for him."

"Michael Aloysius Xavier. Tricky, an acronym, MAX. Michael, the warrior archangel, was the only angel with any real guts, though. The rest—and the saints and martyrs—are wishy-washy window-dressing."

"I don't think any saint is window-dressing."

"I'm just trying to warn you. About Kinsella, and not as a police officer. He knows his way around women. Do you?"

"No, but maybe that's an advantage. Besides, I'm not in a contest for Temple's regard."

"You are if Kinsella's back, whether you want to admit it or not." She sat up and leaned forward, elbows on knees, her hair falling forward on her cheeks. "Just how good a priest were you?"

"Are you asking about the quality of my vocation and my commitment? Or are you asking if I could give an articulate sermon, or sing mass on key?"

"None of that. I'm asking if you were all you were supposed to be."

His jaw almost dropped. Molina was a policewoman, yes. She was used to asking people hard, invasive questions. But why him? He wasn't a suspect for anything. Then it dawned on him. Maybe he was a *candidate*. Maybe Molina wanted him to be the Judas goat that drew Max Kinsella into the open, and jealousy was to be the bait.

"I was faithful to my vows, yes. Though it's none of your business."

She suddenly smiled. "It wouldn't be any fun asking rude questions if it really were my business. You need help, Matthew."

"My given name isn't Matthew."

"That's right. Matthias. He who replaced Judas." She nodded, satisfied, then sipped deeply again from her glass. "I suppose, being so virtuous, you wondered that I even asked."

"I guess I did, and why."

"Still unused to my high-handed ways, huh? I need to get the lay of the land, for professional reasons. You're right; I'd love to have Kinsella in an interrogation room downtown. I wanted to know how big a threat you might be to him."

Matt turned his hardly touched glass in his hands, enjoying the cool condensation on his palms. It kept him alert.

"You don't understand, Carmen. I'm no threat at all. Temple and Max were all but married before he disappeared."

"That's a big 'but.' "

"Not to me."

"A priest says this?"

"A former priest. Theirs is the primary relationship in this whole mess, and I have to honor that."

" 'Honor.' " Molina stretched out long legs and crossed her feet at the ankles. Matt wondered if she wore a gun somewhere, maybe around an ankle. "That's a word you don't hear much nowadays, except among gang-bangers who use it as a synonym for 'macho.' If you worry too much about honor, Matthias, you ain't gonna get Cliff Effinger, and you ain't gonna get the girl."

"How did you get so cynical?"

"About honor, or about priests?"

"Both."

She shrugged. "I may be half-Anglo, but I grew up in a Hispanic culture. We don't sweat the small stuff, like sins of the flesh. A lot of the priests—most—I heard of in Mexico, and even in California, had a woman on the side sometime. It was no big deal. And it was better than boys."

Matt shook his head at her casual acceptance. "I've never understood it. This Mediterranean and South American indulgence of priests who break their vows. I know, I know . . . Americans are descended from Puritans, and are much more straitlaced than our Continental brethren, but still, a promise is made to be kept, not broken—"

"I'm sorry." Molina looked rueful. "I got carried away in my capture-the-crook scenario." She smiled. "It's nice to finally meet an honorable priest at least, even if he isn't a priest anymore. I guess if the good don't die young, they leave."

"I'm not that unusual. The vast majority of priests keep their vows and believe in their vocation. The ones that don't, make headlines."

"Listen. I'll show this sketch around to some of the patrol officers. They're on the Strip every night, so you won't have to bumble into casinos anymore."

"I'll still look. Maybe I'll even get better at it."

"Maybe you'll get better at other things too." She stood, finished her drink. "Go home. I've got to kiss my kid goodnight and get ready for a court appearance tomorrow. This sketch is one more nail in Cliff Effinger's empty coffin. We'll find him."

Matt wasn't sure if the "we" was the police department, or she and he.

"And Max Kinsella?"

"What would you do if he were out of the picture for a good long time?"

"What I've always done. Support what Temple decides to do."

"And if what she decides to do . . . is you?"

Another below-the-belt question. Matt handed back his almost-full glass; Molina wouldn't want to waste it.

"Then I'll have to see what *I* decide to do. You can't play me and Max Kinsella off each other. I don't know what evidence you have against him, but as far as Temple's told me, he's just a magician who did a disappearing act for a little too long. She apparently still has some faith in him, and that's a business I understand: faith when all the facts belie it. Now that he's back, I won't interfere. With Temple, or with him. I won't turn in Kinsella, Carmen. I'd never do that to Temple. Or Kinsella. Or myself. That would be the worst move for all of us."

"Not for me. Remember, triangles are the most volatile configuration of relationship on the planet. Pairs are tough to break up, but trios turn on each other like cannibals. I can always crack a case with three sides."

"Maybe we have more than a triangle here."

"What do you mean?"

She figured out his mathematics while he kept quiet. Her remarkable blue eyes glittered like man-made sapphires, hard and somehow counterfeit.

"You're getting better," she told him, "but don't let it go to your head."

Molina showed him out through the garage, turned on an exterior light and even waited in the open garage door until he had the Vampire started and drifting the driveway.

Matt couldn't decide on the way home if Molina were a mother superior in disguise, or Typhoid Mary.

Temple Starts Cookin'

Temple had Louie home and toweled off from his heroic rescue—all caught on telephoto lens and videotape—by 9 P.M.

His coat was the feline equivalent of a buzz-cut: short, nappy
and quick to dry.

"Two days off, Louie," she told him, ferociously toweling his
tail. "I could use a break. Spending all my time with Domingo
and his minions, Savannah Ashleigh and assorted female con-
sorts of the late Darren Cooke is taxing. At least I won't have to
see the Wrath of Rodeo Drive for a while. Did you watch Savannah light into that director for unsafe conditions? Threatening to sue everybody from the Mirage to the cat-food company
to the cameramen for recording your feat rather than going to
Yvette's rescue?"

Louie, sitting on the area rug washing his already-soaking
feet, sneezed.

"You better not catch something from this! I hope Yvette's
okay too. Savannah Ashleigh would sue us all, every one, if
anything happened to that cat."

Louie, head bent to lick, seemed to be nodding strong agreement.

"You would think her precious cat came into this world spun-dry and was meant to stay that way. Yvette is not above sprinkling in her carrier, you know. Hey! Don't growl. Am I hurting you? Well, stalk off, then."

Temple absently dabbed the damp towel against her own sopping suit-front. Her shoes, J. Reneé snakeskin pumps, lay soaked at her bare feet. She had rescued the rescuer, after all.

Not that Savannah Ashleigh had been at all grateful as she stood shrieking in the key of F-sharp on the lagoon bank. She had snatched the dripping Yvette from Temple's overburdened arms, then carried her Precious at arm's length to the carrier. Once incarcerated, the sopping cat had begun to caterwaul. That was when Savannah had announced that Yvette required at least two days' paid medical leave to recover.

To Temple, this was a welcome break. She was still curious about Darren Cooke's daughter, wishing she had copies of her letters. Even the police didn't have that. Molina had called to confirm their continued absence, only a trace of smugness in her voice.

"Did you look in the hotel safe?" Temple had asked.

"Before you even brought the letters up."

"What about Michelle? Did she say where she found my card?"

"She says it was in the usual place for such fond mementos, under the mattress."

"And your guys missed it. Did you look—?"

"The mattress was lifted off the springs. Nothing there other than some blanket fuzz. You realize that we have only the widow's word on where she found it."

"But why would she lie—?"

"You're the detective," Molina had said smartly, hanging up.

Temple sometimes wondered if the worthy lieutenant didn't use her as a stalking dog to sniff out new directions in such cases. Certainly Molina only fed her enough information to tickle her curiosity bone, which in Temple's case happened to be every bone in her body, plus the calcium supplements she consumed to strengthen her petite frame.

"I don't know what you're going to do on your days off, Louie, but I'm going to find out who has hung around Darren Cooke only recently. Too bad I can't take you along, but this is woman's work."

Louie lay there, licking the coat she had dried, ignoring her every word.

Today, Friday morning, Domingo and his minions would be busy stringing flamingos with fairy lights for a lavish installation around the Luxor Sphinx and grounds.

Although Christmas wasn't that far off, Temple really wasn't in a light-stringing mood. So, leaving Louie to enjoy the quiet comforts of home, she headed for Gangster's. But first she made a telephone call.

By day, the Gangster's layout—like most Las Vegas attractions—looked faded and forlorn. Call it the carnival-funhouse effect. The parking lot was only half full, but Gangster's unique customer pick-up-and-delivery system wouldn't produce a lot full of parked cars. She was pleased to note that a raven Viper lay in wait among the idle black limos parked in an imposing row.

When the Fontana Brother popped up like a chic jack-in-the-box as Temple entered the lobby, she didn't have to guess which one it was. She had spoken to Aldo on the phone.

"Hey, Miss Temple! Hear your pussycat went swimming at the Mirage."

"How'd you hear that so fast?"

"No problem. We are Fontana Communications, Inc." Aldo grinned and produced something from behind his back. The latest issue of the *Sun,* featuring a photo of the crew pulling Louie and Yvette from the lagoon. Nobody, human or feline, resembled themselves in the least . . . except photogenic Savannah Ashleigh, who appeared to be directing the rescue operation, and was so identified.

"Plastic surgery can really get you through those difficult moments," Temple murmured cattily.

"I thought you would like a copy," Aldo announced happily.

Considering that Temple's photo-image looked like a freeze-dried and shrunken mummy, she was not duly appreciative. But she folded the paper into her miscellaneous file cabinet—her tote bag.

"Thanks. What about Darren Cooke's co-workers? Did you round some up?"

"Sure thing. They're all sweating like hell to brush up the show with Cooke's replacement."

"They've replaced him so fast?"

"Listen, my Uncle Mario was on the phone to Hollywood, calling in a few markers, first thing Monday A.M. The Fontana family does not mess around in a crisis."

"I have seen that." Temple nodded sagely. "So who did Uncle Mario dig up?" Oops, she had phrased that badly.

Aldo folded impeccably manicured hands in front of his rigidly pin-striped navy suit and donned a Cheshire-cat smile.

"I'd ask you to guess, but I figure you've had a pretty trying night."

"You figure right."

"Steve Martin fell through, so I'll just say: Sid Caesar."

"Really?" Temple couldn't help being impressed. "He'll be perfect in the part. Is he here yet?"

"Naw. He has some things to tidy up. We got a stand-in for now, but Sid's been sent a script so he'll be ready to go."

"Well, Sid Caesar certainly wasn't in Darren Cooke's vicinity lately, so I can't think up any excuse for talking to him . . . "

Aldo took Temple's tote bag from her shoulder and then took her free elbow in hand too. "I've arranged for the director to have a talk with you during the break."

He escorted her past the discreet chime of slot machines and into Hush Money.

"Thanks, Aldo." Temple resisted his polite but firm custody. "I prefer to snoop around on my own on the stage. Ask the stage crew things. You know."

"Miss Temple." Aldo's voice was gently chiding. "Of course I realize that you wish to do your sleuthing yourself. I thought it might help to start with an overview. Additionally, once the director has spoken to you, he will not question your presence on the set, and will let you go about your business."

"I see. Very diplomatic of you, Aldo."

"We Fontanas are nothing if we are not diplomatic. Now, have a seat and I will get the director-dude."

Seating her with the courtliness of a papal legate, Aldo proceeded to ruin the effect by absently patting his jacket as he left. He was not searching for something like a Cuban cigar, but more like an Italian automatic.

Temple hoped the director was not being coerced into seeing her. Reluctant witnesses were the worst kind.

She ordered the Lady in Red Clamato juice, it being a bit too early for lunch, and recalled coming here with Matt. That, naturally (or not so naturally) got her wondering why she hadn't heard from Max lately. He was probably burrowed away in the Welles/Kinsella/Randolph house burning the literary lamp as he toiled to complete The Great Gandolph's nonfiction exposé of the séance game. Max an author! Really! She supposed he might need some organizational help, but wasn't about to volunteer. After all, she was apparently in high demand lately, so let Max wait and wonder and stew. Except she didn't think he was doing any of those things, drat.

Aldo returned in ten minutes, tenderly escorting a sixtyish man whose gray hair was cut close, in a Roman-emperor style, to hide a receding hairline. Nothing he could do would hide his receding chin. His bony features didn't profit from the severe haircut, nor did his chin benefit from a Benetton cashmere turtleneck in a shade of green that too closely made one think of a . . . well, a turtle.

Temple braced herself. She'd seen this theatrical type before and knew that he compensated for behind-the-curtain looks with high-theatah mannerisms and energy, energy, energy.

He descended like a pine-green tornado, that being the color he had chosen to set off what was left of his silver locks. He came shaking a finger at her.

"You can't keep your shabby little secrets from me anymore.

I wondered what you were doing coming in and out of the theater, and now I know."

Temple swallowed a gulp of Lady in Red.

"But, Miss Barr, you look so young to be a producer!"

He pumped her hand and sat opposite her at the table for two.

Temple gave Aldo a poisonous look, but he merely rocked back and forth on his slick Italian heels and soles, like a boa constrictor that had swallowed a whole flock of canaries.

"Miss Barr, this is Manny Kurtz, the stage, screen and television director who is mounting the Gangster's revue."

What kind of producer was she supposed to be? Temple asked herself—and Aldo—internally. She smiled, pumping up her energy to match Manny Kurtz. Wilt before all those kilowatts, and you were lost before you started.

"Oh, Mr. Kurtz. You know what they say: kids are running everything these days. Even the studios."

He raised a dramatic eyebrow, a gesture the Mystifying Max put to much better effect. "Even the TV studios, they tell me. I think it's wonderful that *60 Minutes* is doing a retrospective on poor Darren! Feel free to tromp all over my set to find your interview subjects—I myself have several theories on poor Darren's . . . er, death. Who will do the actual on-camera stuff? Morey? Ed?"

"Umm, maybe . . . even Ted."

Kurtz frowned.

Temple rushed on. Aldo was apparently taking lessons from her Aunt Kit Carlson in the telling of Really Big Lies. The last time Temple had been introduced as a *60 Minutes* field producer, she'd had to carry out the impersonation for a massively egotistical overmuscled cover hunk, the male equivalent of a blond bimbo. Kurtz was full of himself, but he was several million brain cells ahead of Fabrizio.

"It'll be as much a surprise to me as to you who will front the story," she replied quite truthfully. "This is just a background expedition, to see if there's story enough here. I'm looking for people who knew Mr. Cooke for a long time, and some who just knew him recently. We hope to get a three-dimensional take on his life and times that way."

"Three dimensional." He nodded, enraptured. "Very good idea! You know, of course, that nobody really knew Darren well, over a long period of time. He was a comic. He required a fresh audience for his same old jokes. He moved on."

"Especially with women." Temple hoped she had managed a confidential leer. "Darren Cooke was the last of the great Hollywood lovers, after all. I've seen his widow, Michelle, of course," she reported with haughty honesty, "who was well aware of his . . . special relationship with the opposite sex. She accepted his inclinations and even gave me permission to explore the real Darren Cooke."

"What a remarkable woman! French, I believe. Trust Frenchwomen to be broad-minded."

"Apparently her late husband was also."

"Broad-minded, you mean?" Kurtz withdrew an antique silver cigarette case from the inner pocket of his cream linen blazer and tapped out a nasty little cylinder that Temple seriously suspected of being a Gauloise, a French brand.

"Darren made no bones about it," he went on after lighting the stunted little thing with a sterling-silver Zippo. He flashed Temple a sharp look from behind his screen of serpentine smoke. She doubted he inhaled, which ought to do his lungs some good.

He was already tapping nonexistent ash from the cigarette end. The entire ritual was a prop with him, providing enough stagy business to keep him in the spotlight anywhere he went.

"Darren and dames." An uproarious laugh. "We're so soaked in the gangster atmosphere for the revue that sometimes we talk like them. He liked his women young, so I was surprised when he actually married and she was over thirty."

"Michelle is an international beauty, of course."

"Quite a catch for Darren, if he were going to be caught. And I know he adored his daughter. Cutest little kid! Don't care for rug rats much myself, or anything that crawls on four legs." His thin frame shuddered.

Temple was glad Midnight Louie was no longer on the stage set, or present to hear this.

"Of course, it's easy enough to get in touch with his official associates. Yourself, for example. His wife and daughter. The less public liaisons are no less integral to the man's life and work, but far harder to ferret out."

"Oh, indeed!" Kurtz turned his unfortunate profile to her while he blew out a huff of smoke in an ostentatiously sideways direction.

Temple waited.

Kurtz leaned in, confidential. His raucous baritone voice lowered to Crawford Buchanan–level. "Actually, my dear, poor Darren had one of his exes on the set last week. Slinky number with the IQ of an onion but a plastic surgeon from heaven. Although she is over his age limit now, I was betting on them reviving the embers. So you might want to talk to Savannah Ashleigh."

Temple dutifully wrote the name on a notepad she had extracted from her tote bag immediately upon being informed that she was a producer for a national news show.

"I've heard of her," she murmured.

"Amazing! I'm impressed. Savannah hasn't done anything to hear about since her last face-lift."

"Was there anyone else in his life this past week, or month?"

"Well, we haven't been rehearsing a whole month, dearie!" He was half-talking and half-inhaling on a new cigarette, his lighter flame ebbing and flaring like a candle in the wind. "Oh, the chorus cuties were always around Darren. He radiated charm. Girls seemed to jump into his bed like lemmings into the sea."

"An interesting analogy. Are you implying that getting involved with Darren Cooke was self-destructive?"

"No! No, no, no. I meant that they had very little concern for their reputations. I suppose he was a fairly major star, and these starry-eyed young things like to say thirty years later when they're knitting booties for the grandbrats that they once had an affair with a star. One-night stand usually, with Darren. But nobody ever complained, as far as I knew."

"Really! What a remarkable man." Temple cupped her face in

her hand and placed her elbow on the table to lean in closer. "What about women who were strangely . . . unsusceptible to Darren Cooke? Any of them around?"

"Well, nobody really notices the losers . . . but we have a new costumer who seemed quite inoculated against his charm. And Darren's personal assistant is quite a striking creature, yet she broadcasts such an icy air of pure business that I doubt even Darren tried the Romeo act on her."

"Personal assistant," Temple repeated, writing and remembering. "I really should contact her. Where would she be now that he's . . . dead."

"Why, his office, I expect. Tidying up the files for the widow."

"Office? Where?"

"He appeared here so often that he maintained a small Strip office. Somewhere on Charleston. Surely you have assistants yourself who can look it up."

"That I do." Temple finished her Clamato drink and shut her notebook.

"I'll buy you another Bloody Mary," he said, pointing, obviously uneager for the interview to end.

"Thanks, but I must get to work. I'll just poke around backstage, if you don't mind. Interview the 'little people' who are so often overlooked in media biographies."

"Excellent idea! Our set is just crammed with the little people—crew and hoofers and floor-sweepers. If you want an overview, don't hesitate to come to me."

"I won't," Temple promised as sincerely as he had offered.

When she rose, Aldo slipped into her seat.

"I would like a Bloody Mary," he told the director, deadpan.

Obviously, Aldo considered his next assignment to be keeping this camera-hound out of her way while she snooped around. Manny Kurtz was in fine (and persistent) Italian hands for at least forty-five minutes.

Once in the theater itself, Temple mentally changed identities and brought forward a new rank of half-lies.

"Where's the cat?" an idle dancer called as she approached the stage.

"Resting at home like a movie star." She climbed the few steps to the stage. The empty staircase reminded her of Midnight Louie's almost-tumble down those homicidally long risers . . . could the cat have tripped on something? The next person down that stairway would have been Darren Cooke.

"I've enjoyed watching the company rehearse," she told the marooned dancer, crossing to where he lounged in the wings.

That was an old theater person for you: she "crossed" the stage, didn't "walk."

He nodded. "Would have been a good show with Darren. It'll be great with Caesar."

"Was Mr. Cooke . . . uneasy at all before his death? Did the average co-worker have any suspicion about what was coming."

"Co-worker? We were just the chorus. He did seem a little withdrawn for Darren Cooke, the world's first wild and wonderful guy. I noticed that he played footsie with the blond chick with the cat commercial, but he didn't seem too pleased about it."

"Darren Cooke pretending to be interested in women?"

"In that woman, anyway. Hey, she was a silicone babe; I don't blame the guy. You seemed to be more his type."

"Me?" Temple hoped she didn't look as guilty as she felt.

"So how come you're asking about all this?"

She sighed. "I'm helping a friend with a book." True, although in the future. "It looks at true-life situations that end in death." Half-true. "Nobody can figure out why he killed himself. I'm looking for a little insight. And, then, I actually met him during the commercial shoot. I'm an ex-reporter. I guess I'm like everybody else. I want to know why."

"Guy had it all. Model wife. Kid. Money enough for a nanny to look after the kid, which is the best part. His show was going to do well. Gangster's is a great venue. I can't figure it."

"Nobody ever—"

"Ever what?"

"I know you've just been around for this show, but did one of his ex-girlfriends or one-night stands get ugly about her built-in obsolescence?"

"Nobody I ever heard of, and the hoofers hear a lot about the headliners, believe me. Except that Ashleigh bombshell. I saw them coming out of his dressing room, arguing about someone. Drew, that was it. The name! By God, I remembered it."

The dancer straightened his spine and grew an inch in an automatic physical expression of his psychological exuberance.

"Do you suppose that's important? That he and this Ashleigh woman were arguing about some other woman named Drew. Could be a last name, or a first name. What do you think?"

That everybody thinks he's a detective, Temple told herself sourly.

"Should I tell the police?"

"I doubt it. I'm going to look around during break. Thanks."

She walked backstage, imagining this sudden windfall of information getting to Lieutenant Molina. She imagined Molina finding out that the "Drew" under discussion was "Nancy." And finally, of course she'd realize, that the person was her, Temple Barr. She couldn't help wincing as she thumped down the narrow backstage stairs to the dressing rooms below.

Dressing the Part

If Temple knew how to do anything, it was how to schmooze up theater people, especially crucial backstage personnel.

Like support staff in any endeavor, these folks were often taken for granted or even snubbed by visiting stars. For a little attention and commiseration, they could tell a lot about the stellar personalities with whom they had passing, but intimate, contact.

So Temple spent the next hour gossiping with Mike the stage doorman, the janitor, a few more lingering chorus members who weren't needed until the next number and the all-important hairdresser and costumer.

"I had standing instructions to let any pulchritudinous females into Mr. Cooke's dressing room," Mike admitted.

"Pulchritudinous? He really said that?"

"No, I said that."

It soon came out that Mike, at seventy, was studying English at the University of Nevada to make up for a scanted education (in sixth grade he had dropped out to help support his family).

"Really?" Temple asked, not knowing anybody who hadn't been forced to go through high school, and often college. "What could you do at age . . . eleven or twelve?"

"It was the Depression. Lots of things. You don't want to know."

Though Mike looked like a stunt double for Santa Claus, with his trimmed white beard and trifocal glasses, Temple took him at his word. In Las Vegas, the Capital of Present Tense, you often don't want to know people's past lives.

"So, did any of these pulchritudinous females slither on in?"

"You didn't," Mike said gallantly. "But that Hollywood harpy sure did."

Temple almost purred. Mike's English classes were making him quite a hand with a cutting phrase. "You mean Savannah Ashleigh, who's managed single-handedly to raise her breast measurement to match her IQ?"

Mike had to think that one through, but then he grinned, showing some black holes where teeth should have been. "That's the she-devil herself. Boy, did they carry on in there! Mr. Cooke always looked very cranky after she came shooting on out. The only rendezvous those two were having was in the boxing ring."

Temple paused to contemplate the lovely notion that Savannah Ashleigh had been Darren Cooke's Sunday midnight visitor, and had driven him to suicide . . . or helped him leave the planet in the guise of suicide.

But why? "Hell hath no fury like a woman scorned," was a pretty good motive. No other woman had gone ballistic when the affair was over, but Savannah had the temper of a born pouter. She might have been hanging onto him like a piranha.

"Anyone else?" Temple asked. "Females, I mean."

"That trim little personal assistant of his. Great gams."

"I hadn't noticed, but then I'm not supposed to. I saw her at his Sunday brunch. She seemed almost fanatically all business."

"That's what she did here. In and out in five minutes, and the same stiff, stern look on her mug. She never even nodded to me as she went by, just trundled past with her briefcase and papers."

"And?"

Mike frowned and adjusted his pistol holster in the groove beneath his Santa-jolly beer belly. "Now we're down to staff. No, wait! Some elf in a miniskirt cut up to her hair-length came in once to see him. Didn't stay long enough for any hanky-panky."

"I've seen the assistant but what did this one look like?"

"Brown hair, not much makeup, flat shoes. And that miniskirt, black-and-white checks all over. Sure could move in that walking-chessboard thing, though. For such a mousy girl, there was something about her."

"Do you remember what day she came in?"

"Friday maybe."

"Nothing really memorable about her?"

"Not with all these showfolk types around. You in show biz?"

"No. My cat is, though."

"Cat? Don't like 'em. Always jumping on cupboards and eating food."

Temple could not deny it, especially since Louie would rather eat almost anything other than Free-to-be-Feline.

"Mind if I poke around down here a little?"

Mike pursed his lips and shook his head. Temple proceeded to poke.

Darren Cooke's dressing room had been stripped of his effects; probably by that haughty but efficient personal assistant.

Temple regarded the garment rod with its few askew wire hangers, a sad smudge of clown-white makeup smearing the neighboring mirror. If only mirrors could record what went on before their cold glass surfaces. Could one of Darren Cooke's female visitors have been his daughter? Had there been any hints that she was stalking him? Was that why he had pounced on Temple in the theater house that day and asked her to brunch?

She went into the hall to look for the costume room.

A faint buzz of industry drew her finally to a pair of shut doors. Her knock didn't disturb the sound of work within, so she pushed open one door.

Worktables filled the space, not much staff. A rainbow of zoot suits lined a hanging rack against the wall, and more costumes decorated other racks. Decapitated heads lined tabletops like leftovers from the French Revolution; some wore wigs fanciful enough for 1790-something.

A small, stout African-American woman bent over a pattern laid atop fabric, her mouth bristling with straight pins.

She was working, alone and so intently that Temple tiptoed closer.

"Pardon me. Are you Minnie? Mike the doorman said you might talk to me."

"Nmmmph like ifff," she mumbled through her mouthful of pins.

Temple hefted herself onto a nearby stool and prepared to wait. A radio somewhere played soft-rock classics.

The woman began spitting out pins one by one as her flashing hands nailed the pattern to the fabric like a human staple gun.

This was a veteran. Temple loved to watch seamstresses work. She herself could barely thread a needle and run it through a buttonhole, but real sewers had an almost balletlike economy and certainty of movement.

"Done." The woman swiftly stuck leftover pins into the cushion attached to her wrist. "What might be your name, mite?"

"Temple Barr. And I don't like being stereotyped by size."

She nodded. "Why're you such a *big* friend of Mike's?"

"I took the time to talk to him."

"That Mike! Always jabbering. Me, I can't usually. What's the fuss? I have to remake this costume right soon."

"Actually, I'm asking about poor Mr. Cooke."

"Poor Mr. Cooke! I don't think so, honey. I know you're trying to speak nice about the dead, but there was nothing poor about that man. He had the cars, the clothes, the cash, the chicks and maybe the boy chicks too, if he'd awanted them."

"You do know all the dirt, like Mike said."

"Mike. That blabbermouth. When I sew, it's quiet, I'm quiet. Everybody forgets about me. I hear more than I should, but it's all just noise to me."

"Now that Mr. Cooke's dead, though, you must be thinking over what you might have heard. You must wonder what drove him to suicide."

Minnie folded fabric and pattern into loose squares. Her huge brown eyes were as sharp as pins, and her unwrinkled complexion was the warm, comforting color of cocoa. "Girl, I don't wonder. That's why I like this job. I been doing costumes in Las Vegas for almost forty years, and I ain't never been required to wonder. You got a reason I should change that?"

"Yes, ma'am, I do."

"You do? Just who are you to go round asking questions? You work for these folks that own Gangster's?"

Temple took a deep breath. "In a way. I work for Nicky Fontana at the Crystal Phoenix, and his brothers have an interest in this place, so—"

"The Fontana Brothers? Why didn't you say so up front, girl?" Her face unfolded in laughter, producing its first creases. "They are too much. Too much. Them and their family Viper. That is one bad automobile."

Temple smiled. You had to love the Fontana Brothers, especially when the mere mention of their names served as an "open sesame" in the unlikeliest places around town.

"I do their tailoring for them," Minnie confided. "Why do you think they look so good in those Italian suits? You should have seen them as whippersnappers. Cute as a litter of hound-dog pups."

"I bet," Temple said.

"You date one of those boys?"

"No, I don't."

Minnie frowned, as if any female who neglected her boys was suspect. "What you want to know?" She plucked an iron from its resting place to press a length of fuchsia suiting material.

Temple could tell that Minnie was queen of her backstage domain, and had been so for far too long to fool. "I've got a bad feeling about that death. I think a woman was involved. A young woman. I'm trying to find out who might have seen Darren Cooke during the last days before he died."

"This any of your bizness?" Minnie looked up, narrow-eyed, from her ironing.

"No."

She nodded. "You one of his girls?"

"No!"

Minnie glared at her.

"He asked but I just said no."

Minnie nodded. "He never missed a young thing that came within fifty feet."

"Someone thought he might have killed himself because the young things weren't saying yes as often as they did when he was younger."

Minnie made a dismissive sound. "There's always enough young things around dumb enough or greedy enough to say yes. This trip I count three girls in the chorus, and maybe some dark horse from outside. She came and went too fast, though."

"Brown-haired girl, quiet except for a sassy miniskirt?"

"That's the one, Temple. I never forget a skirt like that."

"Maybe she wanted to be noticed," Temple speculated.

"Sure. Anybody who wear a skirt that short wants something to be noticed. I don't know about her. Could be a—what you call it?—red herring."

Temple smiled. Minnie was getting mystery fever.

"Wasn't that other one," Minnie muttered, "with the cat that was more stuck-up than her. I bet that woman's hair turned white from her looking in the mirror so often and scarin' herself."

"You mean Savannah Ashleigh."

"More like born Betty Lou Kravitz. Savannah's too nice a town to be associated with her. She was in and out for days, screaming and kicking. Then it was 'Poor Mr. Cooke.' I never seen one of his exes come round acting up before. And I been working all over this town, must've worked maybe eight of his other gigs. He was a favorite in Las Vegas, Mr. Cooke."

Minnie tabled her iron and lifted a creaseless garment for inspection. She frowned.

"One thing bother me. Day after he died, his wife came in for some of his things. She was a classy lady. I read about that, their getting married and having a baby. Why would that man keep on slipping around on the side with a famous model for a wife?"

"Habit. A habit as hard to break as heroin."

"Go on wi' you, Temple Barr. I don't believe that."

"But his wife was here? What time? She supposedly had just flown in from France."

"She was by about, oh, six o'clock in the afternoon. Before the joint really got jumping. Long, tall thing, my goodness! Not like you and me."

"What did she take from his dressing room?"

"Odds and ends. I moved out the costumes, but his makeup case was gone. That's all."

Maybe, Temple told herself, and maybe not. She jumped to the floor.

"You're not leaving?"

Minnie liked an audience, or liked *giving* audiences, rather.

"Yup. I have other errands to run. Thanks!"

Temple retraced her steps in a hurry. Her first date would be with the phone book—to find out what flights arrived from Paris on Monday.

Chapter 29

Office Affairs to Remember

Nobody was saying Darren Cooke had been killed, but Temple compiled a suspect list anyway.

Her home office desk was littered with papers, notes and the latest copy of *Elle,* which featured a full-page ad the color of a Midnight Margarita with Michelle Bonard's pale face as a centerpiece. The widow's long, graceful, sinfully toned arms were sheathed in elbow-length, indigo-blue velvet gloves. Her velvet fingers held up a crystal flacon of "Secret" perfume like an offering from—and to—the gods.

Temple sighed. Three of the suspect women were not the right age to be Cooke's daughter: Savannah Ashleigh, his ex-fling; Michelle Bonard, his wife; and Domingo's lost leech, Verina.

The library had produced an excess of birth dates for the cagey Savannah (who had greeted the world thirty-five, thirty-one or thirty-eight years ago, and those dates were probably shaved before they were allowed in print). Savannah Ashleigh could be past forty! Temple crowed to herself.

Michelle Bonard's true age and name were matters of record.

Teenage Michelle Bonard apparently hadn't expected the graying of America to prolong her modeling career, and had been honest from the outset. She was a wonderfully well preserved thirty-eight.

Darren Cooke was officially fifty-two years old, give or take two to four years more. Entertainers are multiple personalities when it comes to reporting birth dates.

Even so, he would have had a hard time fathering a woman in her late thirties. The daughter must be younger, twenty-five to thirty-five years old.

Three pages of Temple's legal pad were scribbled from top to bottom with the things she hated most: numbers. Words were her bailiwick. Numbers were for the birds. For the flamingos!

She listed her mystery women, who all seemed to be twenty-somethings. A provocative finding. They were: assorted young things among Domingo's volunteer crew, Cooke's personal assistant and the mysterious brown wren in the checked miniskirt. The assistant could be checked out, but the brown wren . . .

She flipped a yellow, lined page, and winced. Lines and lines of flight times and time-zone calculations. Even looking at it made her head ache. While she was browsing the Yellow Pages of the phone book, she looked under entertainment.

After much reading of fine print, her forefinger pinioned an address on Charleston: Laughalot Productions. Darren Cooke's Las Vegas business office.

Her watch said it was only 4 P.M. If she hurried, she might find the assistant in and closing down the office.

She hurried.

Traffic was horrible, but within twenty minutes the Storm had snuggled up to the parking block in front of the usual one-story Strip shopping center. They all looked alike, this one a close twin to Matt's home away from home, ConTact. Temple had never officially visited there, but had driven past out of rank curiosity. Or rank infatuation.

So why was she sitting outside the late Darren Cooke's office thinking about her love life? Her potential love life? Get with it, girl! You're here to Nancy Drew.

She wondered if anyone had ever used a proper name as a verb before. She jumped out of her sleek little roadster, and approached the office of Carson Drew, her tall, distinguished father . . .

Darren Cooke had been neither particularly tall nor distinguished. The vertical blinds on his office windows were drawn against the late-afternoon sun, or against the casual observer.

Temple had parked beside a red Miata that she hoped belonged to the assistant, because she certainly didn't want to encounter someone official in the office. Maybe it was the wife, cleaning out, or cleaning up after her husband.

Her knock was ignored at first, until repeated enough times to show she wasn't going to fade away.

The door finally jerked open. *Voilà.* The very woman, still as trim, fashionably redheaded and hostile as ever. The most unpersonable personal assistant.

"Hi. I'm Temple Barr."

"I remember seeing you Sunday."

"I remember seeing you too, but I didn't catch your name."

"It wasn't thrown."

"Well, maybe you'd toss it out now."

"Darby. Alison Darby. What are you doing here?"

"Actually, I'm on a mission of mercy for Mrs. Cooke. Michelle. I had dinner with her—and darling little Padgett, of course—Wednesday night. She asked me to see that her husband's affairs were wrapped up. Ooh, that was a bad choice of words, wasn't it? Affairs, I mean."

Alison Darby had grown visibly frosty as Temple gave her false credentials. She positively froze on the word "affairs."

"You should know," she snapped, still refusing to step away from the door.

Temple regarded her furious face. Why did the cool and aloof Miss Darby care who had vanished into Darren Cooke's bedroom of a Sunday noon? Besides, she should know there had been hardly time enough for even the most fast and fevered affair.

"No, I plead innocent," Temple said. "Mr. Cooke asked me to the brunch to consult with him on a personal matter—not between us, between himself and a third party."

"A third party?" Alison looked shocked. Her pale skin was white-marble against the burgundy tint of her salon-styled hair.

"The matter was confidential, and still is, even though Mr. Cooke is dead."

"What are you?" She backed into the room as if Temple were a ghost she feared would touch her. "I know everything about Mr. Cooke's undertakings. That was my job."

"Ah, but did you approve of them?"

"Approval was not a requirement of my job."

Temple was far enough into the office to study it. Pretty mundane. A wood grain–topped desk awash with files. A swordfish on the wall that looked like molded plastic, that looked a lot like a lawn-ornament plastic flamingo. Temple knew it was partially the real fish skin preserved to resemble painted fiberglass.

A silk ficus tree anchored a corner between two cheap upholstered chairs. Semi–Swedish modern best described the furnishings. Altogether a depressingly tawdry place.

Miss Darby thought so too, from her disclaimer. "This was a . . . branch office. With Mr. Cooke's frequent performances in Las Vegas, he needed a base." Alison Darby was apologizing, a weak position, which was just where Temple wanted her to be.

"You must be exhausted!" Temple guided her onto a chair. "Let me get you some water." She filled a tiny paper cup at the bottled-water dispenser. "You must have been working on all this nonstop since Mr. Cooke's death was discovered last Monday."

"Well, yes." Her face lost some of its taut strain.

Temple examined her features for some trace of Darren Cooke. It wouldn't be too farfetched for the vengeful daughter to have insinuated herself into his entourage. Though her attire was often theatrically over the top, Alison had cultivated a forbidding, all-business air unusual in a young woman, one which made her an exception to the rule: Darren Cooke left her alone. That was something his daughter would want to ensure if she joined his inner circle.

Temple sat on the adjoining chair, peering around an inconvenient branch of silk-leaved ficus. Her continuing silence stimulated the other woman.

"There were engagements to cancel, accounts to get in order for the lawyers, for the estate, you know. Someone must do it. Someone must attend to practical matters. His wife—she's a foreigner and knows hardly anything about his affairs . . . his business. I've got to go."

"Miss Darby." Temple sat back in her uncomfortable chair, possessed of an insight. "Are you closing down his personal life before the lawyers and his wife have a chance to see any traces?"

"I . . . covering up?" Her laugh rode the razor's edge of amusement and distaste. "I hardly approved of his lifestyle, but he was my boss."

"And you hardly approve of what you're doing now, but you're doing it. He was your boss. Is it a little black book on computer you're erasing? Records of flowers and hotel rooms? What?"

Her breathing accelerated until the bodice of her conservative beige linen dress heaved like a trapped rabbit's body. Temple had caught her at something. Whether she told the truth about her purpose or not, it was at least clandestine.

"You have no right! I'm only doing my . . . job."

"I'm warning you. Cooke's death is a police matter, whether it's the suicide it appears to be, or something else."

"Something else?" She jumped up. "No. You saw more of him on Sunday than I did. Everyone left after the brunch. He was alone. He must have become despondent for some reason. Maybe he drank. He could drink a lot, you know. Then . . . it happened."

"Did he always keep a revolver in his hotel room?"

"Absolutely. This is Las Vegas; there's a criminal element that preys on tourists. In the dark they might mistake Mr. Cooke for just anybody, for a complete nobody. He took care of himself."

"Yes, I think he did. That's why suicide seems so unlikely."

"Don't say that! The police are perfectly content with their diagnosis. Their conclusions! No one has bothered us, until you."

"Us?"

"I mean, those of us associated with Darren. His wife, his friends, his staff. Why don't you just leave us alone!"

Temple glanced at the desktop computer, its screen filled with a complicated spreadsheet that looked like Sanskrit.

"Maybe I will. And maybe you should leave his office alone until the police are satisfied. They're never perfectly content, you know, even if they let it appear that way."

"*Who* are you?"

Temple knew a great exit line when she heard it. "Someone who's well acquainted with the sins of the father."

Alison Darby blanched. She went as white as a sheet of Neenah bond paper. Her fingers clenched her beige linen skirt until the cords on her hands stood out in bas-relief and the skirt was irreparably wrinkled.

Temple left.

She didn't think about that very odd interview until she was at home again. She pictured that unguarded computer, with the police too disinterested to investigate, and God-knows-what melting from its hard disks under the trembling fingertips of Alison Darby.

Then she eyed the open phone books covering her desk and decided to let her rock-steady fingers do the walking.

She needed to call a number so new to her computerized address list that she had to look it up. That's when she noticed that her own fingers had caught a bit of the Darby tremor.

Temple shut her eyes. This was business. She knew no one else who combined the necessary computer skills with the necessary nefariousness.

Still, calling this number felt clandestine. Even criminal.

All she wanted was some petty breaking and entering, both into a building and a machine. A magician was just the man to do it. Max Kinsella was the man to do it.

She knew why she hesitated. Asking Max for something, especially something slightly illegal, was handing him an edge in the tightrope act of their sundered relationship, and he never failed to use an edge. Turning to him meant she was turning away from Matt Devine, and perhaps the law-abiding side of society.

Come on, she told herself. *Don't make a federal case out of petty snoopery. You're not committing yourself to a life of co-conspiracy. Max owes you, and he knows it.*

Still, she held her breath as the phone rang.

It was answered with an uncompromising "Yes." No hint of question in the word. Just "Yes."

"Max," she said. He'd recognize the voice, just as he'd recognize the opportunity. "I've got a sick computer that needs a magic touch."

"Your place or mine?"

"Neither." Sternly. Flirting was more dangerous than felony for her right now. "And it'll take a magic touch just to get into it."

"You make about as much sense as ever."

"Thank you."

"Temple, is this worth the risk?"

"I don't know. I hope so."

"What are you looking for?"

"Something suspicious."

"Temple, Temple . . . when and where?"

She told him.

He told her that she should stay out of it.

She said she couldn't; only she would recognize what was wrong, if it were wrong.

He again complimented her incisive logic.

She again thanked him.

He told her to wear black.

She hung up, hyperventilating more than an apprentice cat burglar should.

It certainly had been a Gangster's kind of week, and it was promising to be a Gangster's kind of night.

Chapter 30

Could Louie Die for Love?

The life of a TV star is not to be envied.

Here I sit, still a bit wet behind the ears and between the toes after having given my coat a thorough tongue-lashing from stem to stern and from tip to tail. I do not believe that I have even been so wet in my entire vagabond life as I was when Yvette and I were dragged dripping from the Mirage lagoon.

Not that I have not been showered—(oops, wrong word)—provided with all the creature comforts.

Miss Temple Barr has ensconced me in the bed, heaping the covers around my recumbent form, and has moved my food from the kitchen and my litter box from the spare bathroom to the bed's foot. (As if I would set paw in makeshift indoor facilities, or sink a fang into a pile of unadorned Free-to-be-Feline if I did not have to.)

Although I sneeze now and then from my underwater outing, I am fine. People always think a wet dude is in need of succor. What he really needs is a bit of catnip to take the edge off.

So, once my little doll is out, I am up and stretching. Then I scratch in the box until I have removed enough litter to make a pretty sand painting on the carpet. I next walk through it in such a way as to leave a message: will be out until later. Read my feet. Unfortunately, humans are not used to interpreting messages spelled out in spilled litter, and they miss a lot that way.

Finally, I bury the Free-to-be-Feline with a few swift kicks of litter over the loathsome army-green pile. I am not being rude, just expressing myself in the most direct way I know.

Before you can burp up a cricket, I am climbing my favorite route to the spare-bathroom window and eeling out into the wide world. Within twenty minutes, I have leg-rubbed my way into the Goliath Hotel and taken a ride in a linen trolley up the freight elevator. Now I stand, dizzy but triumphant, outside the Divine Yvette's closed hotel-room door.

Here I must wait until some human or other decides to go in or out. (And they call *my* kind indecisive about which side of the door we wish to be on!) While waiting, I clean the litter from behind my nails and generally put the Ritz on my topcoat. A neat appearance does a lot for a gentleman with notions of a romantic nature. I figure that having played the hero and saved the Divine Yvette's life, she should be ready for a very hot reunion. And this time no Midnight Louise lurks to put the kibosh on love and the other facts of life.

At last a maid's cart clatters down the hall. I dash over while the maid is inside a room, and stow away behind stacks of extra toilet paper. As color goes, toilet paper is not the ideal hideaway for me, but it is also stored so low that the maids reach down for a roll without really looking.

I spend an idle hour or two on a slow boat to delight, batting toilet-paper rolls toward the maid's reaching hands, until we are back to Yvette's door. With the turn of a passkey, the maid is in. Behind her back, Midnight Louie is busted out and at large.

I have already explored this public terrain from beneath Miss Savannah Ashleigh's dressing gown, so I streak for the bedroom where the Divine One hangs out. No one is at home but my darling, and she is not in her carrier! My heart and other romantically motivated parts of my anatomy quicken as I leap upon the bed beside her.

Her little pink nose is cherry-red. I detect a pathetic sniffle.

"*Ma cher,* are you indisposed?" I ask with sinking heart and other parts. "Have you been in a blue mood?"

"I am always in a blue mood lately, Louie," she confesses. "I do not know what is wrong. When my mistress took me to the veterinarian yesterday, they did all sorts of nasty tests. My mistress was very upset. I heard her in the vet's private office. I am afraid I might have contracted some dread tropical disease from that phony lagoon. And I am so tired after that dreadful dunking yesterday. It has ruined my hair!"

I see that despite some quick licks and a human attempt at combing, the Divine Yvette's fur still has a shopworn, bedraggled look. Those Persian coats are murder to keep up! I am often glad I wear a close-cropped, plain old American alley-cat coat. Just a shake and a damp-down keeps it glossy and styleable.

"Your hair is lovely," I lie. That is what guys do when the light of their life is growing dim over a hangnail or whatever. "I have heard that the Mirage puts only the purest distilled water in its lagoon, and distilled water was used for bathing in the time of the Egyptians."

"Cleopatra bathed in milk, I heard."

"For her, milk. Yes. But for the queen of our kind, only the purest distilled water."

The tiny black vertical frown lines on my beloved's forehead crease. "Does not distillation take engines and machines and such? Did the ancient Egyptians have all that?"

I can see that she wants to believe me, but needs more reason. "Tut-tut," I say. "The Egyptians did brain surgery. These humans used to be a lot smarter than they look. And, now, if I may just lick a lock of your ruff into place—"

"Lou-ie," she answers with a short purr of forbidden delight. She coils into a kittenish comma, curling her forelegs, in their pale gray striped stockings, against her chest. What a living doll!

I can see my moment coming. For the fact is, in my species the female is not exactly enthusiastic about certain natural acts. She is often not in the mood. Even when the stars and hormones are in conjunction, she is tricky to approach. She is not disposed to let any of the male sex behind her, will even hiss and bat a suitor away, no matter how sincere. Sometimes it is necessary for the male to declare his superiority by taking the bit into his teeth: he nips a bit of skin at the back of her neck and forges ahead, ignoring all yowls, scratches and protests.

I do not know why it is so difficult. But I have never known the male of any species to have an easy time persuading the lady of his choice into the position of his need.

Pardon me, there was one male who apparently had solved the conundrum of the ages: Darren Cooke, by all repute. And you see what happened: he is dead.

I am now licking the Divine Yvette's long silver ruff into order and working my way downward. She twists and turns with delight, I will soon be in a position to . . . well, this is not a how-to book. Suffice it to say that all my dreams will come true in a nip and a tuck.

In fact, I have made so much progress without protest that I am not prepared for the scream when it comes. It is a doozy. I look up to see what has gotten into the Divine Yvette, but her eyes are wide open too, and her little pink mouth is firmly shut.

Then I realize that the scream is inhuman, but that it is coming from a human.

Savannah Ashleigh is standing in the open bedroom door, her purse a heap on the floor, surrounded by its spilled contents, her hands fists of fury.

"You worthless alley cat!" she screeches in my direction. "You ugly, nameless prowler! Rapist! You're the one who made my poor, darling Yvette pregnant!"

I look at Yvette. She looks at me.

Obviously, no one has seen fit to inform either of us.

"Who—?" I begin.

But I have no opportunity to question the only one who would know.

Miss Savannah Ashleigh swoops toward me in her flapping black cloak. Now I know how poor little Toto felt. If there were a yellow brick road leading from this chamber, I would take it. If a twister funnel were making like an egg-beater outside this twentieth-story window, I would leap into its eye without a qualm. If there were a dumbwaiter in the suite, or even an empty elevator shaft, I would plunge into it and take my chances.

But there is none of this. There is only one way out, and Miss Savannah Ashleigh, screaming like a banshee, is blocking it.

I jump off the bed and then slither underneath it.

The springs groan as Miss Savannah performs a flying tackle.

I try to skitter to the bedroom door, but she is across the room like a bullet, kicking it shut with one spike-heeled foot. I dodge the needle-sharp heel that aims at my brain and take cover under the bed again.

Trapped. I know it.

All is quiet beyond the dust ruffle. I wait, then hear a zipper being shut or opened. Can Miss Savannah be calming down and undressing?

I stick a few whiskers out from cover. I see nothing ahead of me. No shoes, no legs. I twist my head to look above. Nothing leans over the bed's edge.

I ease out. The door is still closed. I am ready to take

cover again, when a big pink cloud descends on me like a flock of flamingos. I am smothered in pink, and turn over, wrestling the cloud. In a second my weight overturns it, and I hear a zipper straining shut. Bet Miss Savannah has put on a few pounds, heh-heh. Lying on my back, I kick at the pink cloud with both back feet, shivs out.

They bounce off sturdy canvas as I finally realize what has happened.

The zippers I heard were not in Miss Savannah Ashleigh's clothes, but in something else, something inescapable. I have been scooped up in the Divine Yvette's pink cat carrier. Miss Savannah Ashleigh grunts in a most unladylike way as she struggles to set the carrier upright. I do not give her any help.

"Got you, you molester! Ruin my beautiful, innocent purebred, will you? She was destined for a champion Persian stud. They would have had beautiful babies, instead of the mongrel spawn my poor baby now will have to labor to deliver. Those offspring will go off to the pound as soon as they're old enough, do you hear? As for you . . . "

I see her legs scissor back and forth in front of me. I have heard the anger in her voice and seen the madness in her eyes. Poor Yvette. Her mistress has gone over the serrated edge. She is loony for real this time.

"I have had it with your gender, buddy." She stops to lean her face way down to the mesh side of the carrier. "First that jerk Darren makes it pretty clear that he considers me over the hill! Me! I am almost young enough to be his daughter, yet I am 'too old' for him. And now you. You will never see Yvette again."

I hear an anguished mew from the bed, very faint.

Miss Savannah Ashleigh hears nothing but the madness of her own heart beating.

"What to do with you that's vile enough? The pound would be too easy. Someone might find you, or even adopt you. No, I need something permanent, a punishment that fits the crime—"

Inside the carefully applied black eye makeup, Miss Savannah Ashleigh's eyes are bloodshot and deranged. They suddenly squinch almost shut with an idea.

Her face vanishes as she stands. I feel a jerk on the carrier handle, then am lofted a full four inches from the floor. "I am going to take care of you, Mr. screw 'em and leave 'em to have kittens on somebody else's bed. I am going to fix you forever."

I yowl the entire way down the elevator to the parking garage, but people in the elevator, people we pass on the way out, only shake their heads.

"Does not like to travel?" they ask, smiling.

"He will get over it very soon," Miss Savannah answers grimly. Every time.

In front of the Goliath she hails a cab and gives an address on the professional side of town. Not a bad neighborhood at all. She places the carrier on the cab floor. Her toe kicks it every now and then, keeping time while she sings a little song about boots made for walking, stomping all over you.

I do not believe that there is a rodeo in town at the moment, so she cannot mean to throw me into the bull ring. Of course, there are greyhound training stables, and illegal pitbull fights, where she could also import me at great risk to my handsome hide.

There is no doubt in my mind. Miss Savannah Ashleigh is in a killing fury, and I am completely under her control at the moment.

It will take an act of Bast to save Midnight Louie this time.

Chapter 31

Break In and Press Enter

"A Strip shopping center, for heaven's sake, Temple!"

They sat in Max's black Ford Taurus (courtesy of the late Gandolph the Great) a block from Darren Cooke's office.

"Nothing but flat open spaces and street lights," Max continued. "Does it have a back entrance?"

"I don't know. I didn't think of breaking in until I got home. Don't you have a—you know—bag of tricks?" She examined the car's front seats, then leaned over the headrests to study the backseats.

"No. Stop jumping around like a four-year-old. Simple is best," he added. "And the less incriminating evidence on you if you're caught, the better. Houdini used picks so tiny he allowed himself to be searched naked."

"Gee, I hope it doesn't come to that. Molina wouldn't know what to make of it."

"How about a case of breaking and entering? Along with the usual murder."

"Stop acting so martyred, Max Kinsella. You know you love this sort of challenge."

He suddenly grinned. "Yes, I do. Impossible tasks are the spring board of my life. Where'd you get that rather clingy cat-suit? I don't remember it."

"Didn't have it in your day. You said black. I don't have much black. I needed this for a Black Cat wine promotion earlier in the fall."

"Speaking of black cats, where's that one of yours?"

"I left Midnight Louie lying quietly tucked in my bed after a difficult drenching while shooting a cat-food commercial at the Mirage lagoon. I can count on knowing where he is nights," she added, untruthfully but with great righteousness.

"You always knew where I was: at the theater, until I had to duck out."

" 'Duck out.' You make it sound like you took a little run to the men's room. Six months, Max."

"We didn't argue like this before."

"*We* didn't know the whole truth about you before."

"You still don't." He grinned again.

"I know."

"And you love it. You love a mystery."

"I know, I know. Okay, let's start cracking this one."

He put the idling Taurus in gear to cruise past the deserted shopfronts once more, peering over the steering wheel at every door.

Finally he nodded. "None of the neighboring businesses have a reason to have anyone there at this time of night. That's a plus."

As the car turned the corner at the block's end, Temple saw that the building backed up on the rear of a similar shopping center. Though no loading dock loomed into the space between, there was plenty of room to park delivery trucks.

Max made a U-turn in midstreet and parked the car on the side street facing the main drag.

Although only a couple above-door lights lit this service area, the concrete paving was so starkly pale and bare that Temple couldn't imagine crossing it in her black cat-burglar suit; she would be like Midnight Louie trying to be invisible on a glacier.

"Come on," Max urged, "and no banging the car door."

"How am I supposed to shut it?" Temple had never heard a discreet car door.

"Leave it not-quite shut, if you have to. Nobody's going to steal the car in twenty minutes."

"Trust a crook to trust a crook to be predictable." Temple came around to the car's street side on soundless, catlike feet.

Max glanced down. "Much better. When did you get black tennis shoes?"

"I didn't. I used black shoe polish on one of my pink metallic pairs."

"One of—?" Max lowered his voice even more. "From now on we only whisper, and not much."

She nodded and crossed the street beside him, wishing for the cover of a nice midwestern avenue arched over with veiling elms . . . only most of those had succumbed to Dutch elm disease, so even midwestern streets weren't the sheltered spaces she remembered from her childhood.

Max's shoes were black and as well mannered as hers. They walked like ghosts, Temple trying to recall how many shops Darren Cooke's office was from this end.

Apparently Max had taken care of that detail already. He stopped at a nondescript metal door, and pulled something pale from somewhere on his person. "Surgical gloves. Put 'em on."

He did himself as he had advised her, then gave the door an examination such a plain entrance hardly deserved, examining even the roofline for security devices and wires, she supposed.

"Turn around," he whispered. "What you don't witness you can't testify to."

Shivering in the lower night temperatures, Temple crossed her arms over her chest and obeyed. The neighborhood was deadly quiet. She heard every small noise behind her, the occasional brush of clothing on itself, snicks and scrapes. Unconsciously, she braced for the sudden blaring shriek of an alarm system.

Finally, she leaned against the building. Not watching was worse than watching, because she could only imagine what Max was doing and when it might be critical. She didn't know what particular moments to dread, so she dreaded the entire, unseen exercise. Maybe Max loved this stuff, but she loved the prize at the end of the hunt, not the means of getting to it.

She pictured Matt here at this moment; he would be mulling over the situational ethics. To break the law to break a case, or not. He wouldn't even be here.

So why was she?

She heard a snicking sound, and then the doorknob turning.

"Get in fast," Max advised, so she did, the black shadow that was her merging with the black shadow that was him and both disappearing through what seemed a literal crack in the door.

When he shut it behind her, the darkness inside was total.

Temple let out a ragged breath.

"Don't worry." Max's voice echoed a little. "This little light of mine will guide us."

It flashed on, the beam of a pencil-thin high-intensity flashlight. The light whipped around the room, showing Temple three plain doors leading to other rooms, some empty worktables, a disconnected table lamp, cardboard cartons and a pyramid of toilet paper and paper-towel rolls against one wall.

Max followed the dancing beam around the perimeter, returning to her in two minutes flat.

"Bathroom, storage room and outer office. You notice whether the exterior windows have any coverings?"

"I can't remember, but they must. The sun glare would hit them hard at either morning or evening."

"I'll check out the office. Stay here."

"In the dark? Alone?"

"You saw it; nothing here but paper products."

She nodded, but he already had flicked the light toward one of the doors. Then it went out.

Temple waited. In the dark her hearing grew more acute. She now discerned the eternal rumble of a ventilation fan, which snapped once in a while from something caught in it. And smell!

The bathroom broadcast that awful, fruity, sweet-strong air-freshener scent used in cars. Flamingo-pink stuff, now that she remembered it, that smelled like . . . dead flamingos, for sure. Dead ducks. Her and Max, if caught. Red faces, and worse.

The wait and the silence grew intolerable. Time seemed motionless. Surely Max had been gone at least twenty minutes, maybe thirty. An occasional muffled thump from the other room offered some reassurance, until she wondered who else it might be.

She heard the door crack open, then a cue stick of light pointed to the floor.

"It's clear. I've got a desktop lamp on, but we don't dare use the overheads. And I turned the ceiling fan off because they might move the vertical blinds apart."

She followed his harsh whisper into the other room, but it wasn't the one she had visited more officially earlier today.

Her heart began thumping with dismay. Max was bending over the laptop computer on a desktop corner.

"What are you looking around for?" he asked.

"This isn't the office I was in today! This is the wrong place."

"Inner office. Check beyond that door, but don't open it too wide. Those vertical blinds would move at an angel's sigh."

Peering through as he had instructed, she saw Alison's desk and the copier. "I never suspected an inner office."

"Had to be someplace where the boss could duck visitors if he had to. I doubt Cooke came here much. Let the help run his business. The big computer out front is full of booking dates and tax returns. All the routine business stuff. This is where he'd stash anything private. So what are we looking for?"

"Number one, a thick manila envelope filled with letters."

"You do the drawers while I try to figure out if there are any safeguarded areas on this computer."

He put the laptop on his knees and pushed the cushy leather desk chair away from the desk the length of his long legs. Temple searched the office furniture to the accompaniment of clicking keys and the occasional balky beep of an operating system that was being pushed against its inclinations.

She took Max's nasty little flashlight to examine the inside of every drawer, then the underbelly of the desktop and the drawer bottoms. She pulled each one out to study the drawer backs.

She crawled into the kneehole and felt all the exposed and hidden surfaces. She lifted the plastic chair mat. No hidden manila envelope. She took apart the small bookshelf the same way. She even lifted the silk jacaranda tree's pot and looked beneath it; only rusty water stains on the cream-colored carpeting. Who would water a fake plant? Maybe an office cleaning service. She poked through the real bark surrounding the phony trunk, dislodging a small spider.

The desktop was bare as Mother Hubbard's cupboard, but she checked under the deskpad and protective paper tucked into its four leatherette corners. She eyed the desk lamp, a Danish modern affair that hid nothing. The countertop under the small bookcase bore the most office litter: a coffeemaker, empty plastic-cup holders. Temple shook her head at the unreal real world. O-ring padded folders, piled up. An electric shaver, still plugged in. A recipe box painted with tole flowers, probably a silly gift put to office use. And a huge Rolodex.

Temple jumped on the Rolodex like Midnight Louie on a morsel of meat. She took it to the desk lamp and crouched down to examine the alphabetized entries under the brightest light available.

"What is Darren Cooke's daughter's name?" Max's voice sounded strained, he had been silent for so long.

"The sicko one? I don't think she used one on the letter. Just 'your daughter.'"

"No, I want the baby one, the apple of his eye."

"Oh. Um . . . Padgett."

"You can spell that?"

"You can't? P-a-d-g-e-t-t. If they didn't get New Age Hollywood and change it to something like P-a-g-e-t."

Max hit a short riff of keys. "They didn't." He sounded pleased with himself. "Found a password area. Might contain some interesting stuff. You turn up anything?"

The CRT screen lit his face from below, highlighting the concentration lines etched deeply into his features. Computers were just another complicated cryptogram for Max to solve. Temple liked to use computers, but she never went more than screen-deep into their mysteries. Wait a minute! Max had never even met Darren Cooke. How did he know what the password would be?

Temple crouched there pouting a little at the patented Kinsella enigma: the windmills of his mind were always hidden within boxes within boxes. Sometimes the closer she got to Max, the farther she got from the real person.

He must have used logic to find the password, must have read articles on the tendency to choose family names. She knew a little more about Darren Cooke than he did. Maybe she could pull a rabbit out of a hat too. But what—? She shoved the Rolodex away. It was crammed with business cards, erratically filed. A manila folder would never fit there, anyway.

Max's irritating whistle signaled he had found something juicy on-screen and she was supposed to go over and gawk at it.

"What?" Temple asked, not moving.

"Doing business with insider traders, looks like. The IRS would love to break into this area. If the assistant were erasing anything—and more likely she was transferring it to floppy first and then erasing—this is it."

Temple stared at the small, hard square disks piled beside the computer. "Why do they call them 'floppies,' anyway, when they're as hard as Mexican tiles?"

"Didn't used to be." Max looked up. "What's the matter? Couldn't find anything?"

Now he was reading her moods! Temple got up and wandered around the desk. She went to the bookcase and pulled out the books again, this time looking inside every one. Just computer manuals and reference books, the kind of things you'd expect to find in an office.

She frowned and looked down at the counter's littered surface. There was one thing you didn't expect to find in an office, especially Darren Cooke's office, since he was notoriously *not* the domestic type. A recipe box. But it was the right size for office index cards.

She opened the lid. Flower-decorated labels popped up above the level field of index cards like spring crocuses. "Appetizers. Main Courses. Hot Tamales. Pastries. Sugar-and-Spice. Sweetmeats. Exotic Drinks."

Well, the exotic drinks probably fit in with his lifestyle, at least.

Temple suddenly clapped the box shut, as if it were Pandora's hope chest.

Max bolted up from the chair. "What is it? You heard something?"

"Yeah, my little gray cells turning pure silver and hitting pay-dirt."

"All the secrets I'm finding on this computer are financial manipulations. What have you got?"

Now he was coming over to gawk at her find, and she didn't even know what she had. Just suspected.

Temple took the box to the desk lamp, set it down and opened it as if she expected a rattlesnake to pop out.

"Recipes?"

"Maybe."

She pulled out an index card behind the label "Sugar-and-Spice." A smaller white card was taped to its lined face, a hand-written "For my only darling!" scrawled across it. Underneath was hand-printed: "Miranda Cummings," then an address and phone number. And a notation: "A sultry dish with paprika hair and legs long enough to make an octopus jealous." And a date.

Temple pulled out another index card. This one had a business card affixed, but a similar coyly written summary.

"Cooke!" she said. "This is Darren *Cooke*'s little black book! His wife must have found my card in here, not at the hotel room, as she said. I didn't think the police would have overlooked searching under the mattress." She looked up at Max. "That must have been an eerie task, his widow coming here to go through this box of . . . forbidden treats. And, look, the dates are sequential in each category—aha, three days before I was hit on . . . Dana, the nanny! His own daughter's nanny. Did that man have no sexual conscience?"

Max took the box and began paging through. "Of course not. He was infamous for it."

"The nanny could have been the mousy miniskirted woman who visited Cooke's suite last week!"

"His wife?" Max wasn't really paying attention.

"No, the nanny."

"What category do you suppose you were under?"

"I don't know, maybe 'Appetizers.' Is there a section for food allergies?"

"Let's see what 'Desserts' is like."

"Let's not." Temple snatched for the box. "This is a lascivious little stockpile. It could be used to blackmail a lot of women."

"I know. It's always handy to have something on the rich and famous."

"It's not our business to read it. We'll have to turn it over to the police. Why do you suppose Michelle left this here?"

"Safer. Hardly anyone knew about the office. And she didn't want to make the personal assistant suspicious; just told her to transfer the computer financial records to those piled disks, checked the front of all the categories to see who was most recent on her husband's Hall of Fame recipe files and used your card to contact you."

"Why would he put me in here with all these pushovers? And when?"

"He could have come here Sunday between brunch and midnight."

"Why?"

"To look at his records. Maybe to meet someone in a discreet place."

"Maybe . . . he liked to play games, and if you like to play games, you don't cheat at them. Maybe he had my card along because he intended to contact me again, and whoever met him here didn't know and put me in the file."

"Someone who knew about it."

Temple nodded. "*I* figured it out." She eyed the dark office lit by the lone island of light. "But no manila envelope."

"That he'd put somewhere really secure, like a literal safe. His conquests were not a secret. Nothing here. I checked the walls and floors when I first came in."

"That's why it seemed you were gone forever!"

"Maybe you just missed me."

She ignored that. "But the police checked with the Oasis front desk. Darren Cooke hadn't rented a safety-deposit box."

"Maybe not there. If he kept his black book at the office instead of in the bedroom, maybe he kept the letters in another hotel safe."

Temple nodded. "With all the hotels in town, it'd be like searching for one lightbulb in a whole galaxy."

"Not necessarily. He couldn't resist the Cooke recipe box. It's a pun of sorts, it refers back to himself. You might think of someplace significant to him right now."

"Not right now. It's too late to think. What do we do? Leave the box?"

"We have to. But . . . there's a copier in the outer office."

"Copy the cards? There must be dozens and dozens. The machine will make a heck of a noise in this tombstone area at this time of night."

"We can lay out several to a page. We'll set up a system and it'll go fast." Max checked his glow-in-the-dark watch face. "It's after one. Should only take half an hour or so. Then you won't have to worry about clues and evidence vanishing."

Temple nodded.

They hurried to the outer office and warmed up the machine, which made a telltale wheezing sound in operation.

"Wait!" Temple stopped Max from laying out the cards. "This machine has a reduce feature. We can get more cards to a page that way." She adjusted the setup, then Max began dealing out index cards faster than the eye could see.

Temple pushed the copy button, kept the paper feeder full and stacked the finished pages.

They worked fast, with a sense that the activity might attract someone at any instant. The cards seemed endless, even copying eight to a page. Temple felt feverish. She felt like a robot stacking the copies. Max was a machine himself, slapping cards to the glass copier surface in supernaturally neat rows.

"Had a lot of practice at this," he said once.

It took forty minutes, but the recipe-box contents were copied and back in their categories, and Temple had a sheaf of something to take out of the break-in site.

"Copier off. Paper tray refilled to the previous level," she announced.

They both studied the outer office for anything out of place.

"No discards in the wastebasket." Temple nudged it with her foot.

"Lights out here, then." Max snapped off the outer-office desk lamp.

They edged their blind way to the inner office, where the box was replaced, the clutter was reinstituted, the laptop and desk chair replaced and the desk lamp turned off.

The flashlight flared at the same instant.

They edged through the rear storeroom and out the back door.

"Go to the car," Max said. "I'll reset the alarm."

Temple went, counting the moments until she was off the street, with her armload of white papers, and safe within the Taurus's dim interior . . . which was still there, not stolen, hallelujah!

Temple scrunched down in the front seat, watching Max's dark figure fuss around the light-colored door. A car drove by on the main street. She hadn't dared slam her door shut, so she still felt vulnerable.

Any moment a bogeyman could spring out of the dark and jerk her door open . . . A bogeyman filled the passenger-side window even now. Temple jumped. And then Max slid into the driver's seat, leaving his door unslammed, and stripped off his thin latex gloves.

"You can toss yours now too." He glanced at her hands clutching the papers on her lap.

The latex gloves still felt oddly creepy. They hit the floor as soon as she could yank them off.

The Taurus, once started, crept onto the better-lit main street.

After a couple of turns and a few blocks, they entered Charleston Boulevard. More cars joined them. Soon they were merging with Strip traffic.

Max had been right, as he had been all too often lately. She was back at the Circle Ritz by 2 A.M.

Max parked beside her Storm.

"How's your book going?" she asked.

"A mess, but mine own, now that Gandolph's gone."

She nodded. Trying to organize a dead man's notes and computer files must be maddening. "I could look at what you've got, divide it into sections."

"Maybe we can use index cards, like Cooke's recipe book?"

She laughed. So did Max, but then he sobered.

"I've used my international contacts to check on the psychics present at the séance when Gandolph died. Oscar Grant of *Dead Zones* and D'Arlene Hendrix made several trips to Russia and Eastern Europe before and after the Iron Curtain collapse, investigating psychic phenomena."

"Isn't that routine for them?"

"Possibly. But they could have encountered terrorist agents. Maybe someone offered tit for tat: kill Gandolph and get Russian trade secrets from their years of secret psychic research."

"You still think Gandolph was murdered?"

"I'm still not satisfied that he wasn't."

"And until then, you're not going to let it go?"

"Would you?"

"No, but it isn't personal for me."

"You were there. Don't you hate being hoodwinked?"

"Not as badly as a professional magician might." Temple smiled. "I guess I came through my first breaking and entering without any neurotic damage."

"You found something, which is more than I thought possible. And keep trying to think of where Cooke might have hidden those letters. They could be the key to his death."

"Another maybe-murder."

Max shrugged. "Life is not as neatly compartmentalized as Cooke's recipe box. Neither is love."

She looked at him.

It felt just like it had in Minneapolis when they had first started dating . . . what, almost two years before? Coming home to her apartment in a warm cocoon of car, the winter night as close as the frosty rolled-up windows and as far away as Mars.

People courted in cars in a northern state like Minnesota, risking carbon-monoxide poisoning. She remembered the engine idling in park, the heater blowing, the headlights off and the conversation not stopping because nobody wanted to open a car door and let in the cold. Because then they would have had to dash through the subzero weather for her apartment-building door, and dashing always ruined the moment. Lingering on the stoop was impractical, so he'd drive away until the night the moment was right to not drive away.

No, it all had to happen in the car, with the engine off but the dashboard lights on, with the radio playing so low it was almost inaudible.

Max leaned forward to turn on the radio, but not very loud.

Temple felt like Pavlov's dog, her figurative tongue hanging out. When he pulled her across the center console like a rag doll, she felt an aching rush as if they had never made love. Yet their mouths meshed like gears, and the kisses never seemed to stop. They knew how to maximize each move and moment, and how to avoid each other's noses. Soon they were bumping the steering wheel and shift stick. Max's hands were finding areas they shouldn't have been able to reach in such close quarters, and Temple was rediscovering the pleasures of pent-up desire. It was like the very first time, the outcome was inevitable and the feeling was divine.

Uh-oh.

Temple disentangled herself.

"Wow. Max, give me a moment to think."

"I've had too many moments to think about this. Don't think, Temple, just let me love you."

She melted at his voice, his dimly seen face, the hands that had given her pleasure. They belonged together and came together again, until their breaths were deep and shaky.

"Let's go in," Max said.

And Temple hesitated.

His hands tightened. "Why not? We don't even have to practice safe sex. Do you know what a gift that is nowadays? Do you know how hard it was to be without you all that time I was gone?"

"Of course I do. I felt it too. It isn't sex, Max."

"What? Still out of trust because I didn't tell you my background? I've told you now. I shouldn't have, but I did."

"I know." She couldn't say what stopped her. She couldn't say anything, just choked on a lump of indecision.

Max's hands left her to bang down on the steering wheel. "Damn Devine!"

"It's not Matt, either."

"Isn't it? You keep saying he's not the rival I think he is, but you won't say why. Something is holding you back."

"Maybe . . . it's reality. When you left I couldn't fantasize that we were the real thing. You mentioned marriage again, at the Welles house, but now you're caught up in whether Gandolph was killed or just died, and that kind of quest could go on forever."

Max stared ahead, his hands on the wheel as if he were still driving. His eyewhites glistened in the light of a streetlamp. Otherwise, she could hardly see him, and certainly not his expression.

"My mistake," he said finally. "In Minneapolis I thought I could do it: lose the past, start a future with you. I still think it sometimes. I'm not just trying to avenge Gary, if he were killed. I'm worried that if someone got him in that clandestine way, someone could get me. And then getting married is a fantasy; besides, you don't trust me—"

"I don't trust myself anymore."

"It would clear up matters if you'd just tell me Devine's big secret."

He was right. She swallowed, licked her lips. No words came.

"Then you're more loyal to him than you are to me."

"No! I just can't betray a confidence."

"Would you tell him my history if he asked?"

"No."

"If a lot depended on it, like he might go away and you'd never see him again?"

"No."

"Your loyalties really are divided, right down the center. It can't be pleasant. How did that happen so fast, Temple?"

"It wasn't fast. It was worry so constant I couldn't stand to think about you anymore. It was Lieutenant Molina always probing about you, showing me how little I knew. It was those men in the parking garage. Everything would have been bearable, Max, if I'd had even a rough notion of what was wrong. I wouldn't have told."

"You can't know that. You can't imagine the extreme methods to make you tell that exist in the shadow world next to this one. Now you do know. You have something to not tell. You're worse off than before, and so am I if you punish me for protecting you. So now what?"

"I need to think about it. Maybe go away for a while."

"I think you need to go to bed with me, to remember what we had feels like."

"That's so tempting . . . that's why I hesitate. I shouldn't be just tempted, I should be jumping at the chance."

"I still say Devine is playing a bigger part in this than you admit."

Temple shook her head in the dark. She didn't know anymore. "I was considering going away for Christmas."

"Home to Minnesota?"

"No. To see my aunt in New York."

"City?"

She nodded slightly, then realized he couldn't see the gesture. "Yes."

"Temple, don't cry."

"I guess I will if I have to."

"I'll miss you."

"There's always New Year's."

He sighed, a huge heave of frustration. He was entitled to it,

Temple thought. Great erotic moments that go awry always turn into great letdowns.

She opened the car door. "I'll let you know . . . if I go."

He was silent. Then, "I love you."

"I love you too," she said before slamming the door shut.

She was glad he didn't walk her in; she could hardly see for the stupid tears and stumbled like a drunk on the low threshold.

She turned in the doorway, and saw the Taurus's headlights abruptly spear the darkness. It began to nose away as her door shut.

You could be upstairs in bed with Max right now, she berated herself in the elevator. *You could be setting records in the sexual Olympics. That long separation, the tension of the break-in tonight cutting loose. As Michelle put it, oh-la-la. Instead you need a cold compress and a pain pill and your head examined.*

She let herself into the dark apartment, not bothering to turn on lights, just feeling her way blindly to the bedroom. *Instead, all you have in your bed is a black cat who tries to ease you right onto the floor.*

Temple turned on the overhead light, wincing as the bedroom leaped into immediate clarity. She could see Max walking toward the bathroom, bare as Hamlet's bodkin.

Ghosts she could conjure. What she suddenly realized she couldn't see was Midnight Louie. She scanned the room, called his name. He liked his comforts enough to come home nights. Where was he? Drat! Temple realized that if Max *had* come up, they wouldn't even have had to worry about dislodging Louie.

Temple nearly hit the ceiling. She had finally fallen asleep when the phone rang in the dark of night. The wriggly red numbers on her bedside clock read three-thirty.

Had Max—?

She answered, her heart still drumming from the abrupt awakening.

"Temple."

Matt's voice. Or was she confusing the two men? Now she could understand how Darren Cooke might feel.

"Matt? You must be just home from work."

"Yeah. I hate to disturb you, but I tried calling all night. From after midnight on, anyway. You must have had the phone ringer turned off."

That sounded lame even to her. No use trying to fool a professional phone man.

"Not really. I was . . . out," Temple said.

"Out?"

"I can't say where or why, but it involves Darren Cooke."

"Can you say 'with whom'?" he asked pointedly.

"Ah—"

"None of my business," he added. Too hastily. "I thought you'd want to know this as soon as possible."

"Know what?"

"Tonight. He called."

"He called?" She was thinking of Max again, for some reason. And was confused.

"Him. My regular. The sex addict."

"But . . . Darren Cooke is dead. I may not be sure why, but I sure am sure of that. Mr. Cooke, he dead."

"So they say, but my chronic caller isn't. He also isn't Darren Cooke, unless they run phone lines from the afterlife."

"Matt! Then you didn't hear the last person to visit Darren Cooke arrive. You heard some other floozie arriving at some other Lothario's door."

"Sounds reasonable to me."

"This . . . ruins everything. My whole case."

"Maybe it shouldn't be your case, Temple. Maybe it's a sign to retire from the Nancy Drew business. We were wrong, all the way. Just plain wrong. And you're just as wrong about Darren Cooke's death being suspicious."

Temple couldn't think of a thing to say.

Everything Matt said was absolutely right.

Maybe.

When he hung up, she recalled that something (besides the Mystifying Max) had troubled her presleep mind. She often got her best ideas in that foggy limboland between wakefulness and sleep. Now, fully awake and almost as disturbed by what Matt had just told her as she had been previously by her Mexican standoff with Max, Temple felt her barefoot way into the main room. Still no Louie. Great; another problem to worry terrierlike at her overcharged mind. Where on earth was Midnight Louie?

The copied entries from Cooke's recipes-for-rendezvous file lay dumped on the coffee table. She had skimmed them at the office, recognizing some names, not most. But she had recognized something else without quite knowing it. Yawning, she stood next to the lit floor lamp, staring down at the pages. Should have set the copier's darkness feature higher. Some of the writing faded on upper and lower loops, making it almost cryptographic. She kept looking for the discrepancy that was bothering her unconscious mind.

Something was . . . different. Temple's glance lingered on the famous name of a West Coast TV talk-show anchorwoman. Why did *she* need to do the bedroom boogie with Darren Cooke?

"Midnight rendezvous in a limousine," was scrawled across the woman's embossed business card. "Great traction, but a sticky carburetor."

Temple frowned at the crude summation, then realized that the crassness didn't bother her as much as the handwriting. Was it really Darren Cooke's? She had seen a sample of his writing somewhere . . . when?

She yawned. Where? At his brunch. On what? Then her eyes opened wide enough to let in too much lamplight. She rushed squinting back to her bedroom. What had she worn to Gangster's the first day she had watched Louie?

She must have absently tucked away Cooke's card, the gag one, on which he had scrawled his hotel-suite number for the brunch. She remembered consulting it before leaving for the Oasis Sunday morning and slipping it into . . . no, she hadn't taken her tote bag for once, and she had worn leggings . . . no pockets there, but the Big White Shirt she almost never wore had one tiny breast pocket for effect. Could she have slipped it in there, then returned the shirt to the lost-and-found department in her closet for another three years?

Turning on all the bedroom lights only made her eyes water, but she paged, blinking, through the hangers until her hand closed on the slightly wrinkled shirt.

A hasty pat-down revealed something flat and sharp-edged inside the pocket. Either a forgotten calculator or . . . She reached in with a gingerly forefinger and thumb, and pulled out . . . Cooke's card!

She didn't compare it to the copy paper she'd brought into the room until she was sitting on the bed. The handwriting on the recipe cards and Cooke's card were identical. But, Temple recalled, on *her* card, the one Michelle had found, it had *not* been quite the same. More heavily pressed down, slanted less, not exactly right at all. If only she could see her card to be sure! Who had it now? Cooke's widow or Lieutenant Molina?

A slight difference in writing, if genuine, would explain why Temple was erroneously labeled for the trysting pile: Cooke didn't do it. Someone else did, either assuming that their brief bedroom interlude was romantic rather than of a business nature, or wanting someone—people, the police—to think that Temple was Darren's last lover.

She had to see her card again. And there was something else she ought to look into. Who had any business imitating a busy man's handwriting? Who had any chance to become adept at it? No one but his very own personal assistant.

But not until morning. Temple settled down again in the dark.

"Goodnight, Max," she whispered. "Goodnight, Louie."

Wherever you are.

Chapter 32

Louie Is Knocked Out

I awake, prone. I expect to be in a cage, but it is worse than that. I lie in a sort of homemade pen.

I recognize the room right off: small, pale, with a long table covered in white cloth and a smell of rubbing alcohol and disinfectant.

Despite the long, cloth-covered table, this is no dining room. There is only one chair, a rolling stool, in the corner. There is a built-in cabinet full of things that smell harsh and antiseptic.

Every bone in my body aches, and every muscle, and my head most of all.

I know I have been put into an artificial slumber with chloroform or some more powerful anesthetic. My memories of my arrival here last night are confused. This Mickey Finn they pumped into my veins is not helping me any.

The cab ride cost eight dollars and seventy cents. Miss Savannah Ashleigh tipped the driver a buck. I made sure to remember the amount in case I need to retrace my route here. I remember the driver grumbling about cheapskates. (As far as I know, skates are not very cheap these days; those on-line blades cost a small fortune.)

Uh! Why can I remember the small stuff and not the big? The room goes in and out of focus, like the walls are breathing and I am not. All right. The office was officially closed. I remember the doctor, a man in a white coat, (really precise ID, Louie!) complaining that he had no staff, no nurse.

"I will be your nurse," Miss Savannah Ashleigh had volunteered in an iron tone.

He had fussed some, about not being licensed for this. About criminal mischief. What about my owner? he had asked.

"He is a stray. An alley cat. No one owns him," she had answered honestly enough, vitriol searing every word.

The thing is, Miss Savannah Ashleigh believed that she was lying, that she was concealing Miss Temple Barr's relationship to me.

I can read the handwriting on the prescription pad. I am here to be put to death. It may be a private execution, but it will be as final nevertheless. I wonder what the Divine Yvette will be told. Probably that I ran off, never to return. What will Miss Temple Barr think? That I was run over or lost. She will search every crack in the Las Vegas concrete for me, leave no grain of sand unturned, but it will be useless. No one knew of my mission to the Goliath. No one will suspect that I was carried off by a vengeful, crackpot film star. No one will know. Ever.

I sigh. I plan to fight every inch of the way, but suspect I will not be given much chance. I may even be gassed in the Divine One's carrier, oh irony of ironies!

Now would be a great time to deliver one of my favorite closing speeches. "It is a far, far better" et cetera.

But there is nothing better about this predicament.

When the doctor comes at me with the needle, I duck and twist and buck, but ultimately feel the final prick. I do not understand why he is so reluctant. Surely he performs such nefarious acts every day. I must be at a shelter, accused of being rabid or some such story. Certainly Miss Savannah Ashleigh acts as if she has some say-so over the doctor's actions.

But that was then . . . and this, much to my surprise, is now. I find myself awake, as I did not expect to be ever again.

Now I feel pain.

And I realize that my fate is to be far more horrible than a quick anonymous death in a neat little room.

I am to be kept alive. I am to be tormented. I am secretly in stir. But while there is life, there is a chance of escape, however slim. I am still a fighter.

And yet it strikes me, as I gaze at the merciless fluorescent light above me, that I am paying the ultimate price for something I did not do. I never once successfully touched the Divine Yvette. Not through any failure of my own intention, but through mere circumstance.

For the first time in my life, or what is left of it, I am able to state: I am a completely innocent dude.

Chapter 33

At the Drop of a Card

Temple awoke the next morning with flamingos on her mind.

Dream fragments still floated on the out-of-focus white screen of her ceiling. Oh, yeah. She had been doing a fandango with Max, for an audience of flamingos, who were swiftly grabbed by passersby for use as . . . golf clubs.

Then Midnight Louie had waddled by, upright on two feet, wearing an orange vest and top hat, clutching a pocket watch and complaining that he was late for work. Electra appeared out of nowhere as the Red Queen, followed by a pack of Darren Cooke's conquest recipe cards. Matt had been nowhere in sight in this Mad Hatter's dream, which was typical.

She sat up in bed, donning her glasses to inspect the coverlet for Louie. He seldom stayed out all night anymore, but he had now.

Flamingos. Things had been so hectic lately that she'd forgotten to check in with Domingo. And she hadn't gotten a message from the À La Cat film crew, so she didn't know when Louie would be needed next. Perhaps not until Yvette had recovered from her dysentery or distemper or whatever was supposed to be wrong with her, besides sprinkling in her carrier and shrinking when wet. Meanwhile, Temple could laze in bed a little and speculate on all sorts of things that were none of her business, always the most fascinating topics of consideration.

Had Sid Caesar stepped into Darren Cooke's soft shoes yet? Did it feel creepy to stand in for a dead man? Omigosh! She'd neglected to ask the director for a free show pass for Electra. Even with Cooke dead, she was sure a devoted fan like Electra would want to see what he *would* have been doing if he *weren't* dead.

Snatches of the chorus production number swirled in her head, the human hoofers intermixed with quick-stepping flamingos. Pretty good show. Clever idea to hark back to Las Vegas's colorful days of yore, when larger-than-life figures like Bugsy Siegel and Howard Hughes had made Las Vegas their private playpen, then ultimately the world's.

Actually, the revue, with its tribute to Bugsy and the Fabulous Flamingo hotel that he founded, was more appropriate to the current Flamingo Hilton. The one that gave Domingo's installations such a run for the money with its lavishly lit façade of a flamingo chorus line. Bits of the original 1946 structure still lurk within the thrice-rebuilt hotel today. And Temple had learned why Bugsy (who hated his nickname) had named his hotel-casino the Flamingo: Flamingo was a nickname for his feisty girlfriend Virginia Hill! Virginia apparently turned a vivid shade of red when she drank, which was often. Temple would have to tell Domingo sometime . . .

Flamingos. So many feathers to cover a gawky-graceful bird that only weighed three to seven pounds, including lightweight, long neck and legs—even the six-foot-tall ones, which would almost match Max's height . . .

Temple's hand drew patterns along the comforter's zebrastripes. Darren Cooke had almost been ready to perform that revue for an audience. He'd been drenched in Old Las Vegas flavor for weeks. He used a recipe box to hold Cooke's cookies and their cards. Why wouldn't he use a flamingo box to hold the missing manila envelope?

Nothing to do with Domingo's presence here. That was coincidental. But the Flamingo Hilton's safety-deposit boxes . . . Cooke must have stayed there before, been "comped" as a celebrity. Wouldn't the management have let him use a hotel safe for a few weeks if he had asked? Treating celebrities with discretion had been a Las Vegas password even before Sinatra's Rat Pack ran up tabs and tabloid coverage in the sixties.

Temple checked her clock face in the harsh light of day. Ten-thirty. Time to rise and shine, Lt. C. R. Molina!

Temple speed-dialed the police number, and was lucky enough to reach Molina eventually.

"Barr," Temple said as brusquely as Molina announced herself. "Have you tried the guest safes at the Flamingo?"

"For what? Being broken and entered?"

"Not tried in that way. Have you checked to see if Darren Cooke kept a box there?"

"Why would he? He wasn't registered there."

"Maybe not this trip, but I've got a hunch he might have hidden the envelope of letters there."

"You left out 'crazy' in front of 'hunch.' We don't have time—"

Temple cut her off. It felt good. "Only the police could find out for sure. What would it take? A phone call? I'd be happy to identify anything you find."

"It takes a warrant too. And I bet you'd be—" Molina began, but Temple hung up.

Being a chicken, she had mumbled " 'Bye" first.

Temple figured she could handle the second stage of this paper chase herself. She called the Oasis and asked for a room. The operator put her call through, but the phone rang until it tripped a voice-mail request to leave a message.

No way, Temple thought, with all the savvy of a PR veteran. Leaving messages gave people time to think about what they'd say to the message-leaver. Temple didn't want that. Surprise was paramount when you wanted to elicit a confession. And she did think one aspect of the Darren Cooke death called for a confession.

So she decided to take a chance on trying another likely site in person. She went on a whim. She had a hunch, and a nagging, itchy hunch is as demanding as any unsatisfied drug habit.

The drive wasn't long, but it gave Temple time to plan her approach. She would be matter-of-fact, but nonaccusatory. The idea was to confirm a suspicion, not to stir up defensive anger.

She parked in front this time, in plain sight, and neared the windows with their blinds drawn tight against the . . . *overhead* sun, which wouldn't hit the glass full on until late afternoon. A little early to be so discreet.

Temple's knock set the closed miniblinds shimmying against the door's inset glass. She knocked again. And again.

Finally she walked to the corner, counting and studying cars, and down the side street to the building's rear. Parked halfway down that side, all by its lonesome, sat an old Volkswagen Beetle convertible painted a dazzling new white.

Her hunch already paying off, Temple marched back to the Strip shopping center's front façade and the blind-shrouded office.

She knocked again, waited, then said loudly, "I know you're in there, and I won't go away. You could leave, of course, in the car parked out back, but I'd just find you someplace else."

She waited, forbearing to knock again.

Finally, the door blinds rattled. A lock clicked. Temple turned the knob and entered.

The outer office seemed almost as dim as last night, even with all the tabletop lamps on. Against one wall, the copier wheezed. Temple could see its tiny green operating lights from the door.

Alison Darby looked hot and bothered in a shapeless gray jogging suit with baggy pants. Her fashionably cut, burgundy-tinted salon hairstyle was flat on one side and pushed into an inappropriate pouf on the other, as if slept on. Her face was in similar condition, puffy and hollow at the same time, making her look far older.

"Did you often sign documents for Darren Cooke?" Temple asked, figuring her victim was stressed enough to tell the truth without thinking about it.

"Sign? What are you talking about? Why are you here? I've got to finish up the office work quickly, because I certainly can't afford an Oasis room now that Darren's dead."

"A lot of secretaries do it, forge their bosses' signatures. I bet they get pretty good at mimicking their handwriting too."

"Personal assistant," she corrected. "I wasn't just a secretary, though it sure looks like it now." She eyed the office and rubbed a sweatshirt sleeve against her damp forehead, making the improbably magenta bangs stand up like soldiers on parade.

"Why kill yourself? Surely his widow will want you to stay on as an employee and sort through things."

"No. I don't think she will. And, anyway, I don't want to stay any longer than I have to." Harried, she eyed the idling copy machine.

Working over a warmed-up copy machine under a deadline can be a sweaty job. Temple knew, having done it just the other night. But she guessed that something else might be making Alison Darby so hot under the collar.

"Just tell me if you wrote Sunday's date on my card in Darren's bedroom that day. Because it isn't quite his handwriting."

"How do you know?" The tone was sassy teenage challenge.

"Because," Temple said gently, "I looked at Darren's other cards, with his real handwriting on them, in the box in his office, right back there."

Alison glanced backward, as horrified as if the ghost of Cooke had strolled out from the office.

"And I copied them, like you're doing now." Temple nodded to the pile of index cards beside the copier. "Look. I know you were trying to protect your boss. I don't know what you thought you'd accomplish by making me seem like one of his conquests, but that won't hold up. Michelle has my card now, and the police will have it soon."

"Michelle!" Alison cast anxious glances from Temple to the copier. "Why would *she* have it?"

"I'm not quite sure. You may have left it in his bedroom to be found, or have brought it here to the recipe box, where it was accidentally found. Michelle might have come in one day—"

"I couldn't refuse her the keys to the office."

"No. But you didn't have to point a finger at me through my card. I was only in the bedroom with Darren for a few minutes—"

"That was always enough for him!" she spit out.

"But it wasn't enough for me. And all the time in the world wouldn't have been enough for me if the man were Darren Cooke."

"You . . . didn't like him?"

"Let's sit down at the desk, at least. Oh, I liked him. He could be very charming. But I knew his reputation, his game, that's all. I wasn't about to play."

Alison regarded her with a certain numb approval. "You would have been an exception."

"You were an exception too, weren't you?"

She paused on the brink of saying something, then broke into wild, almost operatic laughter, too forced to be genuine. Maybe it was early hysteria.

"A notable exception," she finally panted between the gusts of harsh laughter that rocked her. "To the end."

"You know what I think?" Temple said, keeping her voice even and low. "I think you marked my card because you were trying to protect him."

"Protect him?" Her light eyes stared as if Temple were speaking Urdu.

"I think you found his body that Monday morning before anyone was alerted. Maybe you went back to the suite early. He had to be at Gangster's by nine. Maybe he usually went over the schedule bright and early every morning.

"Only this morning, he was dead. When I left Sunday noon, he was depressed. He could have gotten a lot more depressed by midnight. I think you didn't want it to look like a suicide, so you marked my card and brought it here and put it in the box, hoping suspicion would fall on me, a handy stranger. That's why you didn't destroy that incriminating recipe box. You hoped that if the police suspected something other than suicide, they would hunt farther afield, learn about Darren's office and then find my card, dated the last of all his ladies.

"You didn't know that I would be the last person to be suspected of anything, since I'm known to the local police already—"

"You are? My God, what are you?"

Temple shrugged modestly. "What my card says. A PR freelancer. I help the police sometimes. I can help you now, if you'll just confirm my scenario. Then all the pieces will fit together. I'm not angry that you tried to implicate me, I just want to know why you wanted to implicate someone in what was so clearly going to be declared a suicide."

"Why?" Her fingers drove into her scalp at the temples, pushing her short hair spikes into a punk Mohawk. "You're right. I found him. That morning. Such a shock. Such a surprise. I didn't expect him to escape."

"Escape—?"

"I had to think. I didn't know what the police would conclude. If they'd realize it was suicide, or wouldn't know he had a motive—and then some!—for that. I wanted to cover everything. So I did what I did, don't even remember half of it, except I handled everything with a plastic bag left over from the party." She glanced up, smiling crookedly. "I even wrote Sunday's date on your card with that damn plastic around the pen. That's why the writing wasn't perfect! Usually my imitations of his handwriting are perfect."

"We—"

"You're not alone?" Alison looked wildly around the office.

"My associates," Temple went on, giving an unforgivably wrong impression, but beginning to feel a bit uneasy. Alison appeared to have emotions and motives Temple hadn't dreamed of. "They thought for a while that Darren made a call late that night, just as someone unexpected was arriving. A woman, of course."

"He . . . called someone that night? At midnight?"

Temple nodded, watching Alison unravel with every revelation. Amateurs should never involve themselves in criminal matters; they have no idea of the consequences.

"That lead turned out to be . . . unreliable," Temple said. "Still, you should know that . . . we have a fair idea of why he killed himself, and there's no sense in letting it go public. Such a sad, private story should remain private."

"You . . . idiot!" Alison was standing, her hands still clawing her scalp, as if they would start pulling out hanks of hair at any moment. "Keep it private! I don't want it private. I want the world to know what he was, especially now that he's escaped. What have I got to lose, lady? You tell me. You think you know why he committed suicide? Well, think again. I *know.*"

The intensity of her furious, taunting tone startled Temple. Everything she said to try to make things better seemed to madden Alison more.

"I'm only trying to handle this delicately—"

"There's no delicate way to handle it." Alison began pacing behind the desk, back and forth like a caged hyena. "Delicate?"

"Then you know about the letters?"

"Of course I do. First of all, I was his personal assistant these last nine months. Nine months. Such a nice, round number. I got all the mail. He couldn't get there first without making a suspicious fuss about it."

"You didn't . . . read them first?"

"Yes, I did. I read them first, because I wrote them first."

Adrenaline pushed Temple to her feet, although that didn't do her much good. She suddenly realized that Alison Darby was bigger-boned and taller than she, and much more agitated.

"How did you know that the call was made at midnight?"

"Because it was around then that I arrived. I wasn't exactly checking my watch, but I should know roughly the time for the most important moment of my life."

"You found him at midnight, then? Dead?"

"No." She came deliberately around the desk, ready to push her face up against Temple's to make herself exactly clear.

Temple forced herself not to back up, knowing any weakness would only undermine her position. Tracking a woman who had hastily implicated her in a suspicious death was one thing; confronting a possible murderer was another.

"He was alive then, our Darren," Alison said, seeing him again. "Very much so. A little drunk, but he was used to functioning that way. And seeing me really perked the old guy up. Pulled out all his energy and charm. He'd been working on me for months, for so long that he'd given up. I had been the one Untouchable around him, and then there I was, in my French negligee I'd paid half a month's salary for, and he paid me pretty good. That's the only thing I'll miss. The salary."

"*You* were his midnight visitor?" Temple sounded more confused than she meant to.

The Voice had called Matt since Darren Cooke's death, so how could Matt have heard a woman arrive during a call from some other sex addict, at the same time as this woman here actually did visit Darren Cooke's suite?

"And how! He was ready. He went from the dumps to the Alps in five seconds flat. It gave me a sense of power. Him needing a woman that bad. Needing me." She sat suddenly on the desk's front edge, all threat gone.

"So we went into the bedroom, and did it."

Temple, her legs as weak as Jell-O straws, sat again in the chair.

Alison knew she had a paralyzed audience. She went on with a kind of holy satisfaction.

"This is what I trained to do since I was fifteen, and Mama finally told me who my father was. I went to secretary school not only to get the skills to get close enough, but to get an idea of how to dress and groom my nails, how to speak and write properly. It would have been so easy to grow up like I really was from the gutter he left us in, but I knew I'd never have anything better, never have any peace, until I prepared for my Plan, and executed it."

"He was your father, and you had sex with him?"

"*He* thought so, but I wasn't really there," she said witheringly. "I was back in junior high, where they made fun of me and my clothes and ways. I could even smell the lead-pencil shavings in the dirty, smudgy sharpeners."

"And that was your plan, always?"

"Part of it." She looked sly and smug now.

Temple could think of nothing more to do than to interview her. She knew how to keep people talking about themselves. Although Alison had no obvious weapon on her, she was armed with obsessive years of vengeful plotting. It made her formidable beyond any gun or knife.

While she had talked, and Temple had asked, Temple had been studying the room in quick glances. Matt's voice came into her head: "Anyone who attacks you knows what weapon he'll use; only you know what weapon you can *find* and use."

Temple hadn't sat down out of shock, or a wish to give Alison the advantage of a greater height over her. She'd sat because the chair had rollers. On the vinyl-tiled floor she could suddenly push off and get away, or get to something, faster than Alison could react. But what to flee to? What to use to overpower this demonically driven young woman?

"So after you and he were through—"

"I told him who and what I was. He was . . . sputtering. He couldn't believe it, but I convinced him. Before she died, Mama had given me the date he was in town, what show he had been doing, what he drank that night, everything. From the day she told me, I kept a scrapbook of anything I could find about him. Old stuff, new stuff. Where he went, I went in my mind. The letters didn't start until I was almost ready. I wanted to let him know what he had left out there. *Who* he had left out there, alone."

"But neither your mother nor you gave him a chance to know you."

"Did he come back to his one-night stands to see how they were doing a year or twenty later? This man was a machine. A jackhammer just loose on the street, smashing into anything around it. If you were a woman, and got in his path, you got drilled and were supposed to like it. And, then, after all that damage, he had the gall to get married."

The words "get married" rang with contempt.

"To have 'a baby.' His first baby, the papers said. Not quite. That's when I began the letters, a couple of years ago. Then I tried to get a job with him. I had to make him think I would be another easy one, but just a little bit hard, so he'd actually hire me to wear me down. Boy, did it bother him to find me so hard. I could see it in his eyes. So I tormented him for nine months, and kept sending my letters and watched him fall apart."

"I still don't understand what you got out of all this, besides revenge."

Alison picked up a letter opener that Temple had been discreetly eyeing. The pewter handle was molded into the masks of tragedy and comedy, so it was probably an award Cooke had won.

She laughed, throwing her head up as if to defy a higher power. "I was going to get money, honey. Lots of money. That's what I told him. This was gonna be the most expensive night in his whole life. He was going to pay for sex, for once. If he didn't want me telling my story to all the tabloids: I SLEPT WITH DADDY DEAREST! If that would hurt his career, or his reputation or his marriage or his new little girl, why then he'd have to pay me. He'd have to give me half of everything he had, and then he'd give me the other half."

She shrank into herself a little. "For a while there, I thought he was getting so freaked out that he'd kill me, especially when I told him Stage Two of my Plan." Her face screwed into distaste. "But he caved in. He started whining and swearing that if he'd known I existed he would have been there. Sure. He said I couldn't hurt innocent people, and I said I was innocent before Mama told me and before people started hurting me."

She shook her head. "He was pathetic when I left, but I never thought he'd kill himself. What a stupid thing to do! He had a show, he had lots of money. I woulda left him keep some. I woulda kept quiet. Did I want the world to know this creep was my father? That I had to screw him to get anything out of him, any time, any attention, any money? It would have worked fine! But then he had to get dramatic and go kill himself."

She glanced at Temple. "So he left your card on his nightstand.

For all I knew, you'd let him drill you, so I wrote the date down, just in case they could tell he'd had sex, so they would think you were his last woman. Then I'd be clear, and a lot poorer." She sighed. "It was over too fast. It wasn't any fun. He wasn't even a good lay."

"That's not the way genetic evidence works," Temple said, surprised to find her voice hoarse. She hadn't said much in a long time. "They'd have had to test us pretty quickly to prove anything. Besides, he'd showed me your letters. That's why I was in the bedroom, as I told the police. The daughter would have been a suspect sooner than any woman in the vicinity. You had a built-in alibi; you didn't have to use me."

"You read my letters?" Her face twisted with anger again.

"Skimmed a few, that's all."

"Those were private! I can't believe he showed them to anyone. And to you, a stranger. Or are you lying? You could be lying about everything."

She stood up, the pewter dagger in her hand jabbing toward Temple.

"He was honestly upset by those letters, Alison. And not just because you might have frightened him. He was trying to straighten out, trying to make his marriage work. I do believe that. He did love his baby daughter, and I think he would have loved you if he'd known about you. Babies were the only women he didn't have to perform for. Why didn't you just write him, nicely, when you first found out?"

"Because my mother said he wouldn't care. He'd been a young man, and young men don't look back. He was too rich and famous to care. He probably didn't like children."

"Maybe. But he did finally marry a woman, and have a little girl. Maybe he was thinking about getting older, and leaving all he had earned behind him. Maybe he wanted a little boy or girl to leave it to. Maybe that could have been you."

"No!" She stabbed the letter opener into the wooden desktop so hard it stuck there.

Temple had been hoping for that when she goaded her. Hoping that she'd strike the desk and not Temple. The letter opener might pull out easily enough, but Alison would have to go for it, and by then Temple would have propelled herself back to the copier, and pushed it over at Alison if she followed. Then she could spin the corner water cooler into the center of the room.

. . . by then she should be able to reach and unlock the door, get out into the street and daylight and—

"It never would have been me!" Alison buried her face in her hands. "Mama was just a pretty girl, she wasn't no French model. She wasn't good enough for him, even I knew that when I looked at her, later. We were a step up from white trash, that was all."

"You're better than that now, because you hated him," Temple pointed out.

"What?" Alison looked at her suspiciously, through wet fingers, like a difficult child.

"You made something of yourself, out of hatred. You can type, spell, use a computer, run an office, stand in a roomful of celebrities and come off as a sophisticated woman. You can get another job, just because you can do it. You can go somewhere."

"I had no place to go, ever, but here! Here to get him. And now I have, and it's nothing, like everything else. You are downright crazy, lady!"

"You can't be prosecuted for a man's suicide. You can't be prosecuted for incest. The blackmail isn't in the letters, as far as I saw. There's only your word on it, and why would you incriminate yourself?"

Alison took a deep, ragged breath.

"Oh, that's right. For vengeance, to expose him. But you say he was mad enough to hurt you, but didn't. He hurt himself instead. Maybe if you'd come at it another way, it wouldn't have been like this. I suppose you could humiliate his widow and child. They have a lot more than you, so maybe they deserve it. But they're just a Mama and her Baby alone now, trying to make a go of it. And sure, you could have taken the sleazy tabloid coverage if it had hurt him, but he's dead. He can't be hurt. Only the Mama and Baby he left behind. And you, you'll find that the tabloids leave you feeling dirty all over finally."

"So what should I do?" she asked quietly, like a child.

"Take some time. Think about it. You should talk to somebody about everything. A doctor or a shrink. There are women's centers with groups."

"I been alone on this."

"Maybe you don't have to be alone on the aftermath." Temple stood. "I'd better take the file box and the cards. What were you copying them for, anyway?"

"I was gonna give 'em to her, to Michelle." She hung her head. "But something's been bothering me, ever since he died on me. It's like I've lost a reason to go on. Like I been cheated. I don't care anymore. I been trying to go through the motions, thinkin' and schemin' and plannin' how to make everyone pay. And I just don't care anymore. Maybe he was . . . too easy."

Temple nodded. "Maybe you're better than he was." She got up, fetched the recipe box, with its syrupy floral paintings, and collected the loose cards by the copier.

Walking to the door made her feel like a target, but when she had opened it and turned, Alison was still sitting slumped on the desk, the letter opener impaled beside her. Hmm, like father, like daughter, perhaps.

Temple walked back and took it, wresting it from the Danish modern teakwood.

Molina would hate having Temple's fingerprints over everything, but Temple thought she'd better preserve the evidence, even though she doubted that there was a case to be made from it.

Chapter 34

Cut to the Quick

"Hey, dude. What are you in for?"

"I do not know," I answer the guy in the adjoining cage.

From what I can see, he is an orcaesque individual with white and black splotches all over, and I am in a new place I know too well: some veterinary facility.

"Bet it is the Big One," my cellmate says.

"What is the Big One?"

"Boy, are you wet behind the tail! Did not your mama tell you anything? You look old enough to know the score. You heard the song about what happens when those cotton balls get rotten: they pick 'em right off. You had your fuzzies plucked, right? So did I. It does not hurt too much, and it sure will make my people happier about my territory-marking habits, but I will miss the good old days. Freedom of the city. Going to the fights now and then, especially when I was on the bill that night. Romancing a sweet young thing. Even visiting the road ladies. But it is better for the planet, so I cannot complain!"

"Well, I can!" I reply, appalled. "I am not remotely interested in the betterment of the planet, never having seen it. I believe this planetary good is a mythical entity invented to make poor dudes like us happy with our lots. Are you saying I will not be the dude I used to be?"

"Not if you were neutered."

"Neutered!" The word sears my soul. This is the end. I will yawn when I gaze at the Divine Yvette, and ask her to pass the saltpeter. I will lounge about the Circle Ritz, counting flies that land on the birdbath. I will grow fat. Shall I wear my whiskers curled? Dare I eat a cockroach? The carp will not swim for me. I will be a House It forever.

But how else to explain the pain in my posterior? The smell of anesthetic and my foggy memories of Miss Savannah Ashleigh's mad doctor? This is what she has done to avenge a crime that was not mine (though I certainly gave some thought to committing it). She has altered me forever! I will be fit for nothing but some light surveillance work. Who will protect Miss Temple Barr now?

Sadly, I lean back to try to gaze past my stomach to the area in question. Come to think of it, since I have been eating Yummy Tum-tum-tummy, it has been impossible to see anything but tummy in that vicinity. In fact, my usual fastidious grooming has not quite been able to reach the forbidden zone. Now there is nothing there to reach anyway.

What kind of street-smart detective has no balls, even if it is a girl? I know that mystery fiction features more oddball dudes and dudettes nowadays, with an admirable array of varying characteristics, including the occasional handicap. The handicap I could live with. Tear out a nail! Go ahead. I will even wear glasses. But when has anyone ever heard of a eunuch P.I.?

I am so unutterably sad about this forced emasculation

that I cannot even bestir myself to answer the cad in the next cell.

Midnight Louie as we know him is no more! Rest in peace. If only I knew where they were buried, I would visit them.

Chapter 35

Three's a Crowd

"I wish to hell," Molina said over the phone, "that you'd left the evidence, if it is such, in place."

"I called you the first moment I could."

"And you left her—?"

"Sitting in the Laughalot office on Charleston."

Temple herself was sitting on her bed, the recipe box and the letter opener beside her.

"I'll wait here for someone to collect these things. And, Lieutenant," Temple rushed on, detecting the preparatory rustle of an imminent hang-up. "I'm really worried about something. Midnight Louie has been gone for over twenty-four hours. It's not like him. He always comes home, at least to eat. Since I started adding some Yummy Tum-tum-tummy over his Free-to-be-Feline he's been much better about eating at home too."

"The cat? Cats . . . go places. Call the pound."

Temple sighed and cut off her side of the connection so she could do just that.

But first she called Max.

"You went back alone when you knew this woman was there?" he asked.

"I thought at the time that she had tried to implicate me in Darren Cooke's death to protect his reputation. I didn't realize she had caused it. His death, not his reputation."

"And you left her there alone?"

"I was hardly equipped to take her into custody. And lucky to get out of there, frankly."

"And you just called up Molina to tell her all about it?"

"Max, can you speak in something other than questions?"

"No. Are you all right? I mean, physically. I'm not so sure about the other."

"Well, I'm a little wobbly. And I'm worried about Midnight Louie. I've haven't seen him since . . . early yesterday."

"Forget the cat! Nobody knew where you were. We could have been wondering into next week if anything had happened."

"It didn't. Not really."

"I'll be right over."

He hung up as abruptly as Molina.

Temple flopped open the huge Las Vegas telephone book and hunted through the White and Yellow Pages until she finally found the animal facility listed under "Animal Shelters."

The animal pound, after what seemed like twenty-nine rings and a voice-mail program with a roster of innumerable numbers to describe and hit, finally took her recorded message of Louie's description and her address and phone number.

Temple sighed, and called Matt.

"Sorry to bother you on your afternoon off."

"No problem."

"I wondered if you'd seen Louie anywhere around the place? He's been missing for almost thirty-six hours—"

"Cats roam, and you do let him out. I'm sure he's fine and will be back in no time."

"Oh, dear. I'm not. Anyway, I have some new information on the Cooke case that's very puzzling, given that you've heard from your famous sex-addict client since Cooke's death.

"I talked to Darren's illegitimate daughter, the one who's been sending him the hate mail. And she says she came to his room at midnight Sunday night, just like you heard on the phone, only it can't be her you heard arriving, or him you were talking to, since that man is still calling you, and Cooke's dead. Unless he's a ghost. Or could she be one?"

"I'll be right down." Matt hung up the phone as abruptly as Molina.

They all had hangupitis, Temple concluded, sighing again. She felt so terribly, terribly tired, and wasn't thinking too clearly. But she understood that was because she'd had to deal with a deranged personality for a long time all by herself.

What really worried her was not what she had just been through, but the empty, undented space on her coverlet that testified to Midnight Louie's even longer absence.

The doorbell rang.

Listlessly, she got up to answer it.

"Temple, you're not making sense."

Matt backed her into the room and actually pressed the back of his hand to her forehead as if she were an ailing child. Then he pushed her gently onto the sofa.

"Yes, I am," she answered. "In my way. You of all people should understand how taxing it is to talk to a compulsive, especially when you're trying to outthink one and you have no grasp of the real picture."

"You mentioned Cooke's daughter. You found her?"

"Right in the family circle, so to speak. His personal assistant. She's the one who marked my card and slipped it into the recipe file. I figured she wanted to protect her boss's reputation as a ladies' man, so no one would think he killed himself for impotence or something. But the real motive was quite the reverse. She wanted to ruin him, and didn't care who she used to do it."

"Card? Recipe file. And this daughter came to his room at midnight? But on the phone I heard a man welcoming a woman who had obviously come to sleep with him."

"Yeah. Well. That fits."

"Temple, you are really ragged out. You're not making sense.

You implied that Cooke's secret daughter came to sleep with him."

Temple nodded. "Which she did, and then told him who she was and that she wanted all his money on top of it. No wonder he killed himself."

Matt literally drew back. "That's . . . horrible. She must be completely demented."

"No, not as much as before, maybe. I mean, when she went for that pewter letter opener, I thought I was dead meat. But I remembered what you said about an attacker having already chosen his or her—I suppose I should use that weasely phrase here—weapon, but that *I* had a choice of anything in the area. It really helped. She was no problem, really. At the end, I just took all the evidence, walked out and left her. You would have been proud of me."

"Proud of you? I'm appalled. Where did all of this happen? What made you think you could go off alone and confront her?"

He had grabbed her shoulders, but Temple just stared confusedly into his shocked face. She thought she was being admirably coherent considering how she had spent the last couple of hours.

"The office was on Charleston," Max said, stepping in from the patio behind them. "And we'd both been there the night before."

Matt's hands loosened. This time he drew back with edgy caution. Temple blinked and looked away. Now the cat was out of the bag.

"Why are you wasting your time asking questions?" Max continued. "Temple's obviously shocked and exhausted. Where's the medicinal brandy? Same old place?" He eyed Temple for a response she was incapable of making, then vanished into the kitchen.

Matt stared at Temple as if he'd seen a ghost.

She shrugged. "I had to let him know, seeing as he broke us into the office in the first place."

"Broke you in?" Matt whispered in disbelief. "This entire . . . scenario is nuts."

"I agree." Temple leaned against the sofa back, feeling too lethargic to sit up. "I wish I knew where Louie was."

Max had returned with a juice glass full of something clear, no ice.

Temple squinted at the blue grass, from a set colored in various jewel tones. "What's in there? Amber or white?"

"Just drink." Max knelt beside her to chime the glass against her teeth.

All this solicitation was most uncomfortable.

Matt, still sitting beside her, watched in disapproval. "Temple doesn't need alcohol right now. She needs to talk out her severe emotional strain."

"Nothing cures 'severe emotional strain' better than a bolt of booze."

"This stuff tastes like rubbing alcohol!" Temple protested after one swallow, pushing it away.

"That's what you get for buying cheap vodka," Max said. "I've told you time and again."

"It's always mixed with something else. Who could tell? Unless they were forced to chugalug it straight. Listen, guys." She looked left and she looked right. "I appreciate you both being so concerned, but I'm all right. I called Lieutenant Molina like a good citizen, and the police are sending someone over to get the goods, and will probably pick up Alison Darby for her own safety. Maybe suicide runs in the family. I wouldn't want her to kill herself because she told me the truth. Now I just wish someone could help me find Midnight Louie."

Blatantly, in front of her, Matt and Max exchanged a glance of complete harmony: she was not herself. Temple had flipped.

Before she could protest this outrageous collusion among rivals, someone knocked on the door. This time, everyone exchanged glances.

"I'll get it," Matt said, since he was the only one who really could.

After he opened the door there was a moment's silence.

"Good afternoon, Lieutenant," Matt said loudly.

Max eeled out the patio doors so quickly he seemed like merely a passing sun shadow.

Temple sneaked another swallow of the awful vodka, then Matt led Molina into the room.

"I never dreamed you'd come yourself," Temple said, pulling herself together. "How nice you're worried about Midnight Louie too."

The lieutenant and Matt exchanged a significant glance.

Temple could have screamed, but she didn't want to be mistaken for a crazy woman, although it was a little late to worry about that.

"I should have called you in the first place," Temple told Electra when Molina had left, and Matt had left and Temple had finally called someone who was fascinated instead of appalled by her story.

"You just go to bed, dear. Gracious, talking to that poor girl would have been like watching five years of soap-opera plots on fast-forward. Such a lurid tale! And so interesting."

"But what about Louie?"

"You're right. It's not like the big black bozo to be off so long. Do you have the phone numbers of the people connected with the film commercial anywhere? Maybe he returned to the places they were working. You know Louie, always likes to be at the scene of the action."

"Yes, Electra! You're the only one who's been able to handle my story without hysterics or to see that something must have happened to Louie. Let's see . . . the numbers are on the Rolodex on my desk under 'À La Cat.' Would be right after 'Alabama' . . . if I had such a category on file, which I don't, but I can't remember what would be ahead of or behind it. Maybe I'm not making sense."

"Understand you perfectly, dear. I'll go hunt, and then call around. Now you just settle down. I'll call everybody I can about Louie."

At last, a woman of action!

Temple edged down in the bed covers, too weary to wonder

at the fact that her living room had almost hosted Matt Devine, Max Kinsella and Lt. C. R. Molina all at the same time. Now that was really frightening!

Electra had figured that out too, because when she came back to report that the film crew had been inactive that day, she sat on the bed's edge.

"I know you're tired, but what did Matt have to say to Max when he showed up?"

"Nothing much. They were too busy making faces over my head."

"And then the lieutenant came?"

"In person," Temple mumbled from under a warm roll of sheet and blanket. "Max was outta there like . . . like Louie. Then Matt and Molina made faces over my head, as if I were some certified idiot."

"They just don't have much imagination." Electra pondered for a bit, while Temple flirted seriously with sleep.

A nice warm, white silence hovered everywhere.

Electra hovered in that vague cloudy limbo too, present but unintrusive. Temple was finally slipping back into the flamingoland from which she'd awakened this morning when—

Someone rang her doorbell.

Oh, it was loud! Oh, it had jerked her back to reality. Who had the gall to be at her door now?

She heard Electra trying to rush quietly to answer the doorbell before the offender could ring again. Temple was still too dopey to move.

Until Electra screamed.

Temple sat up, scrubbing her face to brush away the cobwebs.

She stumbled out of bed, lurching in Electra's footsteps. When she got to the main room, she found her landlady, her back pasted against the closed apartment door, her muumuu looking like a floral stick-on decal.

"Who's out there? Electra, is somebody bad trying to get in?"

"Don't look. Let me call Matt. You don't want to see."

Of course, nothing would have snapped Temple into full, alert consciousness just then, except the assertion that there was something she shouldn't see.

"It's my doorstep. Although there's no step, really. So . . . step aside and let me see," Temple ordered with all the articulate authority of a drunken sailor.

"Really, no. I'm terribly afraid—it's just better to let a man handle this."

Another set of fighting words. "Stand back, Electra, or I'll—"

Temple grabbed the doorknob, leaned back and pulled with all her might.

The door gave not a whit, but Electra was intimidated enough to move away.

"You'll wish you'd listened to me. I'm calling Matt."

She was at the kitchen phone punching in the number before Temple had opened the door enough to see a white bundle lying on the floor of the dim hall cul-de-sac.

"Laundry?" she asked. "Somebody wants me to do their laundry? It had better not be male!"

She heard Electra blathering behind her.

What was so horrifying about a pile of dirty clothes?

And then the bundle moved.

Or something inside it did.

Temple would have screamed, but choked it off. Anyone who had walked away from an incestuous psychopath only hours before was not about to be spooked by a post-Halloween ghost.

She crouched down. The bundle was really only one pillowcase. A white satin pillowcase, as a matter of fact. The contents stirred again. Frankly, Temple was thinking . . . snakes!

But as the pillow shifted, she saw that something dark sprinkled the white surface . . . Oh, boy. Blood. In nice fat droplets.

What kind of a sadistic prank was this?

She found the pillowcase's open end, tied into a pucker by a . . . pink velvet headband? She was about to try the knot when Matt's footsteps came pounding down the muffling hall carpet.

"Don't do it!" Electra urged hysterically behind her.

"I wasn't going to open it. I know it might be snakes."

"Snakes!" Electra wailed. "Oh, I do dearly hope so."

A hiss from within the bag appeared to answer her prayers.

Temple jerked her hand back, and cocked her head at Matt as he knelt down.

"Better get a bucket or something in case it is snakes," he said, looking at Electra.

"Who would leave a bag of bloody snakes on my doorstep?" Temple asked.

"Maybe some of the snakes you've been stirring up lately." Matt was grim. "You'd better brace yourself—"

He was working loose the velvet band, and stopped only to take the plastic bucket Electra had found.

"Use these," she said, tossing him a pair of rubber dish-washing gloves. "All I could find."

He hesitated, then donned them awkwardly. They really were too small, but fairly thick rubber in a protective sense.

Then he opened the mouth of the pillowcase wider and wider. Something came writhing and slashing out, hissing to high heaven.

Temple, startled, jumped back with an indrawn breath.

"I was afraid of that." Electra began a soprano wail that went up and up the scale.

It was Midnight Louie, reeking of chloroform, twisting and turning like a black tornado, his claws making coleslaw of Matt's rubber gloves.

"What have they done to him?" Temple wailed.

Matt finally released the cat. The hisses subsided to a long aria of dull growl. Louie lay twitching and blinking in their midst, his eyes wet and shut, his fur matted and unkempt.

"He's alive," Matt pointed out. "We need to examine him in the light. Get a towel, Electra."

She raced for the bathroom.

"Louie." Temple reached a hand to his disheveled head.

He snarled, and she snatched it back.

"What have they done to him?" she asked, whispering.

"He seems disoriented. I think he's been knocked out."

"But why? Just to . . . scare me?"

"Whoever did this was sick." Matt took the two thick bath towels Electra offered. "Talk to him, Temple. We don't want him any more agitated than necessary."

Matt dropped the towels over Louie's huddled form, then gently tucked them under the cat and lifted the whole package.

Black feet flailed as the growls rose to another deafening shriek.

"Get the pillowcase," Matt yelled at Temple as he rushed inside.

She snatched it up and followed. Electra, on the phone, nodded as she listened. Her mouth pantomimed the word "vet."

"Any apparent broken bones?" she asked.

"He's still kicking," Temple said.

"Visible wounds?"

"Hard to tell," Matt announced.

Electra nodded one last time. "Okay. We'll bring him right in." She hung up. "I don't think Temple should drive."

"Oh, for heaven's sake! I drove home after the assault in the parking garage. Besides, I doubt that anyone but Matt can hold him. Grab my tote, Electra; I'll open doors."

The trio hurried outside as fast as their routine allowed: Temple leading and opening, Matt holding the protesting wad of towels, Electra in the rear, toting Temple's tote bag, digging for car keys and closing doors behind her as she went.

The keys were ready by the time they reached Temple's car. Electra opened the passenger door to seat Matt, then struggled into the less capacious backseat.

Temple was awake and then some. She revved the Storm so fast it almost choked, and burned rubber out of the lot.

"Ooh," Electra murmured as the sharp turn onto the side street shoved her all the way to the opposite window.

But nobody dared criticize Temple's driving, and they did arrive safely at Dr. Doolittle's in record time.

"This seems familiar," the receptionist said as she waved them into the first consulting room without a pause at the desk. "What's wrong with this little guy?"

Nobody corrected her. "We don't know," they all said at once.

Louie's feet, battling to escape the confining towels, made skid marks on Matt's arms.

Dr. Doolittle came in, her white lab coat flapping with haste, the vet tech behind her toting Louie's slim record file.

"What have we got here?"

Matt described how Louie had been found, while Temple produced the bloody satin pillowcase.

"Those blood drops came from the outside, not the inside," Dr. Doolittle said with a frown, gingerly peeling back tangled towels to unveil Louie.

He sat blinking under the fluorescent light, ears back, eyes squinting almost shut, fur wet and full of cowlicks. His hind feet splayed out, while his forelegs would hardly brace his solid weight.

"Hmmm. Quiet down, boy. You're gonna be all right." Dr. Doolittle concentrated only on Louie, gently feeling each of his legs. (He didn't like that, and said so.) Then she hefted him onto his feet and felt his torso. He lowered his head like a big black bull and snarled. She even ran her hands over his tail.

Then out came the stethoscope and finally the thermometer.

"Uh-oh." Temple was quick to grab Louie's shoulders. The tech held his head so he couldn't bite, while Matt grabbed his hind legs so he couldn't kick and scratch. Electra, watching from a corner of the room, seemed to enter a meditative trance.

The insertion of the thermometer nearly sent Louie up the wall of human flesh holding him down. Waiting for the instrument's beeped "done" signal seemed an endless ordeal to one and all.

"Everything looks normal," Dr. Doolittle said finally. "Heart's a little fast, but this struggle could do that. He's obviously been anesthetized." She ruffled the fur of a foreleg until she saw something. "An injection hole. He seems a bit touchy in the rear area, but that could have been the thermometer. I'd say that some do-gooder mistook him for a feral cat and picked him up for a quick neutering, but I did a quick check while he was flailing; all his equipment is present and accounted for."

"People would snatch and alter other people's cats?" Temple asked, incredulous.

"Animal-lovers would. You might consider neutering Louie now," she added sternly. "It would keep him from roaming and getting into trouble like this. And it would certainly keep more unwanted kittens from entering the world only to leave it in short order at a shelter, or after a harsh, unhappy street life."

Temple nodded soberly. So much had happened in her personal and professional life since Louie had showed up five months ago. She'd always meant to do the neutering business. . . .

While she wallowed in guilt, Dr. Doolittle considered Louie from a safe distance. He was still snarling and thrashing.

"I can't find a thing wrong with him," the vet said, "except for being woozy from anesthetic and roughed up from fighting the bed linens. We'll keep him under observation overnight—"

"Louie will think I've abandoned him!" Temple fretted.

"I want him on an IV to make sure he gets plenty of liquid. You can visit him tomorrow."

"But there's no visible damage?"

"Not on first examination, under these less-than-ideal circumstances. I want to see how he'll act in the morning."

"Still mad as hell," Temple predicted.

She ventured to pat Louie's ruffled head as the tech carried him off, growling, wrapped in the terrible towels again.

"We'll call if there's any change," Dr. Doolittle promised. "Whatever happened on Louie's recent adventure, only he can say. "Now go home and get some rest," she prescribed for Temple, "with plenty of liquids and someone to watch over you."

She quirked a smile at Electra and Matt, then bustled off to wherever veterinarians go when they leave consulting rooms.

"I've got just the liquid," Electra muttered on their exit. "Bottle of cherry brandy I saved since my last husband."

"You'll have to watch over Temple," Matt told her. "I can't cancel out of work on such short notice."

Electra patted his arm as he opened the Storm's passenger door for her. "You just trundle off to your phone lines, Matt. We girls will sit at home sipping brandy and talking about you guys."

"No brandy for me," Temple said. "I want to find out if the

police picked up Alison Darby. Would she have been demented enough to take my snooping out on Louie? If she's still on the loose—" She picked up the satin pillowcase she had thrown on the shift console. "Something is crusted near the open edge. Ick!" She looked closer. "Embroidery! Initials. Who would be dumb enough to dump a kidnapped cat in a personalized pillowcase? Electra? Matt? Can either of you make out these letters?"

While Temple got the car in gear and going, Electra hunched forward in the backseat so the two could consult over the front seat back.

"Maybe it's a hotel insignia," Electra suggested. "An S. Don't you think, Matt?"

"An S could be the Sands."

"Torn down," Temple reminded them, turning onto the Strip.

"This middle initial is an I," Electra went on, deciphering as much with her fingers as her eyes.

"And," said Matt, "the last one must be an A."

"SIA," Temple mused. "A sister organization to the CIA? Is that why the satin pillowcase? Just kidding. Usually the last name is in the middle, so it really should be SAI."

"Unless," she added, "the person who ordered this attack is so dumb that he or she—and I lean to a she—didn't know that."

She hit the brakes so hard her seat-belted passengers barely caught themselves from being hurled into something hard.

"Sorry," Temple said. "Speaking of dumb . . . it just occurred to me to wonder what Savannah Ashleigh's middle name is."

Chapter 36

Temple Goes a Few Rounds

Temple spent Sunday taking care of old business.

She paid a special visit that morning to Midnight Louie at the vet's, when only the weekend staff was in.

"You are my main man, Louie," she told him. "Who needs a sex life, anyway?"

She went home to while away the night eating frozen yogurt and salted peanuts and watching public TV.

Temple awoke Monday morning a new woman.

She glanced at the empty coverlet just once, then got dressed. She bypassed the spikes in her closet for a sensible pair of two-inch heels. She loaded her tote bag of the day, then called the vet's office as soon as it opened.

The receptionist said that Midnight Louie was the same: somewhat depressed. He had not touched a bite of food. Temple could visit him again in late morning, after surgery was over.

First Temple headed to the public library. In the reference section, she looked up the stock of celebrity address and biography books. For once in her life, she found herself wishing that Savannah Ashleigh were not a total has-been. That she still might be listed in one of these books.

Three gave her the brush-off, but an older edition of *People Who Are Somebody* did list Savannah. "Birth date: February 3, 1959." Savannah was only thirty-seven? Come on! "Born: Farleigh Heights, New Jersey, Susan Imogene Isch." Ischleigh? But . . . Imogene! Awful name. Wonderful name. A culprit was born! Now Nemesis would track her down.

Temple drove to police headquarters downtown. She would not allow Molina to not be in. Positive thinking. It worked on finding parking spaces. Sure enough, one open street spot waited outside the entry tower. The Storm just fit.

Temple crossed the street to the plaza. In the lobby, she asked the desk sergeant to call Molina, if she were in. Temple Barr was here to see her.

He did, she was and Temple did.

Molina came out to the worn leather couches in the visitors' area.

"More evidence? More suspects?" she inquired in greeting.

Temple made a face. "Louie was returned to me yesterday afternoon."

"What did I tell you?"

"In a bloody satin pillowcase stinking of anesthetic and bearing the initials SIA."

Molina actually looked stunned and sat down. "How . . . is he?"

"At the vet's, on fluids. Won't eat. Looks like hell. They say he's 'depressed.' "

"This is awful, but why are you seeing me about it? I don't do crimes against cats and dogs."

"I'm just telling you that Savannah Ashleigh's middle given name is Imogene."

"Ugh."

"I know. She deserves it, unlike my middle name."

"You have an undeserved middle name?" Molina inquired on a lilt of interest.

"Irrelevant. The point is, Savannah resented Midnight Louie's becoming a bigger star than her cat, Yvette, in the À La Cat commercials. There have been several mishaps on the set—a vintage-car brake failed while Louie was in it; he apparently tripped while going down a long flight of stairs on camera; the boat he and Yvette were sailing in on the Mirage lagoon sank."

"Savannah Ashleigh may be a few ounces of silicone short of a full implant, but she'd hardly sink her own cat."

"She might if she were blinded by fury. Her name is all over this pillowcase. I just wanted to warn you that I'm going to have a showdown with her. In case one of us turns up missing."

Molina sat back on the couch. "I'm not too worried. The result of your last showdown with a possible perpetrator has been a total bust."

"How?"

"Number one, the background check on Alison Darby, so far, shows she was adopted. Darren Cooke was indeed in the city where she was born before she was born, but it's likely she built this fantasy of his being her father from that fact. Or her mother may have tried to give her a sense of importance, but I doubt it. Alison's mother was a singularly conservative, unimaginative soul, and so was her husband. They were low-income people. Darby obviously fixated on more glamorous 'real' parents during her tumultuous teen years."

For a moment Molina's face wore a worried look. Maybe she was thinking about her own preteen daughter's forthcoming tumultuous years. She went on briskly.

"Number two, the letters." Molina gathered herself for an unpleasant admission. "They were in a safe at the Flamingo Hilton, and they do match Darby's handwriting, not Cooke's; we compared them to examples among Cooke's files. Darby made some effort to disguise her writing in the letters, or she developed a secondary personality to write them, but nothing flagrant enough that we can even commit her for mental-health treatment.

"Number three, the medical examiner has always been adamant that no crime-scene evidence—not a trace—not the angle of the bullet, not powder burns, indicates that Darren

Cooke did not kill himself. To simulate such a setup, a killer would have to be not only terribly knowledgeable but as skilled as a foreign agent. They've managed some pretty seamless assassinations. This is not one.

"Finally, the sleight of hand with your business card was exactly what you thought: Darby found him dead and hoped to use it to deflect any interest from her. Given her close association and the harassing letters she had been writing, she was in a perilous position, and knew it. She is not as nuts as she has been behaving. She even seems to have mellowed a little. Now that he's dead, she realizes that she's lost something.

"So, congratulations." Molina stood, towering over Temple as usual. "You may have cracked a window of reason in the mind of a troubled young woman. If you do have a head-to-head, or a hair-to-hair, with Savannah Ashleigh, don't expect police assistance. Confronting her could be construed as harassment. On the other hand, I hope you win.

"Finally, I hope you will see fit to tell me someday who ducked out of your place when Mr. Devine so kindly announced me to one and all like a British butler. I have my suspicions, but the police like hard evidence. And the harder it is to get, the more satisfaction there is in getting it.

"Have a nice day."

And that was that.

Dissatisfied, but unable to do a darn thing about it, Temple went on to her next surprise visit. To the Goliath, where Savannah Ashleigh dwelleth like Delilah of old. This time, Delilah was going to get a shave and a haircut, and two bits of Temple's mind.

She had to park the Storm a couple of leagues away from the Goliath entry. While walking in, she felt her righteous anger building up steam like a pile driver.

Savannah had better be in her room.

The desk clerk wouldn't give Temple the room number, of course. He said he would ring Miss Ashleigh's room. Whom should he say was calling?

Temple almost shouted, Miss *Isch*leigh from Farleigh!

But she smiled instead and gave her name: that of one of the few female film producers in Hollywood.

The clerk hung up from calling Miss Ashleigh, his attitude reflecting hers.

"You may go right up. Twentieth floor. The Suite of the Seven Veils."

Temple bestowed a chill nod as she ambled toward the elevators. Nothing like dropping someone else's name in this town.

The Suite of the Seven Veils was not too close to the elevators, but not too far from the ice machine.

The desert did demand its comforts.

She knocked, and waited. The double doors were swept open with a flourish. Savannah stood there in veils of her own, which would have been far more effective with male producers.

"You!"

"You!" Temple replied, sweeping in before the doors could slam shut and sweep her out.

She drew the bloody pillowcase from her trusty tote bag.

"Not every crook is thoughtful enough to use initialed evidence."

"Oh! Take that ugly, messy, reddish thing away!" Savannah averted her supernaturally taut face, her expression perhaps curling a little at the edges to indicate disgust.

How could an actress act through a mask of laser-sculpted collagen?

Not well.

"Sweet dreams, Mrs. Macbeth." Temple threw it down on the pale satin settee nearby.

"I want to know where you kept Midnight Louie, what you did to him and why. I won't leave until I get some answers."

Savannah drew herself up, especially the silicone and collagen parts. She had seen scripts that called upon the heroine to show pride in the face of disdain. She had practiced this particular attitude in the mirror until she had it down pat. This moment was made for her!

"I will give you answers. Do you see that little tiny, helpless cat there? My darling Yvette?"

Temple gazed where directed. Yvette was reclining in shaded-silver languor on a gray velvet pillow atop a chaise longue.

She looked adorable. She looked convinced of it herself.

"Yes?" Temple asked politely. "I imagine she has never been delivered in a pillowcase to your door."

"Deeelivered." Savannah Ashleigh dropped that word with a mannered relish. "She will be deeelivered, poor darling, in not too many weeks. Of a litter. A litter of your evil black cat's Midnight degeneration."

Temple blinked. Savannah's delivery was as overarticulated as any admirer of the Del Sartian school of nineteenth-century acting could desire. But what did 'degeneration' mean in this context?

"Huh?" Temple responded elegantly.

"Oooohf!" Savannah stamped a Frederick's of Hollywood high heel. A full six inches high, like the fetishists get into, quite literally, unlike Temple's usual three-inch models. The stamping high-rise shoe was leopard-spotted with touches of gold lamé.

"Don't play dumb with me! You are up against a master. Look at my lovely babesy-wabesy. She is PG. Pregnant! She will have a revolting litter by your horrible alley cat, not by the Supreme National Champion of her own breed Mumsy has spent weeks and weeks finding. This is Yvette's first litter, and it is tainted! Your beast did it!"

"How can you know?"

"Because he likes her. He is always coming around."

"But you haven't done DNA testing?"

Savannah frowned. "A lie-detector test is not necessary. A mother knows these things."

She beat her breast to indicate the maternal heart pounding away in omniscient knowledge, and Temple feared Savannah's personal Silicone Valley might suffer a major terrain shift.

"So what did you do to him? Drug him and kidnap him? To what purpose?"

"Oh, I had a purpose. I fixed him. I fixed him so he will never do this to another innocent pussycat in all his born days. I found him here, plying his oily wiles on my poor innocent. I took him right to Dr. Mendel and told him to fix that damn cat so he could never impregnate another baby like mine. You don't even have to pay for it. It's on the house."

"You have no right to snatch another person's pet and tamper with it. That's kidnapping and . . . and mutilation. Who is this unscrupulous doctor who'd do such a thing?"

Savannah drew herself up: her high, unfallen frontage, her taut, unlined neck, the taut, expressionless face so like a still photo.

"He is the best plastic surgeon in Las Vegas."

"You had Louie operated on by a plastic surgeon? That's crazy. Veterinarians operate on cats."

"Vegetarians do? I thought they didn't like protein."

"Never mind." Temple was too stupefied to be furious anymore. "I'm going to call this doctor. And if I don't like what I learn, I may sue you."

"You can't. I sue other people. They don't sue me."

"Maybe they haven't yet. But they could, and I will, and maybe the others will get the idea about countersuits before I'm through."

"You have a lot of nerve."

"Yes," Temple said pleasantly.

She left before her nerve reached her fingertips and she did something fatal to Dr. Mendel's other handiwork.

In the lobby, she mauled a Yellow Pages directory until she found the doctor's number.

"Dr. Mendel is with a patient," a receptionist informed her.

Temple was on the warpath. "I'm with the Secret Service. The First Lady is giving a speech in the area, and would like to consult Dr. Mendel on a personal matter. She is not staying in the area very long, but she has heard about him from Cher—"

"Oh! Just a moment."

In just a moment the doctor was in.

"Yes?"

"What did you do to that cat Savannah Ashleigh brought in?"

"I thought you were with the Secret Service."

"I am, and it's a federal crime to kidnap an animal to perform unsanctioned procedures, especially outside your own specialty. The cat was not hers. This incident could cost you your license, Doctor. Depending, of course, on what you did."

"N-nothing. Just what she said to do. I fixed the animal so it couldn't reproduce. Or, rather, so it couldn't father kittens. It's a simple procedure done all the time all over the country on thousands of men. Er, males. I'd never done it before, but I knew what was involved and it was only a cat, after all."

"Only a cat? This cat is a direct forebear of Socks, the White House cat. You have heard of Socks?"

"Yes. Oh, dear. Miss Ashleigh was most insistent, and she is a . . . constant client. I never dreamed the animal was not hers to do with as she would. It was a very simple, uncomplicated vasectomy, I assure you. No undue bleeding, just a couple of internal staples that will dissolve. He should be as good as new in a day or so."

"A . . . vasectomy? Isn't that difficult on a cat's small, er, appendages?"

"Well, he is a rather large cat. And I am used to working very delicately."

"Isn't a vasectomy unusual in a cat?"

"Why should it be? That's the way we do people. It's not my specialty, of course, but I've read the occasional article. I assure you he got the best surgery available. I doubt any other cat has had such a splendid vasectomy performed. My work is virtually invisible. And I even did a small tummy tuck while I was at it."

"Thank you, Doctor. The, uh, First Lady is most reassured. It will not be necessary to subpoena your records, after all. But in the future, I would advise you to perform only procedures that Miss Ashleigh requests to have done upon herself. And, by the way, I do think a bit more collagen in the lips would be an enhancement."

"Aren't they sufficiently plump, as is? I went further than I thought aesthetic the last time, on her insistence."

"Fashions change, Doctor. You might consider more. I understand the First Lady is considering some enhancement in that direction."

"Really? I will, I will consider it, Miss, uh, Service."

Temple hung up smiling. That was one way to give Savannah Ashleigh the fat lip she deserved!

Temple sensed that 11 A.M. was a tad early to call on Domingo. He did not rise with the flamingos, she guessed, or even the mourning doves. Still, she had neglected his interests lately, and thought it only polite to explain why.

She knew his suite, so didn't need the intervention of a desk clerk to get there.

When she knocked she heard some inside activity, then Domingo himself opened the door. He was beaming from ear to ear when he saw who had come to call.

"Miss Temple Barr! I have been hip-deep in flamingos and thought I would never see you again. It's all going beautifully, everything you put in motion. I am having brunch; would you care to join me?"

Temple recalled the last brunch she'd had in the suite of an older, famous, charismatic man and was ready to shake her head . . . when she heard the unmistakable sounds of a child banging a spoon on a dish.

Domingo looked sheepish. "I am not used to it, either, but am told it will pass. Do come in."

At this point, a tank division couldn't have kept her out.

Temple edged in, to see a room-service table set up by the windows from which she had looked down on Las Vegas not many days ago.

A woman sat there, a woman in her late thirties with a cascade of curly dark blond hair like a Renaissance madonna. And to go with the madonna in the flowered sack dress was a toddler in a high chair who was busy turning fruit cocktail into a hat.

"Temple Barr, my guide to Las Vegas, this is my wife, Constance, and our child, Moira. Would you care to have brunch with us?"

Temple could have eaten a plastic flamingo at this point and never even noticed. She edged toward the table sitting in a splash of Nevada daylight.

"How nice to meet you. Domingo never said—" She looked at Domingo.

He shrugged, sheepish again. "This is a different life for me. I am slow to share." He turned to his family. "Temple has been a great help to me, but she was only here to get the project started."

Some worry in Constance's eyes softened. "We're greenhorns about this sort of circus, Moira and I. Domingo thought it was finally time we were introduced to the madness."

"Madness it is, especially in Las Vegas," Temple agreed. "I came here only to tell Domingo that my other commitments are heating up. I won't be able to do much more on this project. Frankly, I don't think he needs my help anymore."

"Nonsense! You were invaluable."

Young Moira had no patience with adult social rituals, or the time they took. She lifted the plastic bowl of fruit cocktail and put it upside down atop her head.

"Oh!" Constance tossed her linen napkin to the table and scooped the child out of the high chair. "A food sculptor in the making, I can see it already. Clean-up trip, if you'll excuse us."

"Sure," Temple said. "I recommend that she keep the maraschino cherry as a beauty mark, though."

Laughing, Constance carried her daughter into another room.

Domingo quickly commandeered Temple's elbow and led her to the windows.

"I owe you a great deal, and have not much time to thank you."

"Thank *me?* I just did my job, ran interference."

"You were afraid I had designs on you," he accused softly.

"Noooo! Well, yes. I'd had a bad experience lately with another famous man also infamous as a ladies' man."

"I know how bad I am considered. But I am that no longer."

"Verina—?"

"My last weakness. I would die if Constance should find out, which is why I thank you for freeing me from the last of my bad habits. I am a new man."

"How did I—?"

"That incident with the hat. It showed me how shallow and

jealous Verina was. Now that I have a daughter of my own, I look at women differently. You are so fresh, so honest. I saw you as my daughter grown, not as a rival of Verina's, as she saw you. This had never happened to me before. It gave me hope.

"My marriage was my first step toward a new, more stable life. Art eats you up. And when you become notorious as a young man, you want to eat everything around you to feed your artistic appetite. It is a wasteful, foolish life, and I lived it for many decades, until the adulation of women became a necessity, especially as I got older and they got younger. I have fought this demon ego that men are encouraged to serve, and I finally think I will win. I am a vain man, but I am also a good artist, and this life will destroy my talent if I do not leave it behind."

"I didn't do this, Domingo. You did."

"With help. I had a very good counselor. An anonymous counselor. I gave him hell, but he never abandoned me."

"Really," said Temple. "And, I was just wondering, when did your wife and child arrive? I never saw them."

"It was a surprise. They flew in from Switzerland. Constance is an accomplished pianist, did you know? It was late, nearly midnight, and one of my darkest hours, I may tell you. And there they were in the hallway, my wife and baby. Just what I needed to banish forever the dark side of my self.

"I had been making progress, but so often when I was alone that dark side took over, goading me. You will never understand the temptations that come to a man in my position, and how easily they overtake him."

"I'm glad you've beaten yours, Domingo."

Temple put out her hand, and he shook it, then lifted it for a kiss.

On that Continental and unexpected parting note, Temple finished the last of her errands, with almost the last of her important questions answered.

Chapter 37

Postmortems

"I'm happy to go with you to the vet's, Temple, but what's your real reason?"

Matt wouldn't take his eyes off her, so she couldn't dismiss his question, though she'd hoped to answer it after all her uncertainties about Louie were answered.

She kept her eyes on the route she was driving, and told him about them all: Savannah, Molina's inconclusive conclusions and finally Domingo.

Matt was shocked into silence.

"He appreciated my help? After wrestling on the phone with me like an antagonistic angel from the Old Testament? I can't tell you how much that man made me doubt myself, my current role, my history. And . . . he's all right now?"

"He believes so. And he admits that the side you saw—or heard, rather—was his demonic other half. You had to do battle with the worst of him in order for the best of him to come out. But it worked, Matt. You're a good counselor. And so am I, by example, of course."

"Take off that halo, Temple. It clashes with your fiery hair."

"I'm just so pleased. Domingo really feels rather fatherly toward me, can you imagine? I remind him of what he hopes his daughter will be one day, if that makes sense. That's so . . . sweet. That's so much better for the self-esteem than being hit on by older men, honest."

"I guess men can't know what that feels like."

"Maybe you can." Temple shot him a look, but Matt was gazing out the window, lost in his own reflections. "All's well that ends well," she said, quoting clichéd Shakespeare and so happy she didn't care.

"And Louie has been vasectomized? What does that mean?"

"I'm hoping Dr. Doolittle will tell us."

"Yes, now that I examine the area—Louie, stay still!—I can feel the snipped ends. Remarkable."

Dr. Doolittle shook her head over Louie's involuntarily prone form. "Marge, you can take him back to his cage."

"Cats can be vasectomized," the vet explained to Matt and Temple. "Though their equipment is smaller than human anatomy, we have the instruments and skill to do it. We just don't, because vasectomy only prevents reproduction. It doesn't end any of the tomcat behavior that pet owners find hard to take."

"What is that, Doctor? I haven't had any problems with Louie."

"Apparently he goes out on his own enough that he doesn't feel the need to mark your living quarters as territory. If he did, the stench would send you to me pronto. And, of course, he'll still pursue females and fight males for the privilege. You'd be better off completely neutering him and confining him indoors."

Temple sighed. Did questions of animal behavior never end, especially among humans? "I'd hate to traumatize him again, after what he's been through. If he can't create unwanted kitties, that's the most important part."

"No, the most important part to Louie is he's still a fully functional male." Dr. Doolittle shook her head. "He has always been the most unusual cat, and now he's truly atypical. Well, we'll watch and see. If he comes home with too many claw slashes on his handsome face, you may want to do the more advanced procedure. I really don't approve of cats roaming."

"Louie doesn't actually roam," Temple tried to explain. "He goes places to do things. And he's a media cat now. We don't want to change his personality now that he's a star."

"Maybe not. You can pick him up for good later this afternoon."

As they left the veterinarian's office, Matt frowned.

"Seems you're advocating a double standard here, Temple."

"How?"

"You're allowing the cat to have his cake and eat it too, but we poor human males aren't allowed the same options."

"When you're all fixed like Louie," she said sternly, "and can't leave unwanted children like Alison Darby littered about, we'll see."

Temple dropped Matt off at the Circle Ritz and decided to run one last errand. She smiled en route to the Crystal Phoenix. This was the first time Matt had spoken in defense of the virile male. Maybe he was beginning to feel the advantages of the noncelibate lifestyle.

She didn't know if Michelle would still be in residence, but she called up and heard the familiar " 'Allo?"

Temple felt she owed Michelle an explanation of how her card had been erroneously marked, and by whom. She wanted to clear herself with Darren Cooke's widow, remove any last vestige of doubt. This was an innocent errand, and she thought Michelle should know what demons were on her late husband's back: the letters from the unknown child, who may not even be his child. It would help her understand his suicide. God, Temple thought, putting herself in his shoes. Maybe he had sinned, but the punishment he faced in his last hours of life was more than sufficient payment.

Room 711 was the same, except that signs of packing lay

strewn on the living-room furniture and Padgett could be heard gurgling from the bedroom.

"I'm glad I caught you," Temple said. "You should know some things."

"Yes?" Michelle kept fussing with the baby's things, folding and packing frilly dresses in exquisitely embroidered pastel fabric.

Darling things. A baby would be like doll I can carry. Maybe not so bad. Maybe like a cat, without fur.

"Can I help? Apparently your nanny is busy with Padgett."

"No. She's gone. She was only a temporary."

"Really? It'll be hard, to take a baby on the long flight back to Paris, alone."

"The stewardesses are wonderful. They love babies."

Temple nodded. She had noticed that stewardesses were partial to young flyers. "Adults must be such a pain."

"Adults, yes. A pain."

Temple sat on the arm of a sofa. Michelle struck her as tense. Her long, thin figure moved jerkily, like a puppet, and her eyes never settled on one place, and certainly not on Temple.

"Listen, Michelle. You've been most gracious to me, considering what you had reason to think of me. I . . . wanted you to know that there is proof that my card was tampered with. I am what I said."

"Proof?" Michelle kept moving, folding, packing delicate baby things. The child had a lot of them.

"I've found—the police have questioned—your husband's personal assistant."

"I've met her, yes. Alison. A bit wild in the fashion area, but overall a sensible young woman."

"Not really," Temple said gently. "You see, Darren had been getting letters from a young woman claiming to be his natural daughter—"

"Natural. I do not know that word in this relationship."

"His illegitimate daughter."

Michelle stopped moving, her storklike body bent over one open case. She wore a rosy pink jumpsuit in a metallic fabric,

very space-age and unkind to less than ultrathin figures. She reminded Temple of one of Domingo's flamingos, a plastic ornament of sorts, frozen forever in a certain, graceful attitude.

"Daughter."

"Yes. She's an adult now . . . if she really is his daughter, and
there's no evidence in her background that she is. She may be
simply a demented adoptee who longed for a famous father, and
fastened on your husband, because of his womanizing reputation."

"Reputation."

"She'd been sending him letters. Harassing, ugly, hateful letters. That's why he consulted me in the bedroom, for privacy. He
was brooding about this situation, hating himself for having
abandoned someone he never knew about. I suppose, now that
he had a baby daughter, he pictured himself abandoning her, and
couldn't bear it."

"No, he wouldn't have been able to bear it." Michelle finally
straightened from her interrupted task and looked directly at
Temple. "That was the one thing I thought I could count on, no
matter how much he failed me and our marriage. His love, his
protective love for his daughter."

Temple nodded. "The one, truly sincere feeling in his life,
which is why the existence of this bitter, vengeful adult daughter tormented him. You must believe that."

"Must I?"

"Yes, because that's why he killed himself. She came to him
that night. The one unseduceable female in his entourage. She
was willing, and he was hurting and—I'm sorry—I'd turned him
down and even told him that he'd be getting more of that in future." Temple bit her lip. "I did contribute to his death. I know
that now. I thought I was being assertive. But I was being in-
sensitive too."

"No!—"

"I was there. I know. It wasn't really me, but I was another
feather on the scale that was weighing ever heavier against him.
Because his so-called daughter's revenge was truly demonic. She

went to bed with him, and then she told him who she was. He freaked, naturally. She wanted his money too, but I don't think that made him suicidal. I think it suddenly came home to him that *any* girl could be anybody to somebody—daughter, sister, mother—that these were young lives he played with and that he had a lot to account for. He was feeling low already, so—"

Michelle nodded violently, an expression in her eyes darker than despair. "Yes. He would have killed himself. He was so close." She looked at Temple. "But he didn't."

"How can you know? I doubt Alison Darby did it; she was so shocked by his death. Her plans hadn't included that. And of course she lost the chance to extort money from him, and she wanted it all. Nothing left for you and Padgett."

"So I preserved for Padgett what was perhaps hers, and perhaps not hers."

"*You* didn't. Darren did, by dying."

Michelle turned on her like a furious animal.

"Oh, but I did. I was there, you see. I had come because I had learned he was, had been . . . with Dana, our nanny. With our daughter's nanny! I knew he was not perfect, but that . . . frightened me. If he would cross that boundary, were there not others?"

"When were you there? Before Alison came?"

"No, *cherie*. After."

"But—"

"Yes! I was there when he berated himself. When I unfolded my horror over Dana, he just nodded. The gun was in his hand, in his lap. I had never seen him so passive. He took my anger like rain on dry earth, as if he needed it. When I accused him, revealed my fear that even Padgett might not be safe from him, he had not stomach to defend himself. Now I see why. I knew he loved our daughter, but I knew he could not help himself, could not keep from the sad comfort he got from his endless seductions. And what is child abuse but an unpardonable seduction? Other women I could allow, but our nanny, a girl . . . our daughter, a girl someday.

"He did not shoot the gun. He had it to his head. His temple, the classic target. I could not have stood it had it been in his mouth. But it was at his head, his mind. I touched it to take it from him. He was devastated by what I had said. Now I know why he took it so seriously. If only I had known what she had done *then!* I intended to stop him. Once my hand had covered his on the weapon, I seemed powerless to withdraw it. Instead I found myself pressing my forefinger over his forefinger, pulling the trigger."

"There's no evidence! Only his fingerprints on the weapon."

Michelle held up long arms thin and pale as flamingo legs. "I wear gloves. It is my fashion trademark. I wear them everywhere when I go outside, because I wear them in my perfume ads. I destroyed the gloves. Burned them. I cannot excuse myself. Another self pulled the trigger back. It was hard to do. He must have sensed me doing it, but he didn't move. He just waited. In a sense, it felt like a mercy killing."

Her eyes, haunted, met Temple's for the last time.

"What you have told me eases nothing. No wonder he did not fight my accusations! That girl killed him despite herself, through me. What should I do? Whatever I do, Padgett will have to live with it all her life."

"So will you," Temple said. "If only I hadn't come. You wouldn't know, and I wouldn't know. I can't say what you should do. I don't know what I should do."

"We could tell, each or both of us."

Temple kept silent.

Michelle eyed her aslant. "It will make for an interesting tension. Wondering if one or the other will tell, and when."

"I would have to think about it for a long time."

"A lifetime, perhaps."

Temple stood. In the other room, Padgett was giggling to herself. The tension was already awful, and it would only get worse.

"Good-bye," Michelle said.

Only she said it in French. *"Au revoir."*

Temple left without another word, because no words were sufficient.

Au revoir. She remembered from college French class that it was an uneasy good-bye. The direct translation was closer to "until we meet again."

Temple finally had found a secret too awful to tell another living soul.

Chapter 38

Louie Seeks Solace

I am not one to wash my dirty linen in public, but I am in a quandary.

The À La Cat commercial has been unmentionable ever since my regrettable abduction and alteration.

Miss Savannah Ashleigh and the Divine Yvette left town so suddenly that they may have been abducted themselves by a UFO. (Do not laugh. There is a lot of that around Las Vegas and the nearby Air Force base, the famous Area 51 beloved of alien-intelligence aficionados.) I have had no opportunity to confirm the dread news about the lovely Yvette. Is she indeed soon to become a mother? Perhaps she will lose her kittenish figure and no longer be in demand for television commercials.

I know that Miss Temple Barr has no use for the Divine Yvette's mistress. She is still in a snit about my terrible experience and mutters every now and then about suing the cellulite off Miss Savannah Ashleigh yet. I am certainly being treated like a king around the Circle Ritz, as I should be, but I do miss the action and the limelight.

And one little thing bothers me. Well, maybe two.

While it is true that I am an extremely educated street dude, I have to admit every once and while to a significant gap in my knowledge. In this embarrassing instance, the gap affects a very personal area.

After thinking it over for several days, I see no help for it but to apply to Ingram, the Thrill 'n' Quill mystery-bookstore cat. I do hate to go to an inferior for advice, especially in a delicate area, but I get up and go.

By the time I amble over—and I amble a lot these days, apparently there are some thorny things called "stitches" in my abdomen that make Miss Temple giggle, if not me—Ingram is ensconced in his display-window den.

There he sits and snoozes, collar neatly buckled, rabies tags glittering at his throat like they were medals, shirtfront pristine and tiger-stripes licked into place.

I shudder at presenting my problem to such a stuck-up prig, but at times even the best of us must bow and scrape a little, and ignorance is a terrible condition to be in.

I extend a claw to rap on the window.

Ingram opens one yellow eye and wrinkles the stripes on his forehead. I know what he is thinking: he does not wish to disturb himself to leave his sunny snoozing spot and come out in the November chill to talk to me.

Tough. If he does not do so, I will get in and disturb him far worse.

He knows this, so soon he is mewing at the door until Miss Maeveleen Pearl, the proprietor, is cooing at the open door.

"Your little friend has not come to visit for some time, Ingram. Run along now and have fun, but do not wander too far."

Ingram is constitutionally incapable of wandering any farther than the fish market three doors down. Which is where we stroll to.

"You have been getting notorious, Louie," Ingram notes as he puts one white-socked foot in front of the other.

"I presume you refer to my new career in film."

"Huckstering," he says with a sniff. He sits down to rub a grain of the sandman's sleep out of one eye. "What do you want?"

"I have a technical question. Perhaps I should wait to ask it until we are back at the bookshop. You may need to look up something."

"Spit it out. I do not want you around the Thrill 'n' Quill too much. Miss Maeveleen Pearl is very soft-hearted, and she might give some of my belongings to you. I have never forgiven you for being responsible for those odious stuffed representations of Baker and Taylor, the Scottish fold cats coming to the shop. They sit atop the shelves, flattening their ears at me day in and day out, taking up good snoozing space and attracting attention that should be mine. I would like to claw the stuffing out of them."

"Then why not do so?"

"I am not a violent individual, like yourself."

"That gets to my problem. I am not like myself anymore."

"Oh? It does not show."

"It should not show, as it is in a very private area."

Ingram waggles the whiskers over his left eye, an effete gesture he uses to signal skepticism.

"I understand that you have had the neutering procedure."

"Indeed, and I recommend it highly. No muss, no fuss. No howling in the night, no howling in the daytime when Miss Maeveleen Pearl discovers the places you have marked while night-howling. No females to muddle one's brain and distract it from socially redeeming literature, no nasty seepage of a foul nature. Have you become enlightened enough to undergo the socially responsible procedure? You amaze me, Louie. I thought you far too regressed to voluntarily surrender your lower nature."

"Actually, it was not voluntary. And I am confused."

"Why do you not consult your esteemed pater?"

"My what?"

"Does not your sire reside now at Temple Bar? So I heard on the grapevine."

"Well, this is something I would prefer not to trouble the old man with. He has had an untrammeled life, and does not understand the demands of civilization."

"I could say the same of you." Ingram brushes an immaculate whisker with a pearl-white paw.

I would hate this guy's guts, if he had any.

I swallow and explain my adventure with the plastic surgeon. "Miss Temple Barr keeps using the word 'vasectomy,' and I am afraid I am not acquainted with it. I know I have a few stitches in my tummy, but that does not seem to be what a vasectomy is."

"Yes, I thought your pouch was looking a trifle sleeker. Silly me. I attributed it to a rigorous indoor-exercise program. I should have known better. 'Vasectomy,' you say. That is impossible, my good goon."

I overlook "goon" because the word "impossible" always attracts my attention.

"How so?"

"We of the four-footed kind have a simple, and sometimes brutal, procedure to control our raging hormonal tendencies toward reproduction. Words vary, from 'gelding' for horses to the general 'neutering.' It consists of cutting off the, er, balls is the street word, I believe, and I would never utter it if I did not have the unpleasant task of explaining the facts of life to you at this late date. Are you sure Three O'Clock cannot help you?"

"Quit with the Three O'Clock! And keep talking."

Ingram sighs. I suspect that is another of the many side effects of this neutering he is discussing. But he does go on. And on.

"This rather drastic, but quick and inexpensive, method results in an animal that is neither male nor female, but more properly an 'it.' It also releases the poor beasts from the tug and pull of natural urges that only serve to over-populate the planet and cause untold misery for the un-wanted young. A neutered male will no longer mark territory with pungent . . . er, urinary liquids. He will no longer fight other unneutered males for female favor. He will no longer haunt unwilling females to force his attentions—and un-wanted offspring—on them. You can see that this proce-dure is completely beneficial to society, and to said males, if they only realized it. Once it has been done, we are per-fectly content, I assure you, and much relieved not to be troubled by urges to roam, fight or mate. It is, in short, cat heaven."

I stare at this dude. I cannot believe him. What a happy, dancing robocat.

"Miss Temple seems to think that this vasectomy is something special."

Ingram yawns. "Not really. By being subjected to this surgery reserved for humans, who have a great many psy-chological blocks to tampering with their sexuality, you now have the worst of both worlds. You will still hunt, fight and chase females, but you will be unable to sire kittens. All the mess and none of the warm, domestic comforts of family life. You will still live it up like a rogue male, with no evolu-tion of your conscience or social responsibility. In other words, you will still be the same, selfish, hedonistic slob you always were, except that you will not bring unwanted young ones into the world."

"The dames I see, they will not get . . . you know?"

"Spit it out, Louie! No, they will not get pregnant. Your dubious genes will never be passed on again. Hallelujah."

"There is no need to get religious about it."

I am too excited to stick around for any spare fish heads that may come our way. I thank Ingram for his precious time and skedaddle.

My feet barely touch the ground. I am running before I know it. The air smells crisp and alive with the scents of prey, rivals and nubile females who will never be out of action on maternity row if they stick with Midnight Louie.

I now know what a vasectomy is and am proud to be one of the first dudes of my type to have such a rare procedure. I know what it means.

I have just been given a license to thrill.

About two weeks later I am lounging contentedly at home beside my devoted roommate, who is reading some supermarket rag. (She does have a few lapses in reading taste, but I try not to tell.)

Suddenly, she holds the paper at arm's length from her face. Then she rips off her glasses and brings it right up to her nose.

"Well, I never—!" she says in great indignation.

She turns to me. "What do those look like to you, Louie?"

She is jabbing her forefinger at a photograph on the page, and since it features several of my species, I deign to look at it.

My heart flutters when I see the Divine Yvette looking as sweet and delectable as always. But Miss Temple Barr's forefinger is not aimed at the Divine Yvette. It is not even pointed toward the odious facial image of Miss Savannah Ashleigh, who is also in the picture. (And it seems that Miss Savannah Ashleigh has been stung in the kisser by a mighty big bee, so swollen are her lips. Ugh!)

What Miss Temple Barr is shaking her finger at are some blurry little dustbunnies who—now that I look closely—are striped kittens. Tiger-striped kittens, three of them, all the color yellow.

"Looks like you were falsely accused and assaulted, Louie. Methinks Maurice has been doing more stunt work than he was contracted for. Well, wait 'til I call the director. That'll get you out of the doghouse and put Maurice, his trainer and Savannah Ashleigh in there pronto. My poor baby. Innocently railroaded with no trial. Forcibly sterilized. At least I do not have to take you in for a neutering. And it was free. The worst is over, Louie. From now on, it is all gravy, I promise you."

I know, Miss Temple, I know.

"What a big purrer you have become since your ordeal, Louie! Such a loving boy."

I know, I know.

Midnight Louie: Short, Sweet and His Same Old Self

What can I say?

It was a far, far better thing I did than I meant to do, which is often the case in happy endings. And my end is very happy, I assure you.

Although I did not have much time to assist Miss Temple Barr in her conundrums, I did manage to save my own skin, save the commercials and the Divine Yvette and save my . . . precious orbs. All while becoming even more politically correct than I had been before.

Obviously, in future I will have to deal with the murderous and deceptive Maurice, and reconcile with my sorely injured ladyfriend. In hindsight, I see the symptoms of her unsuspected delicate condition in a few bouts of uncharacteristic temperament. I also remember the poor darling's dislike of Maurice, who no doubt forced himself upon her, thereby soiling her reputation.

I, however, have the smarts to exercise restraint and a

civil tongue. I am also now socially responsible beyond the ken of my kind.

I must say that doing the right thing feels absolutely terrific. I cannot wait until circumstance brings me into contact with Midnight Louise again.

In fact, I arrange to sashay over to the Crystal Phoenix with not one, but two ladyfriends in attendance. Midnight Louise, of course, huffs herself up into a wad of static-ridden hair and prepares to hiss and spit.

I cock my tail-tip in her direction.

"Tut, tut, my good girl," I say. "Do not distress yourself. This is an engagement party."

"With *two* fiancées?" she spits.

"The party is to celebrate my engagement with the world at large, now that I am the accidental beneficiary of a cutting-edge medical technique. I will have you know that I am vasectomized. No female is safe from my amorous attentions, and I must say that they seem happy about that," I add, as my shills (I mean my lovely companions) brush against me to and fro. "But no female will suffer consequences of a parental nature from my advances. You are therefore one of the last of your kind (which is my kind). I hope you appreciate it.

"As for me, I am a new dude, but I expect to be up to all the same old things. No doubt you wish to congratulate me."

She does not.

But the shills sure do.

Very best fishes,

Midnight Louie, Esq.

P.S. You can reach Midnight Louie on the Internet at:

http://www.catwriter.com/cdouglas

To subscribe to *Midnight Louie's Scratching Post-Intelligencer* newsletter, write: P.O. Box 331555, Fort Worth, TX 76163

Look for news about Louie's new T-shirt!

—CND

Carole Nelson Douglas Employs the Kindest Cut of All

Midnight Louie came into my life a tomcat, as a corporeal motel cat in California. He was a hippie in 1973, no doubt about it. Footloose, all for free love, a true gentleman of the road.

The Minnesota cat-lover who saved him from sure euthanasia as a stray found he couldn't adapt to apartment life. She wanted him to have a country home where he could roam—intact, a tomcat still.

In 1973, people were less aware of the horrible price pet overpopulation exacts on strays. Midnight Louie survived well, but he was (yes) unusually strong, smart and unscarred.

Louie's and my association in 1973 was brief and professional. When I first translated Midnight Louie into print for a newspaper, his tough, street-smart voice came through loud, clear—and irrevocably male.

As Louie later made the leap to fiction, I felt obligated to remain true to the original personality. In the same way, when I made Irene Adler, the only woman to outwit Sherlock Holmes, the protagonist of her own adventures, I felt obliged to work with the details of Sir Arthur Conan Doyle's story about her, "A Scandal in Bohemia." This meant working around his error of making an operatic prima donna a contralto instead of the mandated soprano.

Although Midnight Louie's naturally high testosterone quotient satirizes the rogue male model that populates human hardboiled mystery and other fiction—and sometimes even human society (imagine that!)—I knew that, in real life, unneutered tomcats sire thousands of abandoned, hungry, abused and euthanized kittens, and short-lived, feral stray cats. Yet to conventionally "fix" this fictional tomcat, I would destroy the anthropomorphic blend of human and feline that makes the character his own inimitable self.

So Louie has now undergone an unconventional "fixing" that makes him politically correct in the necessary areas both physical and fictional, without diluting his macho personality one drop. But don't try this on your cats at home, folks. Vasectomy is purely a fictional solution.

The Midnight Louie Adopt-a-Cat tour was launched in 1996 in Texas and the southeast. My publisher donated free autographed copies of the *Cat in a Crimson Haze* paperback to animal shelters and humane societies for those who adopted cats while I was making local personal appearances. We held book signings at shelters, and brought adoptable cats to bookstore signings. Many cats were adopted. A huge number were not.

For an animal-lover like me, visiting a series of shelters, even in a good cause, is an ordeal. Despite meeting the overworking, dedicated staffs who fight the tide of unwanted pets with every means available to them, I saw so many animals in need of homes. I saw attractive adult cats with labels: *Owned: 1 year; Age: 1 year.* These are kittens whose families lost interest when they became cats. These are family pets in cages, facing death.

Kittens are engaging and fearless and always adoptable, but there are always so many more than can possibly be taken. Adult cats whose owners have died or abandoned them hunch in their alien cages, needing homes and often not appearing as outgoing and affectionate as they can be. I watched a woman reach into a cage for a sleeping white cat. Startled, it hissed. She moved on. One hiss and you could be history in an animal shelter.

If Midnight Louie, quintessential survivor in life and literature, can do any good in the real world, I hope his popularity will help convince more people to (yes) neuter their cats and keep them indoors for their own safety; to consider adopting adult cats as well as kittens; to learn about feline behavior so that everybody in the household—human, dog, cat or whatever—can live happily together (and they can).

My husband and I had six cats before the tour began, and a young dog I had found dumped on a street corner only a couple months earlier. I saw so many cats I would have loved to take home. Finally, in Lubbock, Texas, a small black one with a scratchy mew and a broken tail became irresistible. We drove over six hundred miles to fetch Midnight Louie Jr. a few days later, and bring him home.

No one needs seven cats. But they need us.